THE DEATH OF THE *KELDA SCOTT*

The aluminum cylinder was a couple of hundred feet away when the pressure inside the casing reached the critical point. A moment later the metal gave way, expelling a superheated fluid stream of phosphorus. The liquid metal instantly ignited the boundary layer of volatile gases that hovered just above the crude oil slick. And a microsecond later the spark flashed across the water surface, igniting the main gas line underneath the drilling vessel.

The *Kelda Scott* was engulfed in a tumultuous fireball that covered the ship from the water surface to the top of the derrick. The instantaneous ignition of the gas cloud surrounding the lifeboat station incinerated everyone inside the escape capsule.

They all burned to cinders in a matter of seconds . . .

BLOWOUT

JEFFREY LAYTON

AVON BOOKS ◆ NEW YORK

BLOWOUT is an original publication of Avon Books. This work has never before appeared in book form. This work is a novel. Any similarity to actual persons or events is purely coincidental.

AVON BOOKS
A division of
The Hearst Corporation
1350 Avenue of the Americas
New York, New York 10019

Copyright © 1995 by Jeffrey A. Layton
Published by arrangement with the author
Library of Congress Catalog Card Number: 95-94143
ISBN: 0-380-78066-6

First Avon Books Printing: September 1995

AVON TRADEMARK REG. U.S. PAT. OFF. AND IN OTHER COUNTRIES, MARCA REGISTRADA, HECHO EN U.S.A.

Printed in the U.S.A.

RA   10 9 8 7 6 5 4 3 2 1

The Kingdom of Heaven runs on righteousness, but the Kingdom of Earth runs on oil.

A British Statesman, circa 1950

PROLOGUE:

THE FLOWERS OF EDO

Tokyo
March 10, 1945

Kiyomi Yoshida heard the rumble of the airplanes several minutes before the sirens finally began to wail. She had felt the deep pulsations of the B-29s many times before, but never like tonight. Something was different this time.

Kiyomi jumped up from her floor bedding and rushed into an adjoining bedroom. *"Bi-ni-ju-kyu! Bi-ni-ju-kyu!"* she shouted, warning her twelve-year-old daughter, Mitsuko, that the Americans had returned.

Mother and daughter hurriedly wrapped themselves in thick nightclothes and then ran into the alleyway next to their tiny house. At half past midnight, the early morning air had a chill to it. The brisk northwest wind, originating out of the bowels of still-frozen Russia, swept over the city as if it were an invisible river.

"Why don't we just stay here?" protested the little girl.

During the previous raids, most occurring in the daytime, Kiyomi and Mitsuko had hidden in a shallow earth pit under the kitchen.

"I don't feel safe here tonight," answered Kiyomi. "We must get to Uncle Ichiro's house. He has a much better shelter there."

"But it's so far!"

1

"I know, honey, but we can make it."

Kiyomi and Mitsuko started running, joining the hundreds of other refugees who had already filled the narrow streets and alleys of the Asakusa Ward. They also sensed that something was terribly wrong tonight.

Maximum Maxine was on the final leg of its bombing run. After flying six hours from Saipan, the entire eleven-man crew was wound up like a coiled spring. No one knew what to expect.

The B-29 was 7,500 feet over Tokyo Bay, heading northward into the heart of the giant city. There was a reddish glow in the distance, but other than that light the city of ten million was blacked out.

Maximum Maxine was part of the U.S. Army Air Force's 497th Bomb Group, 73rd Bomb Wing. Positioned near the front of the pack, it flew independently into the darkness. A couple of dozen other B-29s were already ahead, dropping their bombs. Hundreds of additional bombers followed behind.

The radar operator, located near the center of the fuselage, was now guiding the plane. Because of the darkness, the only way to navigate to the target was to sweep the approaching terrain with invisible radio waves. He had just spotted a series of piers that jutted out into Tokyo Bay near the mouth of the Sumida River. He had been worried that he might not be able to locate the structures. *Finally!* he thought.

"Radar to pilot. I've got the aiming point." The radar operator paused a moment as he adjusted a control that placed the seaward end of the middle pier under the radar's track line. "Come right five degrees," he called out.

"Roger, five degrees right," acknowledged the aircraft commander. The pilot then dialed the course change into the B-29's automatic pilot.

The target was now about five minutes away, and the radar operator and the bombardier were working together. The bombardier, located in the nose of the plane, had his right eye glued to the telescope on his Norden bombsight.

"Bombardier, clutch-in point coming up," reported the radar operator over the interphone. He was referring to a radar sighting angle back to the aiming point.

"Roger, I've got it," replied the bombardier.

For the next several minutes the radar operator and the bombardier continued their team play, refining the aircraft's heading so that when the forty bombs were released they would follow a parabolic trajectory that would land them on target.

As *Maximum Maxine* approached the final checkpoint the bombardier tensed up, knowing that the bombsight was about to automatically release the bombs. Two seconds later the aircraft lurched upward as twenty tons of incendiary bombs dropped through the twin sets of belly doors.

"Bombs away," shouted the bombardier.

Army Air Force Cadet Hiroshi Yoshida sat in the cockpit of his Kawasaki Ki-61 Hein fighter. The Swallow's engine was still warming up and it idled roughly.

One month shy of his fifteenth birthday, the pilot wore a brown leather flying helmet that covered most of his head. A set of goggles were shoved up onto his forehead and a long white scarf was loosely knotted around his neck. Underneath the helmet he wore a *hachimaki*. The brightly colored headband was a replica of the type that ancient samurai warriors traditionally wore into battle.

Cadet Yoshida was both exhilarated and terrified. He had been scheduled to fly a training flight that night, but Tokyo was under massive attack by hundreds of American bombers. Every available fighter in the outlying airfields was being ordered into the air.

Even though Yoshida had not yet officially earned his wings, he was being pressed into service tonight. The Japanese military was desperate for pilots. After devastating losses against the Allies during the previous year, anyone who showed the slightest aptitude toward flying was rushed into flight school. Yoshida, drafted only two months earlier, was a natural pilot candidate. Academically, he was at the top of his school class, and no matter how badly the senior pilots had looped and dived the two-place trainers, he never got sick.

Cadet Yoshida glanced out the right side of his canopy. The other seven Swallows in his squadron were now taxiing onto the runway. Unlike Yoshida, however, the other pilots of the 244th Hiko-Sentai were commissioned officers and had all seen combat before.

Yoshida released the brake and his plane crept forward. He

then advanced the throttle. Two minutes later he was airborne. With no armor or weapons aboard, Yoshida's Ki-61 lifted off the runway two hundred meters sooner than any of the lead aircraft.

While Yoshida climbed above Chofu airfield he looked toward the northeast. The night sky over Tokyo was already glowing. *My God, what's that?* he thought. A moment later he began shaking. His mother and sister were somewhere inside the hell that was now devouring Tokyo.

Kiyomi Yoshida and her daughter rushed down the narrow streets and alleys, heading eastward. Her brother's house bordered the banks of the Sumida River and was now a dozen blocks away. The air was thick with smoke and the terror from above never seemed to stop.

The narrow metal cannisters, each one containing two and a half pounds of a gasoline gel, continued to rain down on Asakusa Ward. Released from the B-29s in five-hundred-pound clusters, each bomb casing would split open at an altitude of 3,000 feet, dispersing several dozen M-69 incendiary bombs. Capable of carrying forty clusters per aircraft, most of the B-29s flying over Tokyo were each releasing over 1,500 individual firebombs.

The M-69 was only twenty inches long and about three inches in diameter. The steel casing looked more like a pipe than a weapon. There were no fins or pointed ends. Instead, as it dropped through the sky a three-foot-long tail streamer would deploy, preventing it from tumbling.

By the time the six-pound bomblet struck the roof of a house or a factory, it had usually obtained sufficient momentum to drive the steel casing through the structure. As the weapon penetrated the roof, a delayed-action fuse was triggered. The five-second delay provided enough time for the M-69 to come to rest. When the TNT charge detonated, a napalmlike substance was ejected out of the tail. Like a giant fireworks display, the burning gel shot outward, reaching as far as a hundred feet away. Any combustible surface struck by the flaming gasoline would instantly ignite.

As Kiyomi and Mitsuko ran through the streets, they heard the tearing and ripping sounds of the firebombs when they crashed through the surrounding structures. The screams were the worst part of their ordeal. The unsuspecting inhabitants often awoke to a room filled with the stink of burning gasoline. In some cases, individuals were incinerated on the spot; others were trapped and subsequently roasted alive.

Thousands of evacuees were now pouring into the streets. Kiyomi and Mitsuko were caught in the flood flow of humanity as the crowds surged toward the river. The firestorm bearing down on the hapless victims would not stop.

"Navigator to pilot."

"Go," replied *Maximum Maxine*'s commander.

"Sir, I recommend that we follow the Arakawa Canal out to the bay. With all the smoke down there that's the only solid landmark I've got right now."

"Radar, do you concur?"

"Yes, sir. The unit's still not responding. The transmitter must have taken one of the hits."

Just after completing the bomb run, *Maximum Maxine* was caught in a deadly crossfire. Five antiaircraft artillery searchlights caught the B-29 in their beams. The plane took three flak hits before the pilot was able to break free of the death lights. To escape he turned the bomber over a fiercely burning section of Honjo Ward. To his utter amazement, the fifty-ton bomber skyrocketed upward. The air turbulence from the building inferno created thermal currents that literally threw the B-29 upward.

When the plane finally leveled off at 12,000 feet, the radar operator reported the malfunction. Because of the thick smoke that now obscured the land below, the flight crew had no idea where they were.

"Navigator, are you sure that canal is the right one?"

"Hell, I think so, skipper. But it's such a bloody mess down there I'm not a hundred percent certain of anything."

The pilot had no choice but to trust his navigator. If they wasted much more time orbiting over the burning city, they would run low on fuel for the return flight.

"Okay, everyone, listen up. We're going to try to bug out of here now so I want all of you to keep a sharp eye out. We could run into just about anyone up here."

* * *

Cadet Hiroshi Yoshida was orbiting over the north end of Tokyo Bay, maintaining an altitude of 15,000 feet. He was alone. The other fighters in his *sentai* had already dispersed to lower altitudes. The Americans had changed their attack patterns with this raid. Instead of bombing Tokyo from high altitude, as had been done in the past, the current attack was being conducted with low-level tactics. As a consequence, most of the fuses in the artillery rounds were set at the wrong altitudes and the night interceptors found no targets at the higher ceilings.

Yoshida could not follow the other Ki-61s from Chofu into aerial combat. Although part of the 244th Hiko-Sentai, Yoshida was assigned to a special attack unit within the 10th Air Division. Designated *Shinten* ("Shaking Heaven")-*Tai*, Yoshida was a *taiatari*—a body crasher. Instead of shooting down enemy bombers, his sole function was to ram them with his stripped-down fighter.

Yoshida scanned the black waters of the bay toward the south. He could see nothing. But when he turned northward, Tokyo was alive with light. The firestorm had now metamorphized into a conflagration; it devoured the kiln-dry houses and buildings with an insatiable hunger.

Kiyomi and Mitsuko made it to Sumida Park, on the western bank of the Sumida River. The tiny municipal garden, only a hundred yards wide, was already filled with thousands of terrified refugees. Kiyomi had abandoned her original plan to seek refuge in her brother's home. It was also in the path of the flames. Instead, with her daughter in tow, she fought her way through the crowds. *If we can just make it to the river, we'll be safe.*

Kiyomi was wrong. Even if they had managed to jump into the river, they would not have survived. The forty-degree river water would suck the life out of a person in just a few minutes.

As terrible as death in the icy river might be, it was nothing compared to what was now happening to the victims of Sumida Park. The rolling flames that had devastated the western sections of Asakusa Ward had not yet descended on the area, but the deadly downdraft of superheated air that preceded them had. Kiyomi didn't even know her thick baggy trousers were on fire until it was too late. The spark landed on a cuff, and in the scorched air the flames raced up the garment at lightning speed. She was a ball of flames in just a few seconds. Mitsuko was consumed almost simultaneously.

Maximum Maxine broke out of the smoke plume just as it passed over the northern shoreline of Tokyo Bay. The smoke-filled air was overpowering. To most of the crew the odor smelled like burning cedar, but to a few it was the stench of death.

"Okay, navigator," called out the pilot, "we're over the bay. Get us home."

"Roger, skipper. Turn left zero-three-five degrees. That should put us on the correct heading."

The pilot executed the course change. They were now heading southward across Tokyo Bay. The Pacific Ocean and their pathway home were dead ahead.

Yoshida spotted the B-29 as it emerged from the black clouds that blew out into the bay. Light from the massive fire backlit the plane's silvery skin. He advanced the throttle to the stops and pushed the stick forward.

Everyone inside *Maximum Maxine* kept his eyes glued to his respective viewport as they flew over the water. Enemy night fighters remained on the prowl, and *Maximum Maxine*—as well as the other 324 B-29s on the bombing raid—was terribly vulnerable. In order to carry maximum bomb loads, the guns and ammunition in the aircraft had been removed. With the excess weight removed, and the decision to bomb from lower altitudes, the bomb loads had been increased to the maximum.

Despite the fact that *Maximum Maxine* was completely defenseless, the aircraft commander wasn't too worried about the Japanese night fighters. Only a few had air-to-air radar capability and even then their equipment was crude. What really worried the pilot, however, was the risk of running into one of their companion aircraft. There were dozens of B-29s over Tokyo Bay right now, some starting their bomb runs while others were heading home. They all flew at different altitudes and headings, each aircraft entirely on its own.

* * *

Yoshida had the big bomber lined up perfectly. He was approaching from the front at a forty-five-degree down angle with a speed of 360 miles per hour. Everything was perfect. He couldn't miss.

Maximum Maxine's copilot spotted the Ki-61 a few seconds before it struck. The flames from Tokyo revealed its presence for just an instant. "One-way Charlie!" he screamed. And without thinking he grabbed the wheel.

Before Yoshida could react the B-29 rolled right and nosed downward. He missed the main fuselage, but his port wingtip clipped the B-29's left horizontal stabilizer.

"Damn! Where'd that sucker come from?" yelled the port observer over the B-29's interphone. He had just seen a gray streak flash by his porthole. The damage to the B-29 was minor.

"I don't know," responded the pilot, "but we're sure as hell going to get outta here before he comes back." He then retook control of the plane, relieving the copilot and advancing the throttles and pulling back on the wheel. The bomber settled into a steep climb.

The pilot turned to face his second in command. "Nice job, Jack. I didn't see that sucker at all."

"I only caught a glimpse—it looked like a Tony to me."

"Yeah, must have been one of those suicide nuts." The pilot paused a moment as he looked upward through the overhead cockpit windows. He could see a cascade of stars. "Once we get above twenty-five grand, they won't bother us anymore."

Although the damage to the American bomber had been negligible, Hiroshi Yoshida's aircraft was in trouble. For just an instant he thought of ejecting his canopy and jumping, but then he remembered that he didn't have a parachute. Like his fellow kamikazes, he had intended to fly a one-way mission.

Yoshida finally managed to regain partial control after tumbling nearly six thousand feet. When the fighter finally leveled out he discovered that he was nearly out of fuel. A fuel line in the damaged wing had been severed, draining most of his reserves. With no other options available, Yoshida finally dropped altitude and prepared to ditch in Tokyo Bay.

The landing was surprisingly smooth. But somehow Yoshida managed to smash his right arm into the side of the canopy. He felt a bolt of pain as a bone snapped.

The Ki-61 floated for almost five minutes, providing Yoshida with enough time to extract himself from the cockpit, broken arm and all. Although he didn't carry a parachute, the plane was equipped with a self-inflating one-man life raft. A minute after he climbed into the yellow raft, the Swallow disappeared into the cold dark waters.

Once the immediate shock of the ditching was over, Yoshida felt the ache in his arm. He tucked the wrist of his broken limb inside his flight jacket, immobilizing it. He then grabbed the one wooden paddle and began dipping it into the water. After a dozen halfhearted strokes he managed to turn the raft around. He was now facing northward, toward downtown Tokyo.

The sight before Cadet Yoshida was nothing less than awesome. The city was being consumed by a man-made hell. Flames rose hundreds of feet into the atmosphere and thick plumes of black smoke billowed upward. Once again the Flowers of Edo were in full bloom.

The feudal name of Tokyo was Edo, and for centuries its inhabitants had feared accidental fires, especially those that occurred at night. Constructed primarily of wood and fabric materials, the city had always been a tinderbox, and the nocturnal fires that plagued it were nicknamed "flowers."

The Flowers of Edo were often disastrous, burning out entire sections of the city. But tonight the inferno that gripped Tokyo had mushroomed into a gigantic avalanche of flame. By dawn, the very heart of the once-thriving metropolis would be reduced to nothing more than soot and ash.

Tears rolled down Hiroshi Yoshida's cheeks. The teenage warrior's mother and sister were gone. He cried hard for several minutes but then suddenly stopped. Noise from above caught his attention. He looked up and spotted the silvery underbelly of the incoming bomber. Another B-29 was starting its bomb run. He raised his good arm and shook it above his head. "You bastards," he screamed. "I'll kill you all!"

1

THE ELEPHANT AT HAMMER FOUR

Captain Daniel P. Barker was on the port bridge wing of his vessel, standing nearly a hundred feet above the placid ocean surface. A baseball cap covered his bald head. Although he was six feet tall, his expanding waistline made him look plump. He needed to lose about twenty pounds.

Dan Barker was alone on the tiny steel deck, looking east toward the distant coastline. The pea-soup-thick fog had finally lifted a half hour earlier. The jagged peaks of the coastal mountain range were now silhouetted against the yellowish red hue of the late morning sun. *Looks like another good day*, thought the fifty-five-year-old former U.S. Navy officer.

Barker had retired from the navy four years earlier. He had served nearly thirty years as an officer; his last command was a fleet oiler. Like most of his graduating class at Annapolis, he had longed for the prestige of commanding a real warship—a carrier, a cruiser, a destroyer, or even a frigate—but that was not to happen. Instead, he was assigned to the navy's surface support fleet, where he served on a succession of auxiliary vessels: tenders, supply ships, tankers, and even a hospital ship.

Dan Barker loved his work, despite its passive role; he continually advanced through the years, always graduating to a larger and more complex command. He even served at the Pentagon as a senior staff officer in the Office of the Chief of Naval Operations. But after three decades of service to his country, the writing on the wall was clear: It was time to leave. When he was passed over for promotion to rear admiral he retired.

Leaving the navy was a bittersweet experience for Captain Barker. His two children—both young women now—were finally out of college. The years of struggling to pay their tuition and the myriad of other expenses that went along with giving them a first-class education were finally over.

Dan's navy pension was adequate when combined with his wife's income as a registered nurse, and they lived well. Within just a few months of leaving the navy, the Barkers bought a tiny waterfront cottage in southern Puget Sound. Dan Barker spent much of his time remodeling and expanding the Gig Harbor residence. He enjoyed the work, and his wife was pleased to finally have a full-time companion.

As much as Dan enjoyed his home life, he frequently found himself reminiscing about his former shipmates. He missed his old friends. Although he longed for his former comrades, that wasn't what really bothered him. It was his old mistress. She beckoned to him every day, constantly reminding him of how good it had been. Barker resisted, but his addiction was hopeless. The lure and magic of the sea were far more powerful than any drug.

Dan managed to remain beached for almost a year before he finally gave in. It was a tiny ad inside a local marine journal that did it. A Northwest-based company was looking for an experienced merchant marine officer to command a new construction rig. More out of curiosity than anything else, Barker responded to the advertisement. Four months later he returned to his first love.

Captain Barker turned to his left, now looking back toward his ship. His charge was no ordinary vessel. It floated all right, but that was about all it had in common with other ships. The *Kelda Scott* was an oil-drilling vessel—it looked more like a floating factory than an oceangoing ship.

Designed as a semisubmersible, the *Kelda Scott* was built to hunt for petroleum in deep ocean waters. Unlike an offshore platform that is rigidly fixed to the bottom, a semi floats on the ocean surface. Its huge superstructure is supported over the water by twin pontoon hulls. When drilling, the pontoons are ballasted down with seawater, causing the vessel to semi-submerge.

The *Kelda Scott* was larger than the average semi. Its square-shaped main structural deck covered more ocean surface than two football fields laid side by side. The platform's first level, the drilling deck, was supported fifty feet above the ocean surface by six immense hollow steel columns. The columns were founded on twin pontoon hulls that were now completely submerged below the water's surface. The parallel steel pontoons were larger than many World War II submarines; each one stretched over three hundred feet in length and had a beam of thirty feet. Located inside the aft compartment of each pontoon were two locomotive-size engines. They could push the semi-submersible through the water at up to fifteen knots.

The drilling deck was crammed with expensive equipment: cranes, winches, racks containing thousands of feet of steel drilling pipe, automobile-size pumps, and dozens of other pieces of heavy gear. The second level contained more machinery, tons of assorted drilling chemicals stored in barrels and tanks, a deepwater diving station, various ship's stores, and laboratory space for analyzing boring samples. A helipad, the bridge, and the living quarters were located on the third level. And towering over everything else was the derrick. The enclosed steel tower, looking like a truncated pyramid, rose over sixteen stories above the main deck. The derrick was the heart of the vessel. Nearly everything that took place on the rig revolved around the drilling gear that it supported.

At first Captain Barker had thought taking command of the *Kelda Scott* would be routine, even boring. But to his surprise he found the vessel fascinating. Although the complex drilling and testing operations were highly technical and intriguing, it was the crew that really piqued his interest. During drilling operations there were over a hundred persons aboard. They ranged from burly young deckhands to seasoned scientists with Ph.D.s.

The *Kelda Scott*'s crew worked together with clockwork precision. Everyone put in long, hard hours and there were few complaints. Barker found the oil patch kids, a nickname he used to refer to the younger crew members, to be energetic and self-motivating. They were fun to be around.

Barker especially enjoyed working with the women. Most of the twenty-seven females were young and nearly all were college educated. They worked primarily in the ship's laboratories and computer facilities. Several of the older women held senior positions as geologists and geophysicists. Their years of seagoing experience impressed everyone, especially Captain Barker.

To Barker's amazement, the *Kelda Scott*'s male crew members accepted their female counterparts with respect and courtesy. There had been none of the trouble that had occurred when the American navy began allowing women to serve on support vessels.

Captain Barker attributed the exceptional crew relations to several factors. First, the owner of the *Kelda Scott* had a strict policy of treating all employees with respect. There was no gray area of tolerance when it came to crew morale; any employee, man or woman, who tried to take advantage of others, would be dismissed. Second, everyone aboard was well paid. Finally, their employer tried to make life aboard the vessel as comfortable as possible. Each person had his or her own cabin. The galley facilities produced remarkably tasty meals. There was a modern gym with the latest exercise and weight-training equipment; a library well stocked with books, magazines, and newspapers; and a TV lounge linked via satellite to CNN and two dozen other channels. There were also hundreds of VCR movie cassettes aboard.

Even with all of the amenities and pay incentives, life aboard the drilling vessel eventually got to everyone. And that's why the company had a policy of rotating crew members on a staggered schedule. Everyone aboard, including Barker, would be sent home for three to four weeks of paid leave after serving a two-to-three-month tour. The owner of the company believed it was important for his employees to see their families as much as possible.

Captain Barker was scheduled to return to Gig Harbor next week. He was really looking forward to spending time with his wife and continuing his remodeling work. But best of all, his youngest daughter was flying in from San Diego for a two-week visit. He hadn't seen Megan in almost a year.

After nearly three months aboard the *Kelda Scott,* Captain Barker was ready for shore leave. Unlike his previous company assignments in the Bering Sea and the North Sea, from which it took him several days to get home, his return trip this time would take only a couple of hours. It would start with an hour-long helicopter flight to Seattle's Boeing Field and end with a fifty-minute drive down Interstate 5 to Tacoma, and then a few more minutes across the Narrows Bridge to Gig Harbor. He could hardly wait.

The *Kelda Scott* was moored off the northwestern coastline of Washington State. Located nearly twenty-seven miles southwest of Cape Flattery, the rig was floating in 935 feet of water. The drilling site was designated as Hammer 4.

The *Kelda Scott* had been fixed into the same position at Hammer 4 for six weeks. It was moored to the ocean bottom by eight anchor lines, two from each corner of the vessel. Despite the strong ocean currents and heavy seas, the mile-long cable-chain assemblies firmly held the $100 million vessel in place.

The drilling had been slow. The dense basalt under the soft marine sediments was difficult to penetrate. Despite the tough drilling conditions, the rig's drill team—toolpusher, derrick-man, driller, roustabouts, mud men, and a host of other technicians and deck workers—all worked around the clock to complete the exploratory well. After weeks of hard work, they had finally reached the target zone, over three miles straight down.

At first Captain Barker wasn't sure if the wildcat well had hit the pay zone or not. None of the rig's crew really knew what they had found because the geologists on board weren't talking. Two of the company scientists, a husband-and-wife team out of Houston, constantly analyzed the cuttings from the bore hole as the drill bit entered the target area 16,500 feet below the ocean bottom. By microscopically studying the tiny fragments of rock brought back to the surface by the bore hole's mud circulation system, it was possible to determine if the drill string had penetrated petroleum-bearing strata.

Captain Barker really became suspicious when, during the second day of target zone drilling, five more geologists were heloed out to the site from Seattle. Three days later the speculation was over. The exploratory well, only the fourth drilled off the coast of Washington, had hit a potentially profitable pay zone. The tailings suggested that the *Kelda Scott* was moored over an "elephant field"—a huge reservoir of hydrocarbons.

Under normal operating procedures, the drilling rig would have been ordered to move to another nearby location to drill a second well. With the data from the second bore hole, the scientists would be able to better define the extent of the pay zone. It typically took three or four confirming wells to determine if a reservoir would be profitable to develop or not. Hammer 4, however, was different. The data from the cuttings and the results from various electronic sensors inserted into the bore hole all pointed to a bonanza: massive quantities of oil and natural gas under enormous pressure. Consequently, the owners of the well ordered the *Kelda Scott* to run a full-scale flow test.

Conducting a field flow test is the best method for accurately determining the development feasibility of a hydrocarbon reservoir. By allowing the oil and gas to flow upward to the rig, and then igniting the mixture to prevent polluting the water's surface, production engineers could monitor flow pressure over a period of several days. If the pressure levels held up, the reservoir might have enormous reserves. On the other hand, if the pressure readings dropped steadily, then the well might be a dud.

Hammer 4's flow test had been running for nearly six days now. There had been virtually no reduction in overall reservoir pressure. The vessel's flare, a hundred-foot-long steel tower that extended horizontally from the stern section of the ship, was a testament to the power of the subterranean energy source. The 120-foot-long flame that shot outward from the flare's nozzle was an awesome sight during daylight hours. At night it was nothing less than spectacular. The small fishing villages and log camps along the coast started calling the Coast Guard during the first night of the test. The callers were certain that a ship was burning at sea.

During the morning of the second day of the test, two Seattle television stations sent out their helicopters to investigate the fire. When the TV crews discovered that the drilling rig was deliberately burning off crude oil and natural gas, they put two and two together: The *Kelda Scott* had discovered oil off Washington's coast. And from then on the boats started showing up. It almost seemed that everyone in the Seattle area wanted to see what the *Kelda Scott* was up to.

Captain Barker had wished the early June weather hadn't been so good. Otherwise the dozens of boats that had hounded him during the past few days would remain in port. But more curiosity seekers would be back today; it was dead calm again and the fog had finally gone away.

Barker had just turned around to walk back into the bridge house when he noticed something in the distance. He walked the half a dozen steps to the far end of the platform for a better look. He pulled up a pair of binoculars to his eyes; he always carried them draped around his neck whenever he was outside. *I'll be damned, there's one here already.* Just off to his right he could see the boat. It was several miles away, coming from the south. *Hmm, I wonder how many more visitors we'll have today.*

The *Victory*'s twin 1,200-horsepower Detroit diesels purred like tigers in heat as the boat charged northward at twenty-two knots. The *Kelda Scott* was dead ahead, now only three miles away. The 120-foot-long yacht had departed from Portland twelve hours earlier.

While *Victory*'s four-man crew kept the boat moving forward, her other three passengers were busy on the spacious afterdeck. They were huddled around a strange-looking object about the size of a large refrigerator on its side. The device had an exterior framework of heavy-duty aluminum tubing. Its interior was filled with an assortment of orange steel tanks, watertight metal boxes, four ducted propeller housings, and half a dozen television and photographic cameras. At the front of the structure, mounted to the frame just below two of the cameras, was a clawlike mechanical arm. It was bent back in the form of a V. It looked like an appendage to some kind of grotesque robot creature from outer space.

Despite the odd appearance of the boxlike device, it was a highly sophisticated machine that had cost nearly $5 million to manufacture. The various onboard electronic computer systems rivaled the technology used in the space program. The ROV, or remotely operated vehicle, was designed to explore the deep ocean.

The ROV was mounted on a steel platform directly over an open well in the deck. Sandwiched between the two drive-shafts from the engines, the well extended through the deck to the hull's bottom plates. A special retractable panel in the bottom allowed direct access to the water. For now, however, the panel was sealed shut and the well was dry.

The underwater vehicle was capable of being remotely piloted from the surface by means of a cable-tether system. A five-foot-diameter spool built into a fiberglass compartment next to the well contained over three miles of neutrally buoyant cable. When the ROV descended through the open well, the tether would pay out, supplying electrical power to the machine's propellers and camera systems, and transmitting navigational control signals from the machine's onboard computer.

The ROV aboard the *Victory* was designed to explore deep wrecks, like the *Titanic* and the *Bismarck*. It was capable of conducting a variety of surveillance tasks ranging from detailed stereo photographic analysis of submerged objects to retrieving hardware and artifacts from the bottom. The underwater mission it was about to embark on, however, was nothing like its designers had ever imagined.

After a quick cup of coffee in the galley—his fourth for the morning—Captain Barker headed down a steep ladderwell that led to the drilling deck. He was looking for Big Billy.

Although Barker was technically captain of the ship, he wasn't in complete charge. William Robinson, the rig's "tool-pusher," was really running the drilling operation. "Big Billy" Robinson was a forty-three-year-old petroleum engineer who had been working in the offshore oil industry for over twenty years. The former all-American lineman from Texas A&M had been hired by the *Kelda Scott*'s owner, Scott Coastal Systems, Inc., five years earlier. Robinson's knack for bringing wells in on time and on budget made him one of SCS's highest paid employees.

When Captain Barker reached the main drilling deck he found Big Billy standing near the moonpool, a ten-foot-diameter hole in the deck where the marine riser rose up from the ocean surface. The thirty-inch-diameter, heavy-walled pipe extended nearly a thousand feet down to the sea floor. Inside was another smaller pipe through which the crude oil and natural gas flowed.

"How's it going today, Billy?" asked Barker.

"Aw, pretty good, skipper. Looks like we won't have any more weather problems for the test."

Barker nodded his head. "Yeah, we should have calm conditions through the weekend. Are we going to shut down on schedule?"

"Yep. I talked with Zack last night and he said to go ahead and conclude the test tomorrow."

"Things must still look good for the well then?" queried Barker.

Robinson smiled. "She's a real gusher. Gonna make the company a bundle."

Captain Barker smiled back. He knew what Billy was implying. SCS owned 75 percent of the Hammer 4 well, and it was company policy to handsomely reward the drilling crew with fat bonuses whenever they brought in a producing well. Zackary Scott always paid the crew immediately after completing the work—not waiting to the end of the year or otherwise delaying payment. Barker guessed that his cut would be around $25,000. Robinson would receive three to four times that amount.

It was now half past two in the afternoon. Several hours earlier, the *Victory* had closed with the *Kelda Scott*, taking up a position half a mile off the semi's southwest quarter. The ROV was already overboard. About twenty minutes earlier, the special well housing the underwater robot had been flooded. A white fabric awning over the *Victory*'s twenty-foot-long fantail completely concealed the wet chamber. No one aboard the *Kelda Scott* witnessed the launch.

The underwater vehicle was heading downward at a rate of fifty feet per minute. A tiny microprocessor inside a stainless steel pressure housing on the ROV was guiding the machine toward the bottom directly under the *Kelda Scott*.

The ROV's three-man support team was in the *Victory*'s main saloon, monitoring the robot's descent. The elegantly appointed compartment was filled with $2 million of electronic equipment: high-resolution depth finders, two computer terminals linked to a minicomputer, several VCR recorders, three television monitors, and a high-resolution sonar unit of military quality.

Dan Barker had returned to the *Kelda Scott*'s bridge. He was sitting in his pedestal-mounted captain's chair working with a notebook full of tables and charts. For the past ten minutes he had been tabulating all of the major consumables that had been used up on the ship during the past twenty-four hours. It was a boring and often long task, but it was a vital part of his duties. Today, however, his job was simple. The rig was running a flow test and not in a drilling mode so there was little to keep track of. The ship's electrical generating plant had used only about a few hundred gallons of number 2 diesel fuel.

Captain Barker stepped off his chair and turned to his right, heading for the coffeepot next to the chart table. As he passed one of the half dozen television monitors he noticed that one of the screens was flickering. That particular monitor was connected to a camera mounted just above the wellhead, a thousand feet below the ship. Barker moved closer to the television screen. He could still see the black-and-white image of a massive pipelike assembly mounted on the wellhead just above the bottom. The display was grainy, the result of poor lighting. Only one of the three floodlights next to the camera was working. The other two had failed several days earlier and Big Billy had not yet sent down a diving team to fix them.

Barker was about to reach for the vertical control on the TV set when the screen turned to a solid sheet of static. "Son of a bitch," he yelled.

Jerry Evans, the rig's assistant engineer, had been standing nearby and moved next to Barker. "What's the matter, skipper?"

"We just lost the frigging wellhead camera."

"Damn, what do you want to do now?"

"Find Billy and tell him we need to get a diving team down there now."

"You got it, skipper."

Captain Barker had no choice. SCS company policy was adamant about the wellhead surveillance camera: It had to be operational at all times. The camera served as a final backup to an elaborate monitoring system designed to prevent leaks.

The old adage "A picture is worth a thousand words" fit very well. Despite all of the sensitive electronic flow-measuring systems, and the multitude of other remote sensors built into the well, the sight of oil seeping upward, mixed with the turbulent venting of natural gas, provided the best leak detection system of all.

The man piloting the ROV sat at a control panel near the aft section of the yacht's saloon. He was young, no more than twenty-five years old. His skin color was surprisingly light for an Asian, but his strong facial features clearly marked him. He wore a plain white T-shirt and a pair of faded blue jeans.

The ROV operator's eyes were glued to a color television monitor built into the console. The underwater probe was now only twenty feet away from the *Kelda Scott*'s marine riser. The operator could clearly see the gray steel color of the thirty-inch-diameter pipe in the foreground.

The ROV's computer-controlled descent had been nearly perfect. The vessel was about seventy feet off the bottom and just a few feet above the well's blowout preventer.

A blowout preventer, or BOP, is a massively built mechanical device that is designed to prevent the escape of pressurized gas or liquid from an oil well. The BOP is mounted on top of the wellhead, just above the seafloor. It looks like an enormous version of a street fire hydrant. The BOP stack is cylindrical in shape, has a diameter of at least three feet, and rises several stories in height. The BOP's casing is milled or forged from high-strength steel and its exterior walls are several inches thick. Multiple pipelike arms, one on top of the other, project horizontally outward along the length of the casing.

The BOP's pipe arms house the emergency devices that are designed to shut in or seal the well. These heavy steel cylinders contain various cutting, sealing, and ramming apparatuses that close off the bore hole when pressure inside the well exceeds safe limits. The sole function of the sealing system is to prevent an oil well blowout.

The BOP's sealing systems are activated by hydraulic pressure from a high-powered pump system located on the surface. Thick steel-reinforced rubber hoses connected to the marine riser transmit hydraulic pressure from the drilling rig to special subsea control pod assemblies located on the BOP stack. The pods, in turn, activate the various sealing devices that are built into the BOP casing.

The BOP stack for the Hammer 4 well was almost six stories high. It consisted of six separate preventers mounted vertically. It was controlled from dual monitoring stations located on the bridge and in a special control room on the drilling deck near the moonpool. The BOP had cost $5 million and was Hammer 4's single most important safety device.

The ROV operator disengaged the computer navigation system and took manual control of the robot. He used a hand-controlled joystick to maneuver the underwater vessel. At first he skirted around the marine riser, testing the four-unit propeller system to make certain it was still operating properly. The ROV flew like a helicopter—rising, descending, turning on a dime, and hovering. Satisfied with the flight tests, he next checked the six-foot-long mechanical arm. He inserted his right hand into a glovelike device on the control panel and began a six-part exercise designed to test the remote unit's dexterity. The man was an expert, capable of picking up a raw egg with the steel finger clamps without cracking the shell.

After a minute and a half of testing, the operator relaxed. The ROV's manual systems were in perfect working order. He swiveled around in his chair to face the man who had been standing patiently behind him. Like the ROV operator, the observer was also of Asian descent, and was about five and a half feet tall. Although the man was only thirty-five years old, he looked much older, primarily because he was almost completely bald. What remained of his jet-black hair was plastered down next to his ears. He wore thin wire rim glasses, and a smoldering cigarette hung out of the corner of his mouth.

"Is it ready?" asked the observer in his native language.

"Yes, sir. The unit is nominal."

"Very well, let's get on with it."

It took the ROV operator only a minute to maneuver the vehicle until it was right over the wellhead television camera. He was very careful to prevent the vehicle or its tether from encroaching on the camera's field of view as he inched it closer. He then extended the mechanical arm toward the BOP and, in one quick snap with the claw, severed the power feed cable to the camera. Next, he moved the ROV until it was just a few feet away from the upper ram preventers on the stack. He was looking for just one thick black hose inside the maze of other hoses and narrow steel tubes that snaked around the BOP. He found it about a minute later. Again using the mechanical arm, he attached a viselike clamp to the rubber conduit. The hydraulic line was now completely isolated from its control panel onboard the *Kelda Scott*.

Within just a couple of minutes the ROV operator cut all of the remaining hydraulic hoses on the stack. Reddish black fluid vented from the rubber and steel tubes, creating a huge plume of discolored water around the ROV. He increased power on the descent thrusters and pushed the craft downward, escaping the turbid cloud. He stopped the robot near the bottom of the BOP stack, just below the last pipe ram preventer. Without turning to speak to the observer he said, "Is this where you want it?"

"Yes, anywhere around there will be fine."

The *Kelda Scott*'s bridge was in chaos. The BOP alarm panel was lit up with warning lights and the loss-of-fluid-annunciator in the overhead was blaring away. Captain Barker was trying to regain control of the situation. There were nearly a dozen men inside the compartment, half of them yelling at each other.

"Harry, kill that damn alarm now," Barker called out to one of the technicians hovering over the BOP control panel.

A few seconds later quiet returned to the ship's nerve center and Barker took over. "All right, gentlemen, listen up." He paused for a moment, looking over the men who were now huddling around him. "I know we've got something very unusual going on with the BOP, but I want everyone to calm down so we can work out the problem."

Before Barker could continue he was interrupted by someone from the back of the group. "What the hell happened, skipper?"

"I don't know much yet, only that we've lost video and hydraulic control of the preventer."

Barker turned to one of the petroleum engineers who was managing the flow test. "John, have we got a runaway?"

"No, Captain. There's no indication of that. In fact, the

downhole pressure level hasn't changed a lick since the event started.''

"Then the well is still flowing normally?''

"Absolutely, like nothing happened.''

Barker suddenly felt a little better. "Good! Then we must have some kind of sensor problem, because if we had had a leak, the BOP's blind ram would have engaged and we wouldn't still be flowing oil.''

"I don't know about that, skipper,'' called out the BOP technician. "I've got zero pressure at the deck pump on all of the preventer's external hydraulic activator lines.''

"No pressure at all?'' called out Barker, clearly astonished at the man's statement.

"That's right, zero pressure. My readings indicate the lines are drained.''

"Have you checked with the deck crew yet?'' Barker was referring to the companion BOP control system located on the drilling deck.

"Yes, skipper. Billy's gang are double-checking everything right now. But so far it's not looking too good.''

"Jesus, then the lines must really be severed.''

"Right, except for one. The line to the wellhead tubing shut-in system is registering in the normal range.''

The tubing shut-in system was designed to be fail-safe. It consisted of two redundant valves built into a special section of the production pipe in the lower portion of the BOP stack. Hydraulic pressure from a surface control line pressurizes the annular space of the well bore, causing the spring-loaded ball valves to remain open, allowing oil and gas to be produced to the surface. When it is necessary to stop the fluid flow, or shut in the well, the pressure is reduced and the heavy springs automatically close the valves.

Captain Barker didn't hesitate at the news. His decision was easy. "Release the pressure now, I want that flow stopped.''

"You got it,'' called out the technician as he started tripping switches on his console. Thirty seconds later he made his report. "Captain, line pressure is now atmospheric. The valves should be closed.''

Barker turned to the man monitoring the flow test. "The flare out yet?''

"Negative, Captain, it's still burning."

"What! How the hell can that be?"

"I don't know. The shut-in valves should have closed by now."

Unbeknown to all onboard the *Kelda Scott*, the clamp around the rubber hose on the BOP stack, clandestinely installed only a few minutes earlier, prevented the fail-safe valves from closing.

"Good God," Barker shouted, "we've got a potential runaway here."

"That's right, Dan," called out a new voice. It was Bill Robinson. The rig's toolpusher had rushed into the bridge from the outside. He was slightly out of breath, having sprinted up the seventy steps of the access ladderwell. Two minutes earlier he had been on the drilling deck, monitoring the other BOP control panel, when he decided to return to the bridge to check the backup console.

"What do you know so far, Billy?" asked Captain Barker.

"The preventer's hydraulic control lines are gone for sure. And we can't maintain any mud pressure in the kill lines except for the shut-in hose." Kill lines are heavy-walled rubber hoses that are attached to the blowout preventer through which drilling fluid, a carefully controlled mixture of clay, water, and other chemicals, can be pumped from the rig into the well. The density of the heavy fluid controls downhole pressure.

"Jesus, all the other choke lines are out, too?"

"Yep, and we also tried to trigger the wellhead shut-in valves from our panel but it didn't work. That's why I came up here—to activate the backup panel, but I gather you just tried it."

"Yeah. Nothing happened. We've got zero pressure now, but we're still flowing."

"I was afraid of that—the valves must be jammed open somehow."

"But what about the BOP hoses—you think they're really open to the sea?"

"Yep, there's a slick of hydraulic fluid on the surface—no doubt about it."

"How the hell could that happen?"

"I have no idea. None of those lines should be giving us trouble. They're all new and have been repeatedly tested." Big

Billy paused momentarily to glance at the BOP panel. "For all of the hydraulic controls to go out plus the shut-in system failing to engage—I just don't know how it could happen. The odds of this happening are just frigging incredible."

"Shit-oh-dear!" someone called in the background.

Captain Barker was equally shocked. They no longer had any direct control over the wellhead. The oil and gas that continued to flow up the steel tubing inside the marine riser could now be shut off only by one of two emergency methods: either by closing one of the several above deck valves on the rig or by engaging a downhole safety valve. The latter was the best way because it sealed up the conductor pipe deep inside the well casing, preventing oil and gas from rising to the surface. Unfortunately, activating the downhole valve required time. The entire production test tubing, all 16,500 feet of it, had to be lifted above the bottom packer about three feet and then reset on top of the seal. By picking up and then setting down the reciprocating test tool, the valve would close.

"Billy, I know it's your call, but I think we should trip the downhole tool and kill the flow test right now. I don't like any of this."

Robinson, as toolpusher and overall boss of the drilling gear, had ultimate responsibility for the bore hole. "We've already started to kill the flow." He briefly looked down at his wristwatch. "In fact, Jamison should have the main deck valve closed off in a minute or so. We're then going to set the downhole tool, but it'll take at least twenty minutes to rig up the gear to pull and reset the tubing."

"Good plan. That ought to cover it," replied Barker. He then turned back to face the flow engineer. "Are we still flaring?"

"Just a minute, Captain. I'll check."

While the man studied his instrument panel Barker realized he could have ordered one of the techs to run outside behind the bridge and see if the flare had stopped burning.

"Got it, Captain. The flow test just shut down—the flare's extinguished."

Barker felt better. *One less thing to worry about*, he thought. He turned back to Robinson. "Billy, how do you wanta handle the BOP?"

"I've ordered the divers to . . ."

For the next several minutes, Captain Barker and Big Billy discussed a variety of emergency procedures until they were rudely interrupted by another noisy bridge alarm. This was a different warning sound—not a horn, but a siren. A moment later a new voice yelled out from the crowd, "Christ Almighty, we've got gas on the drilling deck."

"What?" yelled both Barker and Robinson simultaneously.

"Look here," called out the BOP technician. He was pointing to the H2S warning panel. The analog map of the ship had a series of tiny lights all over it. Five of the lights, each representing a methane-hydrogen sulfide gas sensor near the moonpool, were glowing red.

"Damnit!" Big Billy said. The men he had just sent to close the test valve were working in the area identified by the cluster of lights.

Barker responded next: "That gas can only be coming from one place."

"Yeah, you're right. We've got a blowout and the damn preventer is useless."

Both Barker and Robinson were in shock. The absolutely worst thing that can happen to an offshore oil operation is a wellhead blowout. Although the crude oil that reaches the surface creates enormous water pollution problems, it is the natural gas that rises from the deep that really threatens the humans aboard a drilling rig. Poisonous gases within the raw mixture can kill anyone not wearing a gas mask. But worse, if the hydrocarbon components of the gas ignite, the entire vessel can be consumed in a hellfire of unimaginable magnitude.

Barker took command. His ship was now in mortal danger. "All right, everyone, listen up. I want you to get your gas masks on and stay inside the bridge until we figure out what's going on."

One of the men ran to a nearby storage locker and began tossing out the rubber garments. The men struggled to pull the cumbersome breathing devices over their heads.

Barker next ordered the bridge watch officer to activate the ship's master gas alarm system. A moment later, a special prerecorded warning began broadcasting over the ship's intercom system. The female announcer's voice was specifically designed to be recognized over the normal male voices that dominated the IC system. The message was repeated every few seconds: "Warning—there is poisonous gas on the vessel. Don your gas mask and move to your emergency station."

After sounding the gas alarms, Barker ordered the watch officer to shut down all nonvital electrical systems aboard the ship. Although all exterior-mounted electrical switches were enclosed in explosionproof housings, he couldn't afford to take any chances. One spark from a motor could ignite the gas cloud surrounding the vessel.

Finally satisfied that the ship's safety systems were being properly activated, Captain Barker turned toward Robinson. The toolpusher had stood by silently while Barker called out the orders. The former naval officer's calm voice and deliberate manner in handling the crisis had a calming effect on everyone in the bridge house, especially Robinson. He was glad to have someone like Barker take charge.

"Billy, where are the rest of your men?" Barker asked, his voice muffled by the gas mask.

"Most of them are sleeping, and I imagine a few are in the galley by now."

Barker did a quick mental calculation. Most of the ship's 112-person crew were inside the vessel somewhere. If they remained inside and wore gas masks they might be okay. Anyone caught outside without protection was probably already dead.

"All right, I think you know I've got no choice but to order the crew to abandon the vessel. This baby could go up any second." He paused for a moment. "However, I'd like you and a couple of your best men to stay a little longer. I want to see if we can sever the mooring and break free of the casing before the well goes up."

"You got it, skipper. But first I want to see what happened to Jamison and his crew. Besides, we still might have an outside shot at triggering the downhole valve."

"Do it, but then get back up here in ten minutes. We don't have much time."

Ten seconds later Big Billy was off the bridge, heading for the drilling deck. Two workmen followed in his footsteps. They all wore gas masks.

* * *

The ROV was on its way back to the surface; the operation had gone perfectly so far.

After disabling the wellhead camera and severing the hydraulic control lines to the BOP, the ROV operator had placed a specially designed explosive charge on the outer casing of the blowout preventer. He used the underwater vehicle's remote-controlled arm to wrap the yellow-colored flexible line around the circumference of the BOP, just above the hydraulic connecter to the wellhead. The explosive, shaped like a half-inflated fire hose, was six inches wide and nearly twenty feet long. Magnets built into the charge held it tightly to the BOP's thick steel walls. From a distance, the bottom of the blowout preventer looked like it was being attacked by a gigantic sea worm.

The explosive device consisted of two hundred pounds of Semtex encased uniformly along the length of a polyvinyl tube. The plastic explosive was shaped into a linear, wedge-shape charge. It was designed to focus nearly 90 percent of its energy in one direction.

Two minutes after the charge was detonated, both men were leaning over the ROV's control panel, studying the image on the video screen. The lower half of the BOP stack was in the foreground. They could see a jagged gash running crosswise at the bottom of the stack. A torrent of crude oil and natural gas was gushing from the opening. It looked like an underwater tornado.

"Excellent," called out the older man. He reached over and patted the ROV operator on the left shoulder. "The charge worked perfectly. The production tubing is severed."

"Should I retrieve the clamp?"

"Yes. It's useless now. Besides, we can't afford to leave any evidence behind."

The clamp had been installed only as a backup. If the explosive charge had failed to detonate, the clamp would have kept the well bore open, allowing oil and gas to flow upward. They would have then attached backup charges to the marine riser. The pencil-thin walls of the thirty-inch-diameter pipe would be much easier to sever than the fist-thick steel casing of the blowout preventer.

Five minutes later the clamp had been retrieved and was stored inside the ROV's exterior tool bin. "What now, sir?" asked the ROV operator.

"We've accomplished our work here."

"So I should bring the ROV back?"

"Yes, but first don't forget to release the probe."

"Oh, yeah, I almost forgot."

The operator reached forward and triggered a toggle switch on his console. A moment later the robotic underwater vehicle jettisoned a silvery cylinder about eighteen inches long and eight inches in diameter. The aluminum container was buoyant. It would take six minutes for it to reach the ocean surface—plenty of time for the ROV to get away.

Billy Robinson and two of his roustabouts had made their way to the main drilling deck. It had been tough going, though. There was gas everywhere and they had to take extraordinary care not to create any kind of spark. A doorway opened the wrong way or a tool dropped on the steel deck could lead to instant disaster.

The drillers were looking for the three-man team that had been sent out earlier to close off the flow test line. So far, there was no sign of them.

"You guys head up to level A-one," Robinson said, his voice partially muffled by the thick gas mask he wore.

As the two men headed through a companionway, Billy made his way to the moonpool. He had to see what they were up against. Half a minute later he was standing next to the ten-foot-wide opening in the deck. The ocean surface below looked like a witch's caldron. Huge bubbles of natural gas, mixed with thick releases of hydrogen sulfide and accented by black boils of crude oil, churned away fifty feet below. *My God, it's a total blowout.*

Bill Robinson was just about to turn away from the moonpool when his eye spotted a flash of silver. *What's that?* He looked closer. Something metallic had been brought up in the plume, but it disappeared a few seconds later in the turbulence. Billy spent half a minute looking downward, trying to find the object. He finally gave up and then began heading toward the next subdeck to rejoin his crew.

* * *

The aluminum cylinder launched from the ROV was now on the surface. Strong eddy currents generated by the subterranean flow carried it nearly a hundred feet away before it finally slowed down. A pressure sensor inside the cylinder had just been activated, starting a chemical reaction. It would take a few more minutes before the internal pressure would exceed the bursting strength of the aluminum casing.

Captain Barker was still in the bridge house, manning the radio console. Despite the confines of his gas mask, he had issued a Mayday to the Coast Guard and was now desperately trying to warn any other vessels that might be in the area. The rig could go up at any second and he didn't want to endanger curiosity seekers.

So far, he had managed to contact only a few fishing boats, about five to ten miles to the north. They were in no danger. The only other nearby vessel was the yacht that had appeared earlier in the day. It was still about a half mile to the south. Although it was relatively close by, it was in no immediate jeopardy. The oil slick and gas cloud from the ruptured well were both moving north, carried by a combination of tidal current and wind. Despite the vessel's favorable position, he repeatedly tried to contact it by radiophone, calling on the marine emergency VHF frequency. The yacht did not acknowledge the call so he finally gave up.

Satisfied that he had done his duty, Captain Barker decided it was time to leave the ship. Five minutes earlier he had activated the Abandon Ship alarm. The Klaxon's wail sounded throughout the ship. It had only one meaning: Get to the lifeboats now!

Barker ran out of the bridge house, heading for C deck. It took him about a minute to reach the forward lifeboat stations. The *Kelda Scott* was equipped with four state-of-the-art oil rig escape vessels: two near the bow and two at the stern. Only the bow stations were being used. The escaping gas cloud had completely engulfed the stern lifeboats.

Although only half of the lifeboats were available, it was enough. Designed as floating emergency escape capsules, the quarter-million-dollar vessels each held up to sixty people. The airtight structures were built of fire-resistant composite materials and were equipped with self-contained oxygen-breathing systems.

One boat had already been launched and was now beginning to motor away from the rig. The second lifeboat was in its launch position. The single hatch to its self-contained cabin was still open. As Barker sprinted forward he hoped that Big Billy and his men were already inside. He didn't want to leave anyone aboard the *Kelda Scott.*

Big Billy was still on the drilling deck. He couldn't find the two crewmen he had started out with, let alone Jamison's missing crew. *Shit, they must have already left. I better get the hell outta here too,* he finally concluded.

The ROV operator continued to monitor the vehicle's return trip to the *Victory.* It was almost back. The senior Asian was on the flying bridge of the yacht. He was wearing a baseball cap to protect his bald head from the sun and he held a pair of binoculars to his eyes. He could hardly believe what he was seeing. The lower half of the *Kelda Scott* seemed to be engulfed by a boiling mass of gas and oil. Plumes of black watery oil shot upward ten to fifteen feet under the vessel; it looked like a volcanic eruption.

The Asian looked at his watch. *Should be any minute now.*

Captain Barker was standing halfway in the open hatchway of Lifeboat 2. The vessel was crammed with forty-four men and seven women. The yellow-brown gas cloud had now spread completely across the vessel, invading everything in its path.

Damnit, I can't wait any longer. We've got to go now, Barker thought. He took another step down the ladder and was preparing to seal the hatch when he spotted movement on the deck near a far bulkhead. It was Big Billy. The man was running for his life. Barker held the door open.

The aluminum cylinder was now a couple of hundred feet northwest of the *Kelda Scott* and the pressure inside the casing had just reached the critical point. The metal gave way, expelling a superheated fluid stream of phosphorus. The liquid metal instantly ignited the boundary layer of volatile gases that hovered just above the crude oil slick. And a microsecond later the spark flashed across the water's surface, igniting the main gas stream underneath the drilling vessel.

The *Kelda Scott* was engulfed in a tumultuous fireball that covered the ship from the water's surface to the top of the derrick. Big Billy had just made it to Lifeboat 2 when the explosion occurred. The instantaneous ignition of the gas cloud surrounding the lifeboat station incinerated everyone inside the escape capsule. They were all burned to cinders in a matter of seconds.

Lifeboat 1 survived. It was about three hundred feet away when the rig blew up. Although the oil slick surrounding the boat was on fire, it managed to power away to safety.

The Asian was knocked down by the shock wave from the ignition. He had completely underestimated the power of the explosion. As he picked himself up, he was thankful that he had taken the precaution of ordering the *Victory* to maintain a kilometer's separation from the rig. A minute later he was back in the main saloon. The ROV operator was still at his console. "Have you got it yet?" he asked.

"Yes, sir. It's in the well now, and I'm ready to seal the opening."

"Good, close it up. We've got to get out of here. The American Coast Guard, and the gods only know who else, will be out here soon."

Two minutes later the *Victory* was steaming south at twenty-four knots. The first Coast Guard search-and-rescue helo wouldn't arrive for another twenty minutes.

2

A RUDE AWAKENING

Seattle

Zackary Jacob Scott was alone in his expansive corner office high above downtown Seattle. Elliott Bay, with its magnificent harbor facilities, dominated the view from his windows. The forty-seven-year-old executive was busy studying a thick financial report on the health of his company. He was more than pleased with what the document concluded: Scott Coastal Systems was thriving, generating more cash than a dozen Hollywood blockbusters. He was already a rich man. Soon he would have world-class wealth.

Scott pushed his chair away from the solid oak desk, the focal point of his office, and stood up. He was a quarter of an inch shy of six feet tall and weighed a trim 175 pounds. Although his jet-black hair was just starting to gray, his handsome facial features made him look years younger than his true age.

Zack turned around and scanned the dozen photographs displayed across the top of his long credenza. The framed color prints were of family and friends. Two were his favorites. The eight-by-ten photo of his wife and two young sons on the flying bridge of his yacht was the centerpiece of the collection. Right next to it was a smaller print. It was of Zack with another man. They were kneeling beside the bank of a river in southeast Alaska, displaying their catch of salmon. Zack smiled as he recalled how much fun he and Big Billy Robinson had had on the trip.

Zack placed his hands on his hips. He then slowly bent backward, arching his spine. He repeated the back exercise five times before returning to his chair. Once again he started scanning the report, but he quickly lost interest. His mind was wandering. He was thinking about how lucky he had been.

Zack was fiercely proud of SCS—it was his life. He had spent the past twenty years working twelve-hour days, six to seven days a week, to fulfill his dream. And he was finally there. SCS was one of the top specialty marine construction companies on the West Coast. With over six hundred hard-working and loyal employees, annual revenues of nearly $300 million, and a huge backlog of work, Zackary J. Scott was on top of the world.

SCS specialized in offshore construction. It consisted of three main operating divisions. The Harbor and Coastal Division, the firm's original breadwinner, concentrated on building port facilities, piers, breakwaters, marinas, and other shoreline-related structures. The Bluewater Division, Zack's favorite, specialized in deepwater diving technology, primarily serving the petroleum industry. SCS's third operating section, and Zack's newest venture, the Oil Exploration Division, was engaged in the high-risk business of offshore oil drilling.

Zack dropped the report on his desk and reached for his coffee cup. As he sipped the steaming brew, he couldn't quite get the thought out of his mind that he had nearly lost everything. Years earlier he had taken an enormous gamble, one that he should never have made.

At that time SCS consisted of only two operating divisions: coastal-harbor and diving. Although the company was doing well as a conventional marine contractor, Zack had always been attracted to the really big marine work—offshore oil exploration. However, the American petroleum exploration industry, especially offshore oil, was in a deep recession back then. Crude oil from OPEC and other oil exporters flooded the world market, drastically depressing prices and killing the incentive to search for new sources of oil and gas. Consequently, offshore oil exploration equipment could be purchased at bargain basement prices.

By this time SCS had accumulated over $10 million in retained earnings and it was burning a hole in Zack's pocket. He sensed it was the right time to "go big." Convinced that OPEC would eventually reverse the drop in oil prices, Zack purchased three floating offshore drilling rigs at a court-ordered bankruptcy auction in Houston. The $40 million he paid for the rigs was a real bargain considering that they were all less than 10 years old and had cost over $70 million each to construct. Unfortunately, the previous owners went bankrupt because they couldn't find any work to pay the mortgages.

Scott gambled that the price of oil would turn around within two years, allowing the rigs once again to earn their keep. In the interim, however, he had to find some way to make the interest payment on the $30 million he had borrowed to finance the deal.

Zack's gamble nearly killed his business. Three years later, the price of crude oil was still in the cellar and there was no work for his rigs. And the $250,000 monthly interest payments were sucking up all of SCS's surplus cash flow. Both SCS and Scott personally were only a few months away from bankruptcy.

Scott had become so concerned with his tenuous situation that his lower back once again gave out on him. While some people suffer with migraine headaches when they are under pressure, Zack was plagued with a bad back. He was forced into the hospital for a week of therapy.

A month after his hospitalization, however, Zack's fortunes changed. Another brutal war flared up in the Middle East. The conflict between the feuding Arab states lasted only a few weeks, but the consequences were devastating. Nearly 50 percent of the Persian Gulf's oil production facilities were either lost or so badly damaged that it would take years to replace them. Consequently, the flow of oil out of the Middle East plummeted, causing the price of the remaining crude supplies to skyrocket.

Thank God for the mess in the Gulf, Scott often said to himself. The new war shocked the world far worse than the previous Arab oil embargoes or the Iraqi invasion of Kuwait. Almost instantly, there was congressional talk of gasoline rationing and reimplementation of emergency energy conservation measures. Just two weeks after the fighting stopped, the spot price for crude doubled.

The sudden price increase for oil stimulated the hunt for new offshore petroleum on a worldwide basis. American and Canadian oil companies scrambled to find any available offshore drilling rigs, rushing them to old and new sites in the Gulf of Mexico, Alaska, and the Canadian Arctic. Three months after the war ended Zack was offered $100 million cash for his three drilling rigs. Declining to sell, he instead entered into an agreement with a major oil firm for the exclusive use of his offshore drilling rigs and crews for exploration in Alaska's Bering Sea. The basic agreement was for a five-year period with another five-year option. Never in the history of the firm had it developed such a backlog of work.

With the guaranteed cash flow from his drilling operations, Scott was also able to personally focus much of his energy on completing a research-and-development project he had started a decade earlier. After investing over $5 million, SCS's remotely operated underwater drilling system had nearly reached the prototype stage. If the subsea oil well drilling system worked as well as Scott expected, it would revolutionize the search for oil in deep water. The profit potential was enormous.

Scott's newfound wealth also allowed him to purchase a fourth drilling vessel. And after enduring several years of federal regulatory "red tape" he was able to employ the rig for his own account. The Hammer 4 oil field off the Washington coast was turning out to be SCS's greatest asset.

All in all, Zackary Scott was a very lucky man. And he knew it. Even though he worked hard and was innovative, good fortune continued to bless him. It seemed that he could do no wrong. But that was all about to change.

Zack was just about to reread another section of the report when the intercom speaker on the desk came alive. "Zack, I'm sorry to bother you, but there's a call I think you should take."

"Who is it, Janet?" he asked, knowing that his secretary would interrupt only if there was a problem. Earlier, he had requested that all of his calls be held until he finished reviewing the report.

"It's some reporter from Channel Six. She says it is urgent—something about an accident on the *Kelda Scott*."

Scott sat up straight in his chair at the mention of the drilling rig. The *Kelda Scott* was the flagship of the SCS fleet, named after his wife. He took a very personal interest in its welfare.

"All right, I'll take the call." He reached forward for his telephone handset. "This is Zackary Scott."

"Mr. Scott, this is Susan Harris at Channel Six. We just received a report that your drilling rig, the *Kelda Scott*, has been involved in some kind of accident. Can you give me any details?"

"I don't know what you're talking about—who said there was an accident?"

"I don't have much detail yet. But we believe there had been a major oil spill."

"Impossible. That rig is one of the safest in the world."

"Then you deny your platform is leaking oil."

"First of all, lady, it's not a platform. It floats and it is called a semisubmersible. Second, I have no reports of any trouble from the vessel. If we had had a problem out there, I would have known about it."

Zack was just about to continue with his lecture when Janet Clark rushed into his office. The attractive thirty-eight-year-old woman normally smiled when she was around Zack, but from the frown on her face he could tell something was wrong. He put his hand over the mouthpiece. "Janet, what's wrong?"

"Zack, the Coast Guard's on line four. Something's happened to the *Kelda Scott*."

Scott disconnected the reporter's line and punched in the new number. "Zackary Scott here."

"Lieutenant Matheison, Mr. Scott. About five minutes ago we received an SOS from your drilling rig. Captain Barker reported that he had a wellhead blowout in progress and that he was preparing to abandon the vessel."

Zack was in total shock. His worst nightmare was materializing in broad daylight. "You mean we're losing the well?"

"Yes, sir. Barker reports crude oil on the surface and lots of gas around the rig."

"Stand by, Lieutenant. I gotta check something real quick."

Zack punched the Hold button and turned toward Janet. "Get me Barker on our sat-line right now. I've got to confirm this."

"I just tried, but we can't raise the rig. They're not answering."

"Damnit."

Scott reconnected the Coast Guard officer. "Lieutenant, are you in radio communication with the rig? We can't raise it with our own system."

"Yes, for the time being. The vessel is using VHF channel nine and our La Push station is relaying the signal to us."

"So my people are preparing to abandon the mooring. Can you help them?"

"Yes, we've just initiated a region-wide SAR operation with all of our available units. We've dispatched two helos: one from Port Angeles and another from Seattle. They should be on the scene within a half hour or so."

"I've got over a hundred people out there, Lieutenant. Those helos won't be able to do much good."

"I know, that's why we've got two cutters on the way. One from Neah Bay and another from Port Angeles. But they're still hours away."

Scott looked at the wall next to his desk. A huge chart of the Washington State coastline covered most of it. The hydrographic map covered the entire continental shelf from the southern end of British Columbia's Vancouver Island to the Columbia River. A tiny scale model of the *Kelda Scott* was glued to the Hammer 4 location, just south of the Strait of Juan de Fuca, near the top of the map.

"Do you have any reports of casualties?" Zack asked.

"Nothing yet. Only that the captain has ordered the vessel abandoned. As far as we know the crew is safe at this point. Captain Barker did indicate that they were going to try to jettison the anchors and power the vessel away from the site."

Good thinking, boys, Zack said to himself. He knew Billy Robinson and Captain Barker would try to save the rig after ensuring the crew's safety. By moving the *Kelda Scott* just a short distance away from the well site—only a half mile or so—it might make all the difference in the world. Having a functional deep drilling rig nearby could be vital to stopping the blowout. When control of a subsea well is lost, the usual method of stopping the leak is to plug the casing. That can only be accomplished by drilling a new relief or intercept well and then pumping tons of high-pressure mud and grout into the runaway well bore to create a seal. Unfortunately, the *Kelda Scott* was the only drilling vessel in the Northwest capable of working at the depth of Hammer 4. The nearest other rig was working offshore of southern California, at least three sailing days away.

Zack instinctively sensed that if he didn't immediately stop the Hammer 4 blowout, he would have an environmental disaster on his hands the likes of which would make the *Exxon Valdez* spill look like a walk in the park.

"Lieutenant, have you got any information on the spill?"

"Nothing yet. Only that there's a slick around the rig."

God, please make that BOP work! "Have you called the MSRC center yet?" asked Zack. After the *Exxon Valdez* disaster, the major oil companies created the Marine Spill Response Corporation for the express purpose of managing catastrophic oil spills. Headquartered in Washington, D.C., MSRC has five regional response centers across the country. The closest center to Hammer 4 was located in Everett, twenty-five miles north of Seattle. Although privately funded by oil companies, shippers and receivers of oil, and in SCS's case, exploratory drilling contractors, MSRC operates with complete autonomy, reporting only to the U.S. Coast Guard.

"Yes, they were just notified and have issued a major spill alert."

"Good, how long before they're onscene?"

"The managing director estimated it would be at least eight hours before their command vessel reaches the Hammer 4 site. They've sent out a coast-wide alert for the other vessels they will be mobilizing. Unfortunately, the *Kelda Scott* is so far out at sea that they can't send any of their smaller units out. If the weather kicks up, they'll get the hell beat out of them."

"Yeah, I know that. Look, you've got the full resources of this firm available to you, so whatever you need, I'll get it."

"Well, right now I'd suggest you start thinking about how you're going to seal the well off. If you've lost the BOP or the casing failed, God only knows how long it will take to seal the leak."

"I'm way ahead of you, Lieutenant. I know my butt is

hanging out a mile on this so I'm going to fly out to the *Kelda Scott* and personally take charge.''

"Good, that's what I was hoping I would hear. If anyone's got a chance to stop that leak, it's you.''

"Okay, then, I'm on my way. If you need to reach me, call the office and they can patch you in wherever I am.''

"You got it.''

Scott hung up the phone and stared at the wall map. *Damn! How could that well have blown out?* A few seconds later he turned to face his secretary. "Janet, tell Tom to get the bird ready. I've got to get out there ASAP.''

"Already done, Zack. He's heading to the airport now and will pick you up on the roof in about forty-five minutes.''

"Great. Now where's the *Ranger* today?''

"She's still on station in Rosario Strait working on that new cable-lay project.''

Scott thought for a few seconds as he continued to study the wall chart. "Get hold of Captain Shay and tell him to abandon the cable job. If he has to dump the cable reel overboard with some marking buoys, tell him to do it. I want the *Ranger* steaming to the Hammer 4 site within the hour.''

"Okay, but what should I tell him is going on?''

"Tell 'im the truth. We've lost the Hammer 4 well and I want the *Ranger* available to help salvage the *Kelda Scott*.''

"Okay.''

"Where's Russ today?''

"He's at Metro, going over the contract for the new outfall project.''

"Get someone to find him right now. I want him with me when I helo out there.''

"Okay. Anything else?''

"Please call Kelda for me and tell her that I'm flying out to the rig. I probably won't be home tonight.''

"Will do.'' Janet then turned and walked briskly out of the office.

Zack stood up, pushing his chair away from the desk. He was slightly light-headed and his legs felt as heavy as bags of cement. His lower back was already beginning to ache from the building stress. *Christ Almighty, why did this have to happen? Everything was going so well.*

* * *

The McDonnell Douglas MD500 was racing westward at 120 knots. Zackary Scott was in the copilot seat. SCS pilot Tom Hoop was in the right seat.

Although the sun was now descending in the western sky, several hours of light remained. Even if it had been pitch-dark, however, they wouldn't have had any trouble finding the *Kelda Scott*. She was still moored over Hammer 4, and the fireball that engulfed her was slowly but surely roasting the $100 million vessel. The rig's once brightly painted white-and-red steel superstructure was scorched black from the flames erupting out of the ocean. From a distance of five miles the semi looked liked something out of Dante's *L'inferno*.

"Dear God, what a mess!" called out Russ McMillin. The SCS engineer was in the center of the backseat, leaning forward between Zack and the pilot. "Damnit to hell, Zack, she's a goner for sure. No way we're going to save her."

Zack knew McMillin was right. Big Billy and Captain Barker hadn't been able to move the rig away from the well. "Yeah, the vessel's a total loss." Scott paused for a moment when he spotted an orange object in the water. It was to the left of the burning rig and several miles downwind. "I've got a lifeboat. About ten o'clock, just this side of the smoke plume."

"Got it, skipper," replied the pilot.

"Let's head over there and check it out."

"Roger."

Two minutes later the MD500 was hovering over Lifeboat 1. Despite repeated attempts, Zack was unable to make radio contact with the survival vessel. He could see the heads and shoulders of several people projecting out of the stern hatchway; they were waving their arms wildly. Unfortunately, the lifeboat's radio had been knocked out during the emergency launch—the fiberglass vessel hit the water at a higher angle than expected, and the resulting impact broke the radio's bulkhead housing. It crashed to the deck, shattering its electronic components.

"Where'd that Coast Guard chopper go?" Scott asked as he began moving his head back and forth across the Plexiglas windscreen, searching the sky. Five minutes earlier they had spotted the Aerospatiale HH-65 Dolphin as it patrolled the waters around the burning semisubmersible.

The pilot pointed with his right hand. "It's still orbiting around the rig. You want to talk with them?"

"Yes."

A moment later Zack was patched into the Dolphin, call sign Clearwater One. "Say, Clearwater One, can you raise my people in the lifeboat? We can't reach 'em with our gear."

"Negative. Their radio is nonfunctional."

"Well, any idea when we can get them out of here? Some of the crew might be injured."

"We understand your concern, Mr. Scott. Our cutter, the *Resolution*, will be onscene in about an hour. Until then they'll just have to wait."

"How long are you guys going to stick around?"

"We've got ten minutes before we have to head back to shore. We'll refuel at La Push and then come back out to coordinate with the cutter."

"Okay, that sounds good." Scott paused momentarily. "Any word on our other escape boats? We still don't see them."

"Negative. Before the rig went up, Captain Barker radioed that they only had access to two of the four lifeboats. We've contacted all the other vessels in the immediate area, but only one lifeboat has been spotted. We don't know where the other one is."

Zack had a sickening sensation in his stomach. One lifeboat could accommodate sixty persons, maybe seventy pushing it to the limit. *Where the hell are the others?* he wondered. "Understand. Thanks for your help, Clearwater One. Scott Coastal out."

After signing off, Zack turned toward the pilot. "How much fuel have we got left, Tom?"

"We can stick around for another twenty minutes and then will have to head back to Port Angeles."

"How about La Push?"

"That's strictly a Coast Guard shore base—no civilian aircraft allowed."

"Hell, heading to Port Angeles is going to take a lot of time."

"That's right, skipper. And by the time we refuel, it'll be too dark to fly back here. I don't have any night vision gear for this bird."

"Yeah, I figured that." Zack paused for a moment as he looked down at a partially folded NOAA chart in his lap. "All right, let's make these last few minutes really count. I'd like you to take her up to a couple thousand feet. I want to see where this damn slick is heading. Maybe the other lifeboat is at the end of it."

"Roger."

Several minutes later the MD500 was flying at 3,000 feet about a half mile south of the *Kelda Scott*. The black, sooty plume from the runaway fire rose through the air column another 5,000 feet, finally fanning out against a denser invisible layer.

Zack gasped as he took in the view from below. Much of the crude oil was consumed by the fire—but not all of it. About 20 percent of the escaping oil spread across the ocean surface, carried away from the flames by the wind and surface currents. The black oily water seemed to cover the ocean for miles.

The wind had changed direction several hours earlier and was now blowing lightly from the north. Zack could see streaks of crude projecting southward into the pristine ocean waters. The fragmented black-and-gray slicks pierced the emerald-green water like long stringy fingers. It was an ugly scene. And there was no sign of Lifeboat 2.

Russ McMillin broke the silence. "Well, Zack, at least it's heading away from shore."

"Yeah, I guess that's a good sign." He knew, however, that it would be only a matter of hours before the deadly mixture began flowing onto the beaches, killing nearly every living creature in its path. *Dear God, the environmentalists are going to crucify me.*

As bad as the oil spill was, that wasn't what really bothered Scott. His gut ached out of fear. *Where are the rest of my people?* he repeatedly asked himself as he searched for the missing lifeboat.

Zack finally turned away from the ocean surface, spotting another aircraft in the distance. It was a twin-engine turboprop heading west from the mainland. The pilot spoke next. "I wondered when they'd show up."

"What are you talking about?" asked Zack.

"Bet you anything that's a press charter. Probably loaded with damn newspaper and TV reporters."

Zack could already visualize the headlines: SEATTLE COMPANY KILLING OCEAN!

"Okay, Tom. I've seen enough for now. Let's head to the beach and refuel."

"Roger."

The pilot was beginning to turn toward the northeast when Russ McMillin spoke up. "Hold up a minute. Something's happening with the rig."

The pilot banked the aircraft to the right, bringing the semisubmersible into full view.

"What the hell happened?" shouted Scott.

The *Kelda Scott* was now listing heavily to starboard. The main drilling platform was at a forty-five-degree angle. He could see unsecured equipment and gear rolling off the deck, crashing into the inferno that continued to boil underneath it.

"Jesus, she's losing it," Russ yelled.

McMillin was right. One section of a steel support column on the starboard half of the rig had melted from the heat of the fire. Seawater was now flooding into the hole and cascading downward into the hollow pontoon section.

All three men watched in silence as the deck tilted even farther. Finally, when the list reached sixty degrees, the *Kelda Scott* turned turtle. As it began to capsize, the port pontoon sheared away from its vertical columns. The weight of the normally submerged hull was too great for the supports.

When the pontoon broke away, the main body of the rig sank like a rock. It took only sixty seconds for it to disappear below the ink-black surface. The severed port pontoon followed a minute later.

The one-knot subsurface current pushed the wreckage away from the well site. The remains of the *Kelda Scott* crashed into the seabed about three hundred feet north of the wellhead.

As the hull sank, the thirty-inch-diameter marine riser went with it. And for just a few seconds, the thousand-foot-long pipe functioned like a compression strut, pivoting the sinking debris away from the Hammer 4 site. The force telegraphed to the riser's ball valve connection with the blowout preventer was enormous.

Just before the upper ball joint would have failed, the BOP's lower connection to the wellhead broke. Already severely fractured by sabotage, the remaining undamaged wall sections of the preventer could not resist the massive bending moment that had been produced by the cantilever force. As a result, the steel connection snapped like a pretzel and the entire six-story-tall BOP assembly fell over on its side. Then, as the *Kelda Scott* descended, the riser pipe, still connected to the sinking rig, dragged the twenty-ton BOP along the soft bottom as if it were a flyweight. When the ball valve finally pulled apart, twenty seconds later, the preventer sank into the mud.

The wellhead was now completely severed. The jagged remains of the BOP stack's lower coupling was all that remained. About a foot of the six-inch-diameter conductor pipe projected out of the ruins. Without the presence of the blowout preventer to deflect and disperse the spewing crude oil and natural gas, the high-velocity jet shot straight up. It now looked like an underwater geyser.

On the surface, the effect was even more pronounced than when the *Kelda Scott* had been present. The gas-and-oil-fired flames blasted out of the ocean's surface, taking on a surreal appearance. It looked like something from hell.

Scott turned away from the windscreen, unable to look at the view below any longer. He was sick to his stomach with anger and fear. "Let's get out of here," he finally ordered.

The MD500 raced for shore.

Tokyo

Five men sat around an elegantly crafted pinewood table. The *tsuke* stood only two feet above the thickly cut beige carpet, requiring people around it to sit cross-legged. Silk *zabutons*, stuffed with the finest down, cushioned their legs and buttocks.

The table and cushions were the only furniture in the spacious, square conference room. The two interior walls were tastefully decorated with Oriental tapestries, and there was a four-foot-high bronze sculpture of a great blue heron in one corner. The exterior window walls were completely unobstructed, extending eight feet in height from the floor to the suspended ceiling.

The penthouse conference room occupied the southwest cor-

ner of a brand-new office tower located in the heart of Tokyo's
financial district. The view from the fifty-fourth floor would
have been spectacular if the smog hadn't been so thick. As it
was, a dullish brown haze filtered the vista of the huge harbor
in the foreground, and Tokyo Bay, far in the background,
looked opaque.

Four of the men surrounding the table were young, ranging
in age from the mid-thirties to the mid-forties. The four men
also looked and dressed alike: average height, slim build,
short dark hair, starched white shirts, and conservatively cut,
medium-priced dark suits. All but one wore glasses.

The fifth man did not fit the mold. He was twenty-five years
senior to the oldest of the others. Standing a half inch under
five and a half feet tall and weighing only 130 pounds, he was
small for a Japanese man. Although his stature was slight, the
garments and jewelry that adorned his body demanded respect.
The dark blue pinstripe suit he wore had been custom-tailored
by one of the finest haberdasheries in Hong Kong; the solid
gold custom-made Rolex on his left wrist had cost as much
as a new Cadillac; his diamond-studded tie clasp was worth a
king's ransom.

The combined attention of all five men was focused on a
small circular black object positioned in the center of the conference table. The men listened intently to the electronically
amplified voice that broadcast from the speakerphone.

"So far, everything's proceeding as planned. The device
was successfully attached and then activated."

"Then the well was destroyed?" asked the older, thin-faced
and nearly bald man. He was leaning over the table's edge,
speaking into the box.

"All we know at this point, sir, is that there is a huge fire
and a lot of oil is on the surface."

"Excellent," replied the man. "You've done well."

"Thank you, sir."

"Report back when you have more information."

"Yes, sir."

The elderly man nodded his head at one of the others sitting
on his right. That man reached under the edge of the table and
flipped a hidden switch, breaking the encrypted telephone circuit to the United States.

The senior man leaned back and lit up a cigarette. Hiroshi

Yoshida had smoked at least a pack a day since he joined the army air force in 1945. He often wondered when it would finally kill him.

"Well, gentlemen," he said, expelling a cloud of smoke, "any comments?"

"Do you think this will finally stop him?" asked a man sitting directly across the table from Yoshida.

"Yes, I think he will have his hands full with this mess for a long time." Yoshida paused for a moment as he flicked the ash from his cigarette into a $500 porcelain ashtray. "He will be in the courts for years trying to protect his company."

Another man entered the conversation, grinning as he talked. "The American legal system is a quagmire that will suck the lifeblood right out of the company. It'll cost him millions to defend the lawsuits and pay the fines and penalties. He might even go to jail for a year or two."

The five men laughed in harmony at the last comment.

For the next fifteen minutes, the group continued talking, discussing the next phase of their operation. Then the conference room door opened. Half a dozen women dressed in brightly colored ceremonial *kishi* dresses entered. They carried large trays filled with food and drink. There were seafood delicacies ranging from eel to squid, and a variety of fine European wines and American whiskeys. It was time to celebrate.

After the beautiful attendants served the group and then exited the conference room, Yoshida raised his half-full glass of Jack Daniels. The others instantly stopped chatting as he began his tribute. "Well, my friends, we have much to be thankful for today. Through all of your hard work and by the grace of the Emperor, the company is once again safe and secure. I don't think we're going to have any more trouble from Zackary Scott."

The others nodded their heads in agreement, then clinked their glasses together. There was an air of smugness about the group, especially in the younger men. They were now true believers in the system. They had just seen it work firsthand.

Once again the collective power of the group had soundly defeated an individual rival. It was always the same technique: first infiltrate the adversary's forces, then learn his system, and finally turn his system against him. It seemed the Americans would never learn from their mistakes.

3

LITTLE MIKE

Hammer 4

The *Ranger III* arrived at the Hammer 4 site a few minutes before midnight. The 350-foot-long vessel had been running hard for hours. When it charged past Neah Bay, leaving the Strait of Juan de Fuca and passing into the Pacific Ocean, the SCS helicopter landed on the ship's helipad and Zackary Scott and Russ McMillin boarded the vessel.

Zack and Russ were now in the bridge house, standing next to the vessel's skipper. Captain Jim Shay had been with SCS for over a dozen years. Now in his early sixties, Shay was planning to retire next year. The tall, lanky sailor had been a ship driver for over forty years.

Captain Shay was speaking to his counterpart on the *Resolution*. The U.S. Coast Guard cutter had taken up a monitoring position five hundred yards upwind of the furiously burning oil well. "Commander, any news on survivors?" asked Shay.

"Negative. So far we've only managed to recover the one lifeboat with sixty crew members."

Shay was about to ask another question when Zack spoke up. "Jim, let me talk with him."

Captain Shay handed the microphone to Zack.

"Commander, this is Zackary Scott. I'm the owner of the *Kelda Scott*." Zack paused a moment. "Skipper, we're still missing fifty-two people—they've got to be out there some-where!''

"I understand, Mr. Scott. We've got all of our resources looking right now." The Coast Guard officer hesitated. He didn't want to say what he was thinking but he knew it had to be said. "Sir, we're all praying for your missing crew, but I think you'd better be prepared for the worst.''

Zack shook his head from side to side as he handed the mike back to Shay. He knew that the missing men and women would not be found, but he wasn't ready to give up hope yet.

"Commander, this is Shay again. We know you're doing everything you can.''

"Roger.''

Shay turned to face Scott. "Zack, you still want to pro-ceed?''

"Yeah, we've got no choice now.''

Shay keyed the mike again. "Commander, we'd like your permission to close to within three hundred yards of the well-head. We need to run a side scan sonar survey to check out the BOP.''

"Sorry, *Ranger III*, but I can't let you get that close. It's too dangerous.''

Shay was about to respond when Zack stepped forward. "Jim, let me handle this." Zack keyed the microphone. *"Res-olution*, this is Zackary Scott again. That's my oil well out there and it's my rig on the bottom. If you want to have any hope of getting the spill under control, I've got to get some data on the bottom. I can only do that with our remote gear, but I've got to get closer.''

Commander Welsh waited nearly half a minute before mak-ing his reply. "Okay, Scott. It's your ball game, but you must waive all liability claims against the Coast Guard if you pro-ceed.''

Scott could hardly believe what he was hearing. The man was covering his ass while Zack's was already getting cooked. *Shit! No one will take any responsibility anymore.* "Affirma-tive, *Resolution*, we've been duly warned.''

Scott turned back to Shay. "Okay, Jim, bring 'er in, slow and easy. We've already got the fish streamed. Let's try to get this done in one transect.''

"Roger.''

Ten minutes later the *Ranger* was about a thousand feet upwind of the burning oil. The flame point on the surface generally remained in the same place, but as the tidal current changed, it slowly moved north and south. With over a thousand feet of vertical travel, the buoyant petroleum-based fluids could move several hundred feet away from the bottom before breaking the surface.

Zack and Russ were in the ship's sensor room. With nearly $10 million worth of state-of-the-art underwater electronic sensing equipment onboard, the *Ranger III* was well equipped for the mission it was now undertaking.

Zack's eyes were glued to the output printer of the side scanning sonar unit. A torpedo-shaped cylinder about twenty feet long was trailing off the aft end of the ship. The "fish" was cutting through the water at six knots, five hundred feet off the bottom. High-frequency sound waves were broadcast along both sides of the device. As the sound waves pierced the water column they eventually struck the bottom. Part of the incident sound energy was absorbed by the soft marine sediments but some of it reflected back toward the fish. Special sensors on the probe's body intercepted the return signals and transmitted them to the ship's computers. The returning data was processed and the results displayed on the graphical plotter.

"Got something," cried out Scott as he stared at the paper plot. On the right-hand corner of the twenty-four-inch-wide sheet he spotted a new reflection. It looked like a jumble of lines and shadows, but to a trained eye it was clearly not a natural object.

"Yeah, I see it," replied McMillin. "What is that?"

Zack picked up the plot. "I'll be damned if that doesn't look like one of the pontoons."

"Jesus, I think you're right. But where's the rest of the rig?"

"It must be close by. Tell Jim to set up for another run—a hundred yards closer this time."

"Got it."

Twenty minutes later the *Ranger III* was making its second transect. The radiant heat from the burning oil and gas was so intense during the run that a ten-by-fifty-foot-long section of blue hull paint wrinkled when the ship passed by.

Zack and Russ were still watching the side scan sonar image as the paper plot rolled off the printer. Russ spotted the new target first. Zack saw it, too. This time the image was big—much bigger than the first. "There it is," called out McMillin.

"Yeah, that's got to be the hull," Zack said. He was too stunned to say any more. He could clearly see the ghostlike image of the *Kelda Scott*. It was lying sideways on the bottom. The graphical plot looked like a giant L. The surviving starboard pontoon and support columns were embedded in the mud while the main drilling deck was projecting vertically upward. The derrick had separated from the drilling deck and was crumbled over on the bottom about a hundred feet away.

Zack looked away from the plot, turning his attention to one of the technicians at a nearby console. The twenty-three-year-old woman was manning the ship's GPS navigation system. "Pam, did you get the coordinates of that last target?"

"Yes, sir, I've got it mapped. Target two is in one thousand eleven feet of water. It's approximately three hundred feet northward from the wellhead's coordinates."

"Good, keep tracking. We're going to check the well now."

"Right."

Zack turned back to the side scan output. Russ was still standing beside Zack, but he was no longer watching the bottom plot. Instead, he was monitoring the probe's flight over the bottom. A televisionlike display console plotted the real-time, two-dimensional position of the fish in relation to the location of the subsea well. The probe was closing fast with the Hammer 4 site. Russ made his report: "Zack, looks like the wellhead should be coming on line in about ten seconds."

"Okay, I'm looking for it now."

McMillin's estimate was right on the money. The image of the vertical wellhead structure clearly stood out on the display. It looked like a pipe poking out of the bottom. The steel housing created perfect acoustic reflections on the output plot. The seeping oil and gas, however, were invisible to sound waves. If it had been a real picture, the high-pressure fluids blasting upward would have looked like an underwater volcanic eruption.

"Damn, it looks like the BOP stack is gone." McMillin was referring to the sixty-foot-high blowout preventer that should have been mounted on top of the wellhead. If the BOP had been attached to the wellhead, it would have stood out like a beacon.

Zack was devastated. He had been counting on manually actuating the blowout preventer with one of the *Ranger*'s ROVs, hoping that one or two of the valves would seal the subterranean flow. But without the BOP, his carefully-thought-out plan was useless.

"What the hell do we do now?" Russ finally asked.

"Hell, I don't know." Zack remained silent for over a minute while his mind raced through half a dozen contingency plans. "Russ, maybe we can do something with the casing or conductor pipe. But we've got to get down there to do it. There's no way it can be done remotely."

"So you want me to get *Little Mike* ready?"

"Yeah, we've got no choice. Let's do it."

It took nearly two hours to prepare *Little Mike*. The submersible—really a mini-submarine—was housed on the fantail of the *Ranger III*. It was sixty feet long and had a twelve-foot beam. It looked like a giant beer can with rounded ends. The forward hemisphere was constructed of transparent acrylic, allowing the pilot an unobstructed view of the surrounding water. The rest of the hull was constructed of high-strength steel. Mounted on the stern section were a pair of horizontal diving planes and a vertical rudder fin. A five-foot-diameter ducted propeller projected outward from the very end of the hull. Hydraulic thrusters located along the hull's forward and aft quarter points provided pinpoint maneuvering capability.

Little Mike was powered by an electric drive. Ten thousand pounds of storage batteries mounted to the keel supplied enough direct current to propel the mini-sub at a speed of five knots for over twenty hours.

Zackary Scott and one of SCS's senior ocean engineers had designed the vehicle. It was named after the engineer's first child, born a week before the underwater vessel was launched. Zack gave the christening honor to his friend. *Little Mike* was developed for underwater reconnaissance and construction observation. Capable of diving to ten thousand feet, the submersible had been used extensively to map possible underwater power and communication cable routes in the Caribbean

Sea. Zack had only recently shipped the vehicle back to Seattle. He had planned on using the sub to select a route for a new production pipeline that would link the Hammer 4 well site to the shore. All thoughts of the pipeline project, however, were now forgotten.

"Say, Jim, any word from the Coast Guard on their observer?" asked Zack as he keyed a microphone from inside *Little Mike*'s cockpit.

"Yeah, he's on the way," replied Captain Shay from the *Ranger*'s bridge house. "He landed on the *Resolution* fifteen minutes ago and was transferred to a runabout. It's pulling up to us now."

"Good. As soon as he's aboard, send him here. I want to launch in twenty minutes."

"Got it, Zack!"

Scott replaced the microphone and turned to his left. Russ McMillin was sitting in the copilot's seat. "Okay, Russ, how's everything look?"

"Batteries are up to snuff. Sonars check out, and we have a forty-eight-hour air supply."

"Good. As soon as the Coastie shows up, we'll launch."

"Roger." McMillin then paused for a moment. "Skipper, any word yet on Big Billy?"

Zack wished Russ hadn't brought up the subject. It hurt too much. "Still nothing, Russ. All we know is that he wasn't aboard Lifeboat One."

McMillin sank deeper into his leather chair. He had worked with Billy Robinson for years. "Shit, he didn't make it, did he?"

"No, Russ. I'm afraid they're all gone."

Not only had Big Billy died when the *Kelda Scott* blew up, but Captain Barker and fifty other members of the crew had also expired. The Hammer 4 blowout was turning out to be one of the worst maritime disasters in Northwest history.

For the next eight minutes, Scott and McMillin continued going through a series of predive checklists, double-checking every critical system onboard the mini-sub. And then the Coast Guard officer finally showed up. Zack first heard the footsteps as the officer started climbing down the aluminum ladder of the main hull access hatchway, located ten feet behind the cockpit.

Zack turned around in his seat, preparing to greet his passenger. He was not ready, however, for what he saw. A woman, in her late thirties, stood at the base of the ladder. She had shoulder-length golden blond hair, crystal-clear green eyes, and she wore just a hint of lipstick. Although the blue coveralls she wore were regulation, the way her body filled them out was strictly high-fashion. The silver insignia on her lapels identified her as a full commander and the name tag over her right breast pocket read "Blake."

"Permission to come aboard?" called the woman as she faced the cockpit.

"Sure, come ahead," replied Zack. He then rose from his chair and started aft. He took only one step before stumbling on a loose power cable. Zack just managed to break his fall as the visitor stepped forward, trying to help.

"Thanks," Zack said, clearly embarrassed. "Too much stuff in here."

She smiled at him. Even her teeth were perfect. *God, she's beautiful*, he said to himself.

"Hi, I'm Halley Blake," she said as she offered her hand.

Zack reached forward and returned the greeting. "Zackary Scott."

"Well, I'm really pleased to meet you, Mr. Scott." She paused for a moment. "I think I've read everything your company has published on undersea construction and diving techniques."

Zack smiled. "You're an engineer?"

"Yes, sir. Graduated from the Academy and then took a master's in mechanical engineering at Stanford. I finally finished my Ph.D. at Caltech a couple of years ago."

Zack was impressed—the woman was highly educated. "You have any experience with subs?"

"Some. I've been on a couple of NOAA expeditions in the *Alvin* as well as worked on a number of classified navy projects."

"Good, then you shouldn't have any problem with this boat. It's probably not much different from the others you've been on."

Zack spent the next ten minutes familiarizing Commander Halley Blake with *Little Mike*. When they finished he was even more impressed with the woman. Her questions were nonstop and almost all of them were technical. She devoured Zack's replies with a computer memory.

After assigning Commander Blake to the observer's seat, located just behind the cockpit next to a twelve-inch-diameter view port, Zack returned to the pilot's position. About a minute later, another man climbed through the sub's access ladder. He was skinny, no more than five foot six. His skin was coal black and his equally dark hair was cut close against his scalp, mimicking a 1960s crew cut. Elwood "Ears" Mason, age thirty-one, was *Little Mike*'s chief technician and radio operator.

Mason sealed the hatch and then sat at the engineer's console right behind Halley Blake.

"Ears, meet Commander Blake," called out Zack. "She's our official observer for the dive."

"Pleased to meet you, ma' am," Mason said as he smiled, displaying crooked but gleaming white teeth. He reached out to shake the woman's hand.

Zack turned to face Blake. "Ears has been on the outside running a series of diagnostic tests on *Little Mike*'s remote systems." Zack then turned back to Mason. "Everything okay?"

"You bet, skipper. She's ready to dive."

"Good." Zack paused momentarily, scanning the instrument panel. "Okay, everybody. We're set. Let's get this show on the road."

Ten minutes later *Little Mike* was floating in the dark green waters of the Pacific Ocean. A specially manufactured launching platform built into the stern of the *Ranger III* simply lowered the mini-sub into the water. Once it was buoyant, Zack reversed the thrusters and powered out.

Little Mike was a hundred feet aft of the stern. The glow from the burning oil well lit up the water surface around the tiny submarine as if it was the middle of day. The *Ranger* had managed to maneuver within five hundred feet of the wellhead's coordinates when the mini-sub was released.

"Okay, Jim," called out Zack on his voice-activated headset boom mike, "we're ready to dive."

"Roger, you want us to stick around?" asked Captain Shay.

"Negative, I'd like you to back off about a thousand feet. No reason for you to be exposed to fire and smoke while we're down."

"Affirmative. As soon as you drop below the surface, we'll move away."

"Roger. *Little Mike* diving."

Zack turned toward McMillin. "Okay, Russ, let's do it." The copilot nodded his head and then reached forward, triggering a series of toggle switches. Zack angled the diving planes and advanced the throttle. Within a minute the mini-sub was fifty feet under the surface. Although it was the middle of the night, light from the inferno continued to refract to the mini-sub's depth. Eerie greenish gray shadows loomed in the water as the flames danced on the surface above.

When *Little Mike* passed the hundred-foot level, there was no light at all. Zack then switched on the exterior halogen floodlights. They were mounted around the circumference of the cockpit. The high-intensity illumination proved to be ineffective. The darkness of the deep swallowed up the light rays like a thirsty sponge.

Zack wasn't worried about the visibility, however. *Little Mike* had a set of electronic eyes that were doing the seeing for him. The craft's forward-mounted sonar unit was continuously probing the waters that lay directly ahead of it. Low-frequency pings were broadcast into the water column by an exterior-mounted transducer. When the sound waves hit anything solid, they would create reflections. The echos returning to the mini-sub would register at a slightly lower pitch. The sonar computer automatically computed the distance and bearing between the sub and the reflected object, using the time difference between the incident pulse and the return wave. The results were then plotted on a circular televisionlike screen. It looked like an underwater radar scope.

"Spot anything yet, Zack?" asked Russ.

"Nothing but bottom reflections." Zack paused for a moment as he adjusted a filter on the sonar unit. "Say, Ears, what's the computer say now?"

Elwood Mason was monitoring the vessel's inertial navigator. "Zack, you're right on course. You should be picking up the target within sixty seconds or so."

"Thanks."

Ears's prediction was nearly perfect. The sonar unit registered a strong metallic reflection nearly a minute later. "There it is," shouted Zack. He was really excited now.

"Where is it, Mr. Scott?" asked Halley Blake. She couldn't see much from her position.

"I've only got it on sonar. We're still about two hundred fifty yards away."

While Zack continued to study the sonar's display, Russ McMillin removed his communication headset and then cocked his head to the side.

Zack turned toward him. "What are you doing, Russ?"

"You hear it?" he asked.

"Hear what?"

"Listen. It's getting louder."

In a few seconds Scott heard it, too. It sounded like thunder in the distance.

"My God, is that what I think it is?" asked McMillin.

"Yep, I've head it once before, in the Gulf of Mexico." Zack was referring to a well blowout he had helped cap nearly twenty years earlier. That well had been located in just seventy-five feet of water and had only one tenth of the volume of flow of Hammer 4.

Little Mike finally closed with the Hammer 4 wellhead. The roar from the escaping gas and oil sounded like a racing freight train. It was so noisy inside the submersible that everyone had to stuff cotton inside their ears and use the intercom channel on their headsets to communicate.

Both Commander Blake and Ears Mason moved forward, kneeling just behind the cockpit seats, in order to see the view. It was an awesome sight. The raw power of Mother Nature unleashed was displayed before the entire crew's eyes. The mini-sub's floodlights captured the subsurface discharge taking place less than twenty feet away. Jets of superheated gas, mixed with black streaks of crude oil, blasted upward from the open end of the wellhead casing. The heavy-walled steel pipe projected just four feet above the ocean bottom.

Commander Blake finally broke the tension. "Good Lord! What happened to the preventer?"

"I don't know," replied Scott. "The casing head coupling must have sheared away when the marine riser failed. We figure the riser must have carried the BOP stack with it."

"But that's supposed to be impossible—wasn't the riser equipped with a breakaway ball valve?"

"Yes."

"Well, then I don't understand how the BOP could have failed like this. That ball valve assembly should have failed first when the riser went. The stack would have remained intact."

"You're right," answered Scott. "That's the way it was designed and built. This should never have happened."

"Just incredible," muttered Commander Blake. She was clearly upset at what she was seeing.

Zack inched *Little Mike* closer. He wanted to examine the top of the well casing. Half a minute later Russ shouted out: "Look at that. The BOP's damn coupling is still attached to the casing."

"Yeah, you're right," replied Zack as he pressed his head against the cold acrylic glass of the view port.

The short stub of steel sticking upward from the coupling was actually part of the blowout preventer's base. The heavy milled steel casing of the BOP was several times stronger than the hydraulic coupling that connected it to the wellhead pipe.

Commander Blake spoke up next. "Mr. McMillin, you mean to say the preventer snapped rather than the coupling?"

"Yep, that's exactly what happened."

Halley was even more perplexed now. The BOP was built like a battleship. It was the strongest portion of the entire drill string. For it to fail and the lighter coupling to remain in place broke all the rules. "Gentlemen, there's something very wrong here. That BOP stack should never have failed like this."

"I know, Commander," answered Zack. "We're totally in the dark. Nothing that we see here makes any sense at all."

Commander Blake's suspicions were growing steadily by the minute. It was her responsibility to make a preliminary determination of how the accident might have occurred. Everything she was now seeing pointed to incredible incompetence on the part of SCS and the crew of the *Kelda Scott*. Halley wasn't quite ready to pass judgment, though. She respected Zackary Scott and his company too much to hang them out without examining all of the evidence. "Mr. Scott, do you know where the preventer is?"

"Yeah, we're pretty sure it's a couple of hundred yards

south of here. Our side scan sonar picked up a good reflection that fit the size and shape of the BOP.''

"Then I suggest we run over to those coordinates and take a look at the unit.''

"Yep, I agree. There's not a hell of a lot we can do here right now.''

"Just a second, skipper,'' called out McMillin. While Zack and Halley were talking Russ had been carefully studying the exposed wellhead. He then placed the index finger of his right hand against the glass and said: "You know, Zack, I think the conductor is sticking up a few inches above the lip of the preventer's base. It sure looks like everything's being produced through it.''

Zack turned toward the wellhead. He could just see the severed end of the six-inch-diameter steel pipe projecting upward from the center of the ruptured BOP's casing. The escaping gas and oil appeared to be confined to the internal pipe.

"Hey, I think you're right. I hadn't noticed that before.'' Zack's spirits started to rise.

"What's the significance of that?'' asked Commander Blake.

Russ answered: "If the conductor pipe is intact and the downhole packer is still in place, it means that all of the oil and gas coming up are still confined to the pipe.''

"I see. Then if you can plug the end of the conductor, you might be able to stop the flow.''

"Exactly,'' shouted Scott. "By God, Russ, we might just be able to slip a clamp valve over the pipe stub if we can get that damn coupling off.''

"That sounds wonderful,'' commented Halley. "Can you do the work remotely from this rig?''

Zack thought for a few moments before answering. *Little Mike*'s articulated arm had not been designed for the delicate efforts that might be required. "No, it'll be too cumbersome and slow.''

"So how will you do it then?''

"I've got to get out there and manually work with the gear.''

"But we're a thousand feet deep. You can't dive out there.''

"I've got no choice. If I don't shut the flow off, my company will be ruined.''

"But the—"

"I appreciate your concerns, Commander," interrupted Zack, "but it's my butt that's hanging out in the wind. I know what has to be done and I'm going to do it."

"Whatever you say. I want the well sealed up ASAP, too."

"Good, then if you don't mind, I'd like to postpone our inspection of the BOP and riser for the time being. We need to get back to the *Ranger* in order to prepare for the dive."

"No problem. Let's do it."

Once again, *Little Mike* was on its way to the bottom. It had taken nearly four hours to make the modifications before the main hatch was sealed and the sub relaunched. Russ McMillin was piloting while Commander Blake sat in the co-pilot's seat, serving as observer. Ears Mason manned the engineering console. Zackary Scott was not in the mini-sub. Instead, he was encased inside a special diving apparatus mounted on top of the submersible about ten feet behind the cockpit.

Zack was inside a Newtsuit. The state-of-the-art, one-at-mosphere diving suit looked like something from outer space. The main trunk of the device had a clear bubble helmet section. Enormous arms and legs projected outward, creating the appearance of an obese robotlike creature. The first time Scott saw one of the diving suits he laughed—it reminded him of the giant Pillsbury Dough Boy cartoon character.

Zack and the Newtsuit were parked inside a specially constructed garage on top of *Little Mike*'s hull. Both of the diving suit's remotely activated hand manipulators were locked onto the garage's steel railing, solidly anchoring it to the mini-sub.

The Newtsuit protected Zack from the pressure of the deep. Constructed of high-strength aluminum, the diving suit functioned like a submarine's pressure hull. Designed to resist the sea's hydrostatic pressure to a depth of two thousand feet, the Newtsuit was slowly revolutionizing the deepwater diving industry. By operating at surface pressures the device allows a diver to descend to great depths without having to worry about the dangerous consequences of pressure. Operating like a submarine, the Newtsuit eliminates the need for exotic breathing mixtures, avoids lengthy confinement inside a decompression chamber, and completely removes the danger of contracting decompression sickness, better known as "the bends."

The diver breathes air from three small internal tanks. A CO_2 scrubber on the backpack cleans the used air, allowing it to be recycled. With a nominal air supply of twenty-four hours, the Newtsuit provides plenty of bottom time.

"How are you reading me, Zack?" asked Russ McMillin.

"Five by five. All systems normal."

"Good, we'll be coming up on the wellhead in a couple of minutes."

"Roger."

Zack stared through the acrylic faceplate. He was looking over the forward section of the mini-sub. Its floodlights probed the inky water ahead. The darkness of the depth swallowed up the light like a black hole.

He could hear the soft hiss of *Little Mike*'s main propeller and the occasional higher-pitched whine of the thrusters as Russ adjusted the mini-sub's course.

Zack turned his head inside the large helmet section, scanning the gauges that lined its circumference. He could monitor all of the Newtsuit's environmental controls with a quick glance. His arms were withdrawn from the arm sections and were folded on his chest. He found this position more comfortable when not working. The Newtsuit had a wide trunk, providing him with plenty of room. If he needed to he could reach up to the helmet to turn a switch or scratch his nose.

Although the water surrounding him was only a few degrees above freezing, he was warm. He wore a special insulated nylon garment that covered his body from head to toes.

Zack was checking his oxygen gauge when he noticed a new sound. It was a distant rumble. *Must be getting close,* he thought.

Two minutes later, the rumble had turned into thunder. *Little Mike* was hovering next to Hammer 4. The oil and gas continued to blast out of the bottom. The noise from the subterranean flow was almost overpowering for Zack. No longer protected by the mini-sub's insulated hull, Zack was fully exposed to the noise inside the Newtsuit. It sounded like Niagara Falls.

Zack reached up and increased the volume on his headset

earphones. He began speaking. "Son of a bitch, but it's noisy out here. Can you read me, over?"

"Roger, Zack, you're coming in fine."

"Well, okay. I'm ready to disengage. Are you people set?"

"Roger."

"Good. Just stay put as I launch."

"You got it, skipper."

Scott reached down and inserted his hands into the Newtsuit's aluminum arm sections. He grasped the controls for the remote manipulators. Looking like giant pliers, the clawlike devices projected outward from the blunt-ended arms. He activated both units, relaxing the locking pressure. A moment later he raised the arm sections, freeing the hand clamps from the garage's railing.

Despite the hydrostatic pressure of over a thousand feet of water, the Newtsuit's joints were easy to move. Constructed with fluid-filled rotary joints that were patterned after human joints, the special devices linked together the half-inch-thick rigid sections of the suit's extremities. There were four joints in each arm and five in each leg.

No longer anchored to the garage, Zack turned his attention to two small electrically powered thrusters mounted on either side of his waist. By manipulating a control device inside the suit he was able to power away from the mini-sub, heading for the wellhead.

"Okay, *Little Mike*. I'm unlocked and starting to maneuver."

Although no longer directly attached to the mini-sub, Zack maintained contact with the sub by means of a small tether line. Two communication wires were weaved into the synthetic cable. Linked to a reel on the garage, the tether could be remotely activated by McMillin to pull Zack back to the submersible in an emergency.

"Roger. We're waiting for you."

A minute later Zack swam by the view ports of the mini-sub and then maneuvered the Newtsuit until he was opposite the wellhead. The noise was deafening and he could feel the vibration of the well's uncontrolled turbulent discharge.

"Okay, Russ, I'm just about in position now."

"Roger, skipper. I'll bring you the hose." McMillin was

referring to the high-pressure hydraulic hose that was mounted on *Little Mike*'s manipulator arm. Linked to a port on the side of the submersible, the oil-filled hose could be compressed to ten thousand pounds per square inch by a hydraulic pump located inside the vessel.

While Zack waited for McMillin to maneuver *Little Mike,* he examined the remains of the BOP stack. There was only two and a half feet of the heavy-walled preventer left and most of it was covered by a massive hydraulic clamp. The cylindrical device mated the base of the BOP stack to the underlying steel casing of the wellhead. *How in the hell could that preventer ever fail like this—it just doesn't make sense.*

Zack inched closer to the jagged edge of the BOP's remnants. *What the hell is that?* He could see dark black streaks alongside the steel-gray surface of the preventer. The discoloration looked like scorch marks from a fire. *How could that happen?*

Zack was perplexed. It looked like part of the BOP stack had been burned, but there wasn't any way the escaping oil or gas could ignite down here—there was no oxygen to support the flames.

Zack's concentration was broken by his helmet intercom speakers. "How's that, Zack?" asked Russ McMillin. The mini-sub was now a dozen feet away, its eight-foot-long mechanical arm completely extended.

"Good, stay put."

It took Zack almost half an hour to remove the hydraulic clamp that anchored the hydraulic coupling of the wellhead to the BOP stack. He was now ready to attach the kill valve to the exposed production pipe.

"Here it comes, Zack," called out Russ McMillin over the intercom system.

Zack turned his head and spotted the mechanical arm as it rotated toward him. Hanging from the articulated claw was a cylindrical object about three feet long and a foot and a half in diameter. "Good, bring her a little closer and then let me take a look."

"Roger."

Thirty seconds later Zack was examining the kill valve. Machinists aboard the *Ranger III* had spent hours manufacturing the device that Russ and Zack conceived during the first dive. The kill valve was designed to slip over the exposed portion of the conductor and stop the runaway flow.

Zack maneuvered the Newtsuit until he was right under the suspended valve. He tilted his head inside the helmet in order to examine the underside of the fitting. "Okay, Russ, looks like the bore is completely open. Go ahead and center it over the conductor."

"Roger."

It took only two minutes to position the kill valve. Russ expertly maneuvered the five-hundred-pound fitting, slipping it right over the exposed pipe. The bottom end rested on the rim of the hydraulic coupling. The escaping oil and gas continued to erupt through the open end of the valve as though it wasn't there.

"Great job, Russ," called out Zack. "It looks like a perfect fit."

"Well, let's hope that friction coupling works, otherwise we've been wasting our time."

"I hear you loud and clear," replied Zack. He then set about securing the kill valve to the conductor pipe. He reached for the impact wrench.

The kill valve was actually split longitudinally into two halves. A dozen high-strength steel bolts, located on each flanged side of the fitting, held both hunks of metal together. The bolts were just loose enough to allow the valve to be slipped over the six-inch-diameter conductor pipe. By tightening up the bolts, the two interior half sections of the valve would be forced against the steel pipe, forming an enormous friction bond. A series of offset internal rubber gaskets located at the top and bottom of the device would provide the final fluid seal.

It took Zack nearly twenty minutes to tighten the two dozen bolts. He alternated between sides in order to evenly seat the valve to the conductor. During the entire operation, the pipe discharged another 65,000 gallons of crude oil and thousands of cubic feet of gas.

"Okay, Russ, that should do it," Zack finally called out as he backed a few feet away from the work area.

"Good job. You ready to activate that valve now?"

"Yep."

A new voice called out to Zack. "Good luck, Zack." Although Commander Blake sat next to Russ McMillin and had watched Zack install the valve, she had remained silent until now, not wanting to interrupt his work.

"Oh, thanks, Commander. Guess it's really crunch time now."

Zack disconnected the impact hammer from the hydraulic line and inserted a new tool into a quick-connect fitting on the end of the hose. He then inserted the male end of the fitting into a hydraulic port on the kill valve.

"Okay, Russ, the tool's engaged. I'm now releasing pressure." Zack turned a small hand valve on the tool, allowing pressurized hydraulic oil to flow into a hollow chamber in the top half of the device. The force of the fluid simultaneously rotated a special ball valve housed inside the fitting a foot above the terminal end of the conductor pipe. It took only five seconds for the valve to close.

Zack could barely believe it when the thunderous roar stopped. The silence was overwhelming. It took nearly half a minute for his hearing to adjust. Then he heard the wild screaming in his helmet speakers.

"Zack, you did it. You killed the son of a bitch!" yelled Russ.

"It's a miracle," called out Halley Blake.

"Nice going, skipper," Mason said.

Thank God! thought Scott.

4

AN OLD ENEMY

Hammer 4

After shutting in the Hammer 4 wellhead, Zackary Scott and *Little Mike* spent two hours searching for the remains of the blowout preventer. They eventually found the twenty-ton BOP stack and a hundred-foot section of the marine riser pipe, both buried deeply in the soft marine sediments. After precisely noting the location of the subsea hardware, the mini-sub headed topside.

When *Little Mike* finally surfaced, Zackary Scott was still parked on top of the hull, enclosed by the Newtsuit. The submersible was a hundred yards off the stern of the *Ranger III*, gently rolling with the swells that relentlessly flowed southeastward. It was almost eleven A.M.

Despite the restricted field of view from the diving helmet, Zack noticed the change the second he broke through the interface. The fire from the Hammer 4 well had nearly extinguished itself. Without the natural gas to fuel the flames, the remaining film of crude oil on the water's surface burned slowly. And whitecaps were just beginning to form on top of the rollers as the northerly wind gusted to twenty-five knots. The increased agitation would help to further disperse the oil slick, making it harder to ignite. By early afternoon the fire would be extinguished.

Zack would have preferred to let the oil burn, knowing it

66

would reduce the amount of crude that would eventually reach the shore. But that didn't matter much anymore. The battle line had now shifted from the undersea wellhead to the beaches of the Washington State coastline. The first elements of Hammer 4's thirty-five-mile-long slick were already washing up on the shore.

"Where's the oil hitting the beach?" asked Zackary Scott as he spoke into the radio telephone microphone. He was now standing in the wheelhouse of the *Ranger III,* looking at the *Resolution.* The U.S. Coast Guard vessel was running on a parallel course a quarter of a mile to starboard.

"Ground crews report they've got oil at Moclips and Pacific Beach," replied Commander Welsh. He was also standing on the bridge deck of his patrol vessel.

"How bad is it?"

"So far it's a fairly light coating. They've lost about a hundred seabirds but no mammals have shown up yet."

"What about cleanup crews? Have the MSRC people shown up?"

"Yep, they have a full beach team on scene right now. And they've also got several inflatables and work boats offshore deploying booms and absorbents."

Damn, that was quick, thought Zack. He was more than pleased with the money he'd contributed to the Marine Spill Response Corporation. "How about the skimmers and other cleanup vessels, where are they?"

"They're on the way," replied the Coast Guard officer. "The first units from Gray's Harbor will be working within the next hour or so. The Puget Sound Co-op team is about three hours away from our position."

Even though MSRC had most of its own prepositioned equipment and personnel available for the Hammer 4 spill, it

still relied on the existing spill cooperatives and independent response contractors in each regional area. MSRC employs the smaller organizations as subcontractors for major spills and frequently trains and drills them.

"Okay, Commander, I guess that's about as good as we're going to get. If the weather holds, then we just might make it out of this mess without too much damage."

"Keep your fingers crossed, Mr. Scott. We've been lucky so far."

"I hear you, Commander," replied Zack. He then paused a moment as a new thought formed. *Lucky? How can you call any of this luck?* As bad as the oil contamination might be, it was nothing compared to the real horror of the Hammer 4 blowout. Zack keyed the mike again. "Ah, Commander, any more news on my crew?"

"Yes, sir. One of our helos spotted another body about five miles south of here." The Coast Guard officer paused as he checked a clipboard. "That makes fourteen so far. We have a recovery vessel on the scene right now."

Zack felt sick to his stomach. The reality of the tragedy was really starting to hit home now: There would be no survivors from the missing lifeboat. Fifty-two of his employees—many of them his friends—were gone.

Zack depressed the transmit switch. "You're going to keep searching, aren't you? Some of them might have survived!"

"Of course, Mr. Scott. That's our highest priority."

Zack thanked the officer and then signed off.

It was now late in the afternoon. It was dead calm; the wind had died an hour earlier. The *Ranger* continued to patrol through the oil-coated waters, looking for victims. Five more corpses had been recovered. The charred bodies were covered with white sheets and stored on the fantail, near the helipad. A Coast Guard helicopter would recover the victims in an hour.

Zackary Scott, Russ McMillin, and Captain Jim Shay were all standing together on the forward bridge wing. The stink of crude oil permeated the air. No one spoke as each man searched the waters with binoculars.

Russ finally broke the silence. He wanted to get his mind off the grim task at hand. "Say, Zack, will MSRC pick up the tab for the cleanup work?"

"No. Unfortunately we're totally on the hook for the spill. MSRC just functions as the prime contractor."

"Jesus, this is going to cost the company a lot of money."

Zack didn't really want to talk about that right now. Even though he had insurance and was a member of several local cleanup co-ops that shared spill response cost, SCS's financial exposure was significant. Between the deductibles and liability limits, he guessed that SCS would have to come up with at least a couple of million dollars in cash. And that was if the spill was cleaned up quickly.

"Yeah, well, that's why we have insurance and rainy day funds. Besides, we've still got a hell of a well field at Hammer 4."

Captain Shay spoke next. "Zack, I don't want to dredge up old war wounds, but I have a feeling that we're going to get clobbered by the green bigots again. They fought us tooth and nail during the federal lease hearings, arguing that we'd end up with a major spill."

"Yeah, I know what you mean. I'm sure we're going to hear from them."

During the three years it took Zack and the other oil exploration companies to win approval for drilling offshore of Washington State, they continually fought with local and national environmental groups. If the Arabs hadn't started fighting each other again, Zack would never have even tried. But when half of the Persian Gulf's oil production was destroyed, the search for oil within United States territory took on a new urgency. The president quickly issued an emergency executive order that superseded Congress's Olympic Coast National Marine Sanctuary. That legislation had barred oil exploration off most of Washington's coastline. SCS subsequently won the lease for the Hammer tract.

Although SCS and several other oil companies had won the battle over the right to drill offshore, Zack wasn't so sure he was going to win the new war he knew was coming.

Tokyo

"What did you just say?" asked the bald-headed man; he was clearly startled by what he had just heard. He was sitting at the head of a short-legged table, about to consume a bowl of rice.

The man he was addressing had just walked in and kneeled down at the opposite end of the *tsuke*. He was at least thirty years younger. Although his voice was calm and even, the tremors in his hands gave away his fear. "Sir, the oil well leak has stopped."

Hiroshi Yoshida shoved the nearly full rice bowl away. The normally pallid skin of his face was now beet red. He could barely contain his anger. "The oil is no longer flowing?"

"Yes, sir. I'm afraid so."

"But how is that possible? You assured us that the blowout would last for at least two weeks."

The younger man, obviously embarrassed, looked away from Yoshida as he responded. "We don't understand what has happened yet. Only that CNN is reporting that the Hammer 4 subsea blowout was successfully sealed about three hours ago."

"But the drilling rig from California hasn't even reached the site yet!"

"Yes, Yoshida-san. That's true. And according to our own estimates, as well as the American press reports, when it finally arrived it should have taken about fifteen to twenty days to drill in a new intercept well."

"Something's not right here. We were counting on a lot more oil being spilled before the well was capped."

"I know, sir. But we just don't have an answer yet. All we know at this point is that one of Scott's ships—the *Ranger*, I think it is called—arrived at the site late last night and that it sent down some type of diving team to check the wellhead."

"How did you find that out?"

"Our people have been monitoring the Coast Guard radio communications. There's been a lot of cross talk between the onscene Coast Guard vessel and the SCS ship."

"Well, what could they have done to stop the leak so quickly? Your own experts guaranteed that the explosives would permanently disable the emergency shut-off valve system."

"We just don't have any facts yet. Our current thinking centers around some new type of downhole safety valve that SCS was able to trigger remotely."

Yoshida pushed away from the table and stood up. He rose smoothly and effortlessly, like a man half his age. He was in near-perfect health and remained an active golfer, sailor, and pilot. "Well, it would seem that our 'friend' Zackary Scott has pulled another rabbit out of the hat."

"Sir?" asked the subordinate, not understanding Yoshida's translation of the American idiom.

"Scott is much more clever than we anticipated. Obviously he figured out another way to stop the blowout."

"Yes, sir. I think you're right."

Yoshida looked the man directly in the eye. "Then don't you think it would be wise for us to know exactly what he did?"

"Of course, I'll begin the investigation immediately." The man bowed and quickly exited the room.

The co-founder and CEO of Yoshida Heavy Industries walked toward the expansive window wall of his high-rise office. He looked toward the southeast. Tokyo Harbor stretched out in front of him. He momentarily dismissed the problem with Scott. His thoughts were now focused on a tiny piece of the bay, about ten miles out. He never forgot that night in March 1945, when he crashed-landed his fighter into *Tokyo Wan*.

Yoshida was rescued later in the day. After having his broken arm treated, he made his way back to downtown Tokyo. He never found his home. Nothing was left, not even the building's brick foundation. That portion of Asakusa Ward had been burned to a crisp.

Hiroshi never learned the fate of his mother and sister. They simply disappeared that fateful night—along with 100,000 other souls. He next searched for other family members—uncles and aunts and cousins—but again, he found no one. His entire clan had been wiped off the face of the earth.

Young Yoshida took solace, however, in one recurring thought: *At least I know what happened to Father*. Hiroshi's *otosan*, a torpedo bomber pilot, had preceded them all in death. His plane was blown apart during the sea battle for Midway Island.

Hiroshi eventually returned to Chofu airfield. When his arm finally mended, he again climbed into the cockpit of a Ki-61. It was early August 1945, and Japan was now bracing for the invasion that was destined to come. Cadet Yoshida was one of the five-thousand-strong kamikaze force ready to pounce on the American invasion fleet. The bloody fight for Okinawa would be child's play compared to the reception the invaders would face when they tried to land on mainland Japan.

But the invasion never came. Instead, a single bomber, another one of the dreaded B-29s, changed the art of warfare forever. Virtually untouched during the course of the war, Hiroshima was a thriving manufacturing and port city when the *Enola Gay* dropped its atomic bomb. In less than a heartbeat, the weapon burned the heart right out of the beautiful metropolis. And just a few days later, another bomber blasted Nagasaki into oblivion. Japan's will to resist withered, and by the end of August the war was over.

It wasn't until almost a year later that Yoshida discovered he wasn't alone. One of his father's brothers, Tetsuo, had survived. Originally listed as killed in action during a land battle in New Guinea, the army sergeant hid in the jungle until the war ended. He remained in a POW camp until he was finally repatriated home.

Tetsuo and Hiroshi lived together in a shack on the outskirts of Joto Ward, near the Nakagawa Canal. Tetsuo Yoshida, a University of Tokyo–educated mechanical engineer, started a small shipbuilding company with his nephew, using a small inheritance as seed money. The company's first contract was to build a fifty-foot-long steel barge for the U.S. Army's Occupation Force.

Within just two years the fledgling company grew into the Yoshida Shipbuilding Company. It was building modest-size fishing vessels and small cargo carriers. Another two years elapsed and the firm blossomed into a major industrial enterprise. Now headquartered on Yokohama's newly rebuilt waterfront, the Yoshida Shipbuilding Company had its first contract to construct a medium-size oil tanker. It would prove to be the first in a long succession of highly profitable ventures.

As the company grew, Tetsuo, along with Hiroshi, now a full partner, poured all of the profits back into the company. They wanted to maintain the firm's meteoric growth rate—they could both see that economic victory was just around the corner. And the overseeing Americans frequently pointed to the Yoshidas as a model example of how to bring Japanese industry into the fold of Western ways.

The uncle and nephew continued to live together, rather modestly, until Tetsuo decided to marry. He and his young bride then moved into a new home on a hill overlooking Tokyo Bay. Less than a year later, the rebuilding of the Yoshida clan started. Kei Yoshida was born in July of 1952. A sister and three other brothers followed, with one born every other year.

Hiroshi Yoshida married several years later. His attempts, however, to replenish the family ranks were in vain. He was sterile, the result of a genetic defect he had inherited from his mother's side of the family.

Hiroshi eventually took control of the company as his uncle devoted more time to his family. One way or the other, Tetsuo had been at war for over ten years, and all of the fight had been drained from him.

Under Hiroshi's guidance, the company flourished. With cash pouring in by the shipload, Yoshida expanded into new markets: electronics, automobile parts, and forest products, to name a few. He was a success in nearly every venture he started. Ultimately, he changed the firm's name to Yoshida Heavy Industries. YHI was a world-class industrial giant.

Hiroshi Yoshida turned away from the magnificent view of Tokyo Bay. His eyes were now puffed up as his thoughts turned to a postage-stamp-size lot in the Asakusa Ward. He had never rebuilt on his parents' homesite. Instead, he turned the two-thousand-square-foot plot of land into a simple but elegant memorial. Fresh flowers were delivered daily, and he visited it at least once a month.

Yoshida would never forget his loved ones, nor would he ever forgive the Americans for taking them from him. It was his *unmei*, his fate, to avenge their deaths.

5

LAST RITES

Seattle

For a solid week, the crisis at the Hammer 4 site consumed nearly
every minute of Zackary Scott's time. After securing the subsea
well blowout, he devoted himself to coordinating the spill
cleanup operation. Although the Coast Guard was in overall
charge, MSRC had the principal responsibility for managing the
response teams. Zack trusted both organizations implicitly,
knowing they would do a good job. But because of his company's enormous financial exposure, he took it upon himself to remain fully committed to minimizing the environmental damage.
Consequently, he treated the entire cleanup operation like a war.
The main battle was being managed by the Coast Guard and the
Marine Spill Response Corporation, but the little skirmishes that
continuously broke out were his charges.

Zack was in SCS's main conference room, standing next to
an elegantly crafted oak table; it seemed as long as the flight
deck of an aircraft carrier. The exterior window wall of the
spacious room faced Elliott Bay, but he wasn't enjoying the
view. Instead, his entire attention was focused on the fourteen
SCS employees who sat and stood around the conference table. SCS's Hammer 4 blowout coordination center was in high
gear. Every member of Zack's handpicked team was busy.
Their individual tasks ranged from examining aerial photo-

graphs and nautical charts to monitoring computer terminals packed with weather and tidal current data.

Zack was more than proud of his employees—he was eternally grateful for their loyalty and enthusiasm. To a large extent, SCS's fate as a corporate entity was in their hands. And they were helping win the war.

"What's the latest on team six?" asked Scott, directing his question to one of SCS's senior operations managers.

"They're on the beach, right about here," replied Susan Frost as she pointed to a large-scale map spread out on the huge conference table.

"Is there much oil on the beach?"

"Some, but it appears to be a very fine surface layer—more like a sheen than a true slick."

"Good, then it sounds like this stuff is really starting to break down."

"Yes. Both the Coast Guard and MSRC have reported a noticeable decrease in apparent surface contamination." The thirty-one-year-old engineer paused momentarily as she reached for a set of color aerial photos. "If we compare these two photos of Copalis Beach, I think you'll see what I'm getting at." She handed him a nine-by-nine contact print.

"This was flown about noontime yesterday. Most of the slick was still a mile or so offshore, but notice how bright the main body of the slick appears." She again paused as she reached for a loose-leaf folder. After turning a few pages she found what she was looking for. "There was a lot of oil out there then. Surface samples collected by the Coast Guard at that time indicated a concentration of around five hundred parts per million."

"Okay," replied Scott.

She then handed him the second color print. "This photo was taken at noon today. See the difference?"

Zack scanned the photo. He could hardly distinguish the oil slick. It was there all right, but it was only a shadow of the previous day's image.

"Damn! It looks like it's dissipated a huge amount."

"Right, I just talked with the Coast Guard and they report the concentration is no more than twenty parts per million."

Zack remained silent for a few seconds, thinking about what the ocean engineer had just said.

"Susan, are you sure the main body of the slick hasn't

moved off to another location and we're just picking up a residual?''

''Yes, the rest of the photos confirm that the slick is still sloshing around in the same general area, about ten miles off-shore. The winds are keeping most of it off the beach while the tidal currents seem to string it out in a north-south orientation; it's about seventy miles long now.''

''Then the oil's evaporating like we hoped.''

''Correct. In fact, if the hot weather holds for another day or so, our computer model now predicts that nearly seventy-five percent of the spill's original volume will either have evaporated, been skimmed up, or been contained in booms.''

''That's great news, Susan. You're doing a wonderful job.'' Zack hadn't counted on such an optimistic report.

''Thanks. But we've got a ways to go yet. There's still a couple hundred thousand gallons of crude out there.''

''I know. Just keep plugging away and we'll get most it.''

''We will, Zack.''

Scott turned away and walked out of the operations center. As he headed for his nearby office he couldn't help but think of his good fortune. *Damn, am I ever lucky. We just might get this sucker cleaned up and put to bed without getting totally screwed.*

The young woman was on the bedroom deck of her con-dominium home, facing the blue-green waters of Lake Washington. The high-rise towers of downtown Seattle were in the distant background. The sun was directly overhead and she was starting to perspire. Her long dark hair was spread evenly over her shoulders as she lay back on the foam mattress. Her mirrored sunglasses reflected the ripples from the lake's surface; a gentle breeze blew across the water from the north.

She wore only the lower half of her bathing suit, enjoying the warmth of the sun on her exposed breasts. Her figure was perfect: tall and slim. And she was naturally tan all over.

Like her body, the thirty-year-old woman's face was near perfect. It was a magical blend of East and West. Her Euro-pean heritage dominated, but the underlying hint of the Orient was always there. Men found it hard not to stare at her; they were mesmerized by her beauty.

Cindy DeMorey's mother was largely responsible for her

spellbinding beauty. Born in Quebec and descended from a family with roots in the Bordeaux Valley of France, Suzanne De-Morey was strikingly attractive. When she turned twenty-one, during her junior year at Stanford, she moved in with her lover. Her roommate, an engineering student, also at Stanford, was a Japanese national. They secretly married a few months later, knowing that both families would not approve of the union.

The young interracial couple lived peacefully through their senior year, both graduating with honors. A year later, when he was working on his master's degree at Berkeley as she continued to study literature at Stanford, disaster struck. He was killed in a freeway accident during his daily commute back home to Palo Alto.

Suzanne was eight months pregnant when she learned of Kei Yoshida's death; the shock sent her into early labor. The baby nearly died during the first week after her premature delivery. But thanks to Stanford's fabulous medical school, tiny Cynthia survived. Not wanting to further burden her child with the stigma of mixed bloodlines, Suzanne DeMorey gave her own surname to the baby.

During Cindy's early years she had virtually no contact with her father's side of the family other than the occasional letter. It seemed that none of her blood relatives across the Pacific cared about her welfare. Consequently, she grew up in a cultural vacuum. Despite her obvious Asian features, she was as American as apple pie.

When Cindy turned thirteen, she began to wonder more about her lost heritage. Something inside of her—it was almost like an instinct—told her to find the missing pieces. Cindy's mother, now remarried, encouraged her interest.

After re-establishing contact with Kei's family, Suzanne arranged for Cindy to spend part of her summer vacation in Tokyo. Cindy was never the same again.

At first the Yoshida family was cold and aloof to the American half-breed. Mixed-race children are especially frowned upon in Japan. But the facade eventually melted away when the pretty little girl charmed their hearts.

Cynthia loved her Japanese legacy. It was as if she had discovered a new part of herself that had been locked away in a dark, dusty room. She continually asked questions about her father and the other family members, devouring every story and fact with a computerlike memory. She especially enjoyed the customs and ceremony that are such important elements of Japanese life. And she took to the complicated Japanese language with a proficiency that astounded all of her newfound relatives.

When young Cynthia climbed aboard the jet to return to San Francisco, she knew that she would be back. And so did the Yoshida clan. She was now one of their own.

Throughout her teenage years, Cindy spent every summer in Japan. After graduating from high school she moved to Tokyo, enrolling at the University of Tokyo. She obtained a degree in finance and then went to work for YHI. After completing an eighteen-month training program, she was transferred to Seattle, where she worked for a trading company. The firm specialized in importing Japanese computers and was personally owned by Hiroshi Yoshida. Within just a few years she was promoted to general manager.

Cindy frequently returned to Tokyo for meetings, allowing the relationship with her great-uncle to blossom. Despite her Western looks, Yoshida no longer thought of her as an American. She would never be a true Japanese—that was impossible with her tainted bloodlines. However, she did think and react like a Japanese, and that impressed Yoshida. Each time he gave her more responsibility, she rose to the challenge. There were never any questions about her assignments or political loyalties. YHI always came first. She would do anything for him.

Cindy DeMorey leafed through the *Seattle P.I.* looking for news on the oil spill. Unfortunately, there hadn't been much lately. The morning television news reports were equally sparse. Two weeks had passed since the blowout. After the subsea well was sealed and the main body of the spilled crude oil remained offshore, the local press lost interest. The cleanup was proceeding routinely and the damage to the environment was not nearly as bad as was first thought.

She threw the paper aside and stood up. *Damn it. It's not going to work.* She walked back into her bedroom and sat down next to her vanity. She glanced at the clock; it was half past one. *He should be awake by now.*

Cindy reached for a nearby phone and punched in a series of numbers, long ago committed to memory. Twelve seconds later the phone began ringing inside of a huge luxury apartment in downtown Tokyo. It was answered on the second ring. *"Moshi-Moshi,"* said a male voice.

Cindy switched her thoughts from her native English to her second language, Japanese. *"Ojisan,* did I wake you?" she asked. Even though Hiroshi Yoshida was her great-uncle, she always referred to him as *ojisan*—uncle.

"No. You know I'm an earlier riser." The sun was just rising in Tokyo as the man looked through his bedroom window wall. Mount Fuji was visible in the distance.

"Well, I've been thinking about what you said last night and I think it's time that we move to the second stage."

Hiroshi Yoshida was not surprised at the woman's decision. He had been expecting the call, but wanted her to initiate the plan. It was important that she continue to maintain her personal interest in the operation.

"I agree with your decision. When do you plan to start?"

"It'll probably be a couple of weeks. We don't think they'll be ready to start the recovery operation until then."

"Why the delay?"

"The Coast Guard is taking its time. Apparently they want to make certain the well is thoroughly sealed up before starting any salvage operations." She paused. "But that's okay. I can use the time to get our people in place. And then, once we know for sure, we'll be ready to act."

"Very good. I'll be waiting to hear from you."

"Good-bye, honored uncle."

"Good-bye, my child."

Three weeks had now passed since the sinking of the *Kelda Scott.* And it was the worst day of Zackary Scott's life. The memorial service at Fishermen's Terminal was a terribly depressing affair. Even the weather was dismal. It didn't rain, but the thick gray clouds that blanketed Seattle reflected the mood of the hundreds of mourners who had gathered to honor the fifty-two victims of the Hammer 4 blowout.

It took nearly every ounce of Zack's strength to walk up to the outdoor podium to read his message. His words were simple and were spoken from the heart. Somehow he managed to keep his composure during the five-minute-long address.

The priest, the rabbi, and the minister who followed Scott

did their best to console the families and friends of the deceased. Their combined message was one of profound respect for the dead and hope for the living.

Zack thought he could hold himself together through the remainder of the service. But when the governor began reading each name from the long list of victims he lost control. It was the children that did it. Nearly a hundred youngsters, kindergartners to teenagers, were assembled on a large pier near the base of the podium. They were the sons and daughters, nephews and nieces, and grandchildren of the *Kelda Scott*'s missing crew. As each name was called out, one or two of the children would walk a few steps to the end of the pier and toss a bouquet of wildflowers into the water. Some sobbed as they did their duty, but most remained stone-faced, too emotionally worn out to react anymore.

During the entire roll call, tears cascaded uncontrollably down Zack's cheeks. He hadn't cried in years—and before today never in public. But he didn't care. He knew every man and woman who had been killed—some better than others. He felt for them all. And when each individual name was called out, that person's face flashed into his mind. He remembered something about each one—a smile, a joke that had been told, a personal problem. It tore Zack apart to think they were all gone now.

Zack wanted to die when Big Billy's twin teenage daughters walked to the pier end. The Texan had been one of his most loyal employees, working his heart out for the company. He had also been Zack's pal. Zack would miss the man's companionship for years to come.

And then there was Captain Barker. Dan had been a good, decent man. Anyone would have been proud to have had him as a friend.

When the ceremony finally ended, all fifty-two names were formally entered into the official log of casualties. The long list of names that preceded the *Kelda Scott*'s crew honored the men and women who had lost their lives while working in Pacific Northwest waters. The sinking of the *Kelda Scott* was the single worst maritime disaster in the log's sixty-year record.

6

DEEP-SIXED

Hokkaido, Japan

The helicopter flew low to the water surface, paralleling the long and narrow peninsula that jutted out into the North Pacific Ocean. A minute earlier the aircraft had passed by Nemuro, a small fishing village. It was the last major settlement at the northeast corner of giant Hokkaido Island. Off in the distance, beyond the end of the Nemuro peninsula, was another series of islands. They looked like mini-mountains, thrusting upward from the sea for several thousand feet.

Until recently, the collection of islands that lay off the north shore of Hokkaido had been controlled by the Russian Federation. The Soviet Union had claimed the southern Kuril Island chain at the end of World War II and the Russians held on to the war booty for over fifty years. But after the demise of the USSR, the Russian Federation eventually returned the islands.

Kunashiri, Etorofu, Shikotan, and the Habomai Islands group, all collectively known as the Northern Territories, now belonged to Japan. The incentive to give up the southern Kurils had been too enticing for the Russians to resist: Japan paid billions in cash and trade credits for its former territories.

Hiroshi Yoshida sat alone in the comfortable passenger section of the corporate aircraft. Even though the helo was cruising at almost 150 knots, the cabin was remarkably vibration free and quiet. Soft classical western music from a built-in stereo system was playing in the background. Despite the spectacular scenery that cascaded across the cabin windows, Yoshida dozed. He had seen it all dozens of times before.

Yoshida was jolted awake when the pilot's voice was broadcast through the cabin intercom. "Yoshida-san, we'll be landing in five minutes."

The CEO of Yoshida Heavy Industries stretched his arms and then looked out to starboard. The aircraft had turned and was now running perpendicular to the coastline. In the distance he could see several structures projecting out of the ocean surface. The huge steel platforms, ten miles off the shore of Hokkaido, were founded on the ocean bottom. Towering between six and seven hundred feet above the bottom, the eight steel jackets of the Nemuro Oil Complex all surpassed the height of Tokyo's tallest building.

The helicopter landed on the largest platform. The companion structures, all spaced seaward of the main platform up to two miles away, were only a fraction of the size of the main platform.

Nearly ten acres in surface area, the Nemuro Command Center was like a small city. Several hundred men and women lived on the steel island. It had everything: spacious living quarters, excellent galley facilities, a movie house that showed the same feature films as in Tokyo, several retail stores, a hospital, and extensive recreational and exercise facilities.

Yoshida believed in taking care of his employees. His dedication to *amae* was legendary. Once an employee was hired, he or she had a job for life.

Amae is a state of dependency. It dominates the Japanese culture. Inherited through hundreds of years of collective living, most Japanese expect to be taken care of for their entire lives. In many instances, it is the employer who plays the role of the ultimate father figure.

Five minutes after landing, Yoshida was ushered into the Nemuro office complex. He took his position at the head of the elegant oak table in the main conference room. He was surrounded by a dozen mid-level managers and technicians. The floor-to-ceiling window wall behind his chair provided a breathtaking view of the Pacific Ocean.

"All right, gentlemen," Yoshida said, "how's our production rate?"

The man sitting three chairs to Yoshida's right looked up. The production manager shuffled a few papers on the desk top and then began speaking. "Sir, we've been consistently pumping six hundred ten thousand barrels of oil a day."

"Good, that's right on target. Any problems?"

"Not many. We are getting some fluctuations in our well field from the northeast quadrant."

Yoshida raised his right eyebrow in response. "What kind of fluctuations?"

"Well, we're not sure, but it seems like the reservoir pressure level has dropped some."

"You mean we're starting to get noticeable depletion already?"

"Maybe. We're running some tests and should know in a few days. It could just be some sludge in the lines creating more resistance."

"Well, let's hope that's all it is. The geologists swear that field has enormous reserves."

Yoshida listened to the rest of the hour-long briefing, occasionally asking questions. Satisfied with the operations summary, he concluded his monthly visit to the artificial island complex by having lunch with several of the workers. He made a point of visiting the full range of his employees, from division managers to roustabouts. Yoshida eventually returned to his helicopter at two P.M. It promptly took off, heading back to the northern end of Hokkaido. His corporate jet was waiting on the runway at the Kushiro City airport. Still an avid pilot, Yoshida would personally fly the Dassault-Breguet Falcon 20 back to Tokyo. He would be home by dinnertime.

While the helo flew toward shore, Yoshida reflected on the meeting's results. The production manager's comments about low pressure readings for the northeast field clearly worried most of the management team. Yoshida, however, wasn't concerned. He had been advised of the problem before his trip and knew it would be rectified in just a few days.

Other than the sporadic pressure readings from some of the wells, the Nemuro Complex was running like clockwork. Yoshida's company was raking in hundreds of millions of yen each day. Although he had invested heavily in the project, the Japanese Central Government had poured far more money into it. The joint private-government venture was one of the largest petroleum complexes in the world.

Several years earlier, when Yoshida's petroleum exploration teams discovered oil within Japan's own territorial waters, everyone practically bent over backward to get in on the deal. Yoshida eventually decided to take on only one partner. His deal with the Japanese government allowed him to remain in complete control of the venture while guaranteeing him a minimum of 50 percent of the oil.

As far as the rest of the world knew, the rich petroleum-bearing fields surrounding the Nemuro Complex had barely been tapped. Official YHI corporate reports estimated that when all of the subsea oil wells were finally installed, the Nemuro wells would be capable of supplying almost half of Japan's petroleum needs for decades. Accordingly, the central government treated the Nemuro Complex as a national economic treasure. Finally, after centuries of relying solely on foreign imports, Japan had its own oil supply.

Hammer 4

The *Ranger III* was almost directly over the Hammer 4 well site. The diving support vessel had been operating in the deep ocean waters for nearly two weeks. After successfully cementing in the wellhead, permanently sealing the casing and the conductor pipe that passed through it, the SCS ship had been in the process of recovering the remains of the blowout preventer. For the past six hours, a three-man team of highly trained saturation divers had been on the bottom, a thousand feet under the ship. They had just completed their final task. The diving bell that had carried them to the seabed was now on the fantail, securely anchored to its cradle. The divers had already transferred to a massive steel cylinder located next to the bell. They would remain in the deck decompression chamber for the next seventy-two hours.

The twenty-ton blowout preventer was resting on the steel deck just forward of the diving bell. The multimillion-dollar device was lying on its side; it looked like something a plumber turned artist would create after an all-night drinking binge. The huge collection of pipe sections and massive valves filled up most of the vessel's open deck space.

Sitting on the deck next to the preventer was the BOP's base section. Zack had disconnected the 350-pound chunk of metal during the emergency shut-in of the wellhead. The SCS divers eventually found it buried in the mud next to the casing and had it hauled topside.

Commander Halley Blake and Captain Jim Shay were now on the fantail, examining the blowout preventer. They were both looking at the jagged end of the BOP. The forty-inch-diameter cylinder looked like it had been torn apart. "Jesus, what a mess," Shay said.

Halley leaned forward to examine the torn metal. "This looks worse than when we observed it from *Little Mike*." She paused as she touched the wounded steel. It was ice-cold. "I've never heard of a failure like this—what could have caused it?"

"I don't know, but if that flange blew out during the flow test, that would explain it."

"Yeah, no kidding. Even if they managed to trigger the rams or the annulus preventers, they wouldn't have done a thing."

"That's right. The oil and gas would have squirted out that hole like a frigging fire hose."

"But what about the downhole valves? Shouldn't they have been engaged?"

Shay squatted down and looked farther into the open end of the BOP. "Well, yes. The production string should have had a couple of control valves right in this area." He pointed. "There should have been two hydraulically activated in-line valves just above the flange line."

"Yes, I remember Zack commenting on that. They were supposed to be some kind of hold-open valves, the type that would automatically close if the control lines lost pressure."

"I know. That's what's so puzzling. Several survivors from the *Kelda Scott* reported they lost all hydraulic control of the BOP."

"Then the valves should have engaged."

"Yeah, they should have, but didn't. The well was leaking like a sieve before the rig blew up."

Halley shook her head from side to side. "Captain, there's something very wrong here. Equipment like this just doesn't fail in this manner."

"I know, Commander. None of this makes any sense."

Halley nodded her head. "All right, Captain. I'm beginning to see what you and Zack have been preaching to me for the past week. This all looks mighty suspicious."

"What do you plan to do then?" asked Shay.

"As soon as the tug and barge show up, I want this equipment transferred. Then we'll haul it down to Portland and have our forensic people go over it with a fine-tooth comb. If it was tampered with, we'll know about it real quick."

Captain Shay was reluctant to turn over the blowout preventer to the Coast Guard, despite the federal agency's jurisdiction. The physical evidence might be the only way to prove SCS's innocence; Zack had instructed him to guard it with all of his resources. "Commander, no disrespect intended, but we sure as hell don't like the idea of turning over our gear to your people. Why not let us take it back to Seattle to our yard? Your experts can look at it there."

"Captain Shay, think about my position a minute. Right now SCS and Zackary Scott are on every Northwest environmental group's you-know-what list. If I allowed you to conduct your own investigation of the only available physical evidence, we'd never have any credibility. Besides, if the *Ranger* hadn't been the only vessel around that could salvage the gear, plus the fact that I actually witnessed the condition of the BOP during the blowout, there's no way you or your people would be this close to the equipment right now."

Shay sighed. It was no use arguing anymore. "Okay, whatever you say, but make darn sure that hauler knows what he's doing. We can't afford to lose this gear."

"Don't worry. Your property will be in good hands."

The tug and tow barge arrived at half past three in the afternoon. The BOP and riser section were transferred to the barge. Commander Blake then assigned one of her staff officers to accompany the tug to Portland. The Coast Guard had officially taken possession of the evidence.

Captain Finn Sorenson was in command of the *Odin*. His sixteen-year-old tug was a monster. Its 130-foot length and 30-

foot beam dwarfed the typical 80-foot harbor tug. Its huge turbo diesel generated 6,000 horsepower. It could pull almost anything.

Although the football field–size barge that trailed behind the *Odin* was ocean rated, its mass hardly challenged the tug. With only the BOP stack and riser pipe for cargo, it floated high out of the water. It was like towing a kite in the wind.

Captain Sorenson was in the darkened pilothouse, standing behind the solid oak steering wheel. It was almost nine P.M.; the sun had just disappeared into the ocean. The afterglow filled the western sky with brilliant hues of orange and yellow.

At age forty-one, Finn Sorenson was one of the best tug masters in the Pacific Northwest. He was tall, a couple of inches over six feet, and his massive bulk made him look like a football lineman. He had long fiery red hair and a matching full beard. He was a dead ringer for an ancient Viking warrior.

Astoria, Oregon, was Sorenson's home port, but he managed to remain there for only a few months of the year. Most of his time was spent towing cargo up and down the coastline. He and his two-man crew traveled as far north as Alaska's Bering Sea and as far south as Mexico's tropical waters.

Three weeks earlier the *Odin* had returned to Astoria for bottom painting and new zinc anodes. When the Coast Guard called Finn, asking him pick up the Hammer 4 equipment, he jumped at the chance. Sorenson needed the money. He loved the freedom of owning his ship, but the cost was high. He had to constantly hustle to make ends meet.

After a four-year apprenticeship with the Foss Tug fleet, and then twelve years with Crowley Maritime, he finally went out on his own. Everyone said he was crazy to give up such a good job, but he was a maverick. He wanted to be his own boss. The *Odin* cost him a cool million when he bought it three years earlier, but so far he had managed to make the mortgage payments and even pay himself a small salary now and then.

Although Sorenson wasn't getting rich, owning the *Odin* did have one huge advantage: It allowed him to use the tug as his home. As a single man, living aboard fit his lifestyle perfectly. His spacious captain's cabin, located in the bow, was a waterfront legend from Puerto Vallarta to Anchorage. Unlike the rest of the vessel's interior, his cabin was extravagantly appointed. Trimmed with the best hardwoods and outfitted with tasteful but definitely male-oriented decorations, it was striking. The huge waterbed, built-in stereo, and VCR-equipped television only added to the mystique. The women who were allowed to visit with him never, ever forgot the experience.

Captain Sorenson turned the wheel a half turn to starboard, continuing to maintain a southerly heading. He was guiding his vessel toward the mouth of the Columbia River, now about twenty miles away. Standing beside him was a twenty-four-year-old Coast Guard officer. Lieutenant (jg.) Tim Oliver was enjoying his conversation with the colorful master mariner.

"You operate this rig down in Mexico?"

"Yeah, sure. I've done a lot of hauling for Pemex. Taking gear out to rigs in the Gulf."

"Well, how do you like that compared to Alaska?"

"I like 'em both. You can't beat the scenery up north—the mountains, glaciers, rivers—it's fantastic. And I get along real well with the folks up there. A lot of them are rebels like me."

"What about Mexico?"

"Hey, man, as much as I love Alaska, I couldn't hack it in the winter. So I head south. God, I love it down there—Mazatlán, Puerto Vallarta, Cozumel—they're all great."

Oliver was impressed with Sorenson's lifestyle. He envied the man, but knew that he could never lead such a vagabond existence. The young officer was married and had a six-month-old daughter. He had just put down a rental deposit on a three-bedroom house in Beaverton and was looking forward to moving in next week. He hated his tiny Portland apartment.

"What are you folks going to do with that gear back there?" asked Sorenson, nodding his head toward the trailing barge.

"Hell, I don't know. Commander Blake told me to baby-sit it. I guess we're going to run some kind of tests to see what went wrong."

"How do you like your lady boss?"

"Oh, she's fine. She's an expert in oil spills and I've learned a lot."

Sorenson was momentarily lost in thought. He wondered

what it would be like working for a woman. Somehow he didn't like the idea. He then reflected on the huge oil spill that had been in all of the papers recently. "Did they get that oil well all plugged up?"

"Oh, yeah. The divers finally finished pumping the bore hole full with concrete a week ago, and most of the oil's been cleaned up by now."

"Well, I'm glad to hear that. I don't like to see anyone hurt with an accident like that. Besides, it doesn't do my business any good." Finn had towed SCS's barges to Alaska in the past and liked working for the company. They always paid their bills within thirty days.

Lieutenant Oliver turned away from Sorenson, looking to starboard. Even though the sun had just set, there was enough residual light to reveal the presence of another vessel. "Say, skipper," he said, "looks like we're not the only ones out here."

"Yeah, I've been watching it. Looks like some kind of yacht." He then picked up a pair of binoculars. He focused on the vessel. "Yep, it's a big sucker—looks expensive."

"You think it's heading for the Columbia, too?"

"Probably."

A mile to the west, the yacht plowed into the seas, running at a leisurely ten knots. A sixteen-foot-long Zodiac inflatable boat was trailing behind, its bow cinched up tight to the mini-ship's swim step. Two men were sitting in the Zodiac; they each wore black garments and carried waterproof backpacks. When the outboard motor burst to life, the mooring line was released and the inflatable veered toward the east.

Although the inflatable sped through the water at thirty knots, it was virtually noiseless. Sound from the specially muffled engine was barely audible above the hiss of the rolling swells. And the exposed engine housing and all other metallic elements on the inflatable were coated with thick sheets of rubber; the craft was virtually invisible to radar.

"Hey, looks like that boat is heading back out," Oliver said as he looked toward the west.

"Yeah, I guess they're not heading over the bar after all." Finn was pleased to see the vessel turn toward the open ocean.

He didn't want to worry about it when he started to line up with the buoys marking the entrance channel. Navigating the treacherous Columbia River bar, even during the calm summer season, took a lot of skill and concentration. It was much easier if no one else was around.

For the next fifteen minutes Sorenson prepared to enter the Columbia. He took a series of radar fixes and was planning his first course change when he heard the noise. It sounded like a stack of dishes in the galley had crashed to floor.

"What was that?" asked Oliver.

"I don't know. Maybe Billy and Jack are up."

Finn was referring to his two crewmen. Both men were still suffering from hangovers from the previous evening's binge. The pair hadn't returned to the *Odin* until sunrise.

"Why don't you go down and see what they're up to. Damn guys, they've been drinking too much lately."

Oliver headed down the steep narrow ladderwell that linked the wheelhouse with the tug's interior cabin. When he arrived at the base of the steel stairway he spotted the men. Standing only a few feet away, both men had their backs to him. They were dressed solidly in black from head to toe. Even their heads were covered by full-face black masks.

As Lieutenant Oliver stepped off the last stair step he called out: "What the heck are you guys doing, getting ready for Halloween?"

The nearest man to him, a huge hulk of a man, whipped his head around when he heard Tim's voice. And then he raised his hand. Tim spotted the pistol in a heartbeat and instinctively lunged for it. He wasn't fast enough. The man pulled the trigger as Oliver clawed at the gunman's outstretched arm. The silenced nine-millimeter coughed twice.

The momentum of the hollow-points rocketed the officer backward. Just before he slammed into the galley's six-foot-high refrigerator, Oliver's hands somehow locked onto the right sleeve of the gunman's black shirt. The garment ripped apart under the strain, revealing a well-muscled arm. And on the biceps, running back into the remaining portion of the shirt, was a massive tattoo. The body art depicted the head of an ugly green dragon; yellow and red flames blasted from its obscene nostrils.

Tim Oliver slowly collapsed to the deck as his legs lost

strength. Blood from the fist-size exit wounds in his back streamed down the white enamel of the appliance. He was dead by the time he slumped to the tile floor.

"What about the others?" asked the man who had just killed Lieutenant Oliver.

"They've been taken care of," replied the other intruder.

"Good, then the helmsman is the only one left."

Finn Sorenson was standing at the top of the stairwell, looking down. Despite the underlying din of the tug's engine he could hear strange voices. Although the voices were not loud, he was certain of one thing—they weren't speaking English. And then he spotted the blood. Oliver's corpse wasn't quite visible from the wheelhouse but the blood that pooled beside the refrigerator was. A few seconds later, the *Odin* rolled hard in response to an unusually large swell. The Coast Guard officer's bloodstained corpse rolled into Sorenson's view. *What the hell?* thought Finn.

Out of instinct Finn stepped away from the companionway, moving back into the pilothouse. He then kneeled down next to the kick plate just forward of the wheel and pulled away a six-inch-wide by five-foot-long panel of wood. Hidden inside was a twelve-gauge shotgun. With six double-ought rounds in the magazine, the Remington was instant death. He yanked the weapon free from its foam housing, chambered a round, and released the safety.

Finn Sorenson bought the weapon in Tijuana after he heard about the pirates that patrolled the coastal waters off Mexico's southern shores. He had never been bothered and often wondered if the stories he had heard about the waterborne bandits weren't based more on myth than hard facts. Nevertheless, he always kept the deadly weapon aboard.

Finn held the shotgun at waist level as he stood by the open companionway, looking downward. His left hand steadied the barrel while his right hand grasped the wood stock; his index finger pressed against the trigger. When one of the killers stepped into the stairwell and started up, Finn let him have it. The blast hit the man squarely in the chest, knocking him back into the galley.

The loud report from the shotgun was still ringing in Sorenson's ears when the second man moved into position. The intruder was standing just to the side of the stairwell inside the galley; only his now-bare arm was exposed. Finn saw the tattoo just as the man squeezed the trigger. The intruder blindly fired half a dozen rounds.

Finn pulled away as the silent bullets bored into the wood just inches from where he was standing. The windscreen to his rear shattered from another volley.

Sorenson stuck the barrel of his weapon down the stairwell and pulled the trigger. He waited for return fire, but heard nothing. At first he was tempted to head down the companionway, but decided against it. *Shit, that bastard might still be alive. Better try another way down.*

Finn pulled open the heavy port pilothouse door and was just stepping onto the exterior deck when he heard a thumplike sound as something landed on the wheelhouse floor. He turned to look and nearly froze in his tracks. A green object about the size of a small apple was still spinning on the mahogany deck. Fear engulfed him like a tidal wave.

Finn just managed to back out of the doorway before the grenade exploded. The shock wave propelled his dense body through the top member of the wooden guardrail.

The intruder climbed up the ladderwell, his reloaded pistol firmly held in both of his hands. When he reached the wheelhouse he carefully looked around. He expected to find the broken and torn body of the helmsman. Instead, the compartment was empty. The man cursed silently, wondering how the American could have survived. But when he spotted the broken railing opposite the open doorway, he understood. The man had been blown overboard.

The gunman walked out to the open deck and looked aft. The night was pitch-dark and the tug was still miles from shore. The intruder quit worrying about the helmsman. If he wasn't already dead, he soon would be. The near-freezing ocean water would finish him off.

Fifteen minutes after storming the vessel, the intruder turned the *Odin* about and ran due west. Although the hand grenade had blown out all of the pilothouses' windows, most of the ship's electronics and engine controls survived. The explosive had been a stun grenade; it was designed to knock people out rather than to kill.

* * *

The *Odin* and her tow continued heading westward. Just after four A.M., the tugboat turned into the wind and stopped. The luxury yacht that had launched the raiders was standing off to the starboard, about a hundred yards away. The surviving killer launched his inflatable and powered it toward the waiting vessel. The corpse of his partner was lashed to the Zodiac's bow.

Five minutes after boarding the *Victory,* the assassin triggered a portable radio transmitter, detonating a series of charges that had been planted against the hulls of the tug and barge. Both vessels disappeared within ten minutes. They finally came to rest on the ocean bottom over a mile deep.

Nearly forty miles east of the *Odin*'s grave site, and about five miles north of the entrance channel to the Columbia River, Finn Sorenson fought for his life. Although the bitter cold sea had nearly sapped all of the strength from his once-powerful body, he continued to swim. The Long Beach peninsula was only a quarter of a mile away now. In the predawn darkness he could see nothing. But the dull roar of the breakers told him he was getting close. *Gotta keep moving,* he continually repeated to himself.

7

MISSING IN ACTION

Seattle

"What do you mean the tug didn't show up?" Zackary Scott said, his voice clearly agitated. Zack was in his office. The handset of his phone was glued to the right side of his head. A chief petty officer from the U.S. Coast Guard's Portland District was on the other end of the telephone line.

"I'm sorry, Mr. Scott, but we don't know what has happened. The *Odin* was scheduled to arrive at our pier in the early afternoon, but so far she's a no-show."

"For crying out loud, man, it's nearly five o'clock! The boat should have shown up by now."

"I know, and we've been trying to reach her by radio since three, but there's been no response."

"She doesn't answer your radio calls?"

"Affirmative. Our last radio contact was yesterday evening, when Captain Sorenson called to check on the Columbia bar conditions. We haven't heard a word since."

Zack was fuming. He had made special arrangements for a forensic engineering team from San Francisco to meet the tug and barge when they arrived. He wanted his own independent investigation of the salvaged equipment from the Hammer 4 site. There was too much at stake to rely on the federal investigators.

"Well, is the boat just late, or did it have some kind of trouble?"

"We're checking now. We've got a chopper running down the length of the river from Portland to Astoria. I should have an answer in about an hour."

Zack could already picture the situation in his mind. *I'll bet the damn skipper ran the tow up some sandbar and is trying like mad to get it off before the Coasties find out.*

"Okay, Lieutenant. Sorry to yell at you, but that equipment on the barge is vital to me."

"I understand, sir. Do you want me to have your investigation team stand by?"

"No. Tell 'em to go back to their hotel and we'll hit it tomorrow morning, assuming the frigging boat finally shows up."

"Will do. And I'll call you the minute we find her."

"Thanks."

Zack waited until six-fifteen P.M. for the Coast Guard to report back. But the call never came. He was tempted to telephone the watch officer but decided against it. He would wait until tomorrow morning. Besides, he was late. Tonight was his oldest son's seventeenth birthday and Kelda was throwing a party for him.

Zack wasn't much of an entertainer, but his wife, Kelda, loved to invite guests to their new home. She had helped plan the huge waterfront home on Hunts Point, emphasizing its beautiful western exposure. With over two hundred feet of low bank shoreline, the Scotts' home was one of the best on Lake Washington's gold coast.

Zack was watching the teenagers swim in the pool. There were nearly two dozen kids running around his backyard, yelling, screaming, and generally having a blast. Tim Scott was in the middle of the crowd. He was thoroughly enjoying himself.

Zack turned away from the teenagers and walked back into the kitchen. Kelda was standing next to a serving countertop, placing candles on a huge chocolate layer cake. Her slim back was turned toward him, and she was slightly bent over the table. She wore a cotton halter top with matching shorts. Her long auburn hair cascaded down her shoulders, enhancing her tan skin. Mrs. Scott was still stunning by anyone's measure.

Zack came from behind her and slipped his hands around her waist and then reached up, cupping her breasts.

Kelda stiffened, startled by the sudden affection. "Zack, not now! There are a million kids around here."

"Yeah, but they're all outside now."

"Forget it, buster. No way!"

"Okay. You can't blame a guy for trying."

Kelda turned to face her husband. Her face still looked young and smooth, even though she had turned forty the month before. "Honey, why don't you help me with the candles. When the party's over we'll discuss that subject in private."

Zack grinned as she handed him a handful of red, blue, and green candles.

As they worked on the cake, Kelda decided it was a good time to question her husband. Zack hadn't said anything about business lately, and the only way she would find out what was happening was to ask. He didn't like to bring his work home.

"Zack, are those environmental groups still threatening to sue us?"

"Yes, I'm afraid so."

"How awful. That's just not fair. It was an accident!"

"I know. Nothing's fair about this whole situation." Zack paused as he turned away from Kelda, staring out the kitchen windows toward the lake. "Hell, I don't want to spill oil— none of us in the business want that. It's in our best interests to take care of the environment."

"Don't they know how much we've given to the Nature Conservancy?" Kelda asked.

For years the Scotts had generously supported the national conservation group, helping it to acquire estuaries and intertidal wetlands throughout the Puget Sound region. Zack and Kelda donated their own money for the cause—not SCS's. They both loved the Pacific Northwest and did more than their fair share to preserve its wonderful waterways and shorelands.

"I don't think they care about that. They probably think I'm just trying to buy influence."

"Well, that's not right," protested Kelda.

Zack shrugged his shoulders. "Yeah, I know."

Kelda moved closer to her husband. She decided to change subjects. "Honey, I called Mary Lou Robinson today."

Zack turned away from the window. "How's she doing?" he asked.

"Good. She didn't sound nearly as depressed as she did last week."

"And the twins?"

"They're visiting with Billy's parents in Dallas."

Zack still thought about Big Billy every day. He missed his friend. "Is Mary Lou still planning to move back to Texas?"

"Yeah, I think so. All of their relatives are back there."

"I guess that makes sense."

Kelda could see the grief in Zack's eyes. "Honey, will she and the girls be okay—financially, I mean?"

"Yes, Billy was careful with his money. Besides, Mary Lou will receive substantial insurance benefits. Money won't be a problem."

"How about the other families?"

"They should be okay. Between the company's life insurance proceeds and federal benefits, I think all the survivors will be fine."

"Well, I'm glad to hear that."

Zack nodded his head.

"Has the company funded the scholarship yet?"

The day after the memorial service, Zack announced that SCS would establish a college scholarship fund for the benefit of the *Kelda Scott*'s survivors. The $2 million endowment would be used to educate the children and grandchildren of the deceased crew.

"Yes, the money was deposited into escrow yesterday."

Although SCS was having cash flow problems, Zack didn't postpone his commitment. *It's the least I could do,* he had repeatedly told himself.

Kelda smiled. "I'm sure they all appreciate your thoughtfulness." She then reached up to Zack's forehead and brushed away an errant lock of black hair. It was again time to change subjects. "How's the cleanup work coming along anyway?"

"Well, that's been going real well. The MSRC people have done an outstanding job. In fact, the biologists are now predicting that we'll lose only a couple thousand birds and a few dozen mammals—mostly seals and a few otters."

Two thousand birds and a dozen seals and otters! That sounded like a lot to Kelda but she decided not to query him about that.

"So when do you think you'll be able to start drilling again?"

"I have no idea. The EPA and the Coast Guard made us seal up the well with cement for now." He walked to a window and looked out at the pool area, checking on the kids. "I'm sure we'll have to go through a formal Coast Guard evaluation and maybe some other hearings. We'll be lucky to retool the hole in six months."

"Well, I'm sure it will all work out. There's still a lot of oil out there, isn't there?"

"Yes, honey. More than you can imagine."

"Then even if you're set back for a short time, you won't be losing much. With the price of oil still rising, it'll be just that much more valuable."

Yes, unless we go bankrupt first, he wanted to say. But he didn't. "Yeah, I guess you're right. With the mess in the Middle East, this country will need every barrel of crude it can get."

"Well, let's not worry about all that now. Everything's going to be fine." Kelda then gestured toward the mountain-size cake on the counter. "Now, honey, please help me carry this outside."

As Zack helped Kelda maneuver the birthday cake, he couldn't stop thinking about the consequences of the blowout. He hoped the government investigations wouldn't take longer than six months. Zack needed to get the Hammer 4 field online as soon as possible. Even with the oil spill insurance money, SCS's cash reserves were being eroded daily by the expense of the cleanup operations. He had already spent millions and there was no end in sight to the bills.

Unlike Exxon, which paid billions for the *Exxon Valdez* disaster, SCS did not have unlimited deep pockets. If the cash drain continued, he might have to sell his interest in the offshore leases. Despite the enormous potential from the Hammer 4 tract, there was still no solid proof of the reservoir's overall production capacity. Until several production wells were drilled and actual flow tests were made, the value of the find was speculative. If forced to sell without the confirming wells, he might get only 10 or 15 percent of its true value. *I'll be damned if I'll let that happen!*

Long Beach, Washington

The senior night shift nurse entered the darkened room and walked up to the bed. The patient was resting quietly. The man's core temperature was normal. The cardiac monitor, quietly beeping in the background, indicated that his heartbeat had returned to its natural cadence. She moved closer and then leaned over the stainless steel bed frame, looking carefully at his face. The skin surrounding his bushy beard and long hair was still swollen and in several places it had erupted into ugly open wounds. The welts and sores around his neck were even worse—it looked like he had been burned. *You poor thing. Whatever happened to you?*

About half an hour before Finn Sorenson washed up on the Long Beach peninsula, he drifted into a school of jellyfish. The long poisonous tentacles from the primitive organisms relentlessly tore into his unprotected flesh, turning his weathered skin into mush.

It was the pain from the jellyfish attack that saved Sorenson's life. It pumped extra adrenaline into his bloodstream, charging him with just enough reserve energy to regain control of his fatigued and bone-cold body. When the first tentacle stung his hands, he swore at the top of his voice, cursing the unseen creatures. Then, in the darkness, he blindly thrashed about, trying to swim free of the dense formation that surrounded him. Fortunately, he swam eastward, toward the beach, and before he realized it, just as the sun was coming up, he was in the surf zone. The rolling six-feet-high swells that he had grown accustomed to during the long night were suddenly transformed into avalanches of thundering water that crashed violently into the hard-packed sand bottom. Before Finn could react, he was ground into the bottom by a heavy growler, and then another hit, and another after that. He was tossed along the bottom like a rag doll; each time the coarse sand abraded more of his skin. Finally, after struggling for ten minutes, his body was carried by a broken wave and deposited on the beach like a water-drenched log.

A pair of beach walkers from Seaview found Finn about an

hour later. He was suffering from exhaustion and hypothermia. The elderly couple couldn't understand a word of his babbling. When the county sheriff and local paramedics finally reached him, he was unconscious. By the time he arrived at the local hospital he was in a coma.

Finn hadn't been carrying any ID with him when he was blasted overboard. Consequently, he was simply listed on the hospital's patient register as "John Doe."

The nurse gently cleaned the draining wounds. She then liberally dabbed hydrocortisone cream onto his roughened skin. After checking his IV she glanced at her wristwatch. It was six-thirty-five A.M. Her shift was almost over. *Time to get the paperwork ready for the day shift.*

Seattle

Zackary Scott got the bad news a little after eight A.M. the next day. He was in his office when Lieutenant (jg.) John Palmer from the Portland Coast Guard called.

"Mr. Scott, as of six A.M. this morning we're officially listing the *Odin* as missing. We suspect that she went down somewhere in the Columbia or possibly over the bar at Astoria."

"What?" shouted Zack, clearly shocked at the young officer's pronouncement.

"Sir, we haven't been able to find a trace of the tug or the barge. The last confirmed position was off the Columbia entrance."

"How could it go down without any radio calls or other distress signals!"

"We just don't know. We're baffled by the whole thing." Lieutenant Palmer paused as he checked the notes on his desk. "If there had been some unusually large swells when the skipper tried to come over the bar, then maybe, just maybe, it's possible that the tug was somehow over run by the tow. That would account for the loss of both vessels."

"Have you spotted any debris?"

"Negative. No unusual floating material has been recovered at all. We've got a cutter patrolling the bar area right now looking for oil slicks and flotsam."

"How about from the air—you got anything up?"

"Yes, sir. We have two SAR helos patrolling."

My God, what next? thought Scott. "Well, Lieutenant, I can't say that I'm very pleased with your report. I have a lot riding on the gear stored on that barge."

"I know, sir. We also want that equipment. But that's secondary right now. There are four men missing and we don't have a clue as to whether they're alive or dead."

Scott understood. He had forgotten that one of the missing men was a Coast Guardsman. "Lieutenant, do you know the officer who was assigned to the tug?"

"Yes, sir. Tim Oliver. We were roommates at the Academy."

Scott reflected a moment, now thinking about the *Odin*'s skipper—he was also missing. Zack had met Finn Sorenson a year or two ago. He remembered the man's fiery red hair and impressive physique. He had instantly liked Finn. "Lieutenant, regardless of what has happened to my property, I hope your friend is okay."

"So do I, sir. In fact, I'm heading out on a helo later this morning to help with the search."

"Well, thanks for calling. And if you find out anything more, I'd appreciate a call."

"Will do, sir."

Zack hung up the phone and turned to look at a wall next to his desk. A map of the lower Columbia River was pinned to it. *Damn, where could that tug and barge have gone down?*

Zack was scared. His only defense against the fines and lawsuits that would be coming was aboard the barge. *I've got to get that gear back or my goose is going to be cooked for sure.*

8

FIRST CONTACT

North Pacific Ocean

The U.S.S. *Alaska* was 950 feet below the ocean surface, heading west at six knots. The Trident submarine had been on patrol for sixty-two days and was about to begin the long trek back to its home port in Puget Sound. Captain Mark Berry was in command. This was his last patrol as skipper of the ballistic missile submarine. His promotion to rear admiral had been announced a few days before the start of the patrol. When he returned he would be heading for the Pentagon to a high-level staff position in the Office of the Chief of Naval Operations. The forty-eight-year-old sub driver was going to miss sea duty, especially his tour on the *Alaska*. He wasn't sure if he was ready for the beach yet.

Captain Berry was in the control room studying a chart when the intercom speaker came alive. "Conn, Sonar," called out a voice.

The officer of the deck, a thirty-one-year-old lieutenant, responded. "Sonar, Conn."

"Sir, we're picking up an unusual transient on the BQR." The technician was referring to the 1,200-foot-long cable that stretched out from the *Alaska*'s thirty-foot-high sail. The towed array contained hundreds of hydrophones, each one designed to monitor specific underwater sound waves.

Berry looked up as the OOD responded. "What kind of transient?"

"It's weird, sir. I've never heard anything like it before."

Berry's curiosity finally got the best of him. He walked toward the OOD.

The officer handed off the microphone. "Captain here, Smitty. What have you got?" Berry knew every man aboard and recognized most of their voices.

"Sir, I don't know. I'm pretty sure it's mechanical, but it's so deep that I can't figure it out."

"Okay, stand by. I'm on my way."

"Aye, sir."

Half a minute later, Berry walked into the sonar compartment. The compact room was filled with a half dozen consoles, each one manned by a sonar technician. Chief Petty Officer Michael "Smitty" Smith was at the closest unit.

"What ya got?" asked the captain.

"I'm not sure, sir." The technician handed Berry a pair of headphones.

After slipping on the $5,000 headgear Captain Berry adjusted the volume gain on the right speaker. He could hear a faint hissing noise. It sounded like water flowing through a pipe.

"I see what you mean, Smitty. Any ideas?" asked Berry.

"Sir, it's got to be another boat. The sound is mechanical, but it's definitely not a propeller. I've given a tentative designation as Sierra Nine-Seven."

"Where is this thing?"

"We're coming up on it now, but it's deep."

"How deep?"

"I can't say for sure but the computer estimates somewhere around four thousand feet."

"Christ, how can that be?"

"I don't know. Just doesn't make sense. No one is supposed to have boats that can operate at those depths."

Berry understood Smith's confusion. The Russians still had the deepest diving boats, but they all maxed out at three thousand feet. The sounds he was now listening to originated a thousand feet deeper.

"How long have you been monitoring this thing?"

Smitty glanced at his wristwatch. "About five minutes, sir."

"What's its heading and speed?"

"It's moving east at about twelve knots."

Berry was now worried. Something was wrong. There was another submarine near his boat and he had no idea who it belonged to.

"Could that boat be tracking us?" he asked.

"It's possible, sir. But he's not in the best position to do so. In fact, he's starting to angle away from us now and he's so quiet that I don't think we'll be able to track him much longer."

"Then we may have accidentally crossed over his path and he doesn't know we're around?"

"Yes, sir. That's a real possibility."

Mark Berry considered his alternatives. His first reaction was to turn with the contact and follow it, continuing to record its unusual acoustic signature. But his cautious training prevailed. The sole purpose of *Alaska* was to remain hidden deep under the ocean, immune to the prowling enemy boats that might try to track her.

Although the world was generally at peace, the submarine's twenty-four Trident intercontinental ballistic missiles remained ready to fly at a moment's notice. Despite arms reductions and several changes in leadership, the Russians still had over four thousand nuclear warheads. And the Chinese never let up in their nuclear weapons expansion program. Worse yet were the other half dozen third-world countries that had finally developed nuclear weapons. North Korea, Pakistan, and Libya were particularly worrisome. Even though several of the *Alaska*'s sister subs had been mothballed due to budget cuts, the big stick provided by the remaining Trident fleet kept the interlopers at bay.

"All right, Smitty. Let's identify it as Sierra Nine-Seven. Keep recording for as long as possible."

"Aye, sir. Hopefully, I'll be able to hear it for a little while longer." The sonar operator paused as a new thought occurred to him. "Ah, Captain, are we going to wait until we return to Bangor to report this thing?"

Captain Berry waited a few seconds as he considered the question. "No, Smitty. This is too damned important. Somebody's got a new boat out there that we know nothing about. I'm going to have to phone this one in ASAP."

* * *

About an hour and a half later, long after the phantom sub's strange sound print faded into the background noise of the ocean, a special capsule was ejected from the *Alaska*'s hull. The fiberglass sphere, eighteen inches in diameter, was neutrally buoyant, and for three hours it just drifted with the quarter-knot eastward-flowing current, remaining nearly a fifth of a mile deep. Then, after the *Alaska* disappeared from the area, a thirty-pound lead weight attached to the bottom of the globe dropped away. The sphere rocketed upward.

As soon as the buoy broke the ocean surface, a six-inch-long wire antenna on top of the capsule began broadcasting a high-frequency radio message. For the next two minutes it repeated the message ten times and then quit. The radio beacon sank five minutes later after a tiny valve automatically opened, flooding the hollow interior.

A U.S. Navy satellite, parked 22,500 miles over the mid-Pacific, recorded all ten burst transmissions. A few seconds later, it relayed the messages directly to the Pentagon.

Seattle

Zackary Scott was in his office. For the past two hours he had been reading a number of the transcripts from the Coast Guard's preliminary accident report on the *Kelda Scott*'s sinking. The four-inch-thick report had just been released. It was a detailed summary of comments from the drilling vessel's survivors. After receiving medical aid, all sixty men and women were tested for alcohol and drugs, and then thoroughly questioned by a team of federal investigators.

Zack was pleased to learn that none of the crew tested positive for chemicals. *At least I don't have to worry about that,* he thought. But the rest of the report was of little help. Most of the survivors had been below deck sleeping or eating when the blowout occurred. And none of the bridge personnel or drilling crew made it out alive.

"Damnit," Scott said out loud to himself as he tossed the thick report onto his desk. He still had no clue as to what had caused the accident.

The only lead he found from the six hundred pages of interviews was the yacht. Several of the crew clearly remembered seeing a modern power cruiser, around a hundred feet long, take up position about a half mile south of the *Kelda Scott* before the accident. Unfortunately, the vessel was too far away for anyone to read the name, so it remained unidentified. The only hint as to where it might have come from was that it probably didn't originate from Seattle. One survivor, a fifty-one-year-old geologist, reported seeing the yacht head south. She thought it odd that the boat would turn away from the obviously endangered drilling rig. Standard protocol called for the vessel to remain on station, providing whatever assistance it could to the survivors.

Why would it leave without trying to help? Zack thought. *It just doesn't make sense.*

Zack picked up the report again and reread an introductory paragraph on the witness's background. She was a consultant from a geophysics firm headquartered in Los Angeles. He then reached for his phone. Less than a minute later he was connected to Dr. Margaret Hamilton's office. The phone rang five times before it was answered.

"Hamilton here."

"Dr. Hamilton, this is Zackary Scott from Scott Coastal Systems."

"Mr. Scott, ah, hello." The woman was clearly surprised by the phone call. She had never met the legendary Zackary Scott and was impressed that he would call her personally.

"I'm sorry to disturb you, Doctor. I know you've been through a lot, but I wonder if I could ask you a few questions about the accident?"

"Yeah, sure. Fire away. But please, just call me Margaret."

"Okay, Margaret. It's about the yacht you saw."

"Oh yeah. I spotted it from one of the portholes in the lifeboat. That SOB just turned tail and ran away, didn't try to help us a bit."

"Yes, that's what I understand happened and I've had a chance to read your testimony as well as the testimony of the others who saw the boat. Unfortunately, there's nothing in the report that provides much of a description of the vessel."

"As I recall, the Coasties didn't seem too interested in it, so I didn't elaborate."

Scott's interest level surged. "Well, I'm sure interested in it. Do you suppose you could give me some more details?"

"Sure, I can try." Margaret paused for a moment, collecting her thoughts. "Well, first of all, it was big. My dad had a sixty-foot Hatteras and that boat I saw was much bigger. I'd say it was at least a hundred feet long."

"Okay."

"It had a big flying bridge with a couple of runabouts behind it."

"What about masts and antennas?"

"I don't remember much about those. Although I'm sure it had one of those angled-back masts with the usual assortment of radars and radio antennas."

So far Hamilton wasn't much help, but Zack persisted. "Anything else that you can remember?"

Margaret pictured the yacht in her mind, trying to home in on the details. "Well, there was one other thing. It had what appeared to be a helipad over the fantail, aft of the flying bridge and runabout area. It extended clear to the stern. I thought that was unusual."

"Why do you say that?"

"The yacht was big all right, but not that big. That pad couldn't handle a very big chopper. It would have to have been mighty small to fit that deck area."

"Yeah, I see what you're getting at. That does seem odd. Could that deck area have had another use—maybe a sun covering or something like that?"

"Yes, come to think of it. It could have been built to shade the fantail."

"Anything else you can think of?"

Margaret again re-formed a mental image of the yacht. The details were a little foggier each time. "No. I'm afraid that does it."

Zack waited a few seconds, considering what Hamilton had said so far. "One last question, Margaret. You're sure the yacht was heading south?"

"Oh, yes. I'm positive it was heading downcoast. It really took off—like a bat out of hell—just after the rig went up."

"Well, thanks very much for your help. I really appreciate your time."

"Sure thing. Call again if you have any more questions."

"I will."

Zack replaced the handset and turned around to face his desk credenza. It was filled with photographs he had collected throughout the years. One of the photos was an eight-by-ten color print of himself, Captain Dan Barker, and Big Billy Robinson. They were standing on the drilling deck of the *Kelda Scott*. He missed his friends. *Okay, guys, I've finally got a lead.*

Zack picked up the phone and placed another call. He knew the number by heart. A minute later he was speaking with his attorney, Harold Shapiro.

"Harold, I need the name of a private investigator in the Portland area. I've got a lead on the identity of the yacht that was near the *Kelda Scott* when she went down."

"What kind of lead?" asked Shapiro.

"I think it might be homeported some place on the Columbia. I want someone down there to look for it."

"Okay, I'll call some of my contacts in Portland and get you the names of a couple of reputable firms."

"Good." Zack then changed gears. "Now, what have you found about the Minerals Management Services' decision to suspend our lease?"

"My contacts in Washington say that Dr. Patterson's office continues to be barraged by letters and phone calls. Apparently, several environmental groups have gotten together to team up against SCS. They're using computer networks and co-ops to organize."

"Yeah, that's what I thought. And it's pretty damn effective."

"Sure is. They're also inundating the EPA and the entire Washington and Oregon congressional delegations."

"How long do you think we'll be shut down?"

"Hard to tell at this point, but it'll probably be months before the formal hearings are convened."

Zack again changed the subject. "Have you had a chance to review the statutes and regs yet on our overall exposure?"

The attorney stiffened in his chair. The conversation was not going to be pleasant. "Zack, it doesn't look too good at this point. The Coast Guard and EPA both have the ability to level huge fines against the company and SCS is probably going to be liable for all cleanup costs and any subsequent damage awards that might be made by the courts."

"How about the insurance—it'll cover most of that, won't it?"

"Part. But it won't cover any of the fines."

"How much could we get hit with?"

"I just don't know at this point, other than it could be in the millions, especially if they prove operator failure." He paused momentarily to check the notes on his desk. "But there's another problem now."

"And what's that?"

"The company will very likely get hit with criminal charges."

"Christ Almighty! You mean they could throw me in jail?"

"Yes, it's possible. You will likely be targeted as the corporate CJO."

"The what?" asked Zack.

"The chief jailable officer."

"My God, what a fucking mess!" Zack didn't normally swear out loud but he was starting to lose control. "Don't we have any kind of defense?"

"Just one. If we can prove the sabotage theory, then most of the fines and criminal charges will disappear. The rest of the claims will be covered by insurance."

"But to prove sabotage, we've got to have hard evidence, don't we?"

"Absolutely."

"Shit. Right now I don't have a damn thing. The blowout preventer and the riser pipe are still missing, and none of my drilling or rig operators survived."

"So the only lead is the yacht?"

"That's it."

"Well, let me get to work on it. We don't have any time to waste."

"Yeah."

Zack hung up the phone and started squirming in his seat, trying to get comfortable. The muscles in his lower back were tightening up again. He wondered how long he'd last before the stress finally got to him.

Tokyo

Nearly halfway around the world, Hiroshi Yoshida and his senior managers were eating lunch in the YHI dining room.

The huge facility, located in the basement of the office tower, opened at five in the morning and remained open till midnight. It provided inexpensive, high-quality meals for all two thousand employees of the headquarters staff. Yoshida had purposely eliminated the elite executive dining room. Instead, he frequently dined with his employees, using his visits as a way to reinforce his devotion to *amae*.

Today, Yoshida and his charges were seated off in a far corner of the room. The facility was not yet crowded and they could talk freely. Yoshida was speaking. "Mitsui, I trust your operation went well."

"Yes, sir. Mori-san's men successfully intercepted the recovered equipment. The hardware, as well as the tug and barge, were disposed of. "

"Good, so we won't have to worry about that anymore?"

"That's correct. It will never be found."

Yoshida turned to another man, sitting at the far end of the table. "And you, Matsuoka, what do you have to report?"

"All is going well, Yoshida-san. The environmentalists managed to raise enough concern that the federal government has suspended Scott's drilling rights."

Yoshida's eyes brightened up at the news. "Excellent. How long can we expect him to be out of action?"

"Hard to say at this time. But it could be anywhere from one to two years."

"Good, then we won't have to worry for a while. That'll give us time to permanently deal with the problem."

"Yes, sir. It should."

Chairman Yoshida next focused on the forty-four-year-old man sitting directly on his right side. He was the assistant manager of the Nemuro Oil Complex. He had flown in the previous evening just to attend the meeting. "When is our next shipment from California due?"

"It will arrive in five days."

"And from the Spratlys?"

"That one will be docking tomorrow."

"Then our supply lines are back to normal?"

"Yes, sir. Everything is running smoothly."

"Excellent!"

9

RED WILDCATS

Anchorage, Alaska

Zackary Scott stared out of the cabin window of the Boeing 737. The Alaska Airlines jet had just touched down at the Anchorage International Airport. It was eight-ten A.M., local time.

"How long did she say we'd be here?" asked Jerry Dixon, one of SCS's senior drilling supervisors. He was sitting in the aisle seat next to his boss. They were in the first-class cabin.

"About an hour. I suppose they're going to take on fuel. It's a hell of a long flight from here to Magadan."

"Yeah, I guess you're right. It's about two thousand miles, isn't it?"

"Yes, at least that much."

"Well, I think I'll get up and walk around in the terminal for a while. You coming?"

"No. I'm fine right here."

"Okay, see you in a while."

Dixon stood up and stepped into the aisle. Even though Alaska's first-class seats are among the most spacious of any airline's, he filled it up to the max. Jerry Dixon was a very big man. He stood six and a half feet tall and weighed in at 250 pounds. An amateur weight lifter, the thirty-nine-year-old Harvard MBA graduate looked more like a professional wrestler than a businessman.

Zack was really glad to have Dixon's company. Dixon spoke fluent Russian, the product of the U.S. Navy's Monterey Post Graduate School. He had served as a naval intelligence officer for over six years. His specialty had been the Soviet Far East.

Scott and Dixon were on their way to Russia. They were scheduled to meet with a Russian drilling company in the city of Magadan, located on the Sea of Okhotsk. The privately owned company, Okhotsk Sea Ventures, was one of the new oil exploration firms that had the republic's blessing. It had been awarded the drilling rights for offshore oil and gas in the northern Kuril Island chain.

The Russian wildcatters had courted Scott six months earlier, working hard to convince him to invest in their leases. After checking with the State Department and receiving formal approval to work with the Russians, Zack entered into a joint venture agreement with OSV. He would supply one of his semisubmersible drilling rigs and the key personnel necessary to run it for a trial period of one year. The Russians, in turn, would provide all of the roughnecks, roustabouts, and other laborers as well as all materials and consumables. They would then share fifty-fifty in any profits.

The plan was to drill several exploratory holes around a 50,000-acre tract located off the southwestern shoreline of Urup Island in the Friz Strait. Detailed geophysical surveys suggested that a cap rock formation, about 10,000 feet down, might have trapped vast amounts of hydrocarbons.

Zack settled back into his seat and shut his eyes. He ignored the traffic in the nearby aisle as hordes of passengers moved toward the main exit. He was glad to be getting out of Seattle for a few days. He wanted to forget about all of SCS's domestic problems and deal just with an entirely new situation.

Zack managed to temporarily set aside the financial problems from the Hammer 4 blowout. *Somehow I'll figure out a way to keep things going. I've done it before,* he constantly told himself. But as hard as he tried he couldn't keep from thinking about Billy Robinson and Dan Barker and the rest of the *Kelda Scott*'s lost crew. They were all dead. And the more he thought about it, the more convinced he became: *They were all murdered!*

*   *   *

The man sitting three rows behind Scott watched as Jerry Dixon stood up and headed forward. While the huge American lumbered toward the exit the observer turned toward another man, sitting in the seat on the opposite side of the aisle. Both were Asians in their early thirties, had short dark hair, and were dressed in expensive business suits.

The first man nodded his head slightly. Then, without a word in response, the other man stood up and headed down the aisle, following Dixon. Both men had strict orders not to let Scott or Dixon out of their sight.

Magadan, Russia

Zackary Scott and Jerry Dixon sat in the stuffy room with the three owners of Okhotsk Sea Ventures. Their flight to Magadan had arrived on schedule. The OSV partners had been waiting for them at the modest terminal facilities.

Magadan is a port city with a population of 150,000. It is young by Russian standards, only about fifty years old. Originally constructed as one of Stalin's gulags, it eventually was transformed into one of the key economic nerve centers for Far Eastern Russia.

The air was thick with the stench of cigarette smoke. Zack could hardly stand the smell but kept quiet anyway. His Russian hosts were oblivious to the discomfort both Americans were experiencing.

Dixon was speaking in Russian, explaining a technical point regarding the mooring of a semisubmersible drilling rig. Zack sat silently, staring indirectly at his counterpart across the cheap wood table. The man was in his mid-forties, like Zack. But that was about as close as they came. In physical stature, Boris Zarkaroff was a small man—no more than five and a half feet tall—and he weighed maybe 130 pounds. He was nearly bald. His entire face was heavily wrinkled, the consequence of spending an inordinate amount of time exposed to the sun and drinking nearly half a quart of vodka a day for years. The other men were younger, both in their early thirties. Unlike Zarkaroff, the assistants were tall and built like gorillas.

Zack could hardly believe that he was about to make a deal with these men. He had worked with some rough-and-tough characters before, especially in the Gulf of Mexico, but these Russian wildcatters were a completely different breed. The men who owned and managed OSV were aggressive and eager to forge ahead, but they continually wanted to change the deal points. First it was drill string. They insisted that Scott Offshore supply the thousands of feet of steel drill pipe. Zack refused, knowing full well that OSV had fifty thousand feet of perfectly adequate pipe sitting in a storage yard outside the office. Then it was a supply vessel. They wanted SCS to use one of its 150-foot-long work boats to ferry supplies and crews to the rig from the shore base. Again Zack refused. The cost of an American crew to run the vessel would have been astronomical, and there was no way he would turn control of a $3 million ship over to a Russian crew.

Finally, they tried to change SCS's cut. They wanted an extra 5 percent for setting up the deal. Boris called it a "premium credit." Zack called it "bullshit extortion."

The premium credit would have given OSV 55 percent of the profits and a controlling interest in the overall development of the oil field. Zack flatly refused and stood up, ready to torpedo the entire deal. Jerry Dixon grabbed his arm to stop him. "Hang on a minute, Zack, we can work this out."

A minute later the two SCS executives were huddled together in a corner of the room. The Russians remained sitting at the table, jabbering away among themselves.

Zack was shaking his head in disbelief. "Jerry, where in the hell did these turkeys learn to bargain? They're worse than the Arabs."

"I know. But remember they've been cutting some deals with the Chinese lately. I think they got screwed a couple of times."

Zack smiled just a little. One of his competitors from Houston had entered into a JV agreement with the Red Chinese government to develop an offshore oil field in the South China Sea. After agreeing to a series of concessions and then actually mobilizing the drilling rig to the site, the Chinese canceled the deal. They decided to develop the site with their own equipment. It cost the American firm a small fortune in lost time on the rig and nearly half a million dollars in wasted transit time.

"Well, that explains part of it, but I still don't trust these pricks at all. I think it's in their nature to screw anybody if they get the chance."

"That's no different than about half the folks we work with back in the real world."

Zack thought a few seconds. Dixon was right. The oil business was tough, no matter where you were. "Yeah, I know. Now, let's either finish this thing or we're out of here."

"Okay, give me a couple of minutes here. They're bluffing—they need this deal much more than we do."

Scott nodded affirmatively. But he was really beginning to wonder if his Russian counterparts actually understood English. If they had lied and at least one of them was fluent in English, they would know Zack's entire negotiating strategy. Zack decided it didn't matter. When they first started trying to win concessions from Scott, he made up his mind. *I'm not changing a damn thing. They take it or I leave.*

Dixon turned back to face the Russians. The ensuing debate was heated and long.

In the end Dixon was right. Zarkaroff and his comrades were trying to see how hard they could push Scott. It was a test to see if they could manipulate the head man of SCS. If Zack had showed any weakness, they would have exploited the situation—that was their nature. But they also didn't want to lose SCS as a partner. They didn't have the expertise to drill in deep water, nor did they have the capital to lease a $50 million semisubmersible.

The joint venture agreement was finally signed and the five men celebrated with dinner at a local restaurant. During the interval between the soup and the main course, Zack took the opportunity to ask Zarkaroff a few questions about Russian drilling operations in other areas of the Kuril Islands. He was thinking ahead to a future project. Zack was particularly interested in the area around the south end of Shikotan Island. Although the Russians had returned the southern Kurils to Japan, Russia retained the right to develop offshore oil resources around Shikotan, the most easterly of the Japanese Kurils. And OSV had been assigned the drilling rights.

Dixon interpreted the Russian's words: "We've always had a lot of interest around Shikotan ever since the Japs scored a hit with the Nemuro field. Before the island was given back to Japan a couple of exploratory wells were drilled along its north coast. Unfortunately, nothing was found.''

—''But that doesn't make sense,'' replied Zack. ''There's only a couple of dozen miles separating that area from the Nemuro field, and from what I've read the subsurface formations are similar.''

''I know. The Nemuro field must be confined to some kind of pocket on their side of the line.''

Zack couldn't understand the Russians' lack of success. The Nemuro oil field was Japan's first major petroleum find within its own territorial waters. And it was an elephant. Billions of barrels of crude oil were trapped inside a massive formation of reservoir rock. Yet, just north of the field, the Russians found nothing. *It has happened many times before,* Scott finally admitted to himself. Even with modern geophysical tools and supercomputers, luck still remained the most important element in wildcat drilling.

As the huge meal progressed, the five men began to loosen up. Despite the language barrier they continually toasted each other. Three hours later, when it was time to head back to the hotel, four empty vodka bottles were lined up on the table. And Zack was bombed. He had thoroughly enjoyed the companionship once the deal had been settled. All thoughts of his problems back in Seattle were gone.

Jerry Dixon, on the other hand, was stone sober. As a Mormon, he didn't drink, and Zack knew he could rely on the man to take care of him if he drank too much. When Dixon guided Zack out of the restaurant he happened to notice a man sitting off in the corner by himself. The Asian was reading a newspaper. For just a brief moment Dixon thought he recognized something about him. But then Zack tripped and almost fell to the ground. Dixon grabbed him and guided him to the door. All thoughts of the stranger had evaporated.

The man sitting at the table watched the two Americans move through the doorway and then head down the street. There was no need to follow them now. He knew they were returning to their hotel. He had been listening to the dinner conversation with keen interest. Although he spoke a little Russian, enough to get around the town without much notice, his English was much better. Because of the background noise in the crowded restaurant, he couldn't hear a lot of what Scott had said, but he did hear the words *Nemuro* and *Shikotan* several times. He decided it was time to phone in his report.

Tokyo

Hiroshi Yoshida was in his bedroom when the phone rang. He glanced at the digital clock on the wall shelf. It was 11:43 P.M.

He picked up the receiver. *"Moshi-Moshi."*

The caller replied with a code word. It identified him as one of the men assigned to follow Zackary Scott.

"I'm sorry to disturb you at this late hour, sir, but I wanted to let you know what I've found out so far."

"Yes, go ahead."

The spy was careful with his words. Both the Russians and the Americans monitor telephone calls throughout the region. "It appears that both parties came to an agreement today."

"Do you know where they will start work?"

"No. We haven't got that level of detail yet, but I did hear them repeatedly mention future drilling around Shikotan."

Damnit, thought Yoshida. *They're going to try again.* The CEO of Yoshida Heavy Industries dreaded the thought of one of SCS's drilling rigs operating anywhere near the Nemuro Complex.

"Are you sure they mentioned Shikotan?"

"Yes, sir. Many times. I also heard Nemuro, too."

"All right, stay with them till they leave. Then return home."

"As you wish, sir."

After Yoshida hung up his phone he stood and walked into a large enclosure located just off the bedroom. The special room, his favorite, contained an elegant garden with a small rock waterfall. The water cascaded down the granite with the elegance of a tiny mountain stream. Off to the side of the garden room was the *ofuro.*

The circular redwood tub was only three feet in diameter but was over four feet deep, half of its height recessed into the tile floor.

Yoshida stood in the center of the tile and stripped off his robe. He then lathered his trim body with soap and water. After rinsing, he stepped into the soak tub. The simmering water felt wonderful.

Yoshida's ritual of the evening soak had been a mainstay in his life for the past forty years. He cherished the fifteen to twenty minutes he spent in the *ofuro* at the end of each day. It allowed him to focus on business tasks that would be waiting at the office the next day. Despite the group-think philosophy that dominates the Japanese business world, Yoshida preferred to make his own decisions, and most of the important ones were made sitting in his soak tub. Later at the office he would skillfully plant his ideas with the other members of the executive staff. Few of his senior managers ever realized the extent to which he manipulated their thinking.

As Hiroshi relaxed his tired old body, his thoughts were not on Yoshida Heavy Industries. Instead, he was thinking about the Americans. SCS's partnership with the Russians was bad enough, but the talk about drilling around Shikotan was an absolute disaster. Yoshida could not afford to let that happen under any circumstances.

For nearly fifteen minutes, Yoshida evaluated a series of alternatives. None of them were particularly attractive. However, when he finally climbed out of the bath he had made up his mind. *We must continue with the original plan. It's the only way out.*

10

NIGHT WORK

Seattle

"Hi, Zack," Tim Marshall said as he stepped inside Scott's office. "How was your trip to Russia?"

Zack was sitting behind his desk. He glanced up at his executive vice president. Marshall, a retired army bird colonel, was a few years older than Zack. Marshall's once-trim build had filled out in the past few years. He looked a little chunky.

"Hi, Tim," Zack said. "The trip went well. But that Zarkaroff is one tough customer. I see what you've been going through." Zack was referring to Marshall's previous three meetings with the OSV partners.

"Did he try to change the deal points?"

"Yeah, your friend Boris wanted an extra five points plus a bunch of other concessions."

"Damn," Marshall said. He had set up the OSV deal and now pictured it crashing.

Zack continued: "I didn't give 'em a frigging thing. I stood eyeball to eyeball with old Boris and told him to take it or leave it."

"And?"

"He blinked." Zack paused for effect. "You were absolutely right. They need our rig and people too much to queer the deal."

Marshall let out a sigh of relief. "Then we proceed as planned?"

"That's right. Start mobilizing the *Deepquestor*. I told them that we'd have her under way within a week."

"That's great. I'll start making the arrangements now."

Tim had started to leave, wanting to get back to his office, when Zack called him back. "Tim, you heard anything about the *Odin* and our equipment?"

"Nothing from the Coast Guard, but I did get a call from that Portland PI you hired. Apparently they've got a lead on the mystery boat."

Zack sat up straight in his chair. "What kind of lead?"

"Something about a yacht matching the description from that lady geophysicist."

"Dr. Hamilton?"

"Yeah, that's her." Marshall paused as he moved closer to Zack's desk. "Well, apparently the PI found a yacht that looks like it. It's moored at a marina on Hayden Island."

"That's very interesting. Did he give a location?"

"Yeah, it's in their report—on page two, I think."

"I haven't seen any report."

"Oh, sorry. I still have it my office. I'll be right back."

A minute later Zack was scanning the six-page typewritten report. For four days, the investigative firm had canvassed every marina and boatyard in the Portland-Vancouver area. They located eleven megayacht vessels, but only one of those had a helipad covering the fantail like the one Dr. Hamilton had described.

"The *Victory*. That's her name?"

"Yep," answered Marshall.

"Well, Tim, I think I might just have to make a little trip down there this week to check that baby out."

"Okay, that sounds good. You want me to tag along?"

"No. You're already overloaded. I'll handle it."

Long Beach

Finn Sorenson was still unconscious. He would occasionally reach a semiconscious state, usually preceded by a bout of convulsions, but would then revert back to a deep, comalike state. When his waterlogged body was recovered from the bone-cold waters, he was almost dead. In a last-ditch effort to conserve heat, his body had shut down all conscious activities. Despite the emergency measures that saved his life and the continuing care he had received, his mind remained in a state of near-suspended animation.

The nurses who took care of Finn still referred to him as their John Doe. No one had called to claim him and the local police department had no reports of any missing persons that fit his description. Nearly everyone at the hospital seemed content to wait for the mystery man to wake up. The attending physician and the hospital's resident were both certain he would eventually come out of the hypothermia-induced coma.

The hospital administrator, however, couldn't wait any longer. The John Doe's care was costing over $1,000 a day and he didn't have anyone to bill. Until he had a real name to work with, he was forced to cover the costs out of the hospital's indigent care fund. The account was already depleted, and if he didn't find an insurance company or some family members to guarantee payment, his carefully worked out financial plan for the year would be down the tubes. The hospital was already running at a serious deficit and his job was on the line.

Not willing to wait any longer, the administrator took it upon himself to determine the real identity of their guest. Consequently, he faxed a written description and a photograph of the John Doe to all of the surrounding police and sheriff's departments. He also decided to send one to the Portland Coast Guard.

Hunts Point

Zackary Scott managed to get home a half hour before sunset. He was sitting on the spacious timber deck by his pool, facing west toward the Seattle skyline. He sipped from a frost-coated bottle of Budweiser as a continuous procession of sailboats, power yachts, and water-skiers paraded in front of his waterfront residence. Lake Washington was exceptionally crowded this night. The warm weather had pulled boaters to the lake in droves.

Kelda was sitting next to him. She had a tall glass of iced tea in her right hand. She was wearing a tan halter top with matching shorts. Her long auburn hair billowed around her face in the light northerly breeze.

"Beautiful night, isn't it, honey?" Kelda said.

"Yep. So far, one of the best this summer."

Kelda sipped her drink and then turned to face her husband. "Zack, I'm so glad you convinced me to move here—this is such a great place. I just love it!"

Zack smiled.

The move from Seattle to the Eastside had been Zack's idea. At first Kelda resisted—she liked her Madrona waterfront home and had had no desire to move across the lake. But now she felt different. Hunts Point was truly a unique place to live. Despite the vast urbanization of the surrounding areas, the tiny town of Hunts Point had managed to retain its original rural waterfront character. Gorgeous stands of cedars and firs remained, there was virtually no crime, and all of the neighbors were friendly without being too nosy. It was like heaven to Kelda.

The Hunts Point peninsula, only 205 acres in area, juts three quarters of a mile into Lake Washington, just north of Bellevue. Although the minuscule town has just two hundred homes, it has an enormous economic impact on the local area. Hunts Point is one of the wealthiest communities in the United States. Computer software entrepreneurs, rock stars, and professional athletes—along with a myriad of business executives, high-powered lawyers, and world-famous surgeons—call the tiny Northwest community home. And the Zackary Scotts, after hitting it big in the offshore construction industry, were one of the newest families in town.

"I wonder how long this good weather's going to last?" Kelda asked.

"Well, don't be surprised if it starts raining again." Zack took another sip from his bottle. "Remember what summer was like last year."

Kelda didn't need to be reminded. The weeks of solid overcast coupled with fifty degree temperatures and daily showers had been miserable. The Scott family had hardly been able to enjoy the pool and dock that came with their new home.

"Well, keep your fingers crossed."

"You bet."

Kelda stood up and walked over to the edge of the deck, looking toward the water. "Did you see where Tim and Matt went?"

"Last time I looked they were heading toward the bridge."

Kelda turned toward the southwest, looking down the lake. A ribbon of gray at water level stretched clear across the lake. The four-lane Evergreen Point floating bridge was about a mile away from the Scotts' home. Despite the dozens of boats in the distance she spotted the sixteen-foot-long sailboat. Its red jib stood out like a beacon. Both of the Scott boys were expert sailors.

"Oh, I see them now." Kelda paused as she moved a few feet to improve her view. "Zack, they're pretty far out there."

"Yeah, well, don't worry. They know what they're doing."

"I know that, but the winds are awful light. What'll they do if it quits?"

"Then I guess they'll have to paddle back."

"You should get that outboard fixed."

"I know. I forgot about it. Have Tim take it over to the marina tomorrow."

"Okay."

Kelda again sat down beside her husband. She reached out with her hand and stroked his right arm. "Zack, how about the four of us heading up to Stuart Island this weekend? We could all do a little fishing and beachcombing."

"I'd like that. Barring any more disasters this week, maybe I can swing it." He turned away from the lake, looking directly into Kelda's hazel eyes. "But if I have to stay here, why don't you and the boys go anyway? I can get Kenmore Air to fly you up and then I'll come up Sunday afternoon and pick you up."

"We don't want to go without you."

Kelda's sole motivation had been to get Zack away from the office. Their family retreat in the San Juan Islands was a perfect place for Zack to relax. Stuart Island was miles from the more populous and developed islands in the archipelago. And best of all, their cabin didn't have a telephone—not even a cellular phone. That had been Kelda's idea. Short of flying out to the island, it was almost impossible for the SCS Seattle office to contact Zack.

Kelda was worried about her husband's health. Although Zack exercised regularly, watched his diet, and drank moderately, he was under too much stress. Ever since the Hammer 4 blowout, she could tell that he was having problems. His back was bothering him again and he wasn't sleeping very well. Both symptoms were clear indicators that Zack was again having trouble with the business. After eighteen years of marriage she had seen it too many times before. *Darn it, Zack,* she thought, *if you don't slow down soon, you're going to have a heart attack or a stroke.*

"Well, honey," Zack said, "if you don't want to go, I guess we'll do it another time."

"How about our vacation—that's still on, isn't it?" The Scotts were scheduled to spend two weeks at the family ranch in Montana. Zack's uncle, Jason Scott, ran the 50,000-acre spread and the Scotts vacationed there at least once a year. The trout fishing was superb and they all loved riding horses through the woods.

"Well, I think so, but—"

Kelda cut him off. "Zack, you promised. The boys and I have been looking forward to that trip!"

"Don't worry. We'll go—somehow I'll find the time."

"Good." She stood up and reached out with her hand, rubbing his full head of hair. "Now, how about helping me with the steaks. I'm getting hungry."

"Okay, I'll get the grill going."

Portland

The watch officer at the Portland Coast Guard office heard the fax machine's high-pitched tone as it announced an incoming call. Ensign Winston Isdell hardly ever received any facsimile transmissions during the evening hours, so he pushed his chair away from the desk and stood up. Half a minute later he was standing next to the output tray of the machine. *What the hell's this?* he thought as he reached down and picked up the copy of a black-and-white photograph. He retrieved the accompanying letter of transmittal. It was a form letter typed on stationary from a hospital in Long Beach, Washington. The text read:

To Whom It May Concern:

A John Doe was found washed up on a local beach eight days ago. The white male is around 40 years of age. He has red hair and full beard, also colored red. He is 6 feet 4 inches tall and weighs 220 pounds. The individual is currently comatose, brought about by a severe case of hypothermia. We believe this person may have had some type of mishap with a small boat or may have accidentally fallen overboard from an offshore vessel. If you have any missing persons that might fit the above description (see attached photo), please call Mark Littlejohn, Hospital Administrator.

The watch officer scanned the photograph again. *Wow, that's one tough-looking hombre.* His first reaction was to route the fax message to the Operations Division, but then he changed his mind. He remembered a phone call he had had from one of the day watch officers. Lieutenant Palmer had asked him to be on the lookout for the skipper of a tug called the *Odin*. Palmer had described Finn Sorenson as looking something like a cross between a Seattle Seahawk lineman and a real Viking warrior. *Damn, that's got to be him.* He headed for the phone.

Northern Virginia, Near Dulles International Airport

NRO photoanalysis technician Mary Lynn Britton had been scanning the KH-11 satellite images for nearly four hours now. It was a few minutes before one A.M. Mary hated working the swing shift, but this month it had been her turn to work late. Her section was way behind schedule on reviewing the non-essential surveillance photos. They had to catch up somehow.

Mary was just reaching for her coffee mug when she spotted something unusual on her display screen. The image on her monitor was a computer-enhanced electronic photograph of a land target. It had been photographed from a low orbiting spy satellite. She straightened up in her chair and then used her mouse to move the screen's cursor until its crosshairs were directly over the area of interest. Next, she typed a few strokes

on the keyboard. The screen momentarily blinked off to a solid
blue background. When it snapped back on a few seconds
later, the target area was blown up two hundred times. The
black-and-white image was crystal clear.

What the heck is that? Mary said to herself as she stared at
the object.

The twenty-eight-year-old woman had been conducting a
routine review of aerial surveillance of the Yokohoma waterfront. Part of the National Reconnaissance Officer's duties was
to assess the shipbuilding capacities of all major industrial
powers.

Mary moved closer to the screen. She was looking at a
slightly oblique aerial image of the Yoshida Heavy Industries
waterfront complex. She had been checking the construction
progress on a new 250,000-deadweight-ton supertanker located in the main graving dock. The tanker was still there,
about 60 percent complete. The giant ship, however, wasn't
what interested her. There were two huge cylinders floating in
the water next to the shipyard's main wharf. The thirty-meter-
diameter tubes were positioned side-by-side and appeared to
be structurally tied together. A quick scale check on the screen
told her that the cylinders were almost a thousand feet long.
She had never seen anything like it before.

Mary studied the enhanced images for a few more minutes,
trying to figure out what the Japanese were building. She was
puzzled more than ever. *That can't be a ship. There's no bow
or superstructure. But it's floating.*

After a quarter of an hour Mary Britton finally gave up on
trying to identify the new object. *I'm going to have to send
this one upstairs,* she thought. She typed in a series of commands, directing the computer to reproduce the video screen's
image onto a hard copy. It took the printer about a minute to
duplicate the electronic photo. Mary studied the print for a
few more seconds. She then took a grease pencil and circled
the twin cylinders. After typing a brief cover memorandum,
she placed the photo and memo into a top secret interagency
routing envelope and placed it in the outgoing correspondence
basket. It was addressed to the Photographic Analysis Section
of the Central Intelligence Agency.

11

WAKE UP

Zack was back in his office. It was early in the afternoon. Half an hour earlier he had finished playing a vigorous game of racquetball at a nearby health club. Russ McMillin had won again.

Zack was now reviewing a four-page fax from a law firm in Washington, D.C. The firm specialized in oil and gas matters, in particular lease negotiations with the Department of Interior's Minerals and Management Section. Zack had recently hired the firm to help with the Hammer 4 mess. The report was not good news. As Zack had feared, MMS was considering suspending SCS's lease for the Hammer 4 tract.

"Shit!" muttered Zack as he tossed the report onto his desk. He was just thinking of calling Tim Marshall to inform him of the bad news when he was interrupted by his desk intercom. It was his secretary's voice: "Zack, Lieutenant Palmer from the Coast Guard is on line five."

"Thanks, Janet." He reached for the telephone handset. "Zackary Scott speaking."

"Mr. Scott, this is Lieutenant Palmer, U.S. Coast Guard, Portland. We spoke a few days ago about the *Odin*."

"Yes, Lieutenant. Have you any news?"

"We found the skipper, Captain Sorenson."

"Alive?"

"Yes, sir. He's in a hospital in Long Beach, Washington."

"Long Beach! How the hell did he end up there?"

"We don't know. He was found washed up on the beach."

Zack remained silent for a moment as Palmer's words set in.

"You say he was washed up on a beach?"

"Yes, sir. I'm afraid the *Odin* and her tow may have sunk."

"Sunk!"

"Yes, sir."

"Where'd they go down?"

"I don't know, sir. We just don't have any details yet."

"Well, what has Sorenson told you."

"Nothing. He's still unconscious."

"Good God, what's wrong with him?"

"According to the attending physician, he nearly died from hypothermia and then lapsed into a coma. He's recovering physically but hasn't regained consciousness yet."

"Then you have no idea where the tug and barge went down?"

"Not a clue. Right now we're searching with a helo along the Long Beach peninsula. But I'm not optimistic."

Zack silently agreed. The *Odin* and her tow had been missing for days. It would be a miracle if any wreckage were found.

"What about the rest of the crew?" asked Zack.

"Sorenson's the only survivor so far. We don't have much hope for the others."

"Your buddy's still missing, too?"

"Yes, there's been no sign of Lieutenant Oliver either."

"I'm sorry to hear that. I hope he turns up okay."

"So do I but it doesn't look too good."

Zack knew how the man felt. The memories of the missing crew from the *Kelda Scott* were still fresh. "Well, Lieutenant, I guess you know that I was counting on having access to the drilling gear on the *Odin*'s barge. It was the only evidence I had to prove the blowout was caused by sabotage."

"I'm aware of your claim, sir. But unfortunately, I can't help you with it—at least not yet." He paused, carefully thinking his words. "I'm hoping that when Captain Sorenson regains consciousness, he will be able to solve the mystery. If he knows where the *Odin* went down, then we might be able to recover your equipment."

"Okay, Lieutenant, I read you. But the minute Sorenson comes around I'd like to know."

"You'll be notified, sir."

"Thanks."

"You're welcome."

Zack hung up his phone and stared out the windows. He could see the Olympic Mountains in the distance. The brown haze made their usual jagged peaks look rounded, as if blurred. Zack was baffled. *What the hell happened to the Odin? It was calm that day and there've been no reports of any wreckage.*

After a couple of minutes of mental debate, Zack finally came to a new conclusion: *I've got to get down there right away and nose around. Maybe I'll find something.*

He reached for the intercom switch. "Janet, I've decided to head down to Portland tonight. Would you get me plane and hotel reservations?"

"I'll set it up right away."

"Thanks."

Long Beach, Washington

"Where the hell am I?" echoed the hoarse male voice as it boomed down the deserted corridor.

The senior night-shift nurse looked up from her paperwork. She was standing behind the reception counter at the far end of the corridor.

The strange voice called again, this time louder: "Son of a bitch, what the hell's going on here?"

Susan Schroder, RN, tossed her clipboard aside and began heading down the tile hallway. She was almost running by the time she reached the doorway to the John Doe's room. When Susan turned the corner and headed inside, she nearly collided with Finn Sorenson. The bear-size man was standing next to the door, leaning against a stainless steel bed rail. Although he had lost twenty-five pounds and looked like he had just walked out of a sauna, he was still a powerful man. Anyone else who had been unconscious for over a week would have been barely able to crawl.

"Mr. Sorenson, you're finally awake."

Finn looked back at the tiny woman. The thirty-eight-year-old nurse was barely five feet tall and weighed a wispy one hundred pounds. Finn teetered back and forth a few times before responding. ''How long have I been out?''

''It's been nine days.''

''Come on, now.''

''No, really. You've been unconscious for nine days.''

Finn was growing weaker by the moment. ''Damn but I'm winded. I gotta sit down.''

Susan moved forward and grabbed his right arm, wrapping it across her shoulders. She helped him get back in the bed. ''Thanks,'' he said as he collapsed onto the mattress. Despite the cool temperature of the room, beads of sweat glistened on his forehead.

''How do you feel, Mr. Sorenson?''

''Finn, call me Finn.'' He looked up at her face. Susan was beginning to show her age, but he liked what he saw. ''I feel like I've been keelhauled.''

''Well, I'm not surprised that you're not feeling too well right now.'' She moved closer to his side, placing her right hand on his wrist. She then began checking his pulse while simultaneously continuing her dialogue. ''We've tried to exercise your arm and leg muscles daily, but exercises just aren't a substitute for good old walking.'' His pulse was strong and steady.

Before Finn could ask another question Susan produced a digital thermometer. ''Open up, please,'' she said. She then inserted the device and waited fifteen seconds before removing it.

''What's it say?'' asked Finn.

''Your temperature's perfectly normal.''

''Well, that's good,'' Finn replied.

''Yes, very good.'' The nurse next began fitting a blood pressure gauge on his right arm.

As she began pumping up the cuff, Sorenson's foggy mind cleared a little. *What happened to me anyway?* he wondered. ''Ma'am, was I in some kind of car wreck?''

''We really don't know what happened. All I can tell you at this point is that you were found unconscious, washed up on a beach a few miles from here.''

"A beach?" responded Finn, clearly taken aback by the woman's comment.

"Yes. You're lucky they found you when they did. You nearly died from hypothermia."

"Where is this place?"

"You're in Long Beach."

"Long Beach, like on the peninsula?"

"Yes," Susan said as she completed the blood pressure measurement. He was fine.

Everything started coming back now. Just before Finn woke up he had been dreaming. He was in the freezing ocean waters trying to keep his head above the surface. His *Odin* was pulling away from him, leaving him marooned. "My boat, where is it?" he shouted.

"Gosh, I don't know. All I can tell you is that the Coast Guard's been looking for you for some time now. They just ID'ed you yesterday."

"You mean the *Odin*'s missing."

"I'm sorry, Finn, but I don't know what happened to your ship."

Images of the gunmen shooting Lieutenant Oliver and then the grenade blowing up in the wheelhouse flooded Finn's mind. He felt sick to his stomach. "My God, they hijacked my boat!"

"What?" asked Susan.

"The bastards stole my boat!"

Normally, Susan would have given her patient a sedative to help him relax, but she sensed something different about Finn Sorenson. Despite the partially atrophied muscles, he was as healthy as a horse. He was not about to be told to go back to sleep.

"Finn, would you like me to call the Coast Guard? They left a message saying that they wanted to talk with you whenever you regained consciousness."

"Damn right, I want to talk to 'em right now!"

Tokyo

Hiroshi Yoshida had just arrived at his residence when the phone rang. It was almost ten P.M. *"Moshi-Moshi,"* he said as he picked up the handset.

"Good evening, uncle."

"Ah, Cindy. . . ." Yoshida paused as he mentally calculated the time in Seattle. The sun would be rising within the hour. "Is there a problem?" he asked

"I tried calling you earlier, but your office said you were traveling."

"Yes, I was in Kobe all day." *What's wrong?* he wanted to ask but didn't.

Cindy cleared her voice, signaling her excitement. "I have good news."

She then spent the next five minutes briefing Yoshida on the latest news concerning Hammer 4. Like Zackary Scott, she had hired another Capitol-Beltway law firm to check on the status of the Hammer 4 leases. The rumor sweeping through MMS was that Dr. Patterson was going to indefinitely suspend all lease activity offshore of the Washington coast. The $250,000 donation Yoshida had made anonymously to Greenpeace had done wonders.

Yoshida was now preparing for his evening bath. He was more than pleased with Cindy's report. SCS would be stopped cold in its tracks. Nothing would be happening at the Hammer 4 site for years.

At least I won't have to worry about that problem, he thought as he lowered himself into the steaming *ofuro*.

The problem with the Russians, however, would not go away.

12

ANOTHER CONTACT

Portland

It was a dreary, overcast morning, typical for Portland when a new low pressure front moves in from the ocean. Zackary Scott didn't mind, though. It would be the same in Seattle.

He rose early, still tired. He had tossed and turned all night long; he never slept well when he was separated from Kelda.

After a forty-minute workout in the hotel's gymnasium and a light breakfast he headed out into Portland's rush-hour traffic. It took him half an hour to drive to the marina. He found the yacht a few minutes later.

Zack surveyed the forward section of the vessel as he slowly walked along the long floating walkway at one of Hayden Island's marinas. In the distance, about a hundred feet away, he could see the *Victory*. The modern yacht was moored along a side-tie berth at the terminal end of the pier.

Zack stopped walking when he was about twenty-five feet from the end of the pier. The *Victory*'s bow section and the forward half of the main cabin were directly in front of him. The vessel was just as Dr. Hamilton had described it. It was over a hundred feet long. Its glossy white fiberglass hull had the clean sleek lines of a luxury yacht that emphasized speed and power. The main cabin projected above the gunwale by almost ten feet, and it extended nearly sixty feet in length, providing an enormous amount of living space. Positioned on top of the cabin, just forward of midships, was a modern flying bridge.

Zack walked farther down the main walkway and turned right, heading toward the aft section of the yacht. Thirty feet away from the stern, his eyes were automatically drawn to the roof covering the fantail. At first he thought it was a helipad, just as Dr. Hamilton had suggested. However, when he stepped up to the edge of the float for a closer examination he discovered that the roof's supporting columns were constructed of lightweight aluminum instead of the steel he had been expecting. And then, when he looked upward at the underside of the roof, he was dismayed to discover that the roof deck was not solid, but instead was a synthetic fabric stretched over aluminum struts. *I'll be damned. It looks just like a fiberglass roof.*

Someone had gone to a lot of effort to make the false roof look like a helicopter landing deck. It was doubtful that it could support the weight of a man, let alone a machine weighing several tons.

Zack's curiosity was getting to him. *I've got to get aboard this thing.*

He walked to the fiberglass boarding ladder and stepped up. A few seconds later he was standing on the teak deck, knocking on the pilothouse door. No answer.

Zack reached forward and pulled on the latch of the heavy oak sliding door. It wouldn't budge. He then moved aft, walking along the narrow deck until he reached the open stern section. He eventually walked down several stairs onto a twenty-five-foot-long by twenty-foot-wide deck. The hardwood deck covering the open area was meticulously maintained. It looked like you could eat off it.

He was now under the false roof. The fabric was slightly opaque, allowing a little sunlight to filter through. *Maybe this thing is just a sun shade*, he thought. Zack continued to walk around the expansive deck, finally deciding that the awning was strictly for protection from the elements. If this had been his boat, he would have removed the covering, preferring the open air.

Zack moved toward the aft section of the main cabin and knocked on an elegantly crafted glass-and-wood doorway. He waited a few seconds before trying to open it. It was locked. *Well, there's no way I'm getting inside today.*

He had just turned away from the door when he spotted the recessed panel on a bulkhead next to the door frame. Without really thinking about what he was doing, he reached forward and pushed on the panel. It was not locked, as he had expected. Instead, the fiberglass panel slid off to the side into a hidden pocket. Inside were two black toggle switches.

Zack leaned closer, examining the switches. Under each device was a plastic call out. The first one read: "Open"; the second read: "Close." Zack flipped the first switch.

A moment later he heard an electric motor start up. The whining noise came from somewhere under the deck. And then he felt the vibration in his feet. *What the hell's that?* he thought as he turned around. When he looked aft he was aghast to see the timber deck open up like a trapdoor. When the motor stopped, there was a huge hole in the fantail deck.

Zack moved aft a few steps and stared downward into a cavern. Although the ten-foot-wide by twelve-foot-long hole was completely empty, Zack instantly recognized its function. It was a wet well. By retracting the movable bottom plates the well could be flooded, allowing direct access to the sea. His own *Ranger III* had a similar but much larger facility.

Why in the hell would a modern yacht like this need a wet well? When Zack stepped away from the opening, trying to answer his own question, he momentarily looked up. He again noticed the roof covering. Then it hit him. *Of course! That thing isn't a sunshade. It's supposed to hide the wet well when the deck's open. But why?*

"You mean you don't have any idea where the tug and barge are located?"

"Nope. The only thing I remember was that we were heading south, about ten miles off the coast. The entrance to the Colombia was only a few miles ahead."

Zackary Scott was perplexed at Finn Sorenson's reply. *Another damn dead end*, he said to himself.

After examining the mysterious yacht in Portland, Zack called the local Coast Guard office to check on the search efforts for the missing tug and barge. Lieutenant Palmer told him that Finn Sorenson had regained consciousness. Zack cancelled his return flight to Seattle and immediately drove his rental car to Long Beach.

"Finn, I know you've been through a lot, but this really leaves me high and dry. Without the blowout preventer and the riser section that were on the barge, I can't prove a damn thing about sabotage."

"I'm sorry, Mr. Scott, but I just don't know where your gear is. Those fucking pirates must have killed my crew—I think they gunned down the Coastie first."

"Please, just call me Zack." Zack paused as he walked toward the window. It was cloudy and the wind was kicking up. "I know you've gone over this with the Coast Guard and the police, but do you remember anything else about the hijackers?"

"The one I shot wasn't very big. Maybe five foot six or seven. Slight build—no more than one hundred forty to one hundred fifty pounds."

"What about the other one?"

"I don't know. I only got a quick glimpse of him—for just a second. Real big—built like a gorilla. He was the one shooting at me." Finn paused for a moment as a new thought developed. "There was one thing about that guy—his forearm was covered with some kind of weird tattoo."

"Tattoo?" asked Scott.

"Yeah, it looked like a snake or maybe a dragon—something like that."

Zack nodded his head in acknowledgment. "Okay, anything else about him?"

"Nope. That's all I saw of him."

"How about their face and hair?"

"Sorry, I can't help you. They both had some kind of black hood on that completely covered their heads."

Zack continued asking questions for the next few minutes and then it was Finn's turn.

"So you think those pricks that hijacked the *Odin* were responsible for sinking your drilling rig and killing all those folks?"

"Absolutely—this is all tied together."

Finn looked Zack straight in the eyes. "Are you going after 'em?"

"I'm sure as hell going to try," answered Zack.

"Look, I'm getting out of here tomorrow or the next day. I want to help."

"But you've been badly injured and—"

"Don't worry about me," interrupted Finn. "I'm a lot tougher than you might think. It won't take me long to get my strength back."

"Well, okay, as long as you think you're up to it. I can use all the help I can get."

"Good, give me an address and phone number where I can contact you."

Zack removed a business card from his Daytimer and wrote several numbers on the back side. "You can reach me through my business office most of the time. If I'm not available talk directly with Janet Clark, she's my secretary." Zack handed Sorenson the card.

"The numbers on the back side are my home and car phones."

"Okay."

Zack started to leave but then stopped. He turned back to face the bedridden man. "Finn, I know you lived on your boat. Do you have a place to stay when you get back to Seattle?"

"Thanks for asking, Zack, but yes, I do. I've got a couple of friends who'll put me up."

"Maybe I ought to put you on the payroll while we're working together."

"Zack, that's a very kind offer. I really appreciate it. But no, I can't do that."

"I wasn't expecting you to work for nothing," protested Zack.

"I know that. All I want from you is one thing."

"What?"

"When we find those pirates, and believe me we're going to find them, I want the first crack at 'em before we bring in the cops."

"You got it—as soon as they tell us where the *Odin* and her barge are located."

"Deal," replied Finn as he reached out to shake Zack's outstretched hand.

* * *

It was now late in the afternoon. Zack had just returned to Seattle after his trip to Portland and Long Beach. He was sitting at his desk, talking on the phone. His attorney, Harold Shapiro, was on the other end of the line. Zack had just finished briefing Shapiro about his inspection of the yacht and his conversation with Finn Sorenson.

"Well, Harold," Zack said, "how about you? Have you had any luck in tracing the ownership of the yacht?"

"So far, we've managed to penetrate two corporate layers and are now working on the third."

"Good Lord, three separate holding companies?"

"Yes. The first corporation is based in Oregon. Turns out it is a wholly-owned subsidiary of another Oregon corporation."

"And I suppose there's no street address or phone listed?" Zack asked.

"That's right—just a post office box in Portland."

"What about the third company?"

"That's a little more interesting. It's a Washington corporation and turns out that the corp's registered agent is a partner of one of the larger law firms here in Seattle."

"Law firm?"

"Yes. I've got a call in to him. We've worked together in the past and I might have a shot at getting him to reveal who really owns the *Victory*."

"Jesus, you don't suppose he owns that boat, do you?"

"No way. His firm probably set up the corp for the boat owner and now just handles the annual renewal paperwork."

"Okay, that makes sense. Just let me know as soon as you hear back from him."

"Will do."

North Pacific Ocean

The U.S.S. *Honolulu* (SSN 718) was 1,600 miles northeast of its Pearl Harbor home port. The fast-attack submarine was seven hundred feet below the surface, heading east at a leisurely eight knots. Commander Steve Bishop was in the submarine's control room, standing in the officer of the deck's watch station just forward of the twin periscopes. From his elevated perch he could monitor the dozen officers and enlisted personnel who manned the sub's numerous controls. At the moment, every man in the *Honolulu*'s nerve center was concentrating on his individual task. Half an hour earlier Bishop had ordered the boat to General Quarters. It was not a drill.

"Mr. Markley," Bishop said as he keyed his hand-held mike, "has the contact changed course?"

"Negative, Captain," replied the *Honolulu*'s chief sonar officer. He was sitting at a highly sophisticated sonar tracking console in the sonar compartment, about forty feet forward of the control room. "Sierra Three-Five remains on a true heading of zero-six-five degrees. Range eight thousand six hundred yards. Speed fifteen knots."

"Any estimate of her depth, yet?"

"No, sir. All we know is that the contact is well below our depth. We'll have to go active to get a positive fix."

"Very well, stand by."

Bishop turned to his right, eyeing Lieutenant Commander Tim Clack. The *Honolulu*'s executive officer was leaning over a chart table. "Tim, you got any ideas yet on what's going on?"

"I don't know, skipper. The plant signature doesn't match anything in our computer memory."

"Nothing?" asked Bishop.

"That's correct. Right now I don't know what's making that sound. But whatever it is, it sure as hell doesn't put out much noise."

Bishop turned away from the XO for a few seconds and then turned back. "Tim, do you suppose the Russians or Chinese have come up with some kind of new hull design?"

"Maybe, but the noise output is radically different from anything else we've recorded. I can't say for sure, but I don't think it has a conventional reactor."

"What do you mean?"

"There just isn't any plant noise output at all. We're just picking up some kind of weak hydraulic wash. And we're lucky to hear that. The water depth must be suppressing the noise."

"So we don't have any clue as to the boat's identity?"

"That's right, skipper. Whatever's down there sure doesn't sound like any of our boats."

"Then this must be the same contact the *Alaska* reported."

"Could be. It's right on course and the speed is about the same."

Captain Bishop shook his head. "Hell, Tim, that just doesn't sound right. Any sub driver worth his salt would periodically change course to throw off any potential trackers. But this guy's making a beeline on the same heading."

"Yeah, I know what you mean. If it's the same contact that the *Alaska* reported, then that means it's been following the same path for over a couple of thousand miles."

Captain Bishop didn't respond at first. He was lost in thought. *Hell, the only way I'd ever run like that would be if I thought my boat was invisible. Jesus, that's got to be it!*

"Tim, try this on for size. Suppose you had a new boat that was designed to be quieter than anything else ever built?"

"You mean quieter than a Trident or a Seawolf?"

"Yeah. But there's a catch."

"Okay, what?"

"Just suppose that our friendly *Alaska* was on missile patrol at max depth, trolling around at a minimum speed, say five or six knots."

"Yeah."

"Okay, no one's going to hear that baby unless they run into it."

"Right, but—"

Bishop raised his right hand, signaling the XO to wait. "Now, along comes your new boat. It happens to pass within a klick or two of the *Alaska,* but it never hears the Trident because it's basically sitting there, nice and quiet. "

"I see. Just a freak passage."

"That's right. And the *Alaska* is under orders to remain hidden at all times so they couldn't even add more steam to follow it."

"I think you've got something there, skipper. Our contact has no reason to believe it has been spotted since the *Alaska* didn't try to follow it."

"Exactly, and I bet those buggers don't even know we're trailing them right now. In fact, they're probably running on cruise control, heading along some kind of established path." Commander Bishop cracked a smile. "Hell, I'll bet you that the skipper's taking a nap."

Clack grinned in response as he began to understand where the captain was heading. "So we're going to wake him up?"

"Right. I want to goose whoever's down there. When he runs, then we'll know who it is."

Five minutes later the control room crew was ready for new orders.

The captain was speaking to the sonar section, using his hand-held microphone. "Sonar, give me one pulse."

"Aye, sir. One pulse."

A moment later, the *Honolulu*'s bow-mounted spherical sonar dome converted fifty thousand watts of electrical power into acoustic energy, creating a sharp metallic noise: *Ping*. The sound wave blasted through the glass-reinforced plastic bow dome, spreading out radially at nearly 3,500 feet per second. The acoustic front hit paydirt a few seconds later.

Everyone in the control room heard the reflected sound wave as it passed back through the *Honolulu*'s hull: *Pong*.

"Christ, what a reflection," called out Clack.

"Sonar, Conn. Report!" ordered Captain Bishop as he keyed his microphone.

"Conn, Sonar," came the instant reply. "Sierra Three-Five bears zero one five. Range four thousand six hundred yards."

"Give me his depth."

"Working on it, sir." The line remained silent for a few seconds. "Ah, sir, you're not going to believe this, but Sierra Three-Five plots out at three thousand six hundred feet."

"What?"

"I say again, sir. Sierra Three-Five is running at three thousand six hundred feet below the surface."

"Incredible!" muttered Bishop.

"Impossible!" Clack said.

Over the next minute and a half Bishop ordered two more sonar pulses. He was again checking with the chief sonar technician. "What's happening, Sonar?"

"Sierra Three-Five remains on the same heading. Range three thousand nine hundred yards. Speed—" He stopped in mid-sentence and then started up again. "Wait a second. Computer's now showing a new data stream. Wow, I don't believe it. She's starting to dive."

"What?"

"She's definitely going down."

Clack broke in. "Skipper, how the hell can that be?"

Bishop raised his hand, holding him off. "Sonar, are you sure that boat's diving?"

"Aye sir. No change in speed or course but it's dropping down."

"Fire another ping and give me its new depth."

"Aye, sir."

After the next ping the sonar officer called back. "Sir, that boat's now at four thousand one hundred feet and going down fast."

Bishop could hardly believe what he was hearing. He turned to Clack. "Tim, there's no boat around that can go that deep."

"I know, skipper, but someone's got one that can do it now."

Bishop keyed the mike again. "Sonar, what can you tell from the reflection?"

"Captain, whatever it is it's massive. The return signal indicates a huge hull—bigger than a Typhoon."

Bigger than a Typhoon! That's impossible, thought Bishop. The Russian missile submarine was the largest underseas vessel ever built, measuring 558 feet long and 75 feet in beam.

"Sir," called out the sonar operator, "I'm starting to lose its signature now."

"You mean it's slowing up?"

"No, sir. It's just going too deep. The output's decaying linearly with depth."

"Can we follow it from up here?"

"Not unless we use the active again."

"Do it, man, now!"

The sonar ping barely created a return echo. The target had changed course, heading south. It was now four thousand five hundred feet deep.

Bishop ordered the *Honolulu* to dive. After searching for nearly an hour at the boat's maximum operating depth he finally gave up. The target disappeared when it passed through the five-thousand-foot depth.

Damn it! Where'd that bastard go? thought Bishop after calling off the pursuit.

Yosuke Mishima awoke instantly when the first sonar ping reverberated through his stateroom. He bolted from his bed, grabbing an intercom handset from his desk. While standing in his white boxer shorts, he began firing off a series of questions. "Bridge, what the hell was that noise?"

"Captain, we're being tracked by another submarine."

"What?"

"There's another boat behind us. It's twenty-two hundred meters away on a relative bearing one-seven-five degrees. Depth is around two hundred meters."

"Any identification?"

"Negative, sir. We didn't hear its approach so it must be pacing us."

"What about the—"

Ping! Another powerful sonar pulse hammered the vessel, interrupting Mishima's question.

Captain Mishima recognized the sound pattern. *Americans.*

"Run that sonar pulse through the computer," he ordered. "It must be a six-eight-eight."

"Aye, sir. Working on it now."

While Mishima waited for the report, he began slipping on his clothes. With one hand holding the handset he grabbed a pair of gray trousers and slipped them over his legs. Toughened by years of judo and karate, his slim body was well muscled. At thirty-eight years old, he was fitter than most men half his age.

"Captain, you were right. Computer positively identifies the sonar as a BQS. Same type found on the American Los Angeles–class subs."

Good, thought the captain. *He can't get to us.* "Okay, execute emergency dive procedures. Bring her down to two thousand meters. I'll be on the bridge in a minute."

Just as Mishima completed the new order, another sonar pulse reverberated through the hull. *Damnit,* he thought, *they must be right on top of us.*

Mishima threw the handset onto the desk and began pulling a cotton turtleneck shirt over his head. A few seconds later he was running barefoot down the companionway, his sandals clutched in his right hand.

The captain burst into the tiny control room. There were only five other men inside, each one manning a computerized console. "Number One, what's our depth?"

"Sir, we're at eleven hundred meters, descending at three meters per second."

Ping! Another sonar pulse from the American boat probed the waters around the fleeing submarine. This time the principal axis of the sound wave passed over the hull. *Good,* thought Mishima. *They overshot.*

"Right full rudder, continue the dive," he ordered.

Seven minutes later the vessel dropped below the two-thousand-meter depth. "Zero bubble," called out Captain Mishima. "Maintain heading and speed."

The helmsman acknowledged the captain's orders. He then keyed in the new instructions to the automatic helm. Despite the enormous size of the vessel, it responded quickly. The bow began to rise to a level position.

As the boat changed attitude, Mishima began questioning the sonar officer. "Is the American still following?"

"Yes, sir. He continues his dive. We're picking up hull compression noises and I can hear his propeller clearly. Turn rate indicates twenty-two knots."

Captain Mishima mentally pictured the image of the hunter-killer as it circled above. It was like a great white shark that was preparing to feast on a whale.

"What's its depth now?"

"Approaching three hundred meters, sir."

"Good, he'll be leveling out soon."

"But what about torpedoes?" asked the XO.

"They won't fire on us. Their captain is curious—he wants to know who we are."

"But what do we do now? They clearly heard us."

"They know nothing, only that there's another boat out here that can outdive them."

"Then they will try to follow us."

"Yes, I'm sure they will, but we have the advantage now. We're much deeper and the noise output from our drives has been reduced by the pressure." He paused for a moment. "In fact, I bet they can't even hear us now."

Mishima and his control room crew listened quietly as the *Honolulu* continued searching. The American submarine periodically fired off its active sonar in an attempt to find them. The random probes, however, proved useless. Despite the slow speed of his vessel, Mishima expertly maneuvered away from the sub. About two hours later, they lost all contact with it.

"I think we have lost him, Captain," reported the executive officer.

"Yes, it looks that way."

"Captain, we were lucky that they decided to probe us, otherwise we might never have known they were there."

"You're right. We're going to have to change our procedures. From now on we will stay deep."

"But they know about us now."

"Yes, Number One. It was bound to happen. Fortunately, they do not know who we are or where we're going."

"Then you plan to change course."

"Absolutely. We can't continue on the normal route. We're going to divert toward the south for at least a day, maybe longer. Then we'll head in."

"We'll be late."

"I know—it can't be helped."

13

FALSE HOPE

Seattle

Zack was in his office. He had arrived early—a few minutes before seven—and spent the morning hours reviewing SCS's financial condition. The firm was liquid for the time being. But if he didn't solve the Hammer 4 problem soon, there would be a real crisis. And the loss of the *Kelda Scott* was now causing serious scheduling conflicts. To resume drilling offshore of the Washington coast, SCS would have to pull one of its semisubmersibles out of Alaska. That meant the two remaining rigs drilling in the Naviran basin would have to work even harder to stay on schedule.

Although MMS still refused to allow SCS to resume offshore drilling at the Hammer 4 site, Zack was seriously thinking about temporarily pulling the *Timothy Scott* out of the Bering Sea and bringing her home. Zack wanted the vessel back in Washington for political reasons. He planned to moor the semisubmersible in the center of Elliott Bay, directly opposite downtown. Its presence would remind everyone of a potential solution to the oil shortage. The price of crude oil was now hovering near $60 a barrel, and gasoline at the pump cost $3 a gallon. The lineups at gas station pumps were a constant annoyance. And everyone hated the rationing system.

Zack was gambling that public pressure would help reverse the federal government's hard-line resistance to restarting the drilling. Every day there were fewer stories in the newspapers about pollution from the oil spill. Despite the blowout, the spill response system worked. There was minimal damage to the shoreline and the loss of marine life wasn't nearly as catastrophic as had been expected. The technology worked, but the cleanup teams also had luck on their side. If the weather had turned against them, the mopping-up efforts would have been far less effective.

To most people the spill was of little concern, regardless of its environmental consequences. Instead, the talk was once again centering on the worldwide lack of oil and the hope that conservation and alternative energy sources would save the day. Unfortunately for the United States, as well as most of the other industrial nations, the addiction to hydrocarbons was as strong as ever. Only Japan seemed to be coping with the crisis. The huge oil find in the Nemuro basin continued to fire the island nation's economy. Japan was about to surpass the United States's GNP. It would soon be the dominant economic power of the world.

Smart people. They've got their priorities right! Zack said to himself. He genuinely admired the Japanese. They were hard workers, tough competitors, and very, very intelligent. It would have been easy to fall into the popular ritual of Japan bashing, now rampant around the globe because of the island nation's enormous financial strength, but Zack had refused to participate. Instead, he marveled at Japan's ability to continually earn vast sums of money from high technology. Already dominant in electronics and computers, Japanese corporations were now closing in on software development and commercial airplane manufacturing.

But what really impressed Zack was Japan's miraculous transformation from the world's largest importer of oil to a nation that could now supply half of its petroleum energy demands from its own resources. *We could do the same thing,* he thought, *if the Feds and environmentalists would back off a notch or two.*

Zack was expecting that the federal government would eventually give in to public pressure and once again encourage domestically produced petroleum. The Hammer 4 field had enormous potential. And it was sitting right offshore, almost in the nation's backyard. It was potentially another Prudhoe

Bay, and if developed with other offshore oil finds in Alaska and California, it would go a long way to solving America's energy problem.

Unfortunately for SCS, its efforts to lobby the Department of Interior's Mineral Management Section had fallen on deaf ears. The antioil environmental groups were continuing to work overtime, using every means available to force the government into denying permission to restart drilling. MMS's current moratorium on drilling in the Hammer 4 reservoir was based on the *Kelda Scott*'s blowout. Until the cause of the well failure was determined and the negligent parties responsible were punished, there would be no further drilling offshore of the Washington coast.

Zack was furious with the government and his own stupidity. When SCS crews recovered *Kelda Scott*'s blowout preventer, he had had the evidence he needed to prove that SCS was innocent of negligence. The damage to the subsea well equipment could have been caused only by sabotage. But when the tugboat *Odin* and its barge containing the BOP and riser pipe were hijacked, Zack couldn't prove anything. *Damn it to hell, I should have stayed with that gear until it was safely turned over to the Coast Guard in Portland.*

Zack started leafing through another financial report when his intercom speaker came alive. It was his secretary. "Zack, sorry to disturb you, but I've got some man on the line who's demanding to talk with you right now. Something about the oil spill and a sunken barge."

"Is it another reporter?"

"No, I don't think so. Didn't sound like one at all but he wouldn't tell me what company he's with either. All he said was to tell you that it's Finn calling."

"Oh, that's Sorenson. I'll take it."

Zack punched the flashing outside line. "Finn, how are you?"

"I'm great. They finally let me out of that torture chamber. I'm in Portland right now."

"Well, I'm glad you're okay." Zack paused. "Is there anything I can do to help?"

"Thanks, but I'm fine. But maybe there's something that both of us can do together."

"What have you got it mind?"

"I want to find the *Odin* and I think I know where she might be."

Zack sat up straight in his chair, his interest suddenly piqued. "Go on," he said.

"I'm sure those bastards scuttled her, along with the barge that had your equipment. That's why we can't find her anywhere."

"Yeah, I think you're right. But the big question is where."

"Right. Well, it turns out that just before starting that tow, I planned to top off my tanks, but when I got to the fuel pier, they had pump problems so I wasn't able to take on any fuel."

Zack's interest continued to build. "How much fuel did you have aboard?"

"Both tanks were about half full—total of around three thousand gallons."

"So they had plenty of fuel to go a long way."

"Yes, but I don't think they did. I'll bet you a steak dinner they holed her somewhere out on the shelf, maybe twenty-thirty miles out."

"Yeah, but what—"

Finn cut him off. "Those fuel tanks can't take a lot of hydrostatic pressure, especially being half full. They must have ruptured."

Zack finally understood. "Then it might be bleeding off oil!"

"Right. Remember when that Chinese freighter ran down that trawler off the Strait of Juan de Fuca? The fishing boat leaked oil for weeks before it was finally sealed up by divers."

"I sure do, and I see what you're getting at."

"Yeah, well, maybe some of those offshore slicks the Coast Guard's been reporting lately aren't remnants from your oil spill after all."

"I'll be damned. You just might be right. If we can find where the oil's surfacing, then we'll know where the *Odin*'s sitting on the bottom."

"That's right. But the only way to know is to fly out there and look."

Zack unconsciously scratched at his scalp while he spoke. "Where would you start the search?"

Finn was ready. "I've got it worked out based on where I went overboard. I think it might take a day or so in a plane to cover the area. I'd be out there right now but I'm broke."

"Don't worry about that. I'll get us a plane. When can you be ready?"

"Hell, I'm set right now. Just tell me where you want me to meet you."

Zack looked at his wristwatch. It was a quarter to eleven. *Plenty of time.* "Okay, you get over to Portland International, private carrier terminal area. I'll be there in an hour and a half."

"You're on."

Honolulu, Hawaii

It was almost noon and the watch officer at the U.S. Naval Oceanographic Command (NOC) center at Pearl Harbor was thinking about going home for lunch. But before he could leave he had one last task to complete. He once again picked up the top-secret report from his desk. It was a detailed accounting of the U.S.S. *Honolulu*'s encounter with an unknown submarine contact. SSN 718 had returned to base earlier in the day. Commander Bishop personally delivered the report to NOC. The watch officer reread the concluding paragraphs for the third time. *Something's wrong here,* he thought as he tossed the report back onto his desk. He then punched in several digits on his telephone. It was answered on the third ring.

"SUBCOMPAC," replied the male clerk.

"This is Commander Johnson at NOC. I need to speak with Captain Strum. Is he still in?"

"Stand by, sir. I'll check."

The watch officer waited for about a minute before his call was finally answered.

"Hello," called out Captain Mark Strum. Strum was the executive officer to the commanding officer of Submarine Command, Pacific.

"Sorry to disturb you this afternoon, sir, but I have important information for you."

"That's all right, Commander. What have you got?" Strum

was in a good mood. He had just completed his weekly golf match; he beat his partners by four strokes.

"Sir, I've just had a chance to review the *Honolulu*'s report on the bogey."

"Yes, go on," Strum said. His interest suddenly spiked. The earlier radio report from the attack submarine briefly describing the incident had received his full attention.

"Looks like we've got a real problem. There's no doubt in my mind that there's a new boat out there that can outdive anything we've got—even the *Seawolf*."

"Crap," Strum muttered to himself.

"Sir?" asked Commander Johnson, not sure if the captain was speaking to him.

"How far down did it go?"

"At least five thousand feet, maybe deeper."

"Five thousand, that's impossible!"

"I know, sir. That's what I thought. But I've listened to the sonar tapes and reviewed the tracking summaries. It was down there, humming along at about fifteen knots." He paused for effect. "And, sir, it's real quiet."

"How quiet?"

"Just as good as our best gear—maybe even better."

"Commander, I don't like the sound of any of this."

"I know, sir. That's why I called." He hesitated. "Sir, there's one other thing."

"What?"

"Whatever it is, it's a monster. The *Honolulu*'s search sonar painted a target that could be over eight hundred feet long."

"Come on, Commander. You don't really expect me to buy that now, do you?"

"Sir, I was just as skeptical as you. But when I reviewed the sonar signature I was shocked. The one good ping the *Honolulu* generated must have hit it square on the beam. The reflection was positively massive. It has to be a huge hull."

"But the depth, man? That's twice as deep as the *Seawolf* can handle. The size you're talking about, hell it's bigger than a Trident or a Typhoon."

"I know. It doesn't make any sense. But the evidence is there nevertheless. Commander Bishop was not exaggerating when he radioed in the initial report."

"Damn it. Then we've got a new player in town."

"That's right, sir." What the watch officer wanted to add, but didn't dare say, was: *Looks like we're no longer the biggest fish in the pond.*

"All right. Keep all that data ready. I'll be over in half an hour."

"Aye, sir. I'll be waiting." All thoughts of lunch had just evaporated. The watch officer would remain at the base all afternoon.

Portland

Tom Baker had been staking out the *Victory* for several days now. He was sitting in the cramped cabin of a twenty-six-foot Sea Ray, five slips away from the megayacht's end-tie. He could see anyone who might be walking down the floating pier toward the vessel. So far, no one, not even the marina's dock boy, had approached the yacht.

Baker had started his shift about two hours earlier, relieving the private investigator who monitored the yacht at night. *What a frigging waste of time*, Baker thought as he leafed through a magazine. He hated stakeout work. The twenty-eight-year-old ex-army MP much preferred the investigative end of his profession: interviewing people, following up on leads, researching records. But just sitting around, waiting endless hours for someone to possibly show up was not his idea of fun.

Baker was thinking about making a sandwich when he heard the voices. *Someone's coming.* He moved next to a porthole and peered out. Three men were walking down the wood float. A moment later they passed the bow of the Sea Ray and proceeded to the pier end. *I'll be damned,* he thought, *they're heading for the boat.*

He watched the visitors climb aboard the yacht. Two of the men headed aft. Baker couldn't follow their movements; his view was blocked by another powerboat moored alongside the *Victory*. The third man, however, walked onto the forward deck, stopping next to the bridge house. He inserted a key into the lock, rolled the sliding door aft, and stepped inside.

"Damn!" Baker said out loud. He had been too busy

watching the men to remember to use his camera. He reached for the Nikon sitting on one of the bunks. He pulled it up to the window and adjusted the focus. When the telephoto lens burst into focus, Baker was looking at the man inside the wheelhouse.

Baker hadn't seen the faces of the men as they walked by and was surprised to learn that at least one of them was an Asian. He triggered the power drive of the camera. Five minutes later the other two men walked into the pilothouse from inside the yacht. Baker photographed them. They were all Asians.

The PI was loading a second roll of film when he heard the *Victory*'s powerful diesels start up. For about a minute, thick plumes of black smoke were expelled from the twin exhaust ports. But then as the engines began to warm up, the exhaust turned clear. *What are these turkeys up to?* thought Baker as he continued to watch through the porthole.

A couple of minutes later two of the men were on the float next to the yacht. Baker leaned forward, pressing his face against the Plexiglas window. But both men were out of view. When he moved to another window he spotted one of the men. He was holding a loose mooring line.

Damnit! They're taking off. What the hell am I supposed to do now? Baker watched helplessly as the yacht pulled away from the pier. A powerful bow thruster pushed the hundred-ton vessel away from the mooring.

Baker grabbed his portable cellular phone from his briefcase and punched in a series of numbers. After passing through the switchboard and another secretary he finally reached his boss. "That's right, Bill, the frigging boat's heading out of the marina right now. What do you want me to do?"

"You know how to run the boat, don't you?"

"Yes, but—"

The owner of the firm cut him off. "Tom, just follow the damn thing and radio where it's going. Don't lose it."

"Okay, I'll stay with it." Baker turned off the phone and set it back down on the bunk. *Son of a bitch, I'm no sailor.* Baker hated boats. He couldn't swim.

Seattle

Zackary Scott and Finn Sorenson were in a small waterfront restaurant near the downtown Public Market. An hour earlier Zack's chartered jet had landed at Boeing Field. He and Finn had spent all afternoon searching the waters offshore of the Columbia River, looking for leaking fuel oil from the sunken *Odin*. They found nothing.

The dining room was crowded and they were seated in a corner next to a window. The sun was setting over Elliott Bay. Despite the partially overcast sky, the red, orange, and yellow hues cascading over the distant Olympic Mountain range were spectacular. Neither Zack nor Finn, however, paid any attention to the spectacle. They were too busy talking.

"Even though we didn't find anything," Sorenson said, "I'm convinced those bastards wouldn't go too far away. The *Odin*'s got to be sitting on the bottom out there someplace."

"Yeah, you're probably right," replied Zack. He was sipping his second glass of wine.

Finn picked up his bottle of Anchor Stein and took a long pull. He then looked back at Zack. "You said something in the plane about sending that ship of yours out to look for the *Odin*. You still planning to do that?"

"Absolutely. I don't have any choice. The only way I'm going to save my skin is to prove that the Hammer 4 well was sabotaged."

"But how are you going to do that?" asked Finn.

"I've got to find the preventer, so I'm going to order the *Ranger* to start a sonar search of the entire shelf off the mouth of the Columbia. Maybe we'll get lucky and spot the *Odin* and the barge sitting on the bottom."

"Jesus, Zack, if she had been leaking oil, like I had hoped, that would make some sense. But after our little flight today, I'd say this sonar search you're planning is going to be like searching for the proverbial needle in the haystack—it'll take months to cover that area."

"I know, but what else can I do? I'm sunk without the BOP."

Finn nodded his head. "Yeah, I see what you mean."

Zack drained his glass "Finn, how the hell do you think those pirates got aboard the *Odin* anyway?"

"I don't know. They must have come in from behind the tow in a small runabout. Maybe even an inflatable with a helluva motor."

"But you were still miles offshore, weren't you?"

Finn nodded. "Yeah, I see what you're getting at. They must have launched from another ship."

"Do you remember any other vessels around?"

Finn turned toward the window and looked out. His face was scrunched up as he tried to recall that terrible night. "Shit, I don't remember much. No, wait. There was this yacht. Yeah! A big S-O-B. It was running on a parallel course for a while, about a mile or so west of our position. But then it veered off and headed west, out to sea. That was at least an hour before we were hijacked."

"What did this yacht look like?"

"Oh, hell. I don't remember. Looked new. Modern lines. White hull, high sheer with a fly bridge. Maybe a hundred or more feet long."

"Anything else?"

"No." He paused a moment, twirling his folk in a plate thick with pasta. Just before he was ready to take another mouthful, he lowered his hand. "Wait a minute. I remember something now. It had some kind of helideck over the stern."

Zack reached into his pocket and pulled out a Polaroid photograph. He tossed it onto Sorenson's side of the table. "That look familiar?"

Finn picked up the color print and stared at it. His response was nearly instantaneous. "By God, that's it. How the hell did you know?"

"I took that photo last week, in Portland. Just before seeing you in the hospital. Her name's the *Victory*."

"But how did you—"

Zack cut him off. "That yacht was hanging around the *Kelda Scott* just before the blowout."

"Son of a bitch," Finn said. "Then you were right. The same bastards that killed my crew and scuttled the boat must have sabotaged the Hammer 4 well."

"Exactly. I know it in my heart, but I can't prove anything

yet. All I've got is circumstantial evidence. I can't do anything about this yacht until I get more facts.''

"But I'm sure that's the boat.''

"Yeah, but it isn't enough.'' Zack paused. "Can you testify in court that the men who attacked the *Odin* came from it?''

"No, but . . .''

"Don't you see, Finn, it's no different than the survivors of the *Kelda Scott* saying they saw a yacht nearby when the Hammer 4 well blew out.''

"But what else could it be doing there?''

"I know. There's no doubt in my mind that that damn boat is mixed up in this mess.'' Zack picked up his wineglass and took a drink. A waiter had just refilled it. It was his third glass and he hadn't even touched the main dish yet. "Besides, I found something very interesting on it.''

"Like what?''

"Like a wet well in the fantail.''

"You mean a hole in the hull?'' asked Finn.

"That's right. A perfect area to launch divers or ROVs without being seen.''

"But it's a yacht, not a work boat.''

"That's right. But the aft deck has plenty of deck space to accommodate all kinds of gear, and the overhead canopy covers everything from the air.''

"Then it's not a helipad?''

"Correct. It's a clever fake,'' Zack said as he took another sip from his glass. "It's just made of aluminum and canvas.''

"Then it must be a disguise. Without that covering the boat would look completely different.''

"Yep.''

Finn took a long pull from his Budweiser. "Are we going to see that boat again?'' he asked with a grin on his face.

"You bet. I've got a team of lawyers working on tracing the yacht's ownership. And I've got a PI firm in Portland watching it around the clock. It's been deserted, but somebody will eventually show up.''

Finn leaned against the table, moving closer to Zack. His voice was just loud enough for Scott to hear. "Let me have first crack at the bastards. I'll cut their nuts off and cram 'em down their throats.''

"Finn, you're going to have to wait in line. If those bastards are really the ones behind this mess, I'm personally going to take 'em down a notch or two.'' Some of the wine was talking, but Zack's bitterness for revenge was the driving force. ''Remember, I lost a lot of good people when the *Kelda Scott* went down.'' He swallowed the rest of the wine. ''The fuckers are going to pay dearly for that—I guarantee it!''

Finn was startled at Scott's sudden mood change. The man was holding back a volcano of problems. He had just vented off a little pressure.

''Okay then, we'll both beat the shit out of them.''

''Right.''

Zack called the waiter over and ordered another glass of wine. Finn ordered another beer. It would be a very long dinner.

14

SURVEILLANCE

Tokyo

The Northwest DC-10 from Los Angeles landed at Narita International Airport five minutes before noon. The one American military officer aboard the aircraft finally cleared Customs an hour later. He wasn't wearing his uniform, though. Dressed in civilian garb, he fit right in with the other two hundred or so Asian passengers who had disembarked.

Commander Jeffrey Hashimoto, USN, was in his early forties, stood six feet tall, and had a firm, muscular build. Although he looked Japanese, he was a full-blooded American. His parents were prosperous merchants back in Seattle.

When Hashimoto finally walked out of the international arrival terminal he was met by his contact. The Caucasian man, dressed in a dark blue suit, approached from his left side, his right hand already outstretched.

"Good to see you again, Jeff," said the man as he grabbed Hashimoto's hand and shook it firmly. He was about fifty years old, had a full head of dark brown hair with a few slivers of gray around the ears. His six-foot-two height fit well with his 180 pounds.

"Hello, Captain. I didn't expect you to meet me."

Hashimoto was taken aback by the presence of Captain Carlton McClaran. He was the deputy commander of the Office of Naval Intelligence for the Pacific Fleet. Headquartered in Yokosuka, Japan, McClaran was personally responsible for all U.S. intelligence matters in Korea, China, and Japan.

"Well, I was in the neighborhood so I thought I'd welcome you personally."

"I'm flattered, Captain."

"Save the formalities for stateside. Over here, I'm just plain Carlton."

"Well, sir . . . I mean, Carlton, I'm still in the dark about this trip. I was in Washington last night when I—"

"Hold on," replied McClaran. "I'll fill you in when we get in the car—too public around here for now."

"Okay."

"Any baggage?"

"No, just what I brought with me." He lifted a small carry-on suitcase with his left hand. His leather briefcase was on the floor next to his right leg.

"Good," replied McClaran as he grabbed the briefcase, "let's get going."

As the two men walked through the enormous airport, they engaged in small talk, mainly about the Virginia countryside. Hashimoto, eleven years junior to McClaran, had known the man for just over two years. He liked the senior naval officer and guessed that McClaran had requested him. *But why?* wondered Hashimoto as he walked along the endless tile walkways. *What in the world could be going on over here that requires my presence?*

Although Jeffrey Hashimoto was an Annapolis graduate and a full commander, he rarely wore his uniform these days. Originally trained as an intelligence officer and assigned to the U.S. Naval Oceanographic Command, he was an expert in antisubmarine warfare, especially the remote detection of submarines. His last official U.S. Navy command had been as executive officer at an ultrasecret Sound Surveillance System (SOSUS) facility in Puget Sound.

Because of Hashimoto's exceptional technical experience and his investigative skills, the Central Intelligence Agency had asked him to join its Ocean Technology Group when he was promoted to commander. The special three-year assignment was a plum in any intelligence officer's career jacket.

McClaran's government-issued Chevrolet was parked next to the curb opposite the baggage claim area. The driver, a

Marine gunnery sergeant also dressed in civilian clothes, was waiting by the hood. The oversized American car was out of place in the sea of Asian-built vehicles that were queued up, waiting to collect the arriving passengers.

Both officers climbed inside the sedan. The car sped away a few seconds later.

Seattle

"What do you mean you can't find the yacht?" shouted Zackary Scott into the telephone handset. He was talking to the owner of the detective agency in Portland.

"We don't know what happened to it, Mr. Scott," replied Bill Bailey. "Tom Baker tracked it as far as Ocean Shores last night. It was still heading up the coast when he had to quit because of darkness."

"And now you can't find it?"

"I'm afraid not. Tom had a floatplane up at seven this morning, running up and down the Strait of Juan de Fuca. It wasn't there."

Zack remained silent for a few seconds as he studied a chart of the Strait of Juan de Fuca mounted on the wall behind his desk. His anger was subsiding as he began to make sense of what Bill Bailey had just told him. He couldn't fault the private investigators for anything they had done so far. In fact, he was amazed that they had obtained as much information about the *Victory* as they had.

"Geez, Bill, I'm sorry to yell at you like that. I know you and your people have been busting your butts for me. It's just that I was really counting on finding out where that boat was going."

"That's okay. Zack, I know you're under a hell of a strain. I want you to know we haven't given up by any means. Right now I've got people checking all the marinas along the Strait, both Canadian and American. And I've got a man checking out the marinas in Gray's Harbor and Westport. It could have doubled back."

"Good plan. Maybe we'll get lucky." Zack paused a moment and then began laughing.

"What's so funny?" asked Bailey.

"Sorry, I'm just laughing at myself. It turns out we must have flown right over that bastard yesterday."

"You were on the ocean yesterday?" asked Bailey, clearly surprised.

"Over it. We were conducting an aerial survey offshore of the Columbia, looking for an oil slick from that missing tugboat."

"The one with your oil well gear?"

"Right. We didn't find anything, though."

"I'll be darned. That yacht probably did head right through your search area."

"Well, it doesn't matter anymore. I probably wouldn't have noticed it anyway, even if I had seen it. We were pretty high up and all those boats look—" Zack stopped in mid-sentence when a new thought flashed in his mind. *Jesus, of course, that's got to be it!*

"You still there?" asked Bailey.

"Yes. I've just had an idea." He again paused a second or so, collecting his thoughts. "Just what did you instruct your people to be looking for today?"

Bailey was puzzled by Zack's question. "The *Victory*, of course. I gave them photographs of—" The PI abruptly stopped talking when it finally hit him. *They removed the helipad covering!* "Oh, shit, I see what you're getting at," Baily said. "They must have taken down the covering over the stern."

"Exactly. Without that fake awning, the yacht would look different."

"That's got to be it, Zack. Damnit! I should have thought of that."

"Don't worry about that now, just get your people out there looking for it. I'm sure it's some place up north by now. Hell, it may already be moving through the islands, heading north into Canadian waters."

"I'll get right on this. We're going to find that bastard."

"Good," Zack said. "Let me know the moment you locate it."

"You got it!"

Tom Baker was worn out. He had been on the trail of the *Victory* for nearly two days. The chase had started in Portland

and continued down the Columbia River to Astoria. When the yacht headed across the bar, entering the Pacific, he abandoned his tiny Sea Ray. He was then forced to charter a small airplane from the local airport and once again took up the chase. And just before sunset he found it. The mystery yacht was about twenty-five miles offshore, heading northward up the Washington coast. Later that evening Baker returned to Portland and then took a Horizon flight to Seattle. The next morning he was once again airborne—this time in a floatplane.

Baker had been glued to the right-hand seat of the Beaver all day. Despite the contoured cushioning of the seat, his buttocks ached and his legs were beginning to cramp. But the biggest problem was the boredom. For hours on end he stared down at the water's surface, studying every large boat they came across. The marinas were the worst. Baker had to really concentrate whenever they passed over a small craft harbor. The boats moored inside the high-density basins were often packed together, making it difficult to distinguish individual vessels. Anything that remotely fit the revised description of the *Victory* was scrutinized.

Along with the discomfort and boredom of his assignment, Tom Baker was upset with his boss. *Why the hell didn't he tell me this morning that the damn thing might have its stern awning removed?* Baker believed that if he had been properly briefed about the possible disguise he would have spotted the *Victory* if it had sailed into the Strait of Juan de Fuca. But it didn't matter anymore. He had found it.

The yacht was charging up the Strait of Georgia, about a mile offshore of Point Roberts, when Baker spotted it. Within an hour it had passed under the Lion's Gate Bridge and entered Vancouver Harbor.

Ten minutes later, the Beaver landed. As the pilot taxied along Burrard Inlet, heading for the Canada Customs float, Tom Baker kept his eyes on the yacht. It was only a thousand feet away. He had gotten a good look at it a few minutes earlier when the aircraft was on its final approach to the seaplane landing zone.

The *Divine Wind,* formerly the *Victory,* was heading into Coal Harbour, a beautiful bay located at the west end of downtown Vancouver. *I've got you now,* Baker thought.

15

SHOWDOWN

Vancouver, British Columbia

The jumbo jet from Tokyo landed at Vancouver International at precisely ten-fifteen P.M. Within twelve minutes, four additional international flights had arrived. Consequently, the airport's international baggage claim and Canada Customs terminal were a madhouse. Hundreds of tired, worn-out passengers struggled to gain entrance into Canada. The lines seemed to stretch for miles.

Hiroshi Yoshida, however, didn't have to stand in line. His status as one of the world's wealthiest men insured him special treatment. Accompanied by a team of Royal Canadian Mounties, he and his entourage were whisked through a special VIP customs-clearance station. Within just ten minutes of landing he was inside a limousine, heading toward downtown.

He sat alone in the huge passenger section of the Mercedes. The rest of his party, his own personal male secretary, one of his chefs, and a team of mid-level department managers, followed behind in rental cars. The driver and Yoshida's bodyguard were up front.

Yoshida loved Vancouver. Compared to Tokyo, it was tiny, almost quaint, but it nonetheless had a real cosmopolitan feeling to it. To him, it was one of the most beautiful cities in the world. Towering snowcapped mountains on the north and east surrounded Canada's largest western city while a huge emerald inland sea formed its western boundary. Even the city's modern architecture seemed to fit right in with its rugged surroundings. High rises dotted the shoreline of English Bay and Burrard Inlet. Everything looked new—like the downtown sections of Hong Kong.

Yoshida visited Vancouver several times a year. His North American operations center was based in the city. Housed in the penthouse of a forty-story office building in the West End, Yoshida Heavy Industries was a big player in western Canada. The company was involved in a wide range of business enterprises ranging from buying timber products to developing a coal mine in the interior of BC. Gross revenues from the Canadian subsidiary reached $2 billion the previous year and were expected to exceed that record for the current year.

Yoshida really didn't care about the money anymore. He had infinite personal resources that allowed him to have any physical comfort he could ever want. That wasn't what kept him going. It was the power that his wealth represented that was intoxicating. He couldn't get enough of it.

Zackary Scott and Finn Sorenson met Tom Baker at 10:45 P.M. The rendezvous took place in a parking lot near the Coal Harbour shoreline. The bright deck lights from the *Divine Wind* shone in the background. The luxury yacht was anchored a couple of hundred yards offshore.

"That it?" asked Finn Sorenson as he pointed toward the water.

"Yep. She stands out like a carnival with all those lights on," replied the private investigator.

"When did she pull in?" asked Zack.

"About half an hour before I phoned you." Baker paused a moment as he lit up a cigarette. "By the way, how about filling me in on what's going on? All I was told was to find the yacht."

"Tom, you've done a great job," Zack replied. "We'll take it from here, so why don't you call it a night?"

Baker's curiosity increased as Scott evaded his question. *What is he up to?* "You sure you don't need any help watching it?"

"Thanks for the offer but we'll be fine."

"Okay, I'm bushed. I'll be staying at the Pan Pacific, so if you need me, just give me a call."

"Thanks," Scott said as he reached out with his right hand. "I really appreciate your help."

When Baker pulled out of the lot in his rented car, Finn turned to face Scott. "Okay, Zack, what do we do now?"

Zack looked toward the bay, focusing on the *Divine Wind*. "I've got to get aboard that sucker."

"But what can you do there?" protested Finn. "Why don't we just watch from here?"

"My gut tells me the answers to all our questions are on that boat. And the only way I'm going to get those answers is to get aboard her."

Yoshida's limousine pulled into the main parking lot of a Coal Harbour marina at 11:04 P.M. The shuttle craft, a thirty-five-foot power cruiser, was waiting at the dock for him. He stepped aboard, accompanied by two of his guards, three assistants, and a pile of suitcases. Twelve minutes later he was sitting in the main saloon of his yacht. He was about to light up his thirty-fifth cigarette of the day when Cindy DeMorey walked into the cabin. She was wearing a green evening dress cut an inch above the knee. Her dark hair cascaded over her tan shoulders. She was carrying a small gift-wrapped box with a bright red ribbon on top of it.

"Honored Uncle, it is good to see you again," Cindy said as she bowed. She had arrived in Vancouver earlier in the evening, taking a shuttle flight from Seattle.

Yoshida stared at his great-niece for a few seconds. He had forgotten how beautiful she was. "My dear, please, come here and sit down." He patted the chair seat next to his with his hand.

She moved forward and handed him the gift as she sat down.

"What is this?" he asked with a smile on his face. He then began carefully pulling apart the wrapping paper.

Although Cindy hadn't lived in Japan for several years, she never forgot about the little customs and mannerisms that mean so much to the elders. Hiroshi was especially fond of the old ways.

"It's beautiful," Yoshida exclaimed as he examined the porcelain figurine of a pair of dolphins riding the crest of a wave. The artwork was exquisite and expensive. Cindy had spent nearly $3,000 on the original sculpture.

"I hope you like it. The man who made it is a Native American. His studio is in Seattle."

"Ah, an Indian."

"Yes, sir. He's quite famous in Puget Sound."

"Thank you, my dear. It is perfect."

Yoshida took a long drag on his cigarette and then reached into his left-hand coat pocket. He pulled out a tiny package, also gift wrapped. He handed it to Cindy. "For you," he said.

Cindy had been anticipating her great-uncle's reciprocity. She had wondered what he would give her. "Oh, you treat me too well, Uncle. I don't deserve anything."

"Nonsense, open it now." It was almost a command.

Cindy pulled the wrapping off, revealing a jewelry case, just as she had expected. Inside was a pair of earrings, each solid gold with a cluster of perfectly shaped and colored pearls.

"They're fantastic!" Cindy said. She pulled off her own earrings and slipped on the new pair, using a nearby wall mirror to examine the arrangement. "Oh, thank you, Uncle. Your gift is much nicer than my meager offering."

"They fit you well, my darling, just as I had expected. Now, please come sit down. There is much to talk about."

It was almost midnight when Zack and Finn finally made it onto the water. They found a fourteen-foot-long Avon tied to one of the floating piers along the waterway. The inflatable runabout had a twenty-horsepower outboard motor mounted on its stern and the portable fuel tank was three-quarters full. Zack and Finn, however, decided not to use it. They didn't want the noisy engine announcing their presence. Instead, they used a pair of oars that had been stored inside.

Finn was rowing, sitting on the center seat, while Zack sat in the stern. Zack already had his dry suit on. He was working with the valve on his aluminum air tank.

"How far out do you want me to row?" asked Finn, his voice a whisper.

"A little more, maybe a couple hundred feet. I don't want you to get too close."

"Okay." Finn turned his head to look over the bow of the inflatable. The *Divine Wind* was about three hundred yards away. It was still lit up like the proverbial Christmas tree. He turned back to face Zack. "Who do you suppose those people were that went aboard a while ago?"

"Hell, I don't know. But I'm sure going to try to find out."

Finn pulled a few more strokes and then spoke again. "Jesus, Zack, I don't know if this is such a good idea now. A couple of those guys on that shuttle looked like fucking gorillas."

"I don't have a choice. I'm convinced more than ever that the key to the whole damn mess that I'm—" Zack stopped to correct himself—"that we're both in is somewhere on that boat."

"What the hell are you going to look for?"

"I don't know, but I'll know it when I see it."

Finn remained silent as he continued to row. A minute later he shipped his oars. The mystery yacht was about seven hundred feet away. The water surface was still—there was no wind. The only noise came from a railroad switching engine working on the tracks back on shore. It was maneuvering boxcars onto one of the Canadian Pacific Railroad piers for a barge shipment to Vancouver Island.

"How's this?" Finn asked, still whispering.

"Good, let's anchor here."

Finn dropped the makeshift anchor overboard. It was an old rusted steel automobile wheel they had found on the mudflat next to the marina. He cinched up the line. The water was about thirty feet deep. "Okay, Zack," he said, "we're anchored."

"Good. I'll be set in a couple of minutes."

While Zack continued to adjust his diving gear, Finn glanced down at his right side. A leather case, about four feet long and nine inches wide, was wedged next to the rubber hull. "Zack," he said, "where'd you get this thing anyway?"

"It was a gift from my uncle. He won it off some army colonel in a poker game."

Finn shook his head. He had examined the contents of the case earlier. He had been duly impressed. "Well, it's sure as hell put together well."

"Yep, but I don't think we'll need it."

Finn didn't reply. Something told him that Zack was wrong.

A minute later, Zack broke the silence. "I'm just about ready now." He then pushed the purge button on his regulator. A jet of air blasted out. He looked back up at Finn. "Okay, now I'm just going to quietly slip over the side. I'll be gone for about forty-five minutes or so." He checked his diving watch. "It's now twelve-fifteen. I'll meet you back here at one o'clock."

"How the hell are you going to do that? It's so damn dark out you'll never be able to spot me."

"I'll use this," Zack said as he held up his left arm. There was a black plastic box, about the size of a paperback book, lashed to the dry suit. It had several luminous digital readouts. "This thing's a portable range and bearing finder. Works off the GPS satellites. All I have to do is set the coordinates of where we're anchored, like this." He punched in two keys on the waterproof keyboard. "And then when I'm ready to head back it'll tell me the exact course to take."

"You mean that's a sat-nav unit?"

"Yeah."

"It works underwater?"

"No. The satellite signals don't penetrate more than a foot or two below the surface, so I'll have to be topside when I check my position. But once it computes the course and distance I can submerge and use my compass."

"I'll be damned."

"Pretty clever, don't you think?"

"I'll say. Where'd you get it?"

"One of my companies made it under contract for the navy—it's for the SEALs." Zack was referring to the U.S. Navy's elite commando unit.

"That must be some kind of top secret hardware."

"This isn't—it's a test prototype we made. The real ones are highly classified. They have a lot more accuracy plus a bunch of other things on them that I can't talk about."

"I'm impressed." Finn then rotated to face the yacht. It was still sitting quietly at its anchorage. "Well, Zack, looks like we're all set then. I'll just wait here for you."

Zack reached out with his gloved right hand and touched his friend's shoulder. "Finn, I'm glad you're here."

"Just be careful, man. Those fuckers are crazy."

"I will. See you in a while."

Zack pulled his face mask down and inserted the regulator into his mouth. He took two quick breaths before flipping over the side, falling backward into the water. He hardly made a sound.

Finn watched the bubble trail for about a minute, confirming that Zack was heading toward the yacht. He then turned his attention back to the raft. He sat the leather case in his lap and pulled the zipper. Inside was a custom modifed U.S. Army Mosberg 590 combat shotgun.

The water was pitch-dark. And it was cold. Zack had been swimming for about ten minutes, hugging the bottom as he headed toward the *Divine Wind*. However, he was now stopped, his fins buried in the mud. There was thirty feet of water over him as he began to adjust the inflation control on his variable-volume dry suit. Despite the protection of the suit's nylon fabric and its insulating air layer, he felt chilled. *Damnit, I wonder if that zipper's leaking again.*

The twenty-four-inch-long, heavy-duty fastener was positioned along his shoulder blades, providing access into the one-piece garment. The stainless steel zipper was supposed to be watertight but it had failed once before. Zack pushed the purge button on the suit's intake valve, injecting a few pounds of compressed air into the suit. His weight belt was a couple of pounds too heavy. With the leaking water, he couldn't maintain neutral buoyancy.

Zack felt the immediate change in buoyancy. *That's better—not so heavy now.* He next flipped on his diving light. The bottom was soft, and when he grounded out his fins had thoroughly stirred it up. He was engulfed by a cloud of silt.

Normally, Zack would have gone to the surface to check his gear but he couldn't take that chance now. He was only about a hundred feet away from the *Divine Wind*. His hand-held satellite navigator and compass had served him well during the stealthy approach. He would have been under the boat right now if he hadn't had the problem with the leak.

In spite of his years of diving, often at great depths and under enormously hazardous conditions, Zack was scared. He hated diving at night, especially in waters he was not familiar with. But not knowing what waited for him on the yacht was the worst part of it.

Zack flashed his dive light on the tank gauge. It read 1,900 pounds. *Good, at least I didn't burn up a lot of air getting here.* He next checked his compass and then made a mental calculation. *Okay, I need to head out on a heading of two hundred seventy-five degrees for about a minute.* He then began swimming, staying five feet above the bottom. He flashed the light downward to give him a frame of reference.

When Zack finally stopped he could hear a mechanical rumbling echoing through the water. *What's that?* he wondered. He flashed the light upward but its narrow beam was swallowed up by the greenish depths. He remained motionless for fifteen seconds, trying to identify the noise. Then it suddenly hit him. *Of course! It's got to be the generator.* Because the vessel was anchored offshore, it was running an electrical generator for power. *Good, I must be right under the sucker.* He checked his depth gauge. It read thirty-two feet.

Zack started up, kicking lightly with his legs. He had turned the light off. He didn't want its residual refractive light announcing his presence. He swam in a slow spiral, keeping his head cocked back so he could see obstructions. Just before reaching the surface he noticed a slight change in the darkness of the water. *There's some light up there.*

When Zack surfaced he was about ten feet away from the port side of the vessel. A deck-mounted floodlight from the flying bridge was aimed downward, illuminating a lower deck. At least half of its light cone reached the water's surface, right where Zack popped up. *Jesus Christ,* he thought. He instantly flipped over and dove downward, hoping he hadn't been seen or heard. He headed directly under the vessel and stopped. If he heard anything out of the normal, the sounds of footsteps telegraphed through the hull, the engines starting, or the anchor windlass cranked up, he was prepared to abandon the probe. But he heard nothing—only the ever-present din of the generator. *You lucky SOB. No one must have been out there.*

Zack headed aft, following the keel line. Just before reaching the stern he stopped. *There they are,* he said to himself as he spotted the false bottom panels. He removed his knife and slipped its stainless steel blade into one of the recesses. After prying on it for ten seconds he stopped. The underwater doors were sealed tight. *There's no way I'm going to get in that way.*

Zack moved to the stern, swimming past the dual drive-shafts and propellers. The six-bladed screws looked especially vicious in the eerie diffracted surface light. He carefully worked himself under the swim step. The three-foot-wide cantilevered deck spanned the entire twenty-four-foot-wide stern. He looked up through the slots of the step. There was no one around. *Okay, time to do it.*

A minute later, Zack had removed his weight belt, tank, and fins, securing the gear to a dacron line tied to one of the swim step's stainless steel mounting brackets. After making certain that the equipment was hanging freely he took one final breath from the regulator and headed up.

Cindy DeMorey and Hiroshi Yoshida were both sitting at the main dining table. But they weren't eating. Instead, they had a chart of the Washington State coastline spread out over half the table. Yoshida was speaking, in Japanese, while pointing to a particular spot on the map.

"It's right here."

"Now I see why you were so concerned."

"Yes, it would have been only a matter of time before they stumbled onto it."

"But what will you do now? Eventually they will come back."

"Yes, I know, but by that time we will have moved off the main unit to another area, farther away and much deeper. We'll then run satellite lines to the site that will not be detectable."

"So we will be able to continue."

"Oh, yes. Our best guess is that it will be several years before they come back, so we'll have plenty of time to prepare. In the meantime we shall continue as we have."

"That sounds wonderful. Then our plan seems to have worked."

"Yes, I don't think this Zackary Scott will ever recover."

"I think you're right, Uncle. He is finished!"

Zack was huddled on the yacht's upper deck. The walkway was only two feet wide and the knee-high stainless steel guardrail on his side was nothing more than a nuisance. He was looking downward at the dining room table in the main salon. One of the sliding glass windows was cracked open a few inches for ventilation. He could see the back of a bald-headed man sitting near his side. But it was the Eurasian woman who had his attention. *Damn, what a beauty,* he thought.

Zack leaned a little closer to the window opening, trying to eavesdrop on the conversation. It took him about half a minute to discover they weren't speaking English. The man's speech sounded Asian but Zack couldn't tell if it was Chinese or something else.

When Yoshida leaned forward and pointed to something on the table Zack strained his neck for a better view. *Hell, that's the Washington coastline.* Then, when he saw the man's finger over the coordinates of the Hammer 4 site, he could hardly restrain himself. *What the hell's going on here?*

Zack moved back to the opening, again trying to pick up the conversation. About a minute later, he nearly lost his grip on the handrail when he heard his name mentioned. All he recognized were the man's words: Zackary Scott. *These are the bastards after all!*

Zack remained riveted to the tiny deck, staring into the well-lit cabin. When the man pushed his chair away from the table and turned his head toward the window, Zack saw his face. The Asian wasn't as old-looking as he had expected. The man looked like he was maybe in his late fifties. *Who the hell are you anyway?* thought Zack.

The man was now only a few feet away from the window; he was still looking outward.

Zack started crawling backward, trying to escape the man's view, but he lost his footing on the slick deck. Momentarily off balance, he fell against the window. The side of his head smacked into the tempered glass. It sounded like a rifle shot.

Yoshida was startled by the unexpected noise. He moved closer to the window. And then he spotted the black-clad form. "My God, there's a man there," he shouted in his native tongue.

He instinctively stepped away from the window, not sure what to do. A moment later, fearing he was about to be attacked, he launched into action. He grabbed a nearby telephone, punching the bridge intercom button. "Guards, guards," he shouted into the handset, "there's an intruder on the starboard deck. Get him, now."

"Shit," muttered Scott, "now you've done it." Zack had just a second or two to make a decision. When he heard a doorway burst open and noisy footsteps pounding on the decks he made up his mind. *Time to get out of here.* He pulled down his face mask and leaped overboard.

Just as he plunged downward, the first volley of submachine gun fire riddled the water around him. The nine-millimeter bullets penetrated about three feet before they finally lost their momentum. The heavy rounds then began sinking all around him.

Zack's own momentum carried him ten feet below the surface. He couldn't see much of anything, just a blurred green-black void. *Where's the damn boat?* he thought as he tried to reorient himself while slowly rising. Then he heard another barrage of bullets ripping into the water just above his head. He instinctively turned and swam away, kicking furiously. Ten seconds later he collided with the bottom of the boat. *Thank God*, he thought as he pulled himself along the slimy bottom. *They can't get to me under here.*

Despite the darkness Zack could see the hull's red anti-fouling paint as he swam under the boat, following the keel line aft. Without his weight belt, the buoyancy of his dry suit squeezed him against the hull. It was tough going. When he reached the twin driveshafts, he spotted his diving gear hanging below the swim step. His lungs were burning as he forced himself to move faster.

After taking several deep breaths from the regulator, Zack buckled on his weight belt. He then began slipping on his diving fins. The air tank that sustained him was still suspended from the line. He had just managed to attach the second fin when he heard a high-pitched motorized noise. It was right behind him. *What the hell is that?* Zack spun around and looked forward. The starboard underwater recessed panel was opening up right between the driveshafts. The noisy hydraulic actuator inside the wet well telegraphed the whining sound into the water. A few seconds later the noise stopped. The articulated door, about four feet wide and ten feet long, was wide open. He could see light diffusing through the opening.

Zack kept his eyes glued onto the now-flooded hull opening as he struggled with his air tank. He had just managed to secure the tank's shoulder harness when something sank into the water. He saw just a flash of the object as it plunged into the inky depths. It was cylindrical, about four feet long and half a foot in diameter. *What was that?*

Zack pushed away from the hull, propelling himself downward. He was heading for the bottom, thirty feet down. Half a minute later he plowed into the invisible mud. He hadn't had time to flip on his diving light. His heart was beating furiously and he was breathing much too fast. *Slow down*, he ordered himself. *Conserve your air.*

Zack swam upward about ten feet. He was just starting to regain his composure when he heard it. The metallic whine-like noise was somewhere behind him. It was getting louder. He spun around and flipped on his light. The beam penetrated the darkness only a dozen feet before it was swallowed up. The noise level continued to increase. *That sounds like a propeller!*

He spotted the robotic antiswimmer weapon just in time, managing to propel himself backward as it bore down on him. It raced right past him at thirty knots, missing his abdomen by just inches. The twelve-inch-long by six-inch-wide surgical steel blade mounted on the weapon's bow would have cut him in half if it had connected.

Zack was momentarily tossed around by the weapon's turbulent wake. A few seconds later the water calmed down and he sank back to the bottom. Although he couldn't see the robot, he could hear it in the distance. It was circling around, preparing for another pass. *Christ Almighty. What the hell do I do now?*

Finn Sorenson was barely awake. Despite his recent convalescence, he still wasn't back to a hundred percent. He often found himself drifting off. However, when the first volley of machine gun fire broke the late evening silence, his fatigue disappeared. He snapped up from his half-reclining position, looking back across the water at the *Divine Wind*. A torrent of fire erupted along one side of the vessel, followed a second later by the staccato rapid-fire reports.

Damnit! he thought, *they must be shooting at Zack.*

Finn turned around. He set the choke and throttle on the outboard, and then jerked on the nylon start cord. Nothing. He ripped at the line again. It still refused to start. He reached down and reset the choke. *Come on, you fucker, light up!*

The engine exploded to life on the fifth pull. He tossed the anchor line overboard and advanced the throttle to its stop. The inflatable charged forward. With his left hand on the outboard steering arm, Finn reached forward with his other hand, grabbing the Mosberg.

The antiswimmer robot was probing the water column in front of its advancing path. A tiny parabolic antenna inside the bow section of the pressure casing was transmitting high-frequency sound waves. The sonar pulses spread out in a cone-shaped pattern, penetrating the water for several hundred yards. When the incident sound waves hit a metallic object that generated a reflected signal, the weapon's computer would intercept the incoming acoustic data. Anything large, like a boat hull, would be ignored. It was only interested in small metal objects, like scuba diving tanks.

Zack heard the probe as it again homed in on his new position. This time it was approaching head-on. He turned to his right, kicking madly. He had just seconds to react. He swam horizontally for about twenty feet and then turned downward, racing for the bottom. Five seconds later he plowed into the bottom, half burying himself in the soft mud. He dropped his light during the collision but its beam was still on, pointing upward at a forty-five-degree angle. The probe whisked by, passing through the outer edge of the light's beam. It missed Zack by at least a dozen feet. *That's got to be it,* Zack thought. *It doesn't go after bottom reflections.*

Zack was right. The robot's computer brain was programmed to ignore bottom-generated reflections. It only homed in on free-swimming metallic objects. Otherwise the device would be continually impaling itself on the steel and iron trash that littered the bottom. The bottom of Vancouver's harbor, like most industrial ports, was covered with a myriad of steel cables, abandoned anchors, sunken boat hulls, and numerous other discarded objects.

Zack recovered his diving light. He took a quick look at the air tank gauge. It read five hundred pounds. *Damn! I'm almost out. Now what?*

Zack kneeled on the bottom, his legs and flippers bent under him. His mind was racing a mile a minute, trying to figure a way out.

The probe circled overhead, orbiting around Zack's position like a lion stalking its prey. The weapon's liquid fuel engine had another ten minutes of propulsion remaining. Its computer brain told it that the target was still out there somewhere.

Zack was now almost totally out of air, but he could still hear the robot cruising above him. *Damn thing's still there.* He had just barely managed to suck out another lungful when his regulator shut down. The residual pressure inside the aluminum tank was no longer sufficient to overcome the ambient water pressure. *That's it. I've got no choice now.*

Zack had already released the tank's backpack harness, so he simply pulled the regulator out of his mouth and let the tank go. It was now buoyant.

While still sitting on the bottom, Zack took his diving knife and cut a one-inch slit in the forearm of his dry suit. A stream of bubbles headed up for the surface. He next pulled his arm upward, placing his mouth over the hole. His variable-volume dry suit was still charged with air pressure and the hot tap would keep him alive for another couple of minutes. As he sucked on the stale air, he tried to ignore the chilling seawater that percolated in.

The spent scuba tank slowly ascended, moving at about a foot per second. The probe spotted the tank when it was twenty feet off the bottom. The solid acoustic reflection was like a neon sign to the weapon's computer. In a microsecond it calculated the bearing and distance to the target. New commands were instantly transmitted to the robot's rudder and stabilizers and power plant.

Zack heard the robot change power settings. Its cavitation rate increased by 50 percent as more power was applied to the propeller. *Here comes the bastard.* Twenty-three seconds later he heard the impact. The robot slammed into the empty air tank at forty-three miles an hour. The harpoon blade tore through the soft aluminum tank. A microsecond after impact, the probe blew up. Its tiny warhead was designed to finish off any diver who might be impaled on its skewer.

Although the four pounds of plastic explosive in the warhead would create a modest charge at ground level, it was devastating underwater. The shock wave hit Zack with a vengeance, rolling him along the muddy bottom like a bowling ball. When he finally recovered from the turbulence his lungs were burning. He tried once more to suck air out of his suit but it was useless. He then pushed the folds of his suit along the chest and abdomen, trying to force more air toward the opening. He got one more breath of air and that was it. *Gotta do it now,* he said to himself. Zack flipped the quick release on his weight belt and began kicking his legs.

As Zack raced upward, he forced himself to expel air. Otherwise, he risked rupturing his lungs as trapped air inside expanded due to the reduced water pressure.

Zack finally exploded through the surface, sucking in great lungfuls of clean, fresh air. *Thank God, I made it.*

Zack managed to partially recover his composure when he heard the yelling. It was from behind. He flipped himself around. *Oh shit.* The yacht was about two hundred feet away and someone was training a spotlight along the water's surface. It was almost on him.

Finn Sorenson began firing when the *Avon* was two hundred feet from the *Divine Wind*'s stern. With his left leg draped over the steering arm of the wide-open outboard engine, he deliberately aimed high, hoping the buckshot would pepper the deck area where the spotlight was located. It took three shots but he managed to knock out the light. Then, as he sped by the starboard side, now only fifty feet away, he let loose with the remaining rounds. He punched baseball-size holes in the fiberglass superstructure and blew out one entire plate glass window section.

As he raced back toward the main harbor, a gunman on the yacht's flying bridge returned fire. His aim was way off. The bullets thumped into the water twenty feet away from the boat.

Sorenson continued east, heading for the wide-open waters of Burrard Inlet. A couple of minutes later he stopped. He was well out of range of the yacht's gunners.

As the *Avon* drifted, Finn began reloading the Mosberg. He had just inserted the last shell into the under-the-barrel magazine when he heard the yacht's engines. He turned around and looked back toward the west. The *Divine Wind* had reeled in its anchor. It was now charging through the still waters of Coal Harbour. Three minutes later it passed Brockton Point, heading northward toward the First Narrows and the Lion's Gate Bridge.

At first, Finn was tempted to follow the vessel. But he then decided to head back into the bay. *Gotta find Zack,* he repeatedly told himself.

Five minutes later he found him. Zack was so exhausted that Finn had to pull him into the inflatable.

16

RETREAT

Blaine, Washington

The silver Cadillac pulled away from the second holding lane next to the two-story building. There were no other vehicles around. It was a few minutes after three o'clock in the morning. The U.S.-Canada border crossing at Blaine was a ghost town.

"You lie pretty good," Zack said, a smile breaking out on his face.

"Well, I did what you told me to do, didn't I?" answered Finn.

"Yep. And it worked fine."

The U.S. Customs agent hadn't questioned Finn's story about visiting relatives in Vancouver.

Finn momentarily turned to face Zack. "Too bad about the Mosberg. That was a crying shame to dump it in the drink like that."

"Yeah, I know, but it was just too damn dangerous to be driving around Vancouver with it, let alone try to bring it across the border. Anyone could have heard the firefight, and if we got caught with a shotgun in the trunk"—Zack paused—"they'd throw the key away."

Finn nodded as he stared ahead. A few seconds later he said, "Where do you suppose they went with that yacht?"

"Hell, I don't know. Maybe it's heading back to Portland, but I doubt it."

"What do you plan to do when we get back to Seattle?"

"First, I'm going to put another trace on that yacht. This time with its other name. Then I'm heading over to Montana."

"Montana?"

"Yeah, my uncle's got a ranch over there—Kelda and the boys flew over earlier in the week. I'm going to visit them for a week or so." Zack paused. "I really should stay here, but I'll have a revolution on my hands if I don't show up at the ranch. I promised Kelda that I'd be there."

Finn nodded. "Sounds like a good plan. You need the rest." He again turned to face Zack. "Besides, I think it might be a good idea to have your family out of town for a while."

"What do you mean?"

"These fuckers are crazy. Think about what they've done: blew up your rig, killed all those people on it, scuttled the *Odin* and murdered my crew. My God, they're capable of anything—like coming after your family."

Zack was shocked. Finn's words hit home, deep and personal. "You're right. This whole thing is getting out of hand. *They* are going to stay on the ranch until this mess is over."

"Good. And make sure they've got some security there, too. You never know."

"I will. Uncle Jason and his boys will take care of that."

The two men remained quiet for about a minute, each thinking about what had happened back in Vancouver. Zack finally broke the silence. "How about you, Finn, what are you going do when we get back to Seattle?"

"Well, if it's okay with you, I'd like to fly out to the *Ranger* and help with the search. I want to know where those pricks scuttled the *Odin*."

"Great, we could sure use your help. I'll get a chopper for you."

"Thanks." Finn remained silent for about a minute and then once again turned to face Zack. "Any more thoughts about those people you saw?"

"No, just an old man with a young woman."

"And both Oriental?"

"He was for sure—a little bald guy. The woman, though, I'm not sure about her." Zack paused to picture her in his mind. "I'm sure she had some Asian blood in her, but she looked like she might be American, possibly European."

"Good-lookin', huh?"

"Yes, a real knockout."

Finn remained quiet for a few minutes, staring straight ahead as the car proceeded down the freeway. The white lane markers raced by. The Cadillac was doing seventy-five. He turned to look at Zack. "So the *Divine Wind* must be that old fart's boat?"

"Probably."

"So why in the world would someone like him be trying to sabotage SCS?"

"I don't know, Finn." Zack hesitated a few seconds. "I just don't know."

Zack's mind was racing with possibilities as he stared blindly ahead. *Why, indeed, would he want to hurt me and my company? What could I have possibly done to harm him?*

Vancouver

Hiroshi Yoshida and Cindy DeMorey were sitting in the backseat of the limousine as it sped down Highway 99. Vancouver International Airport was just a few minutes away.

The couple had just disembarked from the *Divine Wind.* The megayacht was now tied up to the visitor berth at the Royal Vancouver Yacht Club's English Bay marina. The ship's crew was already busy placing temporary fiberglass patches over the fist-size holes in the cabin walls. By first light, no one would be able to tell that the yacht had been hit by gunfire.

"Uncle, did you see the man's face?" asked Cindy.

"No. He had some kind of black hood over his head. I only saw shadows, nothing concrete."

"And the other one, in the runabout?"

"None of the crew could see him either—he was too far away."

"So who were they?"

Yoshida shook his head from side to side. "I don't know, but I suspect they might have been someone working for Scott."

"Scott?"

"Yes. It would fit his profile." Yoshida then turned toward the side window and looked at the passing roadside lights.

Cindy lit up a cigarette. After expelling her first lungful of smoke she turned to face Yoshida. "How could Scott have tracked you? No one over here was supposed to know about the *Divine Wind*."

Yoshida raised his arms, signaling his obvious frustration. He then looked into Cindy's eyes. "But it doesn't really matter how they found the yacht. We must assume the spy saw both of us—we were face-to-face, only a meter apart."

"So he saw us. They still don't have any proof, and they'll never figure it out."

"I hope you're right. Unfortunately, I can't take that chance. If it was Scott's man, then he may know too much already."

Cindy inhaled another lungful of the acrid smoke. "So what do we do now?"

"First, I will return to Tokyo. I don't want to be in Canada or the U.S. if Scott should start asking a lot of embarrassing questions."

"But your cruise to Alaska—I know you were looking forward to it."

"Don't worry about that. We'll resume the trip when this is all over."

"Okay."

"Now, I've ordered the *Divine Wind* to head for San Francisco in the morning. I don't want the Vancouver police questioning the crew about the gunfire in Coal Harbour. And I expect you to fly back to Seattle in the morning. There's nothing here to link you to any of this, but just the same I think it would be prudent to leave Vancouver."

"Of course, anything you say."

Hiroshi reached forward and removed a bottle of Chivas Regal from the built-in bar on the seatback. He poured the whiskey into a glass and took a sip. The raw liquor had a fiery bite.

"Now, Cindy, when you return to Seattle I want you to do some more checking on Scott."

"What is it that you want?"

"I've got to find a new way to get more leverage on him. I need a weak spot, something that will make him vulnerable."

"We could try the family angle."

Yoshida had rejected that tactic earlier, but now he was desperate. "All right. Anything will help—but you must be discreet. If those men were working for him tonight, then his guard will really be up. He cannot be alerted to our interest. Otherwise, we may never get another chance to act."

Yoshida took another sip of whisky as he looked out the door window. The airport was coming up on his right. He turned back to face his niece. "Cindy, I've got to get him off my back. Otherwise the whole operation may unravel."

"I understand, *Ojisan*. We'll get rid of him."

Off the Washington Coast

"Captain, we're ready to vent tank one through the bypass system. Valves are open to the sea and we're ballasted down to the standards."

"You checked vessel traffic?" asked Captain Mishima.

"Aye, sir. All clear. The nearest vessel is a single screw; it's twenty kilometers to the north." The man paused to scan another monitor. "We're also picking up reverberations from the storm."

"Thunder?" asked the captain.

"Yes, sir. Apparently, there's a squall moving up from the south."

Mishima dismissed the surface conditions. His ship was submerged under a thousand feet of water—it was immune to the weather. "What's the discharge time?" he asked.

"Computer estimates that it'll take about eighteen minutes."

"Very well, proceed."

The cloud of methane boiled up from the depths. It looked like mist hovering over the ocean surface. The gas would have vanished unnoticed if it hadn't been for the lightning. It took only one errant bolt of electricity to ignite the volatile vapors. And in a microsecond, the pewter-black night was transformed into a blinding light that stretched across the horizon.

"Jesus, did you see that?" called out the helmsman of the *Pacific Voyager*. The 850-foot-long container ship was heading southeast as it exited through the mouth of the Strait of Juan de Fuca.

"Yeah, but what was it?" replied the first officer. The two men were alone on the giant bridge deck. The captain had just retired to his cabin.

"There's lightning out there all right, but I've never seen anything quite like that before. I swear it looked like some kind of explosion."

The officer nodded. "You're right, Sam. That wasn't lightning—something blew up."

"But what?"

"I don't know." The merchant marine officer scanned the nearby radar display. "There's nothing out there."

"Nothing?"

"That's right. We're the only ship around." The officer next checked the chart table. The NOAA chart for the Washington coast was laid out on the tabletop. He studied the various notations on the map for half a minute before spotting the erasure marks on a handwritten note. He had written it five weeks ago during an earlier voyage. "I'll be damned," he said.

"What's the matter?" asked the helmsman.

"When we came through here last month there was an oil-drilling rig moored near that flash point area."

"Oh, yeah. That's the one that blew up and sank."

"Right."

"Shit, you don't suppose there's some kind of connection between that rig and what we just saw, do ya?"

"Hell, I don't know." The officer paused for a moment as a new thought developed. He then turned to face the seaman. There was a grin on his face. "Sam, maybe it's a ghost or something like that, rising up from the deep."

Both men laughed at the vivid image.

"Well, sir," the seaman finally said, "do we need to do anything about it?"

"No, not now. Whatever it was, it's gone. No sense alerting the Coasties over something we can't explain—they'll just get excited for nothing."

"But we should report it, shouldn't we?"

"Yeah, officially we should. When we get to L.A. I'll fill out a sighting report and file it."

"Okay, that sounds good to me."

"How much more venting do we have?" asked Captain Mishima.

"All done, sir. We're now ready to top off."

"Very well. As soon as we're fully loaded I want to get under way. We're already going to be late as it is."

"Aye, aye, sir. We should be ready to depart in about half an hour."

"Good, make it so."

17

A LITERARY FIND

Yokohama

Yokohama is a world-class port city. Simply put, it is huge, both in its size and its population. Situated on the west shore of Tokyo Bay, fifteen miles south of Tokyo, Yokohama is one of Japan's most important industrial centers. It is the home base of dozens of shipbuilding yards, oil refineries, chemical factories, automobile plants, and processed food facilities. With three million inhabitants, it is Japan's second largest city and the capital of Kanagawa Prefecture.

The pace of life in the giant city mirrors the expansive industrial facilities that line its waterfront: modern, fast, and efficient. The huge construction derricks that pierce the air, mixed with the endless rows of smokestacks and warehouses, attest to the city's reliance on heavy industry. And the smell of money permeates the air. The giant port city generates more income in one year than the annual gross national product of dozens of third-world nations.

The fact that Yokohama runs like a well-oiled machine is not a surprise. Nearly every facility is new and well planned, incorporating the latest in engineering design and high-tech manufacturing innovations. Almost bombed to extinction at the end of World War II, the industrial heart of the city was miraculously resurrected, largely due to the hard work and enthusiasm of the Japanese worker but also, in part, by the generosity of the American people. The United States encouraged the Japanese government to rebuild its industrial base. Yokohama was its flagship.

Nestled in on the Yokohama waterfront with Japan's other industrial giants was the shipbuilding division of Yoshida Heavy Industries. Occupying nearly fifty acres of prime property, YHI operated one of the world's most efficient shipyards. Three huge ship launching ways lined the nine hundred feet of waterfront. YHI's repertoire of shipbuilding experience ranged from 500,000-dwt supertankers to offshore oil exploration vessels. The yard's motto was "If it floats, we can build it."

Commander Jeffrey Hashimoto walked along the observation deck of the tower. The modern spire had a commanding view of Yokohama's industrial waterfront and the surrounding city. He was duly impressed with the structure. In typical Japanese fashion, the tower served a number of functions: it was a public view point, of course, but it also functioned as a lighthouse, contained a museum, and even had a restaurant.

The American naval officer worked his way to the edge of the deck, looking toward the waterfront. Even in the middle of the week, the public view point was crowded with visitors. But no one paid any attention to him. He fit right in with the hordes of Japanese. His only distinguishing feature was his height. He towered over most of the others. His American upbringing, especially the emphasis on the consumption of milk and dairy products, was largely responsible for his size. At six feet tall, Jeff had been a star basketball player on his high school team back in Seattle.

Hashimoto leaned against the steel rail. He looked toward the bay. YHI's shipyard was about a quarter of a mile to his left. He raised his Nikon to eye level and began shooting a series of overlapping telephoto shots. A minute later he reloaded his camera and fired off another series. He couldn't see anything out of the ordinary. There were two huge ships on the ways. One was some kind of ore carrier and the other was an oil tanker. He could see workmen scurrying all over the partially completed decks. Sparks from the automatic welder machines lit up both hulls at dozens of locations.

Hashimoto's angle of view was not quite high enough to see the waterway in front of the yard's wharf. But that didn't really matter anymore. Photographs from a recent U.S. reconnaissance satellite overflight revealed that the strange floating cylinders spotted by the NRO analyst were no longer moored at YHI's yard. And review of dozens of other surveillance photos of Yokohama Harbor and Tokyo Bay failed to locate the thousand-foot-long objects. Jeff was both confused and mystified. *What the hell did they do with those things?* he wondered.

Seattle

Zackary Scott hadn't been in his office for more than a minute when Tim Marshall stepped inside.

"Welcome back, Zack," greeted the SCS executive as he walked through the open doorway, his right hand outstretched.

"Thanks, Tim," replied Scott. He stepped forward and shook Marshall's hand.

"How are Kelda and the boys doing?"

"Oh, they're just fine."

Zack had just returned from Montana, where he had spent the past week visiting his family. The reunion had been good therapy for Scott—he missed his family terribly—but the visit was too short. He was just beginning to relax when it was time to return to Seattle.

At first, Kelda had insisted that he take a few more days off. However, when Zack made it clear that he was really leaving she changed tactics, demanding that they all return together. Zack's opposition to her new plan was compelling: "Honey," he had said, "you know I want all of you back home with me, but it just isn't safe yet. Those bastards are still out there. I can't take the risk that they won't try to get to me by harming you and the boys."

Kelda finally gave in and Zack said his good-byes at the ranch. He wouldn't allow her or the boys to see him off at the airport. It was still too dangerous for them to leave the sanctuary.

Zack motioned for Marshall to sit down while he moved behind his desk. "So, how's everything been going around here?"

"Good. All divisions are reporting routine operations. No major problems anywhere."

"How's our cash flow?"

"Not bad. We received final payment from Metro yesterday on that pipeline job and BP is supposed to be wiring us a progress payment today for the Alaska drilling work."

"Have you been able to tally up our costs for the Hammer 4 cleanup work?"

"I've got a preliminary number." Marshall pulled out a sheet of paper from a folder he was carrying. "MSRC estimates that our total exposure will be somewhere between nineteen and twenty million. Insurance should cover about ninety percent of that. We eat the deductible."

"I assume you've set aside the deductible."

"Yep, we've got two million in our cash reserve account."

"How much did we spend ourselves on the cleanup work?"

Marshall briefly scanned another document. "Our out-of-pocket expenses—salaries, equipment costs, helo rentals, per diem, et cetera—totaled just under three million."

"Any chance we'll get reimbursed from our insurance carriers?"

"Not much. We're almost to the policy limits right now with the MSRC billing. We might get a little back—a couple hundred thousand."

"Jesus, I didn't realize we had used up that much of our insurance."

"I'm afraid we have. We have a maximum liability limit of twenty million. Anything more than that and we pay."

Zack turned to look out the office windows. A thick bank of low-lying fog blanketed most of Elliott Bay this morning. All he could see from his perch was the brown crests of several peaks from the distant Olympics. "Well, Tim, it sure looks like we lucked out on the insurance."

"Absolutely. If you hadn't killed the blowout when you did, SCS would probably be in Chapter Eleven right now."

Zack didn't want to think about the specter of bankruptcy. He changed the subject. "Any luck with the search for the preventer?"

"No, I'm afraid we're still drawing a blank. We haven't spotted anything that looks like the *Odin* or its barge. The

Ranger did find an uncharted wreck, though. It turned out to be a downed airplane.''

"Airplane?''

"Yep, it looks like a big sucker—four-engine propeller job. We've turned the data over to the FAA and the military. They're checking their records for missing aircraft.''

Zack momentarily shuffled through a file folder on his desk. He scanned the contents but nothing really registered. He was thinking about something else. He tossed the file down and looked back at Marshall. "We're not going to find the BOP, are we?''

"It doesn't look good, Zack. They could have scuttled that tug just about anywhere.''

"Damn it!'' Zack shouted as he simultaneously pounded his right fist on the desk. "Without the blowout preventer, we can't prove the well was sabotaged.''

"But Zack, we've still got the photos and videotapes you made, along with eyewitness testimony—especially Commander Blake. She'll be able to corroborate—''

"That all helps,'' interrupted Scott, "but we've got to have the hard evidence to really prove our innocence. If there's any doubt about how the well failed, you can bet your ass we're going to get saddled with operator error. And you know what that means.''

Marshall nodded his head affirmatively.

"You heard anything new from MMS?'' Zack asked.

"No, our Hammer 4 drilling permit is still suspended indefinitely and the Department of Interior's investigation of the spill is ongoing.''

"What do our legal people have to say about the fine?''

"If we get fined—''

"Tim,'' Zack broke in, "unless we find the BOP, we're going to get fined. Now, how much are we looking at?''

"The attorneys expect that we could get hit with as much as a five-million-dollar penalty.''

"Damnit! More damn money down the frigging rat hole.''

"But that's not all,'' Marshall said, his voice now more serious.

"What do you mean?''

"The real downside is that MMS could cancel our lease in lieu of the suspension.''

"Cancel the lease? They can't do that!" shouted Zack.

"I'm afraid they can, and we'd also forfeit all prepaid lease payments. There are several provisions in the lease, as well as the actual drilling permit, that allow the Feds to cancel the agreement if there's gross operator negligence."

Zack struggled to regain his composure. "You think they might do that?"

"I don't know. All of our contacts in DC can't figure out what MMS is up to. Dr. Patterson has clamped a gag order on all of the section's key employees. No one's talking about the Hammer 4 case."

Zack's temper flared again. "Damnit to hell. I'll bet she's going to do it."

"But why do you think that? She's always been supportive in the past."

"Tim, I've had to deal with her several times before. She's strictly political—doesn't give a damn about finding more oil for the country. She's using this job as a ladder to move up."

"So what," replied Marshall. "We proved there's a huge reservoir of oil off the coast and there'll be a lot of pressure to develop it, especially in light of the crisis in the Middle East."

"Yeah, but you forgot about those environmental groups! You can bet your bottom dollar they're still lobbying behind the scenes, trying to resurrect the Marine Sanctuary Act. If they succeed, you can kiss the Hammer 4 tract good-bye." *And SCS along with it,* thought Scott.

"You think Patterson's listening to them?"

"Damn right. If she feels the public mood is swinging to their side, she'll go right along with it." Zack hesitated a moment as a new thought popped into his head. "Shit, Tim, I can see the headlines now: Dr. Joyce Patterson, former manager of the Department of Interior's Minerals Management Section, has been appointed head of the Federal Environmental Protection Agency. Her controversial decision to permanently cancel all oil exploration leases off the Washington State coastline was instrumental in the president's decision to appoint her to the cabinet post."

At first, Tim Marshall didn't respond to Zack's parody. Instead, he looked at the wall map behind Zack's desk. The model of the *Kelda Scott* was still attached to the Hammer 4 site. He should have had it removed before Scott returned. Tim turned to again face his boss. "Zack, it sounds like you might be right. If MMS is planning to cancel our lease, you can bet they'll try to make their case as airtight as possible before announcing it. And that will take them weeks, maybe months, so it'll give us some time to prepare our defense. We can challenge 'em in court."

"I know all that, Tim. The litigation over the lease cancellation could go on for years. And maybe we'd eventually prevail with the sabotage evidence that we've got right now." Zack paused as he shifted position in his chair. "But we'd still lose in the end."

"I don't understand."

"We're totally screwed if we can't develop the Hammer 4 tract. We paid a fortune for the leases and the predevelopment costs. Add to that the oil cleanup costs, fines, and the litigation expenses, and we'll be facing a cash flow problem for the next decade."

"I see your point."

"Yeah, and you can be sure that no one will loan the company any money until the matter is resolved. And our investor partners in the Hammer 4 tract are sure as hell going to be pissed at us if we lose the lease."

"You think they might sue?" asked Marshall.

"Absolutely. If we don't give 'em their money back they'll be all over us. And don't forget about the commercial fishing groups. You can be sure we'll eventually get sued from some of them over oil damage to their stocks."

"Jesus, Zack, I hadn't thought about that. Those are going to be real ball busters to deal with."

"That's right. If we can't prove our innocence, the company's doomed."

"Then we keep looking for the preventer?"

"Of course. I have no choice, but I also want to try something else."

"What do you mean?" asked the SCS vice president.

"I've got to find out who's behind all of this."

"But how are you going to do that?"

Zack swiveled his chair around and reached for his briefcase; it was on the credenza. He opened it, removing a thick manila folder. As he turned back to face Marshall he started speaking again. "Remember when Finn Sorenson and I went to Vancouver?"

"Oh yeah. I heard you went up there, but I was in Houston at the time. What were you doing?"

"We found the mystery yacht anchored in Coal Harbour."

"The one that was originally in Portland? The *Victory*?"

"Yep, but her real name is the *Divine Wind,* at least it used to be. That's what her name was in Vancouver." Zack decided not to mention the gunplay—for now. It would just complicate matters.

"Jesus, Zack, how come you didn't say anything about that? Maybe we could have continued tracing the ownership while you were visiting your family."

"I've been handling that. In fact, I've had our attorneys and PIs working around the clock since I left for Montana." Zack tossed the heavy folder onto the edge of his desk. "This arrived by Fed Ex at the ranch yesterday morning."

Tim picked up the folder and began thumbing through its contents. Half a minute later he reacted. "Christ Almighty! They traced the ownership to some business in Korea?"

"Yep. Some outfit called Kimco Investments."

"Who the hell are they?" asked Marshall.

"We don't know. The attorneys have run into a roadblock in Seoul. We've now got a law firm over there trying to figure it out, but the real ownership is still buried under multiple layers of dummy Korean corporations. And the parent company might turn out to be headquartered in another country, too."

"Where?"

"Who knows? The people on the boat in Vancouver were definitely Asians, but I couldn't tell where they were from." Zack held his hands up in the air. "Hell, Tim, they might have been from Taiwan or Japan or China. I just don't know."

Marshall shook his head back and forth. "Asians! Damnit, Zack, that's crazy. Why would they be targeting SCS?"

"I don't know, Tim. But we've got to find out. The company's survival depends on it."

Kirkland, Washington

Cindy DeMorey was in her waterfront condominium. For over a week now she and her operatives had been secretly investigating the Zackary Scott family. They had come up dry. Zack's wife and two boys were not in town. All they had been able to learn was that they were somewhere on vacation. Consequently, for all practical purposes, Zack's immediate family members were untouchable at this point. But Cindy didn't give up. She kept searching.

She was sitting at her dining room table. A stack of old magazines, newspaper reprints, and professional journals were laid out in front of her. She had spent nearly two days accumulating the information. She scoured the main branch of the Seattle Library as well as several Eastside branches. But the real bonanza came from the University of Washington's library. There was a whole section in the engineering branch that dealt with Scott Coastal Systems and Zackary Scott. As an alumnus of the Mechanical Engineering Department, Scott had contributed many of SCS's technical manuals and research papers that dealt with offshore construction and deep diving. Cindy had no idea that Scott was so inventive. He had a dozen patents for various apparatuses, several of which were earning handsome royalties.

As much as the technical information helped explain SCS's strong financial condition and world-class stature as a diving contractor, it was an obscure article in an offshore construction bimonthly magazine that really made Cindy sit up straight. It was an interview with Scott. She reread the critical passages:

Q: We understand that your daughter is also following in your footsteps. Mind telling us more about that?

A: Wendy's a grad student at the University of Hawaii. She's studying oceanography.

Q: Have we an heir apparent in the wings?

A: *Laughing now.* Well, Wendy and I are good friends, but I don't think she has the slightest interest in working for SCS. She's really into the biological end of things. Offshore drilling and marine construction certainly aren't her cup of tea.

Cindy tossed the magazine back onto the table. *He has a daughter!*

This was news to her. The background reports on Scott provided by YHI only indicated that he had been briefly married before his current marriage. Cindy had been unaware that he had a twenty-three-year-old daughter.

I think I've finally found the leverage we need. Cindy reached for the phone.

Kaneohe Bay
Oahu, Hawaii

The twenty-foot-long Boston Whaler planed over the blue-green waters of Kaneohe Bay. The sun was just dipping behind the Koolau mountain range. Dark shadows would soon descend on the northeastern shore of Oahu. The young woman seated at the center console wasn't concerned about the approaching night. She had made the same run dozens of times, many after sunset. She guided the craft toward the marina, lining up with several landmarks.

Wendy Alissa Scott had finished her work for the day and was looking forward to an evening of relaxation. Although she was tired—working with the captured sharks in the holding tanks was always demanding—she thoroughly loved her work. Wendy was a graduate student, a Ph.D. candidate in biological oceanography at the University of Hawaii. Her specialty was the physiology of reef sharks. Much of her research work was conducted at the university's marine laboratory on Moku O Loe. The tiny island, locally known as Coconut Island, was situated in the middle of Kaneohe Bay, about half a mile offshore.

Wendy loved the water, and it was only natural for her to pursue a career in oceanography. Her fascination with the sea had started back in Washington State—in the San Juan Islands. Many of her summer vacations were spent cruising through the archipelago with her father and his second family. The rest of the year she lived in Los Angeles with her mother and stepfather.

Wendy throttled back and let the fiberglass runabout glide forward. The floating pier was about thirty feet away. A few seconds later she maneuvered the boat along the edge of the dock. After shutting down the outboard and securing the bow and stern lines she started down the main walk, heading for shore. *I wonder where Dan is?* she thought.

Wendy spotted Dan Wallace just as she stepped off the gangway onto the land. The twenty-eight-year-old man wheeled into the gravel parking lot, braking his ancient VW convertible to an abrupt halt. A cloud of dust rolled from under the vehicle and sailed across the lot toward a dozen parked cars. They were already covered by a thin film of dirt.

Wallace turned off the engine and unsnapped his seat belt. His yellow Bug ran well, but it looked its age. The tropical salt air was hard on all vehicles. He climbed over the driver's side of the car, his long legs easily scaling the distance. His door was inoperable, the result of an accident with another vehicle a couple of months ago—his fault. Wallace didn't have collision insurance and couldn't afford to get it fixed.

"Hi, darling," he called out as he walked toward Wendy. Unconsciously, he reached up with his right hand and brushed a thick lock of light brown hair from his forehead. He looked like a California surfer. "You just come ashore?" he asked.

"Yeah, your timing is perfect."

Dan leaned forward to kiss her. Wendy was only five foot five while he towered over her at six foot four. As their lips touched Dan couldn't help but think how lucky he was. *God she's beautiful!*

Wendy Scott was, indeed, a real beauty. Her near-perfectly sculptured face and long blond hair could have graced any popular magazine cover. And her trim body, tanned by the Hawaiian sun and toughened by her hours of in-water research, was tantalizingly firm.

"Well, how was your day?" Dan asked as they started back to the VW.

"Good, I think we'll be able to save Arby." Wendy named all of her sharks, treating them as individuals rather than numbering them as some of the other researchers did. She tried to personalize everything she did.

"Arby, which one is that?"

"He's the little blue. Remember, I told you about him;

someone speared him and then let him loose. A couple of undergrads found him circling on the surface off of Lanikai.''

''Oh yeah, now I remember.'' He lied. Dan couldn't keep any of Wendy's creatures straight. He hated all sharks, especially the small ones. One of his diving partners had lost half of his foot to a shark in the Marshall Islands. The baby tiger, only three and a half feet long, attacked without warning. It was just fate that Dan's companion had been maimed. It could have just as easily been him.

Dan opened the passenger side of the VW—that door still worked—and Wendy slipped inside. A minute later they were driving through Kaneohe, heading for the coast highway. Wendy and Dan lived together in a tiny rental house just outside of Kahaluu. The hillside cottage had a wonderful view of the ocean.

''So how's the program coming?'' Wendy asked.

''Okay. I think I've finally got the bugs out.''

''That's great. Then you'll be able to finish your dissertation this summer.''

''Yeah, maybe. But there's still a lot more work to do.'' Wallace was also a doctoral candidate, but not in oceanography. He was an ocean engineer. His specialty was studying the complex interaction of large ocean wave forces on submerged structures. Part of his research grant was funded by the U.S. Navy, the rest by a consortium of oil companies.

''Well, you're still a lot closer to finishing than I am.''

''We'll see,'' he replied.

Dan drove through the outskirts of Kaneohe and then pulled onto the coast highway. He shifted into fourth gear and stepped on the throttle. The VW groaned as it accelerated. The air flowing over the windscreen blew his long hair back along his head, making it look like it was glued to his scalp. Wendy's golden hair, however, billowed around her face. It looked sexy—like when a professional photographer deliberately directs a fan onto a model's face.

''You hear anything more about your dad?'' Wallace asked, turning briefly to glance at Wendy's face and then back to the road.

''No, only what we've read in the papers.''

''Well, it sounds like they've cleaned up the oil spill, and from what I've heard around the campus, the environmental damage doesn't sound too bad.''

''I hope so.''

Dan remained silent for about half a minute before again speaking. ''You know, Wendy, it was just an accident. Your father didn't mean for that well to blow out.''

''I know that,'' she snapped back. Dan was on very sensitive ground. Wendy had never thought much about her father's business until all the controversy erupted over his plans to drill for oil off the Washington coastline. She had been working on her master's at Stanford when the first hearings were convened. All of the West Coast environmental groups were opposed. Even a few of her professors voiced their concerns over the proposal.

After moving to Hawaii, Wendy remained isolated from most of the controversy—she was immersed in her research work and Washington State was so far away. Nevertheless, she confronted her father during one of her first Christmas breaks from the islands. On her way back to Los Angeles to visit her mother, she stopped off in Seattle. She stayed with her father and his other family for three days. During one heated debate with her father, she did her best to pin him down. In the end, Zack promised that the drilling program at the Hammer tract would be the safest in the world and that not one drop of oil would be spilled.

Wendy finally broke the silence; she had said it before: ''Dan, he lied to me. My own father lied to me.''

''Come on, honey, I can't believe that. It had to be an accident—maybe even an act of God.''

''Bullshit! The papers say it was gross operator negligence—not an accident.''

''That's just press talk—the official investigations won't be finished for months. I know your dad—he's one of the most careful people around.'' He paused to look at her. ''Just like you.''

''Yeah,'' replied Wendy, ''but all I know is that several hundred thousand gallons of crude oil were spilled. It fouled up everything along the Olympic Coast. The worst oil spill in the Northwest and my father's company did it.''

''But it's basically all cleaned up now—everything's okay.''

"They won't have any idea of the environmental damage for years, and I'll bet that stuff will be haunting the coast for decades, just like after the *Exxon Valdez* mess."

Dan Wallace remained silent. He could see where this conversation was heading—just like all the others. Wendy's environmental advocacy seemed to be increasing by the day, especially after any new publicity about the Hammer 4 blowout. She kept most of it locked up inside, however. Only Dan and a few others in Hawaii knew that her father was Zackary Scott, owner of Scott Coastal Systems. Wendy never mentioned her family's wealth or glorified her father's exalted position in the offshore construction profession; since early childhood she had been reared not to make a big deal about money or to brag about Zack's business successes.

After the disaster at the oil well site, Wendy clammed up even more than normal; she was too embarrassed to admit that Zackary Scott was her father. Dan could still recall with clarity her tirade of a few days earlier: "Here I am, trying in my own small way to save the environment, and there's my big shot father, back on the mainland, dumping crude oil into the ocean and acting like it's no big deal!"

Dan downshifted into third gear as he started up a steep grade. He again glanced at Wendy. She was staring off to the right, looking at the ocean. He could tell she was still thinking about her father and the oil spill. *I've got to get her mind off this thing or she'll end up hating him forever, and he doesn't deserve that—no father does.*

"Say, honey, what do you say we stop off at the Tide's for pizza and beer? Maybe shoot a few games of pool. We could even do a little dancing when the band shows up."

Wendy turned back to face Dan. She was smiling. They hadn't been on a real date for months—they both worked too hard. "That sounds great! Besides, I don't think we have much in the refrigerator anyway."

Dan reached over with his long right arm and gently squeezed her shoulder. "All right!" he said. "Now, prepare yourself, my dear, because we're going to have a hell of a good time tonight."

And they did.

18

THE DOCKING

Off Hokkaido Island

The gray-black hull prowled the depths like a prehistoric creature. It remained perpetually in the dark, never seeing the light of day. Nearly a fifth of a mile in length and over two hundred feet wide, the *Shikoku* was the largest submarine ever constructed. It had been in continuous service for almost three years. It was now on the final leg of its latest transpacific crossing.

"Have you picked up the beacon yet?" asked the compactly built man as he walked toward the high-tech electronic console.

The man sitting behind the impressive instrument panel turned in his swivel chair to face the *Shikoku*'s master. "Aye, Captain. We acquired the signal about five minutes ago."

"Then everything is ready?"

"Affirmative. We should be at the outer marker in about half an hour."

"Very well, proceed to Docking Point One at normal speed. Then I'll take her in manually."

"Aye, sir. Continue under computer control to Docking Point One."

Captain Mishima stepped away from the navigator's console and returned to his command chair. His perch allowed him to efficiently monitor all of the tiny control room's principal stations from one location. The bridge crew's consoles were laid out in a horseshoe pattern centered around his position. Besides the navigator, there was the propulsion officer, the diving officer, the environment officer, the sonar officer, and the tankmaster.

Positioned directly in front of Mishima was the submarine's helm. But no one manned the symbolic steering wheel station. Instead, the collection of computers housed in a compartment directly behind the bridge controlled the vessel. The human crew was only along for the ride, occasionally disengaging the computer controls to test the backup manual systems and to perform routine maintenance.

Mishima was still amazed that his monster-sized vessel—nearly as big as an aircraft carrier—could be controlled by so few men. And the ship's designers repeatedly bragged to him that their next version would be fully automated, requiring no crew at all. But he didn't believe that for a minute. Humans would always be aboard. Besides, hadn't he already proved his worth? The encounter with the American submarine during the first half leg of the voyage had been a perfect example. No computer could have evaded the hunter-killer with the speed and skill that he and his crew demonstrated. *Fully automated—what bullshit!*

"Captain," called out the sonar officer. "I'm holding a steady contact on Docking Point One."

"What's our range?"

"We're five kilometers out."

"Depth?"

"Four hundred and ten meters, ascending under computer control at a rate of ten meters per minute. Speed remains at ten knots."

"Good, continue as you were."

In just a couple of minutes Captain Mishima would step up to the helm and personally maneuver the behemoth into its underwater slip.

After four weeks at sea and a journey that had covered over sixteen thousand kilometers, Captain Mishima was looking forward to shore leave. With any luck he'd catch the company shuttle from Nemuro to Tokyo International. And six hours later he'd be relaxing on the beach in front of the firm's Hawaiian compound. Located on the leeward shore of Oahu near

Diamond Head, the six-acre site and five hundred feet of sandy beach that came with it were pure heaven. Only top company officers, like Mishima and the other skippers, were accorded the privileged quarters. The rest of the crew would be flown to company-owned resorts on Okinawa.

Captain Mishima closed his eyes and envisioned the Hawaiian seashore. He could hear the beat of the pounding surf and smell the salty air. He missed the sea. Despite the fact that he was surrounded by the Pacific Ocean, he had not once laid his own eyes on it since starting the voyage.

"Sir, the *Shikoku* is now at the final marker."

The Nemuro operations manager looked up from the stack of papers on his desk. The young woman standing in front of him was distractingly attractive. She had a cute face with long, silky black hair that cascaded onto her shoulders. It was the seductive curves of her uniform, however, that really caught his attention. He was a breast man, and her amble bosom, unusual for a Japanese woman, was like a magnet to him. He often fantasized about her, but she was untouchable. Her husband also worked on the artificial island. Besides, extramarital affairs were strictly forbidden by company policy. And he wouldn't do anything to jeopardize his position.

"Have you dispatched the tugs?" he asked.

"Yes, sir. They're on the way right now and should be lining up in about five minutes."

"Good, inform the reservoir manager that we'll be ready for offloading within the hour."

"Yes, sir," replied the woman as she turned to leave the manager's office.

He caught himself staring at her backside as she walked through the door. *Damn, she's even got a great rear end!*

"Sir, *Bronco One* and *Bronco Two* are now in position."

"Very well, let's proceed with the docking," replied Captain Mishima. He was sitting at the helm console, staring at a three-dimensional video display screen. The computer-generated image looked like a Nintendo game. The boxlike frame of white lines that repeatedly blinked onto the outer perimeter of the screen and then traveled toward the center created a tunnellike image. A graphic representation of the *Shikoku*'s bow was in the foreground.

Mishima reached for a nearby microphone. *"Bronco One, Bronco Two, this is Shikoku."*

"Go ahead, *Shikoku*," came the instant reply, both submersibles responding at the same time.

"Stand by to slave your computers to ours."

"Bronco One ready."

"Bronco Two ready."

"Very well, taking control now." Mishima triggered a series of switches on his panel. Ten seconds later he had complete propulsion control over the two sub tugs that were moored to hard points on either side of the *Shikoku*'s bow. He now controlled the two-thousand-horsepower electric drive motors on each tug.

For the next ten minutes Captain Mishima expertly guided his vessel into position, using a combination of alternating bow thrusts from the tugs and the *Shikoku*'s own stern-mounted jet drives. He could have let the computer do all the work, but he wasn't about to give up the one cherished duty that set him apart from the crew. He would berth the ship himself!

When Mishima finished, the bow of the thousand-foot-long submarine was moored to a towerlike structure that rose sixty meters above the ocean bottom. Free to swing with the tidal currents that flowed across the seabed, the *Shikoku* looked like an enormous underwater version of a blimp.

"Docking maneuver complete," called out Mishima as he shut down the helm controls. *"Bronco One*, you are cleared to disengage and return to base."

"Roger, *Bronco One* disengaging."

"Bronco Two, disengage your mooring and then redock with our command module."

"Affirmative, *Shikoku*, we'll be locked on to you in ten minutes."

Captain Mishima stepped away from the helm, moving to the tankmaster's console. The engineering officer was busy punching in a series of commands on his keyboard. "Shintaro, are you ready to start pumping?"

"Almost, Captain. The prime movers are coming on-line right now. And the compensating ballast system is all set."

"Good. How long will the transfer take?"

The officer typed in a few keystrokes and then scanned the CRT screen. "Ah, sir, the computer estimates that it'll take about eighteen hours to detank the vessel."

"That's a little shorter than normal, isn't it—especially with a full load?"

"Yes, sir. But the viscosity of the product is slightly lower so it'll flow faster."

"Well, every bit helps."

"Yes, sir."

The *Shikoku* was late. The unscheduled course change during the first leg of the Pacific crossing—the result of the encounter with the American sub—had cost Mishima almost three full sailing days. He had never been late before, not once during his twenty-two voyages as captain.

Mishima returned to his cabin and began packing his overnight bag. Besides his clothing, there were only a few personal items to retrieve. He commanded the ship only part-time. Another captain, along with a fresh crew, would board the ship tomorrow. Once the cargo was off-loaded, the *Shikoku* would once again head back to sea.

Captain Mishima was now topside, sitting in a spacious office. The door to the compartment was closed. The manager of the Nemuro Oil Complex was sitting next to him. Both men had just lit up cigarettes and the room was beginning to fill with smoke.

"Well, Captain, how was your trip?" asked the manager.

"Long."

"So I gather—three days longer than usual."

"Yes, we were forced to take evasive action this time."

The manager sat up straight in his chair. "What do you mean evasive action?"

"We were briefly tracked. An American submarine—Los Angeles class—stumbled across our path on the way out, about three thousand kilometers northeast of Hawaii."

"Are you sure it tracked you?"

"Yes, they pinged with their active sonar for several hours. I'm sure they picked up a couple of solid reflections before we managed to lose them."

"Damnit, this complicates matters."

"I know, but what could I do? That sub was waiting for us. It was deep—near its maximum limit." He flipped the end of his cigarette into an ashtray on the manager's desk.

"But how could they know? We run so deep and quiet that even their best SOSUS gear can't hear us."

"I don't know. Maybe it was just a fluke—they could have been waiting for a Russian or Chinese boat. They sometimes patrol in that area."

The manager turned to stare at a large map of the Pacific Ocean basin; it was taped to a nearby bulkhead wall. "You're sure you lost them," he said as he turned back to face Mishima.

"Absolutely. We went real deep—to the max. We then headed south for a day and a half before turning back to the base course."

"Well, thank the gods that you were able to evade them. That was too close." The manager paused momentarily as he recalled an old warning. "Captain, I guess your earlier recommendation to stagger the courses has merit after all."

Mishima smiled, just a little. "It'll cost another day or so of sailing time, but in light of what happened I think it'll be well worth it. Otherwise, all they'd have to do is track us just once on the return trip and they will know exactly where we're going."

The manager nodded. "Yes, I'll make the recommendation to the board. I'm sure they'll go along with your plan this time."

"Good, that should help a lot."

Captain Mishima stood up and snuffed out his cigarette on the heel of his shoe. After dropping the butt into a wastebasket he walked to the far side of the compartment and peered through one of the half dozen portholes. Ominous-looking black clouds were forming on the horizon. The howling wind blew the whitecaps right off the heavy swells that rolled in from the east. "Looks like a new storm is brewing," he commented.

"Yes, Captain. It started up this morning."

"Another typhoon?" asked Mishima.

"Right now it's just classified as a storm. But it has the potential to turn nasty."

"What are they calling it this time?"

The manager searched through a pile of papers on his desk. Half a minute later he retrieved a single sheet of computer-generated output data. The weather report was updated every couple of hours from on-line data supplied by orbiting Japanese and American satellites, as well as dozens of specially designed weather buoys moored across the Pacific. The two nations shared the data but each prepared its own forecast. The manager scanned the data sheet. "Our people are calling this one storm number three-seven."

"And the Americans?" asked Mishima.

The manager again looked down at the paper. Rather than using a logical numerical system to keep track of the ocean storms, the Americans named them after people, alternating between the female and male gender. *How strange,* he thought. *Naming acts of nature after mere mortals. What barbarians!* A few seconds later he found the part of the text he'd been searching for. He struggled with the English pronunciation of the word. "ZAK-R-Y," he said. "They are calling this storm Zackary."

North Pacific Ocean

The *Deepquestor* rolled slowly from port to starboard, reacting to the huge ocean swells that boiled under its towering decks. The SCS drilling rig was running westward through the storm-racked sea, heading for the Kuril Islands. It was just an hour after sunrise.

Captain Ian Flynn was on the bridge, sitting in his command chair, sipping a steaming hot mug of coffee. The fifty-two-year-old professional sailor had been on the bridge all night, mothering the semisubmersible through the worst part of the storm. His body spilled out of the leather padded chair. At six foot three and 220 pounds, Flynn was a big man. Although his size was impressive, his most prominent feature was his face. His long pointed beard and bushy hair made him look like he belonged on the stage with the rockers from ZZ Top.

Flynn took another sip and then glanced to his side. His navigator was huddled over the chart table, updating the vessel's position. Adjacent to the chart table was the vessel's helm. But the steering station wasn't manned. It didn't need to be. Flynn could dial a course and speed change right from the console that was built into the right armrest of his chair. The *Deepquestor*'s bridge was completely computerized. It took only two men to control the aircraft carrier–size ship.

Captain Flynn again faced forward. The view through the wheelhouse windows, nearly 120 feet above the sea surface, was a blur of gray sky and green water. At times the crests of the mountainous seas looked as if they were almost level with the bridge.

"Jesus, what a bitch of a day," called out a voice from behind Flynn's chair. It was the rig's toolpusher. Pete Miller had a death grip on the stainless steel grab rail next to the chart table. The forty-eight-year-old engineer had just walked onto the bridge from the adjacent galley.

Flynn turned in his chair. "Ah, Pete, this ain't so bad. Last year in the North Sea we—"

"Fuck the North Sea! We're in a goddamn typhoon." Miller was right. For nearly twenty-four hours Typhoon Zackary had been hammering northern Japan and the southern Kurils, especially the waters off Hokkaido. It wasn't a particularly big storm, unless you were caught in it, of course.

Miller moved a few steps forward, continuing to brace himself against the rolling deck. He stopped opposite Flynn. "When's this shit going to stop?"

Flynn laughed. Miller was a hell of an oilman, but a lousy seaman. "The good news, Pete, is that it should blow itself out by noon."

"It's about time. Then maybe I can eat something that will stay down."

"But the bad news," continued Flynn, "is that the seas won't die down till later tonight."

"Shit, you mean we've got to put up with this crap for another day?"

"Maybe not." Flynn swiveled his chair to face the navigator sitting at a console a few feet away. "Bill," he called out, "what's it look like?"

"Captain, we're right on course. If we continue at this speed and heading, we'll be opposite the strait in six hours."

"Good." Flynn turned back toward Miller.

"Well, Pete, maybe you'll get to eat lunch after all. We're on the final leg of our approach to Friz Strait. Once we get past the southern tip of Urup, I plan to turn north. We'll be in the lee of the island by then and things should calm down."

"Fantastic. That'll make my day."

"Good, now why don't you try to get some more sack time until then. Our contacts should be flying out sometime late this afternoon."

"Yeah, okay." Miller was just starting aft when a new thought popped into his mind. He turned around. "Say, skip, how the hell are we going to talk with those turkeys—none of us speak any Russian."

"Jerry Dixon's already with them. He flew into Magadan last week and has been setting everything up. He even has a helo standing by in Podgornoye."

"Okay, good, but what about Zack? You think he might come out here after all?"

"I'm not sure—normally he would. But with all the trouble the company's been having back home I doubt he'll show up."

"Ah shit, that's too bad."

"Yeah, I know. I don't think he's ever missed one of SCS's inaugural spud-ins for a new field. Says it brings him luck."

"Well, I guess there's a first time for everything."

Thirty-five miles southeast of the *Deepquestor,* another vessel plowed into the savage seas. The frigate was taking a beating from the waves. The warship's captain, like Ian Flynn, had been up all night. But his tenure had been much more demanding than the American's. Unlike the semisubmersible that rode the heavy seas fairly well, the 298-foot-long patrol vessel wallowed unmercifully from side to side, like a bucking bronco.

The captain of the vessel was now certain of the radar target's destination. It was time to act. He keyed his intercom mike. "Communications, Bridge."

"Communications," came the instant reply.

"This is the captain. I have a message that I want sent to headquarters."

"Open circuit or secure, sir?"

"Encrypted. Now here's what I want . . ."

Fifteen minutes later the secret message was broadcast upward to a geostationary satellite. It was instantly bounced backward to earth. A special receiving station in Japan's Maritime Self-Defense Forces headquarters in Tokyo intercepted the signal. A computer automatically began decoding the message.

Hiroshi Yoshida was still at his residence when an assistant to the defense minister called. Normally, Yoshida would have never talked with such a low-level government official. But the minister himself was out of the country, attending a conference in Singapore.

"Mr. Yoshida, I have disturbing news this morning," the caller said.

"What is the problem?"

"The Americans! They are moving a drilling vessel into the Friz Strait area."

"What?"

"One of our frigates picked up the drilling vessel this morning. It is heading directly for the southern end of Urup Island."

"Have the Russians said anything?"

"No, nothing. But then they never inform us of any of their vessel movements anyway."

"Are you sure it's a drilling rig?"

"Positively. We just had a patrol aircraft fly over the vessel. They reported sighting a floating drilling vessel—a semisubmersible."

"Have you identified it?"

"Not yet. We'll be analyzing the aerial photos in the next couple of hours. But it was definitely an American vessel—the crew spotted U.S. markings on the hull." The bureaucrat paused momentarily as a new thought struck him. "Oh, there's one other thing. The flight crew reported seeing the letters S-C-S painted onto the helipad."

"S-C-S?" Yoshida struggled to control his emotions.

"Yes, we don't yet know what it stands for."

Yoshida quickly changed the subject. "Do you have any idea if this vessel is just passing through or is it planning to drill near the strait?"

"I don't know yet. Maybe in a few hours I'll have an answer." The man paused. "By the way, if they do start drilling on the Russian side of the strait, what do you think their chances will be of hitting oil?"

"Hard to tell at this point. They've tried a number of times before and have come up with nothing but dry holes."

"Can't say that I blame them. With all of that oil on our side of the line, it must be very tempting to see if any of it stretches onto their side."

"Yes, you're right."

"Well, I thought you would like to know about the sighting. We'll keep track of that rig and let you know what it is up to."

"Thank you. We appreciate your concern."

"Of course, sir. Your Nemuro Complex is one of our most important national assets. You can be assured that we will continue to protect it with all of the means we have available."

Hiroshi Yoshida hung up the phone. *S-C-S. That bastard Scott again. When will I be rid of him?*

19

LOST AT SEA

Seattle

Since returning from his mini-vacation in Montana, Zackary Scott had immersed himself in the day-to-day operations of SCS. Much of his time during the past week had been spent coordinating the final cleanup work for the Hammer 4 blowout. He had also spent a lot of time with the firm's attorneys, reviewing potential liability claims from the oil spill. And today, Zack was reviewing a series of cash flow projections for the firm. The company was losing money like water through a leaky pipe. The federal government's refusal to re-open the Hammer lease tract for drilling was the principal cause of SCS's financial grief.

Zack had read about half of the Coastal Construction Division's operating report when he was interrupted.

"Excuse me, Zack," Tim Marshall said. He was standing in the open doorway to Zack's office. "If you've got a minute, I have some good news for a change."

Zackary Scott looked up, making eye contact with his executive vice president. "Come on in, Tim. I'll take good news any way it comes."

Marshall walked toward Zack. He sat down in one of the two black leather chairs facing the desk. He held a coffee mug in his right hand. The red letters S C S were embossed on its side. "I just talked with Ian Flynn. The *Deepquestor*'s moored and they plan to spud in sometime tomorrow morning, our time.''

Zack smiled. ''I'll be damned. That storm didn't slow 'em up much, did it?''

''Nope. And many of the weather pros thought that blow would turn into a major typhoon. But instead, it just kind of fizzled out.'' Marshall paused, remembering that the storm had been officially named Zackary. He smiled at his boss as he continued. ''Sorry, Zack, but your namesake turned out to be just a plain old run-of-the-mill typhoon. Not the ripsnorter I expected.''

''That suits me just fine. All I need is more problems with one of the rigs.''

''I know. But I think everything's okay with this project.''

''Has Jerry shown up yet?'' asked Scott.

''Yeah, he and old Boris Zarkaroff heloed out last night. The supply vessel's due in today sometime.''

''I hope our Russian partners come through with the drill pipe and mud or we've wasted a lot of money.''

''I know what you mean.'' Tim paused to sip from his cup. ''Ian also said that, according to Jerry, the Russians loaded over thirty thousand feet of drill string and a couple hundred tons of chemicals onto their service boat and scow.''

''Well, that should be enough. I assume we'll use our own casing.''

''Yep, that was all loaded aboard plus another ten thousand feet of drill collars.''

''Good, then we should be in good shape.''

Marshall nodded his head as he continued to sip his coffee.

Zack grabbed a handful of papers on his desk, placing them in his Out basket. He then looked back at Marshall. ''You know, Tim, I just don't understand why our Russian friends insisted on spudding in the first well on their side of the Friz Strait. We should be working up around Sakhalin. The geophysical reports are much more favorable up there.''

''I agree, Zack. They've already drilled six damn dry holes off the southern tip of Urup, but it was their call. They still have the leases down there and according to our agreement, they choose half of the sites.''

''I know. I guess in a way I can't blame them. With all that oil on the other end of the Kurils, the temptation is just too great not to try one more time.''

"Well, maybe we'll find something. The Japanese can't have all the luck." Marshall took another sip of coffee.

Scott glanced at a new map tacked on the wall next to his desk. It depicted the northern half of Japan and the adjoining Kuril Island chain. A series of red dots was inked onto the map, each dot representing one of the ten exploratory wells the *Deepquestor* would drill over the next two years. *I must be crazy to be doing this,* Zack thought as he studied the map. *Joint venturing with a bunch of ex-Communists who haven't got a dime to their name.* Zack next focused on a fat blue circle several inches below the red dot marking the *Deepquestor*'s current position. It identified the Nemuro oil fields.

Zack turned away from the map to face his friend. "You know, Tim, that whole Nemuro operation still mystifies me. For all those years Japan was so dependent on imported oil and then it turns out they have almost as much oil as the North Sea right in their own damn backyard.''

"Yeah, I know what you mean. They seem to be getting all the breaks lately.''

"But it doesn't make any sense. The old surveys over that area never suggested anything as big as they've got." Zack paused to once again examine the wall map. "I would have expected some pockets of gas, and maybe some crude, but nothing like the magnitude of the Nemuro find.''

"But they've got an elephant there, Zack. They continue to pump out at least a half million barrels every day, and according to their press releases, the reservoir has at least thirty more years of production left.''

"Yeah, I know all that, but how could they be so lucky?''

"Geez, Zack, you know as well as I do that wildcatting, especially offshore, is risky as hell. And we're doing real good if one out of ten holes produces." Marshall shifted his lower body to a more comfortable position in the chair. "Even though our remote sensing gear is good—as good as it comes—plain old luck is still our best ally.''

"But such a huge find in an area that had been repeatedly explored before the Russians sold it back to the Japanese— I'm still having a hard time with that.''

"Well, don't let that bug you too much—it'll drive you wacky. Besides, we've got our own elephant. It's not as big as Nemuro, but it's right in our own backyard."

Zack smiled. "Yeah, you're right, Tim. I even wrote off the Washington coast until some of our own people convinced me to give it another look. They were sure right."

"You bet they were, but they only had a hunch—the data was inconclusive. It was your decision to spend the company's money—your money," he corrected, "to check it out. So, by all accounts you're the lucky one!"

"I'm not so sure about all that—remember, we lost the damn well."

"But that's just a temporary setback. The spill's all cleaned up and I'll bet we'll be back on site within a couple of months."

Scott appreciated Marshall's encouragement. His VP was working hard to boost Zack's morale. It was helping, but Zack still harbored fears that SCS was in deep trouble.

"Well, Tim, maybe you're right. But we're still not out of the woods with the blowout."

Marshall nodded while setting his half-full mug on the coffee table. He looked back up at Zack. "What's the latest on our hearing date?" he asked.

"It still hasn't been scheduled. The MMS attorneys hinted to our legal people that they might hold it in December."

"That's not as bad as we originally thought."

"No, but there's something else going on behind the scenes that's really starting to bother me."

Marshall leaned forward in his chair, his attention piqued. "What are you talking about?"

"I got a call from Senator Allen's chief of staff yesterday afternoon. Apparently some of our competitors are really starting to smell blood. They've been making quiet inquiries to certain congressional delegations about taking over our lease."

"The bastards, they can't do that—MMS decides those issues."

"That's right," Zack said, "but you know how the system works. A couple of powerful senators and representatives making a few phone calls to the right people in the executive branch and bingo, we're out on our ass."

"But the Hammer 4 lease can only be cancelled if they prove we were negligent."

"Correct, and our attorneys are telling me that we're vulnerable as hell right now unless—"

"Unless we find the damn BOP," interrupted Marshall.

"Yep."

"I assume there's no news on that front?"

"That's right, Tim. We're still searching but haven't found a damn thing yet. It's like looking for the proverbial needle in the haystack."

"Then if we can't find it in time, how are we going to defend ourselves at the hearings?"

Zack shook his head from side to side. "Tim, I'll be damned if I know."

Yokohama

"Well, Commander, how about we drop it off right about here?"

Commander Jeffrey Hashimoto stared at the chart of Yokohama Harbor. Even though the map's text was printed in Japanese, he recognized where the man's finger was pointing. "I don't know if that'll work or not. Can't you get it closer than that?"

"That's risky. The buoy's not very big and it's painted black, but someone might spot it from shore. If they send out a boat to check, the jig'll be up for sure."

"How much cable have you got on the reel?"

"Oh, there's two thousand feet on it—plenty to get in from there."

Hashimoto looked up from the map, turning his head so he could look out of the cabin window. He was inside the wheelhouse of a U.S. Navy fleet tug. It was slowly making its way up the main waterway of Yokohama Harbor, heading for a berth at a repair facility leased by the American government. Jeff raised a set of night vision binoculars to his eyes and scanned the shoreline. The target was coming up on the port side, about four hundred yards away. A moment later he turned back to the man. "What about other vessel traffic in the channel? If we drop it off there someone might run over it.''

''That's always a possibility, but there won't be too much traffic tonight. We checked all the shipping schedules. Nothing big should be moving through here till about sunrise.''

''Well, Chief, I'd feel more comfortable if we could get closer, but you know the harbor—I sure don't.'' Jeff paused as he looked back at the map. ''So let's go ahead and deploy it where you suggested. The tide will be slack in about an hour. That will give enough time to get set up.''

''Aye, aye, sir,'' replied the chief petty officer. ''I'll set it up right now.'' He reached across the hardwood table, switching off the small incandescent light that illuminated the chart. Five seconds later he disappeared down a steep ladderwell that led to the tug's interior spaces. The fifty-one-year-old sailor would be very busy for the next five minutes.

Hashimoto stepped away from the chart table and moved forward, taking up a position by the helmsman. The wheelhouse was rigged for night running. The only illumination came from the red lanterns that ringed the windscreen. He looked forward, over the bow. Yoshida Heavy Industries' shipbuilding complex was coming into view. *I sure hope this works,* he thought.

Kaneohe Bay, Hawaii

Wendy Scott advanced the throttle and the Boston Whaler blasted across the glassy water surface. The early morning air was still and the ocean unusually quiet. The rollers were low and slow.

It was half an hour after sunrise. Wendy was alone in the University of Hawaii research vessel, commonly identified as Boat 6. She was heading down the coast from Kaneohe Bay to her principal observation station offshore of Wailea Point. Sharks, like many other species of fish, tended to feed during certain times of the day. The early morning hours were particularly popular around Wailea.

Wendy planned to anchor the skiff over a fifty-foot-deep coral reef opposite Mokulua Island, where she would lower a remotely controlled television camera over the side. The TV device, built by her father's company, allowed Wendy to record the shark's feeding habits without having to dive into the melee.

She dropped the anchor a few minutes after seven o'clock, using her fathometer and two line-of-sight reference points on the mainland to pinpoint the mooring point. Then, as the twenty-foot-long runabout rode the gentle swells, she prepared her equipment for deployment. She first triggered the ignition switch on the portable generator. The three-thousand-watt Honda power plant started up without hesitation. Despite the muffler system, the gasoline engine was noisy, drowning out the surrounding sea sounds.

Wendy ignored the noise as she readied the camera unit. Housed in an acrylic sphere that was rated for twenty atmospheres of pressure, the Sony minicam was in perfect working order. She activated the electric winch on the Whaler's built-in steel davit, hoisting the 120-pound camera assembly until it was suspended a foot above the gunwale. Next, she pushed on the J-shaped davit arm, rotating the camera until it was over the water. A few seconds later she began lowering the device; a three-quarter-inch thick bundle of power and control cables trailed behind, paying out from a three-foot-diameter reel that was mounted to the deck next to the engine compartment.

The camera unit "landed" on the bottom almost exactly where Wendy had planned. The observation point was located on a tiny coral head that cantilevered over the steep outer reef edge. She knew the site like the back of her hand. It was perfect for observing sharks as they made their way up from the depths, chasing their prey into the shallower waters.

After verifying that the camera's remote controls were functioning normally, Wendy began preparing to take her observations. First, she donned a pair of Bose headphones. The tiny speakers inside each earpiece were linked directly to the camera's hydrophone. She liked to listen to the cacophony of underwater sounds when making her observations—it made her feel like she was diving. Besides, the thick padding on the outside of the headphones muffled the oppressive generator noise.

Wendy next draped a black nylon sheet over the color television monitor and her upper body. The hood blocked out

most of the unwanted sunlight, allowing her to watch the
screen without having to fight the glare. The setup looked like
one of those old-time cameras where the photographer stooped
behind a tripod-mounted camera with a black cape over his
head.

Perfect, thought Wendy as she adjusted the focus, using a
hand-held control unit to manipulate the camera. The water
clarity was exceptional this morning. The light hues of the
upper waters transcended into the rich, blue-green tones of the
depths. And there were fish everywhere. Yellow, red, silver
ones—every imaginable color, shape, and size. *Should be
plenty of good pickings today, boys. Now, where are you?*

Several hours later, Wendy Scott remained glued to the TV
monitor. Dozens of her subjects were patrolling across the
reef, scavenging for the remnants of a large grouper that had
been attacked by an even larger hammerhead shark. The ensuing feeding frenzy had reduced the three-hundred-pound animal to nothing more than a giant fish head. Torn fragments
of the white and red flesh from the brutal assault littered the
water column. They looked like snowflakes drifting with the
current.

Wendy didn't hear the forty-five-foot Bayliner as it made
its approach from the south. The throttled-down twin diesels
were barely audible above the background noise. The vessel's
stealth, however, wasn't necessary. Wendy Scott's headphones
masked all surface noises and the hood covering her head and
the television screen blocked all exterior views.

The small yacht pulled up next to the Boston Whaler's starboard side. The Bayliner's bulk completely blocked the view
of the tiny runabout from the distant shoreline. A moment
later, a man stepped lightly from the yacht onto the Whaler's
bow. The boat listed a few degrees under his weight. He then
stepped aft, moving to the generator's control panel.

Wendy was completely oblivious to the presence of the
boarder. But when he hit the kill switch on the Honda, everything changed.

"What the heck?" yelled Wendy as she looked at the blank
television monitor. Then she noticed the silence in her earphones. *Darn, the generator must be out of gas.*

Wendy pulled back the nylon covering. The sunlight was
overwhelming, forcing her to blink her eyes half a dozen times

to adjust to the brightness. And then she saw him. The man was squatting on the deck a few feet in front of the console. He was young, Wendy's age, and his build slight, but the muscles on his exposed arms and legs looked like thick ropes.

"Who the hell are you?" she yelled.

Dan Wallace was worried. It was five in the afternoon and Wendy still hadn't shown up.

Dan had arranged to meet her at the marina at four o'clock. When she didn't show, he sat down at a nearby picnic table and began studying a computer printout. Wendy was often late.

An hour later, when Wendy still hadn't turned up, Dan became concerned. He found a pay phone and called her laboratory office number. The phone rang nearly two dozen times before it was answered. "Shark Center, Jim Lampe here," called out a male voice over the phone.

Dan recognized the grad student's name. "Say, Jim, this is Dan Wallace calling. I'm looking for Wendy. Is she there?"

"Just a sec, Dan. I'll check." The man placed the handset on the table. He then went out to check the dock. He returned half a minute later. "Sorry, Dan, but Wendy's rig is still checked out. She must be working late."

Wallace's back stiffened. *Something's wrong!* He and Wendy were supposed to have dinner with one of her professors tonight. She would never forget about that. "Is there anyone else there who might have seen her today?"

"Gee, I don't think so. Everyone else took off earlier. I'm the only one around."

Dan's mind was racing a mile a minute. "Look, there's something very wrong here. Wendy was supposed to meet me well over an hour ago. So if she isn't even back to the lab by now, then she's in trouble."

"Yeah, I see what you're getting at. How can I help?"

"Look, I don't have any transportation. Could you come and pick me up? I think I know where she was going today so we can run out there and check. She might be out of fuel or have some kind of mechanical problem with the boat."

"Sure thing. I'll grab one of the Whalers right now and head back to the marina. Where do you want me to pick you up?"

"I'll be on the outer dock—please hurry."

"You got it."

Eighteen minutes later, Dan Wallace was aboard a Boston Whaler, speeding across Kaneohe Bay. The sun was beginning to fall behind the mountains.

At a quarter past six o'clock, Dan Wallace and Jim Lampe found Wendy's boat. It was right where it was supposed to be, firmly anchored to the reef. The underwater camera was still deployed; its umbilical cord hung over the runabout's gunwale like a garden hose. But Wendy wasn't aboard.

"Damnit," shouted Dan, "where the hell could she be?"

"Maybe she's diving—working on the equipment down below?" asked the student.

"No way. She never dives alone, especially at this site. It's loaded with sharks."

"Well, maybe the engine quit and she got a ride to shore from someone else."

"Yeah, that's got to be it."

Dan climbed aboard. He immediately grabbed the red fuel can near the outboard motor, lifting it six inches off the fiberglass deck. It was heavy. *Plenty of fuel.* He turned around and sat down in the helm chair. A moment later he turned the starter switch. The Evinrude fired up on the first turn. It purred like a tiger. He engaged the forward drive and the boat nudged forward. He slipped it back into neutral and turned to face Lampe.

"Jim, there's nothing wrong with this thing. It works fine."

The grad student remained silent for half a minute before speaking again. "Dan, I hate to say this, but maybe she fell in."

A chill swept through Wallace's body. The same thought had just occurred to him. He reached for the instrument console, punching the emergency channel on the VHF radio. He then picked up the microphone and depressed the Transmit switch. "Mayday, Mayday. This is Kaneohe Bay Research Vessel Six calling Coast Guard. Come in, please."

Zackary Scott was deep asleep when the phone next to his bed started beeping. He woke instantly. He then rolled to the side and switched on the wall-mounted lamp. The clock read 3:10 A.M. He reached for the receiver.

"Hello."

"Zack?"

"Yes, who the hell is this?" asked Scott, still groggy.

"Zack, it's Dan. Dan Wallace."

Scott's mind instantly focused. *Something's wrong,* he thought. "Oh, hi, Dan."

"I'm sorry to wake you," Dan said, "but I've got a problem here that you need to be aware of."

"What's the matter?"

"It's Wendy. She's missing."

Zack sat up straight in his bed. "What do you mean she's missing?"

"She was out conducting research today—solo—and never returned to the lab. I found her boat anchored off Wailea Point around six P.M., but she wasn't aboard."

"Wasn't aboard?"

"Yeah, we think she might have fallen overboard and was carried away by the current. It runs strong along that section of the coast."

"Jesus, why aren't you searching for her right now?"

"I am. I'm with the Coast Guard. Our chopper just returned to the base for refueling. I had a couple of minutes so I decided to call you."

"Just one chopper looking? That's not enough!"

"I know. We've got another Coast Guard helo joining in, plus two cutters are already searching. And the university's got a dozen Whalers out tonight as well."

Zack swung his legs over the side of the bed. "How long's she been missing?"

"We don't know for sure. She left early this morning. I didn't suspect anything was wrong until early this evening—when she didn't show up at the marina."

"Then she could have fallen over hours ago."

"That's right."

"How far offshore was the boat anchored?"

"About half a mile."

"Damn, then she could have been swept out to sea."

"I know. That's why we're expanding the search area. She's a hell of a strong swimmer and if she was wearing her life jacket, she'd be able to stay afloat for a long time."

"That's right, but she's got to be found soon or hypothermia will set in."

"I understand that, Zack. That's what worries me the most."

Zack stood up. While continuing to hold the phone handset, he slipped on a white terry cloth robe. "Okay, Dan. Sounds like you're doing everything you can, but if you need anything—more boats, civilian helos, whatever, you have carte blanche. My firm will guarantee payment for everything, just have them call the Seattle headquarters office for confirmation."

"Thanks, maybe at first light we could get some more eyes in the air."

"Do it—get whatever you need, don't worry about the cost." Zack started pacing back and forth across the room. "Now, I'm going to catch the first flight to Honolulu I can find. Until then push everyone to the limit. If we can find her in the next eight to twelve hours she's got a chance."

"Okay, Zack. I will."

As soon as the line cleared, Zack punched a series of numbers into the handset. The phone rang a dozen times before it was answered.

"Hello," answered an obviously annoyed voice.

"Finn, this is Zack."

"Geez, Zack, what the hell time is it?"

"It's early. Look, I don't have a lot of time but I need your help. Can you . . ."

The jumbo jet freighter touched down at Honolulu's Sand Island International Airport at quarter past seven A.M., local time. The sun was rising and the air temperature was a balmy seventy degrees.

Zack and Finn had hitched a ride on the cargo plane. Scott had called in a favor from a friend, arranging for passage on the only available early morning flight to Hawaii. After thanking the flight crew, Zack and Finn took a cab to the main terminal. Zack rented a new Lincoln from Hertz and set off for Kaneohe Bay. They arrived about fifty minutes later, delayed by rush hour traffic.

Zack stepped out of the driver's seat and searched the marina in the foreground. Finn was on the opposite side of the car, looking north toward the open bay. "That the island with the lab on it?" he asked as he pointed northward.

"Yep, but I don't see any of their runabouts. They usually have one or two at the dock."

"Well, what about one of these?" Finn asked, now pointing to a dozen boats tied up to a floating pier about fifty feet to their left

"They're privately owned—not part of the university."

"Well, just sit tight a minute and let me see what I can do."

Finn raced away.

Zack paced by the edge of the car. He was mad at himself. In his rush to get out of the airport he had forgotten to rent a portable cellular phone. He needed to find out what was happening. He searched the shoreline, looking for a pay phone. *There's one,* he said to himself. The booth was about a block away, next to the edge of the road. He started running. A minute later he was calling the island laboratory.

It took several attempts before Zack finally connected with someone at the Coconut Island lab who knew what was going on. The Coast Guard was concentrating the search off Makapuu Point. Dan Wallace was in one of the SAR choppers.

As Zack hung up he spotted Finn Sorenson standing next to the Lincoln. A moment later Finn saw Zack and began wildly waving his right arm. Zack raced toward his friend. "What's up?" he asked as he ran up to the Lincoln. He was slightly out of breath.

"I've got us a boat: a twenty-eight-foot Shamrock. It's right here. Fueled up, VHF radio, fathometer, Loran—the works."

"Does it have any charts?"

"Yep, full set for the entire island."

"Good, let's go."

Finn and Zack spent nearly ten hours endlessly searching the offshore waters. There were at least two dozen other vessels crisscrossing the search area. In the air, the Coast Guard helos continued to search, aided by a U.S. Marine Corps chopper from the Kanoe Air Station, three CAP spotter planes, and two charter helos. But there was no sign of Wendy. The official search would end at sunset.

"Zack, we're getting low on fuel. I think we should head back now."

"We've still got another hour of light. We'll stay out till then."

Finn didn't argue. *I'd feel the same way if it were my daughter.*

After the sun finally disappeared into the distant sea, Finn guided the Shamrock back to its home port. It powered into the marina on vapors.

Dan Wallace was waiting dockside. He helped fend off the boat as it docked.

When Zack stepped off the hull, the fatigue and tension of the long day finally caught up with him. Although his entire body ached, it was his heart that hurt the most—it was broken.

Dan walked forward and the two men embraced. There were tears in both sets of eyes.

"I'm sorry, Zack, we tried everything."

"I know."

"Honest to God, I just can't believe she's gone—it's not fair."

Zack remained silent, gently patting Dan's back.

Dan continued speaking. "I couldn't get the Coast Guard to continue the search—they said it was useless to go on."

"They did all they could, Dan. Don't blame 'em for stopping—they're just following their regulations."

Dan stepped away from Zack. He wiped the mist from his eyes. "What if she's still alive out there—drifting right now?"

During the slow trip back from the search area, Zack had objectively analyzed the situation. Wendy was probably gone by now. The chances of her surviving another night in the open ocean were dismal. If the cold hadn't sapped away her strength by now, then one of her sharks might have completed the task. He hated to think about that last possibility.

"Dan, we'll continue our own search in the morning. We'll get the planes and helos out at first light. All it takes is money."

Wallace smiled. "Good, I don't want to give up."

"I know. Neither do I."

Dan helped Finn and Zack tie up the boat. All three then climbed into the Lincoln and headed back toward Honolulu. They were going to stay in a hotel near the airport. At sunrise each one would board one of the charter aircraft or boats.

20

AN OFFER HE COULDN'T REFUSE

Honolulu

"Come on, Finn. Let's get going," Zackary Scott said as he stood by the car.

Finn Sorenson ran up to the Lincoln. "Sorry, Zack. I thought I left my shades in the room—they were in my coat pocket all along." He dangled a pair of mirrored sunglasses in the air.

"That's okay. I just want to get out on the water. I've got to know what happened to Wendy today—one way or the other."

"No sweat. I'm all set."

Both men climbed into the Lincoln Town Car. A minute later they pulled on to the Nimitz Highway heading for Honolulu International Airport. The early morning air was a sticky eighty-five degrees. There was no wind.

"Zack, why don't you take the helo this morning? I'll go out in the boat."

"Thanks, but no. I want both you and Dan in the air today. You guys have a lot better eyesight than I do—I'm getting too old to be of much use."

Hardly, thought Sorenson as he glanced at his friend. *Scott may be middle-aged, but he's taken good care of himself.* "Whatever you say," Finn said as he paused to look out the rear window. There was an orange hue on the distant horizon.

"Looks like the sun's starting to come up. Do you think Dan's airborne yet?"

"Yeah, that bird he chartered has night vision capability, so I imagine it's already at sea."

"What about you? You're not going out on one of those dinky Whalers are you?"

"No. After I drop you off I'm heading over to a marina on the Keehi Lagoon. Dan's got a professor friend from the university with a forty-two-foot Grand Banks. He volunteered to help."

"Great, between your rig, the other lab boats, and the helos, we'll have quite an armada out there. And I feel like we're going to get lucky today."

"I sure as hell hope so," Zack said. "Wendy won't last much longer out there—that damn ocean—even at seventy-plus degrees—will suck the heat right out of you."

Finn didn't respond. He held out little hope of finding Zack's daughter—dead or alive.

Zack drove silently down the road, creating a crystal-clear mental image of his daughter's face in his mind. *Please, Lord, don't take Wendy away from me. She's a real good kid, just starting her life. She doesn't deserve to die.*

Zack was terribly depressed. A feeling of foreboding was rapidly eroding his natural optimism. The fact that he had hardly slept a wink during the previous night didn't help matters either.

At a quarter past six A.M., Zack pulled into a tiny asphalt parking lot serving a helicopter charter company. He stopped the car and turned to his companion. "Finn?"

"Yeah."

"You know we've got to find her today or she's lost for certain."

"I know, Zack. I'll do my damnedest."

"Thanks."

Rear Admiral Michael Richardson, Commander of Pacific Submarine Operations—Pearl Harbor, walked into the conference room at 8:05 A.M. The room was full of junior officers. The second his foot passed the door frame someone yelled out, "Attention on deck!"

"Relax, gentlemen," called out SUBCOMPAC as he took

up his position at the head of the table. Admiral Richardson sat down and then all eight members of his staff repositioned themselves. The atmosphere in the conference center was stuffy. The air conditioner was working overtime trying to keep up with the body heat generated by the assembled officers.

"Okay, Mark," Richardson said, "why don't you give me a rundown on the situation."

"Aye, sir." Captain Mark Strum stood up and walked over to a Kodak Carousel slide projector at the end of the twenty-foot-long conference table. The screen was next to Richardson's chair.

Captain Strum triggered a switch on the control panel. The room lights automatically dimmed as the projector's fan switched on. He advanced the selector switch and the first slide popped onto the screen. It was a colored map of Japan.

"Sir, as you're aware, NRO spotted some unusual shipping activity in Yokohama several weeks ago." He again triggered the selector switch. A wide-angle aerial photograph of the huge port city snapped into focus.

"A recon photoanalyst discovered a strange-looking hull configuration in this area." A new slide appeared on the screen. It was an enlargement of one section of the Yokohama waterfront. It showed half a dozen pier and wharf structures along a wide waterway. Two buildings, each one covering several acres, also projected landward from the shoreline.

Strum picked up a light wand and aimed it at the screen. A bright white arrow illuminated the area. "You can just see the object here." It looked like there was a long white line in the middle of the photo. He advanced another slide. The object was now blown up twenty times in size. The image was slightly blurred but still visible. "As you can see, these things are quite large. They appear to be cylinders that are—"

"Just how big are those things anyway?" asked Admiral Richardson.

"Ah, sir, I was just coming to that." He momentarily glanced at his notes. Despite the dim light he could read his own handwriting. "Both cylinders are about a thousand feet long, give or take a few feet. Each one has a diameter of around a hundred feet."

"Jesus, they're huge," called out Richardson.

"Yes, sir. That they are."

"And they're floating?"

"Correct, Admiral. We couldn't tell exactly from the photo but we estimate that they're sitting way out of the water in this configuration, side by side."

"Damn things look like pipes," Richardson said.

"Exactly, that's what we thought they were at first. Caissons for some kind of underwater tunnel or outfall pipe or something like that. But after we ran the specs through our computer files, we discovered that no one—not even the Japanese—has ever attempted to manufacture something this long and wide."

"So what's that mean?"

"They're not for civil construction works, so we decided they must be some kind of new ship hull design. The Japanese have been innovative in tanker construction as well as container ships and other large vessels, so we figured they were experimenting with something new."

Captain Strum paused to sip a glass of water. His mouth was already dry and he was only getting started. "We monitored these two cylinders by satellite for about two weeks, waiting to see how they might be used. But then they disappeared—NRO couldn't find the damn things."

"Then they must have been moved to a new location," Admiral Richardson commented.

"Yes, sir. That's what we thought. We ran a full photo scan search of the immediate harbor area and other outlying areas, but nothing showed up. There was absolutely no evidence of where they had been taken."

"Go on, Captain."

"Well, naturally both NSA and the CIA were curious, so they authorized a covert probe."

"Who'd they send in?"

"Actually he's one of ours but he's been assigned to the CIA. His name is Hashimoto, Commander Jeffrey Hashimoto."

"Well, the name sure fits the assignment."

"Correct, sir. He was a natural for the job. Speaks fluent Japanese, although he's an American. His grandparents immigrated to the States in the early thirties. He's a third-generation Japanese-American. Born and raised in the Seattle area. Annapolis graduate. He spent a lot of time in Naval Oceanographic Systems and had some sea duty before he went into the NIS.''

''Sounds impressive. So what did he find out?''

Strum advanced another slide. The view was from the waterway looking toward land. A huge multistory warehouse building, built along the edge of the water, filled the screen. ''Commander Hashimoto spent a week prowling the Yokohama waterfront, looking for any evidence of where the cylinders might have been berthed. He found them here.''

''In that building?''

''Yes, sir.''

''But how did they get 'em inside?''

''It's a disguise, sir.''

''What is?''

''The building,'' Strum answered. ''It's a shell, a covering over an old graving dock.''

''I'll be damned. You'd never know that from this photo.''

''Exactly. We weren't sure either, so Hashimoto conducted an underwater penetration. He dropped off one of those new remotely deployed ROVs in the adjacent waterway. He then swam it right under the false outer wall and surfaced inside. This is what he found.''

When the new image flashed onto the screen, there was a collective gasp from the entire group. Admiral Richardson spoke first. ''Good Lord, Captain! That's a submarine.''

''Yes, sir. It sure is, and it's the biggest sub that's ever been built.''

''Bigger than a Trident?''

''Much bigger. Two Tridents and a Typhoon could fit inside this monster.''

''Incredible,'' muttered one of the other officers in the background.

''How's this damn thing propelled and where's the frigging sail?'' demanded Richardson.

''Don't know, sir. The probe wasn't able to scan above the water surface very much because of the possibility of detection. What we know is that it does have stern planes and some kind of outrigger pods that look like drive units—but without propellers.''

''No wheels?''

"Well, at least not in this state of construction."

"So you think it's not complete yet?"

"We don't know, sir. In fact, we don't have a clue as to the mission of this thing. That's why I asked you over here today. Whatever it is—it's clearly beyond anything we've ever built." Strum paused. "And we now believe it might be connected with these strange sub sightings we've been picking up in the mid-Pacific."

"The phantom sub contacts?" asked Richardson.

"Yes, sir."

"But this thing's so huge—it couldn't possibly operate at the depths reported by our people."

"I know, sir. That's what's so confusing. The last Honolulu contact painted a pretty solid sonar image with its active unit. The reflection was immense and could conceivably correspond to this type of hull configuration."

"Come on, Captain," Admiral Richardson said. "Let's get real here. In order for a sub, one of ours or a Russian or anyone else's, to be able to operate at five thousand feet or deeper requires a titanium casing—and one that's maybe no more than thirty feet in diameter. These frigging things—these twin pontoon hulls are each a hundred feet in diameter. Hell, I'll bet you a month's pay that they're constructed out of ordinary steel."

"Yes, sir. I agree. That's why we need to confirm it for sure."

"What do you mean?"

"I want to put a team aboard that thing—really check it out." He paused for a moment. "I've got one standing by, as we talk."

Richardson started squirming in his seat. He was going to have to make a tough decision in a few minutes. "What kind of team?"

"SEALs with Commander Hashimoto as an observer. All we need to do is get Hashimoto aboard for half an hour. Then we'll have the answers. He knows subs inside and out."

"I don't think that's such a great idea, Captain. Our relations with Japan aren't so hot right now. If they catch us, the whole thing could blow up into a hell of a political mess."

"I understand, sir. But nevertheless, until we get some real live bodies on that thing, we're going to be in the dark. And if the Japanese have made some kind of major breakthrough in submarine design, I think we should know about it, like right now.''

''When can this be done?''

''Within forty-eight hours, sir.''

Richardson continued to stare at the screen. Half a minute later he turned back to face Strum. ''Okay, Captain. I'll recommend that you proceed, but final approval will have to come from CINCPAC himself.''

''Aye, sir. I'll write up the request for your review as soon as we're finished here.''

''Very well. Have it on my desk by noon.''

''Yes, sir.''

Admiral Richardson stood up and walked out of the room without further comment.

Zackary Scott was standing by the steel guardrail of his hotel room balcony, twenty-two stories up. He was looking out at the sea. The ocean was ink-black, just like the night sky. The only light came from the canopy of sparkling stars that graced the heavens. The rhythm of the surf, breaking on the flat sandy beach below, had a relaxing, almost hypnotic beat to it.

Zack, unfortunately, wasn't enjoying the surroundings. He was suffering from overwhelming depression. Part of him wanted to jump over the steel guardrail. But the other part wouldn't let him. *Damnit! Why did it have to be Wendy!*

Zack had suspended the search for his daughter at sunset. After spending all day helping to coordinate the air-sea search, he finally threw in the towel. It was useless to continue. Wendy was gone—washed out to sea, never to be seen again.

It should have been me. I should have been the one that drowned. All the crazy damn things I've done in the water and not a scratch. And then my sweet, wonderful daughter gets caught. It isn't fair! Zack slammed his right fist onto the rail. He ignored the pain.

Zack desperately wanted to vent his anger and frustration against someone, but there was no one to blame. And in a few minutes he would have to walk back inside his room, pick up the phone, and call Susan. Wendy's mother, Zack's first wife, lived in Los Angeles, and she didn't know that her daughter was missing. Dan Wallace had called Zack first, and they collectively decided to delay notifying Susan until they had more information. But Zack couldn't wait anymore. *Poor Susan,* he thought, *this is going to kill her!*

And then there was Kelda—he'd have to call her, too. Wendy and Kelda had become good friends over the years, each learning how to share Zack.

Zack finally mustered enough strength to make the call to Susan and had just started to head back inside when the balcony's sliding door burst open. Finn Sorenson stood in the doorway.

"Oh, there you are," called out Finn. He was staying in a companion unit that had a connecting doorway to Zack's suite.

"Hi, Finn," Zack said as he stepped forward.

Finn moved aside and then followed Zack into the suite's living room. "I heard your phone ringing so I came into the room," he said. "I thought you had left so I picked it up."

"So who was it?"

"It was the front desk. Apparently somebody dropped off some kind of package for you."

"Package?"

"Yeah. I told 'em to have the bellhop bring it up. It should be here any minute."

"Hum, must be something from the office."

"Yeah, that's what I thought, but Fed Ex doesn't deliver this late, does it?"

Zack glanced at his wristwatch—it was nearly ten P.M. "Yeah, you're right."

A minute later they heard a knock at the door. "I'll get it," Finn said as he headed for the door.

Zack sat down on a sofa, staring at the television screen. The sound was muted but the picture was crystal clear. It was some kind of sitcom. He was searching for the remote controller when Finn walked back in. He was holding a package about the size of a shoe box. It was wrapped in brown packing paper. Zack's name was neatly printed in black ink on the front.

"Who's it from?" asked Zack as Finn handed him the package.

"I don't know. There's no return address or anything."

Zack started to open the package. "What the hell?" he

called out as he uncovered the contents. Inside the cardboard box was a VHS videotape cassette. There were no identifying labels or marks on it—just the black cassette.

Zack held up the tape. "Well, Finn, what do you suppose this is all about?"

"Hell, I don't know, but I guess whoever sent it to you has some kind of message on it for you. It was clearly addressed to you."

"Yeah, I guess you're right."

"Why don't you play it and then we'll know."

"What do you mean—the TV's not set up for a VCR."

"Oh yes it is." Finn walked forward, opening up a cabinet next to the television. There was a VCR inside. Zack hadn't even bothered to look. He'd thought it was a storage shelf.

"I wouldn't have found this thing if I hadn't bothered to read the room guide," Finn said. "I guess when you pay five hundred bucks a night for these units, the VCR comes standard."

Zack handed the tape to his friend. Thirty seconds later a new image flashed onto the TV screen as the tape began running.

"Christ Almighty," shouted Zack as he rose off the sofa. The screen was filled with a close up view of Wendy's face. "That's my daughter!"

"What?"

"That's Wendy!"

"But what's going—"

"I don't know," interrupted Scott. "Check the sound on that thing. I don't hear anything."

Finn picked up the TV remote and disengaged the mute switch. At first there was static and then a soft hum. It was barely audible above the VCR's background noise.

"I don't hear anything," Zack said. "Is it working all right?"

"Yeah, the volume's up and the—"

Finn stopped speaking as the video image changed. The close-up view was replaced by a long-range shot. Wendy was seated on an old wood chair in front of a plain white wall. She was dressed in blue shorts and a University of Hawaii T-shirt. And she held something in her hands—it looked like a newspaper.

"What has she got in her lap?" asked Finn.

Zack was too astonished to answer. He could not believe what he was seeing.

Wendy turned away from the camera, off to her right. It looked like she was silently listening to someone off-screen. A moment later she turned back to face the camera. There was no smile on her pretty face, only fear. She held up the newsprint. The paper's headline was clearly visible: GOVERNOR APPROVES RESORT COMPLEX.

Finn turned toward Zack with an amazed look on his face. The same paper was sitting on the edge of the coffee table. It was the evening edition, only a few hours old.

"Jesus, Zack. That's tonight's paper." Finn reached for it. He held it across his chest, just like Wendy in the video.

Zack still couldn't respond. The joy of knowing that his daughter was alive could not be described. *Thank you, Lord, for not taking her. Thank you! Thank you! Thank you!*

Zack looked like he was going to burst with emotion. "Zack, you all right?" asked Sorenson.

"She's alive. My sweet Wendy's alive."

Zack started to stand, wanting to get closer to the screen, but his legs felt wobbly. He slumped back into the sofa. Just then the audio on the VCR camera came on. There was traffic noise in the background. And then Wendy coughed, like she was clearing her voice.

"The sound's on now," called out Finn.

Zack just nodded his head as Wendy began speaking.

"Daddy, they tell me they're going to give this tape recording to you to prove they've got me. That's why I've got this paper." She tilted it back to glance at the headline. "It's today's edition."

"Read this now," came a muffled voice from the background.

Wendy again looked toward her right and then held out her hand. For just an instant, a brown forearm was visible. She grabbed the sheet of paper it was holding. After scanning the paper for a few seconds, she turned back to the camera. "Daddy, this is addressed to you. They're making me read it: 'We are holding your daughter. She is in a safe place that neither you or the authorities will ever find. We have no desire to harm Wendy but if you contact the police, or any other law enforcement agency, you will never see her again.' "

Wendy paused as the words struck home. She had a bewildered look on her face. Then she continued reading. " 'We will return your daughter to you, safe and sound, provided we come to an acceptable arrangement with you. The choice will be yours. So, if you wish to see Wendy again you must be in the lobby of your hotel at ten-thirty tonight. Wait by the main elevator core. We will contact you. Remember this, though, you will be continually watched from this moment on. If you make any calls from your hotel phone we will know. If you involve the police or the FBI we will know. If you try to use Mr. Wallace or Mr. Sorenson as an intermediary to the police, we will know. And one last thing—bring this tape with you. Don't try to copy it.' "

Wendy looked up from the paper. There were tears in her eyes. And then the tape turned to static.

"Holy shit," Finn called out. "She's been kidnapped."

Zack was confused. He was euphoric that Wendy's body wasn't rotting somewhere on the ocean bottom, but at the same time he was half paralyzed with fear. Wendy's life was still in grave danger. "Oh my God," he said, "you're right. She's been kidnapped."

Finn remained silent, trying to fathom the sudden turn of events. Zack just stared at the static-filled television screen.

"Jesus, Zack," Finn finally responded, "what are you going to do?"

Zack turned away from the TV, glancing at his wristwatch. It was ten-twelve P.M. "Right now I'm going downstairs and do exactly what they tell me."

"You want me to come with you?"

"No! Absolutely not. Just stay here and don't use the phone until I'm back."

"Okay, but if you're not back here in an hour I'm coming down. And if they've taken you I'm going to the police and give them this." Finn held up the VCR tape.

"No, you're not." Zack grabbed the tape. "I don't know what these people want. I may have to take off and I can't have you stirring up the place until I know what's going on."

"But, Zack, maybe they're really trying to get you."

Zack hadn't considered that possibility. He didn't care about his own safety—only Wendy's.

"I don't think they want me personally—they could have killed me anytime. They want something I've got."

"You mean money?"

"What else?" Zack said as he stood up. He grabbed a nylon windbreaker from a nearby table, slipping the cassette into one of its pockets.

Finn shook his head from side to side. "I'm not so sure about that, Zack. None of this stuff makes any sense anymore. I just don't think you should go alone. How will I ever know if they have kidnapped you or not?"

"All right, you've got a point. If I'm not back by nine A.M., do whatever you want."

"Nine A.M.! Hell, that's almost half a day from now."

"I know, but that's the deal. Will you follow it?"

"Yeah, of course."

"Thanks." Zack headed for the door. He was gone before Finn could wish him luck.

The sentry spotted Scott the instant he stepped out of the elevator car. Several hours earlier he had memorized the American's facial features and body build. The dossier on Scott was quite detailed.

As Zack approached the hotel's main lobby, the observer flipped through the newspaper he was holding, turning to the sports section. The fifty-year-old Asian was one of a dozen people sitting in the lobby's reception area. His slight body seemed to be swallowed up by the enormous black leather sofa chair he sat in. Zack didn't pay him the slightest attention when he walked by.

Zack stood in the middle of the hotel lobby, not sure what to do. *Okay, you turkeys, I'm here. Now what?*

He paced back and forth across the marble floor. Hordes of hotel guests, along with assorted hotel staff, were scurrying around the lobby and foyer area. It seemed that everyone was getting ready for a night out on the town.

Come on, you people, let's get this over with. Zack's impatience was growing by the minute. And he was filled to the brim with conflicting emotions. His joy at knowing that

Wendy was alive overrode almost everything. But the bitterness of her kidnapping was beginning to take its toll.

While Scott continued to pace across the lobby floor, the observer, still planted in the same chair, watched. The man glanced at his wristwatch. It had been nearly fifteen minutes since his contact walked off the elevator. He saw nothing to indicate that Scott was being shadowed or that the police had been notified. *It's time*, he thought.

He reached inside his right coat pocket and retrieved a small black object about the size of a cigarette lighter. He pressed his thumb on the top of the device, triggering a switch. An instant later the transponder began broadcasting a short-range radio signal. Scott had taken the bait.

"Paging Mr. Scott, Mr. Zackary Scott."

At first Zack didn't hear the voice calling out his name. The background din of the hotel's lobby partially masked the intercom voice. Besides, his mind was racing a mile a minute, trying to make some sense of what was happening. Finally, he turned to his right and walked to the reception desk.

"I'm Scott," he said, addressing the female clerk behind the counter. "Somebody's paging me."

"Yes, sir. You can use the phone right over there." She pointed to the end of the counter.

"Thanks."

Half a minute later Zack took two deep breaths and then lifted the receiver. "Zackary Scott here." He waited for a response. Nothing. "Hello, are you there?" he asked.

"Mr. Scott," the caller said, "so far you've followed our instructions very well. Keep it up and you will get your daughter back." The voice was male with a hint of an Asian accent.

Who the hell are you? is what Zack wanted to say. Instead, he hid his emotions as best he could. "What do you want?"

"There is a limousine outside—black Cadillac. Get in it, now!" The line clicked dead.

Oh, shit, now what?

Zack stepped away from the counter and then began running toward the hotel entryway. The desk clerk looked up at him as he raced by, but he didn't see her. His handsome face was pale, almost ghost white. *Must have been bad news,* she thought.

Zack pushed his way through the revolving door, rushing out onto the concrete driveway. *There it is!* he said to himself. Although the drivethrough entryway to the hotel was crowded with taxis, shuttle buses, and private cars, the stretch Caddy stood out like a Mack truck.

He started to walk toward the right side of the limousine and the driver's door opened. A large man, at least six feet tall, climbed out. He was wearing a black uniform with a matching cap. The driver moved to the rear of the car and opened the passenger door just as Zack arrived.

The man bowed slightly, gesturing for Scott to enter. That's when Zack noticed that the driver was an Asian. *Japanese,* he thought as he ducked his head to climb into the limousine.

Zack was nearly all the way inside the darkened compartment when he realized that he wasn't alone. A man was sitting on the forward bench. Zack settled into the rear seat, facing the stranger.

"You're right on schedule," the man said.

Like the driver, the passenger was also of Asian descent. But the sheer bulk of his body made the driver look like a puny teenager. The man filled most of the two-person bench seat. His black hair was cut short on the sides but was longer on top. The flat-top cut rose straight up, about an inch above his scalp. It looked slick, like it was oiled. And he didn't have a neck. His huge head seemed to be planted right on top of his massive shoulders.

What a monster, Zack thought as he stared at the man. "Okay, I'm here, now what?" he said.

The man smiled as his eyes looked onto Scott's face. "Mr. Scott, we're just going to drive around for a while and have a little chat." The man pressed a black button on the door console. A clear glass window partition rose from a wall slot located behind the front seat. The passenger compartment was now private. A few seconds later the car began rolling forward.

"Now, Mr. Scott, before we have our little chat, please give me the tape."

Zack removed the VCR cassette from his coat pocket and handed it over.

The Asian inspected the tape, looking for an identifying mark on its casing. A moment later he looked back at Scott. "Thank you. Now, can I offer you something to drink?"

"No," Zack said, his voice clearly irritated. "Let's just get on with it."

The man smiled again, wider this time. His teeth were sparkling white, but were horribly crooked. "No need to be so hostile, Mr. Scott."

Zack finally recognized the man's voice. *He's the one who just called me!*

"Look, just what is it you want from me?"

"We have plenty of time for all that." The man then reached to the side, opening the door to a built-in mini-refrigerator. He pulled out a tray filled with assorted raw fish cuts and sushi rolls garnished with green vegetables. He held the tray in front of Scott. "Sashimi?" he asked.

Zack liked fish, but only when it was cooked. He hardly ever indulged in the popular ritual of consuming raw fish. Nevertheless, he retrieved one morsel—a sliver of salmon encased in white rice and wrapped in nori. He popped it into his mouth. It was surprisingly tasty.

"Now, that's better," the man said. He then reached down with his left hand and grabbed a fillet of tuna.

The man dabbed the white rubbery flesh into a tiny sauce bowl and then chewed on it. Zack was finally beginning to understand what was happening. All of this was a ceremony.

"Where's my daughter?" he asked.

The man glanced at his wristwatch. "Right now, I imagine she's over the Pacific."

"What?" Zack screamed. He started to rise out of his seat.

"Sit down," ordered the man. His voice had fire in it. Zack backed off.

"What have you done with her?"

"Mr. Scott. We know you are very resourceful. Accordingly, we have taken the necessary precautions to insure your complete cooperation." He paused as he reached for another slice of fish. "Until we have concluded our business, your daughter will remain in Japan."

"Japan!"

"That's right. She will be quite safe, providing you cooperate."

Zack reined in his temper. "All right. What do you want? Please tell me."

The man smiled again. "I represent a group of investors who are interested in your business activities."

Investors who are kidnappers. Who the hell do you think you're trying to fool! "Yes, go on."

"We have a proposition for you. We want to purchase your offshore division, including all of your oil leases. We are prepared to offer you—"

"Oh, come on," interrupted Zack. He couldn't restrain himself any longer. "This is pure bullshit. How much money do you want? A million? Two million? What's the damn ransom?"

The man was not used to having anyone talk to him like that, especially from a *gaijin.* "You do not understand. We don't want your money—we will pay you market value for—"

"You fucking monkey! You kidnap my daughter to entice me to sell part of my company. Where do you think we are—back in the dark ages?"

The man's naturally brown face was now turning beet-red. He wanted to pound the insolent American into pulp. Instead, he remained silent, his dark brown eyes locked onto Scott's.

Zack continued his verbal barrage; the anger and fear that had been pent up inside of him spilled out like an exploding volcano. "You asshole, quit your damn charade and get down to business right now. I can get a million bucks in cash by noon tomorrow. Where do you want it?"

"Mr. Scott, I'm only going to say this once more and then we are finished. We will never contact you again. So I advise you to listen very carefully."

"Or what?"

"As I have said earlier, you will never see your daughter again. It's that simple."

Cool it, you fool, Zack said to himself. *This guy's really serious.* "All right, I'll listen."

The Asian settled back in the leather seat. He seemed to relax. "Good. You are to return to Seattle tomorrow morning at eight o'clock, on United. Your reservations have already been made. When you arrive back at your office, we will contact you. The sale will be all cash—the funds are already in escrow in . . .''

Zack listened as the man continued with a series of deal points, outlining certain procedures for the transfer of deeds and lease assignments and the payment of excise taxes and title insurance premiums. The man looked like a gorilla but talked like a real estate attorney.

When the man summed up the intricate series of transactions, Zack finally understood. SCS's offshore division, all of the drilling vessels, and every oil field lease, including the Hammer 4 tract, would be transferred to a new entity based in the Bahamas.

Zack hardly paid any attention to the price the man mentioned—it was ridiculously low for what the offshore division might be worth in a year or so, after the Hammer 4 mess was resolved. And then it finally hit Zack like a ton of bricks. It was almost like one of the scenes from the movie *The Godfather*. *This bastard is making me an offer I can't refuse!*

''Now, Mr. Scott, here's the downside of this deal. If you refuse to cooperate and complete the transaction as outlined, we will be forced to punish you.''

''I know, you bastards will kill Wendy—you don't have to remind me of that.'' Zack slumped into the soft leather seat. He wanted to disappear.

''No, Mr. Scott, you're wrong. We won't kill her, but both you and Wendy will wish we had.''

Zack sat up straight, alert. ''What do you mean?''

''Have you ever heard of the *gaijin* girl circuit?''

''No, what are you talking about?''

''In Japan, white women, especially pretty blond-haired ones like your daughter, are in incredible demand at our, how should I say, less desirable establishments.'' The Asian once again smiled, relishing his next words. ''We will hide your lovely Wendy away in one of our more notorious clubs—in the backwoods, so to speak. A place that is frequented by our less polished citizens. You know the kind I'm talking about: foreign laborers, drug addicts, and hardened criminals. We will make her the prime attraction. And with a daily injection of heroin, one that she will come to value more than her own life, she will be in high demand. At twenty dollars a trick, low by your standards but top dollar to our scum class, she'll make us four, maybe even five hundred dollars a day.'' The man laughed, knowing he had Scott's undivided attention.

"You motherfucker, I'll kill you." Zack lunged for the man but the Asian was ready. He simply raised his enormous right arm and punched Zack in his stomach. The blow knocked the wind out of Scott. He rolled over onto the car seat.

Zack recovered about a minute later and looked up. The man was still staring at him. "Now that wasn't too smart, Mr. Scott. But I'll overlook it just this once."

The limousine rolled to a stop and Zack glanced out the window. They had returned to the hotel.

"Now it's time for you to go back up to your room and pack. You have to fly home tomorrow." The man paused as he triggered the door release. He then pushed the door outward. "The decision to cooperate is yours. If you go to the police or others, we will know immediately and the deal will be off. You know what will happen then. It's that simple."

Zack didn't say anything as he climbed out. He was too stunned to respond.

21

DEEP SECRETS

Yokohama

The sixteen-foot-long boat moved smoothly across the still waters of Tokyo Bay. The eighty-horsepower outboard engine hardly made a sound as it pushed the vessel at nearly thirty knots. The thick padding surrounding the motor compartment, coupled with an electronic antinoise muffler system, produced an exhaust that sounded like a cat purring.

The rigid-hull inflatable was painted a gray-black color; the special formulation was designed to make the vehicle nearly invisible during moonlit sea surface conditions. All exposed metallic parts on the vessel were coated with a rubberized sound-and-radar-wave-adsorbing material. And the engine system, besides being muffled, was shielded and cooled so that it produced no noticeable infrared signature. For all practical purposes, the U.S. Navy SK-V Subskimmer (Mark V) was invisible to conventional monitoring techniques.

The vessel's three-man crew were positioned one after another along the length of the vessel. The helmsman was in the aft position, sandwiched between the engine and the steering console. The next man sat forward of the helm, followed by the third occupant, who sat in the bow section. All three men were dressed in thick rubberized diving suits.

Fifteen minutes earlier, the SK-V had swum off the stern ramp of the U.S.S. *Nassau* as the amphibious assault ship headed out of the U.S. Navy's Seventh Fleet headquarters at Yokosuka. The tiny Subskimmer then raced northward toward Yokohama while the giant ship steamed southward into the Uraga Strait, heading for the Pacific.

At 2:58 A.M., the SK-V entered the outer harbor limits of Yokohama's main waterway. The helmsman slowed the craft to ten knots and proceeded to head down the center of the channel. Six minutes later the man sitting in the middle of the boat spotted the target. He turned to his right and raised his right hand. The pilot backed off the throttle. The inflatable glided through the water for about thirty feet before stopping. There was hardly any tidal current and absolutely no wind.

Commander Jeffrey Hashimoto leaned back until his lips were only inches away from the helmsman. "That's it, Willy. Right up there off the port bow—about three hundred meters."

"Got it. How much farther do you want to go?" replied Lieutenant William Patterson. The twenty-nine-year-old African-American officer was a member of the U.S. Navy's elite SEAL commando forces. He was a platoon leader from SEAL Team One.

"Wait a sec," replied Hashimoto. He made a 360-degree inspection of the harbor area. There was no shipping traffic on the waterway and little activity on the shoreline. He spotted only the headlights of a car as it moved along a waterfront roadway. He could hear the sound of an invisible diesel locomotive as it chugged along in a nearby railroad yard. The naval officer and CIA agent turned aft again. "Let's go another two hundred meters."

"Aye, skipper. Let Jack know, will you?"

Hashimoto nodded and leaned forward, tapping the bow observer on his right shoulder. Five minutes later the Subskimmer was in position. The aft helmsman shut down the engine. He then engaged a series of special valves and covers, completely isolating the outboard engine and its electrical components from seawater.

The man in the bow, another SEAL, took control of the vessel. Besides being able to run stealthily along the water surface, the SK-V was also a submersible. By opening several vents and engaging a bow-mounted electrical propeller drive system, the tiny runabout could completely submerge in about a minute. Once submerged the vessel maneuvered like an underwater airplane. A steering wheel and throttle control in the bow, both separate from the outboard motor system, directed the battery-powered twin bow thrusters, allowing the vessel to fly through the water.

The bow diver, twenty-six-year-old seaman Jack Graham, ran through the dive checklist. Half a minute later he pulled on his regulator and face mask. Hashimoto and Patterson followed his lead.

Each man wore a self-contained, closed-cycle breathing apparatus with a built-in underwater radio. The electronic wireless communication system allowed the three divers to talk with each other while submerged. A tiny microprocessor built into the transreceiver could be preprogrammed to transmit and receive in a variety of coded signals. By using natural biologically produced sounds as the message carriers, underwater transmissions could be concealed, insuring secure communications. Tonight all three units were calibrated to simulate snapping shrimp, a species indigenous to Japanese coastal waters.

The SK-V silently sank beneath the water surface at 3:08 A.M. It was pitch-dark, but the luminous dials on Graham's control panel stood out like a casino marquee. The readouts were designed to compensate for low-light, high-turbidity conditions.

"Can you see the panel okay?" asked Patterson over the radio. His voice was crystal clear.

"Yeah," replied Graham. "Turbidity's not so bad and everything seems to be working."

Hashimoto cut in. "Good, make your heading two-two-eight. That should take us right in."

"Aye, aye, Commander. Heading two-two-eight."

Graham turned the wheel to the left a few turns and goosed the throttle. The ducted propellers bit into the water. The SK-V lunged forward. Although the vessel was capable of running at up to ten knots under maximum power conditions, Graham held back, keeping the speed right at four knots. He wanted to preserve the battery pack for as long as possible, just in case. At the reduced speed, the Subskimmer had enough power to last an hour and a half.

Five minutes later Graham throttled back. The Subskimmer slowed.

"What's up?" asked Hashimoto.

"I'm not sure, but I think we're there. I can just make out some kind of shadow ahead."

Hashimoto looked over Graham's right shoulder. Everything looked black to him. "Let's go a little farther and take a look-see. But take it real slow. I don't want to run into one of those submerged wall panels."

"Understood, we'll go in dead slow."

Graham inched the SK-V forward. A few seconds later he spotted the underwater wall. "There it is," he said.

Hashimoto saw the wall now. It was almost as black as the water, but just enough light from the building's overhead floodlights penetrated to reveal its presence. The submersible was twenty feet below the surface. The false wall panel extended down another ten feet. "That's it," Hashimoto replied. "Let's take her down and head in."

Patterson spoke up before Graham could acknowledge the order. "Commander, do you think they'll have any sensors or barriers across the opening?"

"Doubt it. When we sent the ROV in we didn't encounter anything. Anyway, keep your eyes open—you never know." Hashimoto paused for a moment. "Jack, you ready to go in now?"

"Aye, sir. We're diving." Graham turned the tiny underwater craft to port and rotated the thrusters until they were pointing almost straight down. The SK-V descended like a slow-moving elevator. Half a minute later it swam under the fake building front.

"Okay," called out Hashimoto, "let's set 'er down right here."

Graham eased off the power, allowing the SK-V to slowly sink. It landed on the soft bottom, kicking up a thick cloud of silt. It was like they were inside a glass of chocolate milk.

Two minutes later, Hashimoto and Patterson were ready. The divers pushed away from the Subskimmer, starting their ascent. As they neared the surface, the water clarity improved and Hashimoto spotted the hulking shadow of their target. "There it is," he reported over the radio.

Lieutenant Patterson had been briefed on the size of the hull, but what he was now seeing threw him completely off guard. "Christ Almighty, that son of a bitch is huge!"

Hashimoto was equally awed at the sight but his mind was on other things. "Let's come up along the bottom of the hull to take a look. I want to check out the topside facilities."

"Lead on, skipper."

Hashimoto swam up to the submerged hull. He touched the curved surface. It felt rock-solid. "Willy, this looks like standard steel plating to me. What do you think?"

Patterson stroked the hull with his gloved hands, rubbing away some of the slime. "Yep, looks like a steel can to me."

"Jack, you get that?" asked Hashimoto. Although Graham remained aboard the SK-V, he was still within range of the underwater radio broadcast.

"Roger, skipper. I copy that. Steel hull."

"Good."

"Okay, Willy, I'm going up to take a quick look topside. You stay put."

"Got it."

Half a minute later, Commander Hashimoto's head silently broke through the water surface. He was right under the curved section of the starboard cylinder. Both of the hundred-foot-diameter conduits were riding high out of the water. Only forty feet of the hull projected below the water surface. By using the overhanging hull section as a shield, he remained concealed from the adjacent wharf. A pile-supported timber apron surrounded the berth on three sides, providing access to the exposed sections of the hull. He swam outward about ten feet. *Ah, there it is.* He spotted the ladder that the robot submarine had found during its earlier reconnaissance.

Commander Hashimoto spent another minute looking up and down the length of the vessel. It was quiet as a tomb inside the graving dock. He didn't see any guards. As soon as he submerged he activated the radio. "Okay, Willy, I've got the ladder. It looks like we're alone."

"Good, let's do it then."

It took the divers five minutes to swim to the steel ladder. It rose fifty feet from the water surface up to the wharf face. Each man scaled the ladder, remaining fully suited up. They clipped their diving fins to belt harnesses and disconnected their face masks.

Lieutenant Patterson took the lead, reaching the wharf deck first. Despite the overhead lighting, his black garments blended into the dark background structures. Hashimoto was equally camouflaged, except for his face. The blackout grease he had painted on his tanned skin had partially washed off. Patterson, however, didn't need to worry about face paint. His black skin blended in with the color of his Neoprene diving suit.

"Where do you want to go first?" asked Patterson as he unzipped a plastic bag attached to a shoulder harness clip. He pulled out a stainless steel .357-caliber Smith & Wesson. There was a fat silencer on the revolver's business end.

"Let's cross over to the starboard hull on that gangway over there." Hashimoto pointed with his right hand. "It looks the closest."

"Okay, you want me to take the point?"

"No, just stay back in the shadows. If someone spots me, you know what to do."

"Aye, aye, skipper."

Hashimoto duckwalked along the timber surface of the wharf, leaving a trail of dripping water. His legs were constrained by the cumbersome diving suit, resulting in his funny-looking gait. He headed toward an aluminum gangway that spanned the forty-foot gap between the hull and the pier. Two minutes later he was aboard the phantom submarine, kneeling down on a huge steel deck. *Good God, this sucker looks as big as the* Nimitz. He was standing near the forward section of the hull. The flat steel deck spanning the twin cylindrical hulls seemed to stretch on into infinity. *What the hell is this thing?*

The naval intelligence officer carefully surveyed the entire deck surface; he was looking for some kind of opening. His primary mission was to figure out what the vessel was designed for. That meant he had to get inside the hull.

It didn't take Commander Hashimoto long to find a penetration. He almost fell into the open hatchway as he headed aft along the port half of the hull. The opening was a meter in diameter and there were no barriers around it. Only the top rung of an aluminum ladder jutted out of the hole. He dropped to his knees and leaned his head downward into the opening.

The interior was black as outer space. He then removed a tiny but powerful spotlight from his chest harness. When he directed the concentrated beam into the cavernous interior, the opening swallowed up the light like a cosmic black hole. *Damn, this sucker's hollow.* He could just make out the bottom of the ladder, nearly a hundred feet below. *This is the longest damn ladder I've ever seen.*

Hashimoto looked up, turning toward the submarine's bow. Lieutenant Patterson was supposed to be on the wharf but he couldn't spot him. He raised his right hand, rotating his wrist, signaling the SEAL to advance. Almost instantly, Patterson emerged from the shadows. A minute later he was kneeling next to Hashimoto's side, staring into the hole.

"This is great, Commander. You found us a hatchway."

"Well, I don't know how great it is. This ladder looks pretty damn shaky."

Patterson reached forward and pulled on the nearest rung. It moved. "Yeah, I see what you mean, but it must work. Otherwise why would it be here?"

"Yeah, I guess you're right."

Patterson leaned closer to the opening, aiming his own light into the cavernous hull. "Hum, this baby's clear all the way to the bottom."

"That's right. At least this part of the hull is empty. Whatever they're going to put inside hasn't been installed yet."

Patterson leaned farther into the opening. The cylindrical hatchway extended nearly eight feet downward before the hull opened up into a vast interior chamber. "Damn, this sucker looks like it has some kind of a double hull."

"Yeah, I noticed that. Apparently we're standing on some kind of outer shell. Must be for structural purposes."

"I guess so," replied Patterson. He then looked up to face Hashimoto. "You think this hold is some kind of ballast chamber?"

"No way, it's much too big."

"Maybe it's for missiles but they haven't installed the tubes yet."

"That thought did cross my mind, but the type of building technique is sure contrary to how we or the Russians build missile boats. The missile silos are always an integral part of the hull's design—not some kind of add-on."

"Yeah, I guess you're right." Patterson paused to check his watch. They had been topside for almost ten minutes now. "Well, sir, we've got about thirty minutes left. What do you want to do?"

"I want to get inside this thing and take some photos."

"Good, let's do it then."

Jeff Hashimoto sat quietly as the SK-V planed across the flat waters at twenty-five knots. He had removed his face mask and hood, letting the wind blow through his short black hair. The fatigue and worry that had plagued him only minutes earlier had vanished. He felt wonderful. The mission had been a success. And most important, no one had been hurt.

Just before reaching the outer channel markers of the U.S. Navy's naval base at Yokosuka, Commander Hashimoto's mind wandered back to when he and Patterson were inside the phantom sub. His memory focused on the glass-smooth walls and huge movable bulkhead they had discovered. *What in the hell are they trying to do?* he asked himself over and over.

It had been five days since the abduction, and Wendy Scott didn't have the faintest idea where she was. All she could see out of the window was water, endless green water that stretched clear to the horizon.

The room was minuscule, only eight feet wide by twelve feet long. There was a two-level bunk bed along one side of the room. Wendy occupied the bottom mattress, wrapping both sets of blankets around her slim body to help keep warm. The days weren't too bad but at night she was always cold. Built into the wall on the opposite side of the compartment was a set of drawers and a washbasin with a single spigot that dispensed only lukewarm water. A small oak desk with a stool for a chair occupied the corner. And located just above the desk, on the exposed exterior wall, was an eighteen-inch-high by two-foot-long window. It was bolted to the steel wall frame. Along the interior wall, next to the door, was a four-foot by four-foot enclosed toilet compartment.

Wendy was emotionally and physically worn out. They gave her plenty of food—a tray slipped through a slot at the bottom of the door three times a day—but she didn't have much of an appetite. Wendy had never cared for fish in spite of her professional training. She only managed to eat the rice and a few other vegetables.

At night it was worse. An assortment of strange noises, loud metallic clangs and weird Klaxon-like sounds, frequently broke the background silence. She was lucky if she slept an hour or two without being awakened.

Wendy could deal with the cold, the noise, and the lousy food, but it was the loneliness that was really getting to her. She hadn't spoken a word to anyone since she left Honolulu. She didn't have the faintest idea who her captors were.

She clearly remembered the abduction from her work boat and then waking up in a room where she was forced to make the videotape. At that time, her captors all wore masks so she hadn't been able to identify anyone. And then they drugged her again. When she finally woke up she was in the present room. Her watch and all of her original clothing had been taken away. Her new garment consisted of a full-body jump-suit, blue with a funny-looking Y-shaped logo over her right breast. She was provided with a pair of white panties but they hadn't bothered to give her a bra.

The first day, Wendy repeatedly pounded on the steel door, more out of frustration than anything else. But no one responded. After her hands and arms began to numb she stopped. That was several days ago. She now divided her time between sleeping and staring out the window at the ocean.

At first Wendy thought she was on a ship that was anchored, but the view from the window never changed, not even slightly. And she never felt any motion. She finally figured it out: *This thing's an offshore platform!*

Years earlier, Wendy had visited one of her father's offshore projects in the North Sea. The fixed platforms were like steel islands in the middle of the ocean.

Wendy speculated on where she was being held. At first she thought she was in southern California. On one of her field trips from Stanford, she remembered seeing several oil rigs off the Santa Barbara coast. But she quickly dismissed that idea. *It's way too cold here to be California.* After considering several more possibilities, she finally settled on Alaska. *That's got to be it—I'm somewhere off the Alaskan coast.*

She was wrong.

22

A TIME TO WONDER

Seattle

Zackary Scott constantly fidgeted in the chair. It was the soft, mushy type, and it was murder on his back. Despite his discomfort, Zack continued to tell his tale. He had been home for a couple of days and he was now sitting in the office of the senior partner of a Seattle law firm. Harold Shapiro, Zack's long-time attorney and friend, could hardly believe the story he was hearing.

"What did he look like?" asked Shapiro.

"Hal, that guy looked as big as a gorilla." Zack held his arms out in front of his chest, shaping them like he was holding an imaginary barrel. "He was huge, at least two hundred and seventy-five pounds, maybe even three hundred. And I bet most of it was muscle."

Harold Shapiro rolled his chair back and turned to the side, looking out his office window. He had a commanding view of Elliott Bay—not as spectacular as Zack's, but still exceptional. "So you're certain this guy was Japanese and not Chinese or maybe Samoan?"

"He was Japanese, I'm certain."

"Anything else you remember about him, other than his size?"

Zack thought a few seconds before answering. "His English

was very good and the tailored suit he wore was first-class—must have cost at least a thousand bucks.''

Shapiro nodded and then turned back to face his client and friend. ''Zack, I'm afraid we're into something that's way beyond both of our limits.''

''What do you mean?''

''I don't know if you remember or not, but I spent a year in Tokyo when I was in the navy—twenty-plus years ago.''

''Yeah, sure. I remember. You were assigned to some kind of military court over there.''

''That's right. I was in Yokosuka. Anyway, during my tour I managed to pick up a few things about the local culture—the darker side of their society.'' Shapiro hesitated a moment to think through his wording. ''And from what you've just described, it looks like you've been targeted by the *yakuza*.''

''The what?''

''The *yakuza*—the Japanese Mafia.''

''You mean like our mobsters?''

''That's right, but instead of being run by Italians and Sicilians, the *yakuza* is strictly a Japanese affair. Dates back to the days of the samurai and the shoguns. The *yakuza* were warriors—like mercenaries. Very deadly and brutal as hell.'' Shapiro again shifted position on his chair, leaning back a few degrees. ''Zack, these people are tough sons of bitches. They make the Cosa Nostra look like amateurs when it comes to heavy-duty crime. And they're into everything these days: narcotics, prostitution, gambling, extortion—you name it and they do it.''

Zack shook his head from side to side in disbelief. ''But, Hal, why would they want my company? I'm not doing anything in Japan.''

''I don't know, Zack. I agree that it doesn't make much sense, but everything you've told me points to a classic extortion scam. And from what I've recently read, some *yakuza* factions have been branching out from Japan, setting up shop in this country as well as in other Asian states. They're real heavy in Hawaii—especially Honolulu.''

''You mean the Japanese are now exporting their own criminals, along with all of their cars, computers, and airplanes?''

''No. The *yakuza* leaders have been under a lot of pressure from the government and the public to clean up their act, so to speak. The police have been hounding them for years so they've started expanding their operations—moving into other areas where they have little competition and minimal hassles with law enforcement.''

"So the good old USA lets them in with a welcome hand?'' asked Zack, clearly upset at what Shapiro was telling him.

"No. Not at all, but these people are extremely smooth. I only know a little about how it started, but it basically involved the Japanese tourist trade. It first started off in Hawaii and then spread to the mainland.''

"What did they do?''

"Early on, ten to fifteen years ago, just when the Japanese public was beginning to take an interest in international travel, the *yakuza* somehow got control of several hotels and resorts in Honolulu. With their tentacles already deep into certain travel agencies in Tokyo and other Japanese cities, it was only a matter of time before they started offering special Hawaiian tour packages.''

"So what? We've been selling Hawaii's tourism for years.''

"But not like these characters. Their facilities catered only to the Japanese—no one else is allowed. They provided special enclaves that catered only to their customers, most of whom were young men. They provided Japanese food, Japanese tour guides, Japanese hostesses, Japanese everything. It was kind of like a home away from home.''

"Well, that doesn't sound so bad.''

"On the surface it wasn't. That's why we opened our doors to them. It looked like these foreign tour groups would bring a lot of money into the States, especially helping to boost Hawaii's economy. And everyone knew how polite and sedate the Japanese were—kind of the perfect tourist: spends a lot of money, doesn't create any problems, and then leaves.''

"Okay, tell me what was wrong with all that.''

Shapiro laughed, just a short gruntlike noise. "Well, their tours were popular all right—during the day they took them to all the popular sites: Pearl Harbor, Diamond Head, the Hawaiian Village, and the rest. But at night it was something entirely different.''

Zack stared at his friend, totally engrossed in what he was saying.

"Turns out that as soon as the sun went down, they offered

these young men just about every vice they couldn't get back in Japan: unlimited drinking, wild gambling, and the dirtiest porno movies made. And to top it all off they had a huge prostitution ring set up to serve their customers. Young Caucasian girls, especially American blondes, were their specialty.''

Zack stiffened in his chair as a chill swept up his spine. *Blondes! Oh my God, that's what he said about Wendy.* The man's threats were still fresh in his mind.

Harold Shapiro focused on Zack's face. He could see that he had hit a raw nerve with his last statement. ''What's wrong, Zack? You look like you just saw a ghost.''

''What you just said, about the blonde whores. That guy told me that if I didn't cooperate, he would send Wendy away to one of his clubs. She'd earn him five hundred dollars a night at twenty bucks a trick.''

Shapiro slowly shook his head, not wanting to believe what Zack had said. But he knew otherwise. ''I'm sorry, Zack, but it's all starting to fit together now. For some reason these bastards have started to move into the Northwest. They're already in L.A. and San Francisco, mostly drug related.''

''But why SCS? What do we have that they could possibly want?''

''I can only speculate. Like our own mob, the *yakuza* are trying to get into legitimate businesses to invest their money in order to launder profits. Apparently the tax man in Japan is just as unforgiving as he is here. Many of their leaders have been nailed for tax evasion.''

Zack turned away, looking out the window. ''I don't know, none of this makes any sense. If I had some kind of cash-based business—restaurants, bars, that kind of thing—I could see their interest, because it's possible to hide money in those business. But a construction company and oil exploration company—I don't see that. We hardly ever work in cash—everything's by check or wire transfer. Besides, the IRS watches everything we do with an eagle eye. There's got to be another angle to all this.''

''Maybe there is, but I sure don't see it.''

''Neither do I.'' Zack turned back to face Shapiro and then raised his hands in despair. ''Hal, what the hell can I do?''

Shapiro leaned back in his chair. "Just what have they offered you in return for Wendy?"

"All that prick told me was that when I got back to Seattle, I'd be contacted with the formal terms. They want SCS's offshore division and all the rights to the Hammer 4 tract."

"In return for Wendy?"

"Of course, plus cash."

"Did he say how much?"

"Yeah, it was peanuts. Hell, I don't care anyway. If I have to fucking liquidate SCS to get her back alive and well, I'll do it. It's only money."

Shapiro didn't respond immediately. Instead, he carefully thought through his next response. "Zack, this thing's gone far beyond a simple kidnapping and ransom. There's something going on here that's way over our heads. Now, I know what you said about his warning regarding the police, but you've got no choice in this matter. We've got to get the FBI involved right now."

"No damn way!" shouted Zack. "I'll never see Wendy again if they get the slightest inkling that the police are involved, especially any Feds."

"Okay, Zack. It's your call, but I think you're making a terrible mistake."

"It's my mistake to make." Zack paused as he stood up, straightening out his stiff back muscles. "I expect these pricks will be contacting me in the next day or so about making the transfer. So, please start getting your legal paperwork together for me. I may have to move fast."

"Okay, Zack. We'll be ready here. But just think about consulting with the authorities. They have resources we've never even dreamed about."

"Yeah, all right," Zack said as he headed for the door.

Pearl Harbor

"Admiral, I know this sounds crazy but I think that thing is some kind of underwater transport vessel." Commander Jeff Hashimoto pointed to the black-and-white photograph taped to an easel. He had just returned to Hawaii from Japan, hitching a ride on an air force cargo transport. The CIA operative was now standing in SUBCOMPAC's elegant office.

"To transport what?" asked Rear Admiral Michael Richardson as he stared at the photograph. It was a blowup of one of Hashimoto's clandestine shots from inside the phantom sub.

"That's it, sir. I just don't know. The volume of each twin hull is over five million cubic feet. That's an enormous carrying capacity by anyone's standards."

Richardson looked down at his desk, leafing through Hashimoto's top secret report. The fifty-four-year-old flag officer was commander of all U.S. Navy submarine forces in the Pacific Ocean. Because of his position and his long career as a sub driver, he was familiar with every major submarine system in the world—except for what Hashimoto had uncovered in Yokohama.

"Commander, what's your best guess as to this vessel's cargo?"

"When I first climbed aboard and got inside, I thought it might be some kind of new high-speed transport ship, capable of crossing under the ocean in record time. You know, kind of like their bullet trains. But instead of people, it would carry cars, or VCRs, or something like that."

Richardson just shook his head in disbelief.

"I know, sir. That idea's pretty far out, especially since there aren't any large-diameter access holds in the deck." He paused momentarily as he slipped a new photograph on to the easel. "However, when we spotted this it really started me thinking."

Richardson focused on the photo. It was a little dark, but the details were clear enough. It showed a close-up view of the joint between the curved hull and the aft bulkhead.

"Just what is that?" asked the admiral.

"I think it's some kind of a movable seal."

"A seal? What would that be for?"

Hashimoto pointed to the photograph. "This bulkhead looks like it's made of steel, right?"

"Yes."

"Well, it isn't. It's built of some kind of composite material. I couldn't tell for sure what it was, but it's definitely not steel or aluminum."

"Go on."

"Anyway, despite its massive appearance, the bulkhead is relatively lightweight. And bonded to its entire circumference is this." Hashimoto again placed a new photo on the easel. It was a close-up view of the joint. A black band of material a few inches thick separated the steel hull from the composite bulkhead wall.

"That looks like some kind of gasket," replied Richardson.

"Exactly, sir. That's what I thought, too. And when I probed the material with my knife, I found it to be both pliable and resilient."

"Meaning what?"

"It provides a watertight seal that's adjustable."

"I don't follow you, Commander."

"Sir, I think that bulkhead isn't fixed to the hull but is movable. It can be moved both forward and aft with a minimum force."

Richardson leaned forward in his chair, again studying the photo of the strange-looking wall section. For the first time he noticed the highly polished look of the hull's interior surface. "You mean to say that bulkhead, or whatever it is, can be repositioned along the length of the hull?"

"Correct. Think of it more like a portable dam that—" Hashimoto stopped in mid-sentence as a new thought popped into his mind. "Or better yet, think of the bulkhead as the seal in a hydraulic cylinder. Fluid pressure on the inside of the cylinder pushes against the seal, which in turn is connected to a lever arm that moves something."

Richardson envisioned the concept. "Okay, I see that. But what purpose could it serve? This thing's not a hydraulic ram, it's a damn submarine."

"I know that, sir. But think of this. That bulkhead could be used to separate two different fluids with slightly different densities and viscosities."

"Like what?"

"Like oil and seawater."

"Oil?"

"That's right."

Richardson leaned back in his chair. "Jesus, Commander, do you think this thing is some kind of underwater oil tanker?"

"That's right, sir. By filling the forward section with oil

and allowing the seal to slide aft, it could be bunkered just like a surface vessel.''

"But that would mean it would have to float high and dry after discharging the oil. There's no way the exterior trim or ballast tanks could provide enough displacement for that thing to sink."

"Unless the cargo hold was flooded," replied Hashimoto.

"But that would mean the oil tank would be contaminated."

"Maybe not, Admiral. If that seal is as good as I think, it won't let the two fluids become cross-linked."

"I don't understand."

"Sir, that seal will act like a . . ." He paused for a moment as he searched for the right words. "Like a squeegee, you know, when you clean the windows of your car. The rubber seal carries all of the water and soap away, leaving a smooth, clean surface."

Richardson nodded his head. "I see what you're getting at now. That seal, as it moved back and forth, would scrub the walls clean so there wouldn't be any cross-contamination."

"Yes, sir. And that's why the hull's interior is polished. It provides a perfect medium for the seal."

"I'll be damned. That's clever as hell. To make this thing function underwater, all you'd have to do is pump oil in on one side of the seal while keeping the other side open to the sea. The oil pushes the seal aft, displacing the seawater."

"That's right. And to remove the oil all you have to do is reverse the process. The hull always remains flooded with either oil or seawater."

"But what about oil flotation?" asked Richardson.

"You could easily compensate for the changes in relative buoyancy between the oil and water by using a modest array of trim tanks, maybe even flooding the annular space between the inner and outer hulls."

"Did you see any evidence of that?"

"No, sir. The twin pontoons' hulls were sealed up on both the bottom and topside. They weren't accessible. But I've done a little figuring." He pulled up a new exhibit and placed it on the easel. It was a computer-drawn cross section through the sub's hull.

"Admiral, I plotted this up last night. It's hypothetical, of course, but I think it's accurate."

Richardson caught on instantly when he spotted the open space nestled between the top and bottom halves of the twin cylinders. "So that's where the trim tanks are?"

"I think so. And when I ran the calcs, it turns out there's plenty of space in there to accommodate the required ballast. A couple of compressor units and half a dozen high-pressure tanks is all it would take to control the thing."

Richardson stood up and walked toward the window. It was all becoming clear now. "Commander, from what you've just described, that sub could operate at almost any depth."

"That's right, sir. Those twin hulls aren't pressure casings. As long as the cylinders remain vented to the sea on one end, and the internal seals are free to move back and forth, you won't get any hydrostatic pressure buildup across the seal— just a small change from the different fluid densities."

"So the only limits on depth would be the sub's other components—propulsion and environment spaces. They'd have to be designed to resist the pressure."

"Yes, sir. But unfortunately, we didn't have time to check out those spaces. They were too far away."

Richardson walked back to his desk and sat down. "So what did you see?"

"There was definitely some kind of superstructure near the stern." He paused to pull out another enlarged photograph. "I took this photo looking down the length of the sub."

Richardson could see a mass of steel rising thirty feet above the deck in the distance. It looked like another pipe. "So what is that?" asked the admiral.

"I think it's a pressure casing for the control room and the crew's living quarters."

"But it's so small compared to the rest of the hull."

"I know. But when you think about it, it wouldn't take much of a crew to control this thing—just like surface tankers require only a skeleton crew."

"I see your point. That does make sense." Richardson hesitated as a new thought occurred. "So how is this thing propelled?"

Hashimoto shook his head from side to side. "I don't know, sir. That's still a mystery. There are two large pods on each side of the hull, just aft of the control room, or whatever that superstructure is."

"Nuclear power?"

"We don't think so. The ROV's instruments, as well as our own, didn't detect a hint of radiation in that graving dock."

"Then they're using some kind of closed-cycle system."

"Right. Might be some modification to a Sterling or one of their new superconducting electromagnetic drives."

Richardson shifted in his seat. "Well, Commander, if it's not nuclear then it must move like a slug, even with Sterlings."

"I agree. It probably has a top speed of around eighteen to twenty knots. But when you think about it, they wouldn't have to move very fast. At a couple of thousand feet deep they would be immune to all storm waves and surface-induced currents."

"Yeah, I guess you're right. It could plod along, just like its counterpart on the surface." Richardson paused as he thought about the hundreds of oil tankers that routinely plied the oceans on a daily basis. Oil was still the lifeline to all of the industrialized nations, and despite the problems in the Middle East there were plenty of surface tankers available to move crude oil from the secondary producers to the world markets. "Commander, there's one thing that bothers me about this whole theory of yours."

"Sir?"

"It doesn't make any sense. Why would the Japanese want to invent a submarine tanker when they have more than enough tankships right now? Surely this thing must have cost many times what a normal tanker would cost."

"I know, sir. And I share your concern. I don't know why they'd build it. Especially now that they have their own major oil source."

"You mean the Nemuro field."

"Yes. All they have to do is pump the crude ashore. Their interisland pipeline system will then distribute it to all of their major refineries." Hashimoto glanced at the easel. "And they don't even have one tanker berth at that complex, so I don't understand the need for this sub-tanker."

"Yet this thing really exists," Richardson said as he pointed to the photo of the phantom sub.

"Yes, sir. They're obviously up to something that we don't

know about. Perhaps when they put this prototype out to sea, we'll be able to track it and find out what they're up to.''

''Commander, I don't think this is a prototype.''

''What? You mean there are others?'' asked Hashimoto.

''I now think so. So far we've had three confirmed observations of slow-moving, deep-operating sub contacts in the central Pacific. The contacts fit your description like a glove.''

''Good Lord, I had no idea that these things were operational.''

''Well, we've known about these other boats for a while. However, we haven't had a clue as to who they belonged to. But based on what you've just reported, I think the mystery has been solved.''

Hashimoto was shocked. He had been kept out of the loop regarding the phantom subs. The CIA officer had been operating under the premise that he was spying on an experimental Japanese shipbuilding program. ''But, sir, if they have more of those boats that are now ranging thousands of miles from Japan's home waters, what are they doing out there?''

''I don't know, Commander. But we're sure as hell going to find out, one way or the other.''

23

MR. YAKUZA

Tokyo

Hiroshi Yoshida stood up from behind his desk and smiled when the visitor entered his office. The tiny man hobbled through the doorway. He looked like he was ready for the grave. The little hair remaining on his scalp had turned white and his facial skin had a scaly appearance, almost like it was ready to peel away. But it was his eyes that reflected his inner image. Despite his advanced age, they remained sharp and clear, just like his mind.

"Oyabun, it is good to see you again," Yoshida said as he bowed in respect to the man who now stood in front of him.

Mura Mori lowered his head. "And it is good to see you, my friend."

"Come in and join me. We have much to talk about."

The two Japanese men walked into the adjacent dining room and sat down at the *tsuke.* A male aide discreetly served green tea and then left. They were now alone.

"And how has your family been?" asked Yoshida.

"Fine, I have four grandsons now." He neglected to mention his five granddaughters, but they didn't really count.

"Oh, excellent. Then you will have many to carry on your name."

"I suppose so, but what about you? You still have time."

Yoshida laughed. "I'm too old to pillow anymore. Besides, my seed is rotten. I'll never have an heir."

Mori sipped at his steaming cup. He held the cup between his thumb and forefinger. "It's a shame. You have so much to offer with your bloodline."

"It doesn't matter. The company will live on for generations. That will be my heritage."

"Ah, yes. I see what you mean. Your contribution will indeed be remembered for all time." Mori was sincere. Yoshida Heavy Industries, along with all of its subsidiaries and satellite companies, was one of the largest conglomerates in the world. It was bigger than General Motors and Ford combined. And Yoshida still owned 30 percent of the stock, making him one of the wealthiest men in the world.

"Tell me, my friend," Yoshida said, "what news do you have regarding the American?"

Mori leaned closer to the table, a smile now bursting across his face. "He has taken the bait—you shall have him and his company very soon."

"That is good news. Your people are most efficient in these matters."

"Yes, we have much experience." Mori grinned again as he took another sip of the hot tea.

Mura Mori was a master criminal. Initiated into the *yakuza* nearly sixty years earlier, he rose steadily through the ranks. His brilliant mind and natural instincts always kept him at least one step ahead of his bloodthirsty rivals. And leaps and bounds ahead of the police. Although his body was now weak and frail, during his younger days he was someone to reckon with. His short, stocky build had earned him the title of "The Bull." He had been a tough, mean street fighter, frequently demonstrating his physical power during the gang wars.

But it wasn't just his fighting ability that went with his nickname. Even though he married at twenty-eight and remained with the same woman for almost forty years, until she died, he also slept with numerous other women. As a consequence, he fathered several other offspring in addition to his own legitimate children. It seemed that certain women within the *yakuza* sphere of influence could never get enough of him.

Mori liked to think it was his lovemaking technique that made him popular, but it wasn't. It was his tattoos.

Mori's entire chest, back, and forearms were covered with elegantly crafted, multicolored skin portraits. The theme was the same for all of the designs: dragons. Mori often recalled the times when a new woman he was with saw the *irezumi* for the first time. The effect was nearly always the same— fascination followed by intense passion. The body art acted as a visual aphrodisiac.

Only once had a woman been repulsed by his tattoos. Nearly twenty years earlier, during one of his first visits to San Francisco, he had bought a $500-a-night call girl. The thirty-one-year-old prostitute almost turned green when Mori took off his shirt. She refused to have anything to do with him.

For the first time in years Mori had felt humiliation. He had wanted to kill the woman, but stopped himself. The others in his group never learned of the rebuke—the loss of face would have been catastrophic for Mori.

"Tell me, Mori-san, who did you use for this assignment?"

"Ah, you do not know him, but he is one of my most loyal men. His name is Kato. He's been with me for ten years now."

"Tell me about him."

Mori started to protest. "But . . ."

Yoshida raised his right hand to interrupt Mori. "My friend, I need to understand how Scott reacted to him. I can only know that if you tell me about him."

Mori nodded his head in understanding. "Kato is big, but not like a Sumo. He's mainly muscle and his size is intimidating to say the least."

"Tell me more."

"His English is nearly perfect. He spent a year at the University of British Columbia."

Yoshida's eyes blinked in surprise. "The man is educated?"

"Yes, he graduated from the University of Tokyo and then I sent him to Vancouver to study Western business ways."

"I'm impressed. Please continue."

"Kato's job was to convey your ultimatum to Scott. By sending an emissary who's born from our mold but at the same time has branched out into new areas, I wanted to send a clear signal to Scott. First, he is dealing with a sophisticated party, one who can match him in every way. And second, I wanted Scott to be physically intimidated.''

"And your Kato fits both?"

"That's correct. He's one of my most trusted aides." For the next few minutes Mori continued to recite the man's history.

"Well, my friend," Yoshida said, "your Kato appears to be an exceptional young man. I would like to meet him sometime."

"You will. I will bring him to the next stockholders meeting."

"Ah, excellent idea. We shall all dine after the meeting."

Yoshida and Mori had met nearly twenty-five years earlier, just after Yoshida Heavy Industries went public. At that time Yoshida needed money for expansion. He was forced to sell off part of the company in order to raise capital. And as he struggled to climb over his competition he incurred several years of losses. Most of the new stockholders accepted the devalued stock as a temporary setback and looked toward the future. But a handful of dissidents, ringers for some of his rivals, started making trouble. During the first annual meeting every stockholder was invited. A few loyal friends came, but almost all of the troublemakers showed up. They repeatedly attacked Yoshida for his business practices. The few press people who attended the meeting made sure YHI's embarrassment was thoroughly discussed in the financial pages.

Yoshida had been deeply offended. As a result, he vowed to never let such a spectacle happen again. That's when he met Mori.

Mori's group, like other *yakuza* organizations, offered a very special service, unique to Japanese corporations. For a fee, they would serve as sergeants at arms during stockholder meetings. Called *sokaiya*, the hired thugs attended the public meetings for the sole purpose of intimidating any opposition to corporate policy. Although it would have been unthinkable in the United States, the financial mercenaries often cursed, bullied, and in some cases, beat up stockholders who criticized company performance or asked embarrassing questions of its officers.

When the second YHI annual meeting started, Mori's team was in place. Just after Yoshida concluded his speech, summarizing the previous year's results and forecasting future growth, one of the troublemakers stood up and launched a verbal barrage. The man had managed to speak for only about twenty seconds before he was brutally knocked to the floor by two of Mori's thugs. They then beat the man without mercy.

No one else uttered a word in opposition. The reporters covering the meeting never printed a word of the event. Even the victim refused to press charges. Everyone got the message loud and clear: YHI was now off-limits.

And from that day on, YHI and Mori's organization remained linked. There was never any formal business connection between the two organizations—only an unwritten understanding between its leaders. Each would come to the aid of the other when needed, no questions asked.

"I have just one question about this matter that I would like answered, if you can," Mori said. He and Yoshida were now standing, walking toward the doorway of the office.

"Of course. What is it?"

"This man, Scott, did he somehow offend you in the past?"

Yoshida looked the old man straight in the eyes. "No, my friend, he just happens to be in the way—nothing more than a pesky fly that I will swat into oblivion at the right time."

Mori nodded his head in understanding and headed through the door. His aide was waiting by the elevator. *Pesky fly my ass!* thought Mori as he walked into the open elevator car. *Hiroshi's lying—he's hiding something about this man Scott.*

Seattle

Zackary Scott and Harold Shapiro stood side by side in the elevator car as it raced upward, heading for the top floor of the Seattle high rise. It was a few days after Zack had briefed the attorney on Wendy's kidnapping.

Scott and Shapiro were alone in the oak-lined compartment. Muzak played in the background and both men remained silent. When the elevator finally reached the forty-ninth floor it stopped and the sliding doors pulled back. Shapiro stepped out first, like the point man in a combat patrol. His client followed behind. They were deep in enemy territory.

Shapiro walked up to the reception counter. A pretty brunette in her early twenties sat behind the desk, a headset wrapped around her long hair.

"We're from Scott Coastal Systems to meet with David Wilson."

"Yes, sir. I'll tell him you're here."

Shapiro turned around and directed Zack to sit in the corner of the expansive reception area.

"This must be a big firm," Scott said as he sat in one of the elegant black leather chairs.

"Yeah, it's big all right—they've got about sixty attorneys here. But it's just a branch office. The main office is headquartered in Washington, D.C. They have several hundred back there plus a bunch in San Francisco and L.A."

"Do you think this David Wilson knows what's really going on?"

"No way. No legitimate law firm would have anything to do with a transaction like this."

"Yeah, I suppose you're right."

Zack was just about to ask another question when a man walked up to them. He was in his early forties, tall and thin. His wavy brown hair was cut to a respectable length; his suit was a standard Brooks Brothers attorney cut.

"Good morning, gentlemen. I'm David Wilson." He extended his hand. Shapiro rose first. "Hal Shapiro, and this is Zackary Scott, CEO of Scott Coastal Systems."

The three men exchanged handshakes and small talk, customary for introductions where none of the parties knew each other. Wilson then got down to business. "Gentlemen, my client's in the conference room, so why don't we head over there now."

When Zack walked into the conference room, he expected it to be filled with an army of professionals: tax attorneys, accountants, bankers, and all of the other players who are typically involved in a complicated business transaction. But he was surprised. Sitting at the opposite side of the twenty-foot-long marble boardroom table was a woman. She was in her early thirties. She wore a conservatively cut gray-and-blue dress that didn't hide the attractive curves of her slim body.

Her long black hair flowed onto her shoulders. A pearl necklace graced her tan neckline.

It was her face, however, that really caught Zack's interest. He felt her presence the second he looked into those deep brown eyes. It was almost like being under a spell. The woman's European heritage dominated her magnificently sculptured facial features, but the touch of Asian blood magnified those assets. To say her beauty was striking was an understatement.

"Mr. Scott, Mr. Shapiro," Wilson said as he ushered them toward the woman, "this is my client's representative, Ms. Cindy DeMorey."

Cindy rose and extended her hand across the table. When Zack shook her hand he again felt her presence, but this time it was a different feeling. He studied her face for a moment as she greeted Shapiro and then as all four sat down. A second later, it struck him like a bucket of cold water thrown into his face. *She's the one I saw on the yacht!*

It all flashed back to Scott in an instant. The underwater approach to the yacht anchored in Vancouver's Coal Harbour; watching the older Asian man and this woman; and then his narrow escape, aided by Finn Sorenson's shotgun attack.

"Gentlemen," Wilson said, starting off the meeting, "it's my understanding that we're ready to execute this transaction this morning. All of the details regarding the transfer of assets have been agreed upon in previous meetings by the attorneys, and by signing the agreement today we should be able to close in a few weeks."

Zack was about to respond when Shapiro took over. "Ah, David, I assume Ms. DeMorey has full signature authority for Pacific Venture Holdings."

"Oh, yes. She is the senior vice president of the company. She's also a major shareholder. Cindy has the written authority to execute this agreement on behalf of the board of directors."

Wilson passed an impressive-looking document to Shapiro. Zack's attorney read over the corporate resolution. He didn't recognize any of the signatures. But then he wasn't expecting to. A team of paralegals from his office had spent the better part of the week tracking down the real owners of Pacific Venture Holdings (PVH). Like the ownership of the *Victory,* a.k.a. the *Divine Wind,* the sinuous path of PVH's ownership passed through succeeding American corporate entities. First was the actual holding company, registered as a Washington State corporation. It didn't take long to learn that PVH was solely owned by a California corporation based in Los Angeles. That company was in turn owned by a New York–based firm. And so it went. Shapiro's people finally ran into a dead end when they traced parent ownership of PVH to another holding company based in the Bahamas. In order to go any further, it would require delicate negotiations with certain Bahamian officials followed up with a lot of cash. Shapiro didn't need to go to that extreme, however. He had seen the pattern of ownership before. He guessed they'd probably never find the true ownership. But it didn't matter. One way or the other, the ownership would eventually wind its way back to Japan. The *yakuza* had learned to legally hide assets just like the American mob.

"Okay, this looks in order," Shapiro said as he handed the resolution back to Wilson.

"Good, then I think we should—"

"No," Zack interrupted. "Just wait a minute. Before we go any further, I want a word with Ms. DeMorey—in private."

Cindy turned toward Wilson, shaking her head no.

Wilson started to respond: "I don't think that would be—"

"Either you talk to me right now, alone, or this deal's dead. It's that simple."

"Zack, what are you doing?" questioned Shapiro.

"It's all right, Hal. Now both of you, go get a cup of coffee. This won't take long."

Cindy nodded her head in agreement and Wilson and Shapiro left the room.

Zack stared across the table. Her mysterious spell no longer held him. The bitterness and anger inside of him welled up once again. It was all he could do to keep himself from reaching across the table and wringing her pretty neck.

"Before I sign a damn thing, I want proof that Wendy's alive."

Cindy locked on to Zack's eyes. "Mr. Scott, I don't know what you're talking about." She was a convincing liar.

"Bullshit, you're up to your pretty eyeballs in this. Now, I don't care how you do it, but you go over to that phone and get Wendy on the line. I know you can do it."

Cindy turned to the right and glanced at the telephone on the counter at the head of the table. "Mr. Scott, I assure you that I do not know what you're talking about. I'm simply the local corporate officer of PVH. I was instructed by the board to execute the purchase agreement."

"You're lying through those perfect teeth of yours. I know she's in Japan—your man told me. Now get on the damn phone and call 'em."

"How dare you speak to me like that!"

"Listen, you little bitch, I know who you are and who you really work for." Scott was now on a fishing expedition. He had the woman on the run.

"What do you mean?"

"We've met before. Don't you remember?"

"You're crazy. I've never laid eyes on you until just a few minutes ago."

"It was only a few weeks ago—in Vancouver. On the *Divine Wind*. Does that ring a bell?"

Cindy stirred in her seat. *How could he know that?* "You're mistaken. I haven't been in Vancouver for months."

"Don't give me that crap. You and your Japanese benefactor are behind this whole scheme."

What? How could he know that? Uncle Yoshida has never been linked to any of this. "I'm getting tired of this, Mr. Scott. Now I must insist that you stop badgering me. You've obviously got me mixed up with someone else."

Zack smiled. He was ready to issue the coup de grâce. "Honey, you're some liar, but I want you to understand something. I personally saw you on that yacht. You and your elderly Japanese friend were talking about how you sabotaged my drilling rig, the *Kelda Scott*. Remember now?"

A startled look flashed across Cindy's face. *That was him?* Cindy had caught only a glimpse of the intruder as he spied on their meeting, peeking through the yacht's window. She tried to regain her composure, but the shocked look on her face gave her away.

"I don't know what you're talking about, Mr. Scott. You're not making any sense."

Zack grinned. "Like I said earlier, prove to me that Wendy is alive and we'll continue with this little charade. If you don't, then the deal's off." Zack bit his tongue to restrain himself from adding *and then I'll hunt you down and slit that pretty little neck of yours from ear to ear.* He could barely contain himself now. Not only had this woman been involved in the kidnapping of his daughter and the impending financial ruin of his company, but she had played a role in the sinking of the *Kelda Scott.* Fifty-two men and women had been lost. *You murdering bitch*, he thought.

Cindy didn't respond. She worried that Scott might be carrying a tape recorder. Instead, she stood up and walked to the end of the room, where she picked up the phone. She punched in a series of numbers. Zack counted the digits. There were seven—a local call.

Cindy whispered into the mouthpiece, her back turned to Scott. He heard just enough to know she was speaking in English. The conversation lasted half a minute and then she hung up.

Cindy waited silently at the head of the conference table, looking out the windows. She ignored Scott's presence. Four minutes later the phone rang. She picked up the handset.

"Ms. DeMorey, please," said the law firm's receptionist.

"Speaking," replied Cindy.

"Oh, ma'am, I have an overseas call for you. I wasn't sure if you were still in the conference room. One moment please and I'll make the connection."

"Hello," Cindy said.

"Ohayo," replied a male voice.

"Speak English," Cindy ordered, her voice a whisper.

"Yes, go ahead."

"Is she ready?"

"Yes."

"Then put her on the line."

Cindy could hear noise from the phone being passed about and a moment later Wendy Scott's voice was broadcast through the earpiece. "Hello." Her voice quavered. *Good*, thought Cindy, *she's still scared.*

DeMorey held up the phone and turned toward Zack. "It's for you."

Zack raced for the phone.

When Cindy handed him the handset she made a quick comment, her voice barely audible: "You've got one minute so make the most of it."

Zack pulled the phone to his head. "Wendy, is that you?"

"Yes, Daddy, it's me."

Scott clearly recognized his daughter's voice despite a background hum. "How are you, honey? Have they hurt you?"

"I'm okay. But what's going on—why was I kidnapped?"

Zack didn't answer. Instead he asked another question. "What have they told you about this?"

"Nothing, all I know is what they told me to read for that video—did you see it?"

"Yes and I'm paying the ransom now. I think you should be released real soon."

"When?"

Scott turned to face DeMorey, his hand covering the mouthpiece. "How long before she's released?" he asked.

"We'll be ready to close in about two weeks—if we finish our business this morning."

"*Two weeks!*" shouted Zack. "We can't wait that long."

"That's the deal, Mr. Scott. Take it or leave it." Cindy turned away.

Zack was furious. He wanted to lash out at the woman but somehow restrained himself. He took a couple of seconds to calm down before removing his hand from the speaker. "Ah, honey, it might take a couple of weeks."

"Oh, God, that long?"

"Hang in there, kid. It'll go quick."

Wendy could hardly stand to spend another hour in her prison let alone another fourteen days. But she had no choice. "Okay, but I'll be so glad to get out of here."

"Are they treating you okay?" asked Zack.

"Yeah, I guess so. But no one talks to me and I'm locked in this tiny little room all the time."

"Where are you?"

Silence.

"Wendy, you still there?"

"Yeah, Daddy. I can't say anything about where I'm at—they won't let me."

"They're monitoring this call?"

"Yes."

"Well, okay." Zack paused. He was about to ask another question when Cindy DeMorey started tapping her knuckles against the conference table. Zack turned to face her. She then pointed her right index finger at her wristwatch. Scott nodded his head. "Look, honey, they're making me hang up now. Have you got anything you want me to say to your mother or to Dan?"

"Tell 'em both that I love them." Wendy hesitated a second and then continued. "And tell Dan that I hope he gets the Piper Alpha grant."

What do you mean, Piper Alpha grant? Scott wanted to ask, caught off guard by Wendy's comment. But before he could comment the line went dead. Scott looked back toward Cindy. Her right index finger was pressing down on the phone button.

Zack frowned as he returned the handset to Cindy. She then spoke, her voice strong and steady: "Are you now ready to proceed with the transaction, Mr. Scott?"

"Yes, let's get this damn thing over with."

"Excellent."

Executing the transfer and placing all of the documents into escrow was surprisingly simple. It took only half an hour to complete. The formal transfer of SCS assets to PVH would take place in twelve days.

When the final signatures were inked and notarized, attorney David Wilson was more than a little surprised at Zackary Scott's refusal to shake his hand or that of his client. The rebuke, however, was mitigated a few minutes after Scott and Shapiro left the conference room. Cindy DeMorey informed him that if he continued to shepherd the transaction and personally handled the closing she would pay his firm a bonus of $100,000. Wilson could hardly wait to comply with her request. With a huge killing like that on his side of the partnership ledger, he was a shoo-in to win the firm's upcoming election for the highly prestigious position of Managing Partner, West Coast Operations.

North Pacific Ocean

All eight subthermocline hydrophones on Remote Buoy Station A-119 heard the transient. The underwater sound was just loud enough to be detected over the ocean's background noise. It sounded like a garden hose squirting into a pool of water.

The $3 million sonar surveillance system was moored to the ocean bottom five hundred miles south of Adak Island, near the end of the Aleutian Island chain. The array had been deployed by a special U.S. Navy oceanographic research vessel a few days earlier. A total of ten sonar sensors were attached to the array, spread out uniformly along the length of a Kevlar cable that rose fifteen thousand feet upward from the bottom. The terminal end of the synthetic cable was connected to a ten-foot-diameter solid-foam buoy. The buoy, however, was not on the surface. Instead, it had been deliberately positioned so that it would remain submerged at an approximate depth of a hundred and fifty feet. The buoy's fifteen tons of positive buoyancy held the cable taut, like a helium-filled balloon straining at its moorings just before liftoff.

As soon as the sensors detected the unusual noise, electronic signals pulsed through a fiber-optic cable that was lashed to the Kevlar anchor line. The signals were fed into a microprocessor encased within the center of the buoy. The computer sorted out the various messages, storing them magnetically. It would continue to record the underwater transient until it stopped. Then, if the transient didn't return within a two-hour postmonitoring period, a buoyant probe, one of two dozen attached to the exterior of the buoy, would be jettisoned. The probe, an aluminum cylinder six inches in diameter and twenty-four inches long, would rise to the surface, where a spring-loaded, three-foot-long wire antenna would be released. The probe would then begin broadcasting a coded radio message, relaying the recorded sonar sounds to an overhead satellite.

The highly secret spacecraft, parked in a geostationary orbit 22,500 miles over the central Pacific Ocean, would then use one of its EHF communication payload modules to downlink the signal to the Naval Oceanographic Command (NOC) at Pearl Harbor, Hawaii. The NOC controls the U.S. military's Sound Surveillance System (SOSUS) for the entire Pacific Ocean. The probe broadcasts its message for up to an hour and then self-destructs, sinking to the bottom so it cannot be captured by unfriendly forces.

The sound transient at Buoy Station A-119 lasted only five

and half minutes before it faded away. Precisely two hours later, one of the expendable radio probes was released. As soon as it broke the surface it began sending out word of the discovery.

The state-of-the-art hydrophone system on Buoy Station A-119 provided the NOC computer at Pearl Harbor with sufficient raw data to plot the depth, relative heading, and speed of the contact as it moved past the array. Each one of the vertical sensors heard the transient noise at a slightly different angle than its neighbors. By using a repetitive process of comparing differences in sound signals at each hydrophone it was possible to develop a vertical datum line that could be used to plot the position of the contact. Because of the enormous numbers of calculations that would be required, it might take a man several months to work through the data before coming up with the answer. The NOC computer, however, spit out the answer after just forty seconds.

Seattle

Commander Halley Blake read the report for the second time before tossing it onto her desk. The two-page document had just been delivered to her office. It was an official U.S. Coast Guard incident report that had been filed by the *Pacific Voyager* when it berthed in Los Angeles. The container ship had reported observing a large flarelike explosion offshore of the Washington coast, south of the Strait of Juan de Fuca.

Halley scanned the wall to the right side of her desk. A chart of the Washington coastline was pinned to it. She mentally plotted the earth coordinates of where the ship had observed the sighting. *Good Lord,* she thought as she stared at the map. The Hammer 4 oil field was within a half mile of the detonation point.

Zackary Scott and Finn Sorenson were sitting on deck chairs by Zack's pool. It was a balmy seventy-two degrees. The late afternoon sun was sinking in the west. Each man held an ice-cold bottle of beer.

"Jesus, Zack," Finn said, "I can't tell you how glad I am

that you got a chance to talk with Wendy. At least we know she's okay.''

"Yeah, for the time being."

Sorenson took another sip of beer. "There's got to be something we can do to stop those pricks."

"I don't know what to do. All I can hope for is that they'll live up to their part of the deal."

Fat chance of that happening is what Finn wanted to reply. But he didn't. Zack was already under too much strain. "Okay, hopefully they will. So once you get your daughter back, why not turn the bastards in. No court would ever enforce a contract you signed under duress."

"I know that. Shapiro also pointed it out. But the only trouble with that scenario is that I won't have any legal proof. It'll be their word against mine and Wendy's." Zack took a long drag on his Budweiser. "Besides, if they're really connected with the *yakuza,* I gotta believe they wouldn't hesitate for a moment to take us out—permanently."

"Yeah, I see your point," remarked Finn. "They've got us pretty well boxed in, don't they?"

"Yep. According to Shapiro, if I turned these pricks in, the only real protection I can expect from the government would be to place my family in the federal witness protection program."

"Gees, that's not much of an alternative."

"That's right. We'd have to take on entirely new identities, move to some backwoods berg, give up seeing our other family members and friends. And I'd still lose SCS."

"Damn it," Finn said. "Then there's nothing we can do but accept it."

"Yeah, and that's just what we're going to do—bend over and take it." Zack swallowed another swig of beer. He was silent as he stared out at the sparkling waters of the lake. He looked content as he sat there but his mind was running a mile a minute. *Once I've got Wendy back, I'll find the prick behind all of this. And if it's the last damn thing I ever do, I'm going to tear that guy's heart out!*

24

DOUBLE-CROSSED

Hunts Point

Zack woke up early. It was the same nightmare that had haunted him for years: He was trapped inside the diving bell and his partner had just died. He glanced at the clock next to his side of the bed. It read 5:45 A.M. He thought about getting up but instead just lay there, looking out at the lake. The water had a gray tint to it now, like the clouds that sailed across the Seattle skyline.

The dreary morning reflected Zack's feeling. After Finn had headed back to Seattle the previous evening, Zack remained on the deck, lamenting his precarious situation. The four beers he drank didn't help much either. The alcohol did nothing to mitigate the mounting depression that had engulfed him. He finally went back into his house when the sun disappeared at half past nine.

The only bright spot in the evening had been the phone call to his family. Kelda, Matt, and Tim were all safe and sound, and continuing to enjoy living on Uncle Jason's ranch. That was comforting to Zack. At least for the time being he didn't have to worry about their safety.

Kelda still had no inkling that Wendy was missing, let alone had been kidnapped. The Seattle press had not made the connection that the missing University of Hawaii grad student—now presumed to have drowned offshore of Oahu—was Zack-

ary Scott's daughter. Consequently, Zack didn't have to lie
about that. But when he made his second call of the evening,
to Wendy's mother and his former first wife, that wasn't the
case. Susan and her husband had been in Honolulu for several
days, conducting their own search to recover Wendy's body.

Zack wanted to tell Susan the truth—that Wendy had really
been kidnapped and was being held in Japan for ransom—but
he didn't dare. He knew his first wife like the back of his
hand. Susan was stubborn, demanding, and bullheaded—not
all necessarily undesirable traits, but sometimes she carried
them to extremes. That was one of the reasons they broke up.

Zack couldn't help but imagine what would happen if Susan
discovered that her daughter was being held by a gang of
Asian thugs. *Damn, she'd go ballistic for sure. I bet she
wouldn't hesitate for a moment to call in the police and FBI,
not to mention the military. And then every damn newspaper
and TV reporter on the West Coast would be digging into this
mess. We'd never get Wendy back.*

To keep Wendy's mother in check, Zack and Dan Wallace
had conspired to continue to let her believe that her daughter
was lost at sea. The charade was particularly hard on Dan,
now that Susan was in Hawaii. But he'd come through. Wendy's release was too close to blow now.

Zack had tried to call Dan, to tell him about his conversation
with Wendy. But Dan never answered the phone. Zack would
try again later today.

Zack finally rolled out of bed at quarter past six. He arrived
at his office a few minutes before eight A.M., delayed by a
wreck on the 520 bridge. The remainder of the morning was
uneventful, until just a few minutes after eleven. And then all
hell broke loose.

Tim Marshall walked into Scott's office. "Say, Zack, I just
got a call from a buddy of mine at Fletcher General. He said
to turn on the television. Apparently there's some kind of news
conference going on right now. It's about SCS."

"What are you talking about?"

"I know it sounds weird, but can I turn your set on?"

"Of course."

Zack pushed his chair away from the desk, joining Marshall
by the built-in television cabinet at the far end of the room.

Tim flipped through the channels until he found it. And Zack about had a heart attack. The color image of Cindy DeMorey, standing at a podium, filled the screen. She was wearing a tan jacket with a white silk blouse and a red scarf. Elegant gold earrings dangled from her earlobes. She looked smashing as she read from a set of notes.

"Pacific Venture Holdings is pleased to announce today the acquisition of two divisions of the Seattle-based Scott Coastal Systems. Our company is purchasing SCS's offshore oil exploration and deep ocean diving divisions. Specifically, we will be acquiring all of the company's semisubmersible drilling rigs, SCS's fleet of support vessels, and of course, all of SCS's current leasehold interests in its vast petroleum holdings across the globe."

"What about the Hammer 4 tract?" someone yelled from the audience.

DeMorey looked up briefly. "Please, I'll get to that in a moment." She then continued reading the prepared text. "All employees of both divisions will be transferred to PVH's corporate control next week. We are expecting that there will be no changes in staffing or management. The transition has been designed to minimize disturbances so that SCS personnel can be integrated into the new organization without the typical problems associated with new acquisitions."

"What about the rest of SCS—what happens to them?"

Cindy decided to answer the question before continuing. "The coastal construction division will be retained by SCS. It will be reconsolidating at its waterfront headquarters on the Duwamish. Mr. Zackary Scott and his senior managers will continue to own and operate that division. But Mr. Scott will not be associated with the others."

Cindy ignored another question and again turned to her notes. "Now, I'm sure all of you are acutely aware of the near-disastrous oil spill that occurred at the Hammer 4 drilling site earlier this summer." The background chatter in the room dropped noticeably when Cindy mentioned the controversial exploration site located off the Washington coast. "Naturally, we at PVH are very concerned about the long-term consequences of the spill and have agreed to fund a ten-year, eleven-million-dollar monitoring study to evaluate the impact. We have also agreed to set up a fifteen-million-dollar trust fund with the Coast Guard to compensate fishermen for potential losses resulting from the spill.''

''What about all of the fines and penalties?'' yelled a voice from the audience.

''Our acquisition of the two SCS divisions specifically excludes any responsibility for civil and criminal penalties associated with the Hammer 4 spill. The remaining parent SCS corporation will continue to be responsible for those costs.''

''What about Scott, is he still going to face trial for polluting?''

''I'm sorry, I can't really comment on that, other than to say that it is my understanding that Mr. Scott, along with the corporate management of SCS, continues to remain under investigation by the Justice Department.''

Cindy started to read from her notes when she was interrupted again.

''What about the Hammer 4 site?'' yelled the reporter. ''Are you going to try to convince the Department of Interior to let you start drilling again?''

Cindy briefly looked up, facing the woman sitting directly in front of the podium. ''Your question is timely. I was just getting to that.'' She again looked down at her notes. ''As a consequence of the disastrous spill and the tragic loss of the fifty-two crew members from the drilling vessel the *Kelda Scott*, PVH has decided not to pursue development of the Hammer 4 tract.''

There was a huge increase in audience cross talk after Cindy delivered the bombshell. The same woman reporter spoke up again. ''Miss DeMorey, that's an incredible decision. Are you saying that PVH is not going to try to extract all of that valuable oil off the coast?''

Cindy smiled. The press conference was going perfectly. ''To be quite frank, the economics of the situation also played a role in PVH's decision not to develop the Hammer 4 tract. It turns out that there really isn't as much oil and gas offshore as earlier reported.''

''How can that be?'' shouted another reporter, a man sitting in the back row. ''The Hammer 4 tract was supposed to be another Prudhoe Bay.''

''Yes, we know all of those reports. But unfortunately, the initial production potential forecasts turned out to be grossly inflated. There just isn't that much petroleum offshore of the coast as originally estimated.''

The reporter started a follow-up question, but Cindy raised her hand, heading him off. ''I know what you're thinking. Yes, we could develop the site and, yes, we'd probably make a profit—maybe even a lot of money. But at what cost? The Hammer 4 site has already experienced a near-catastrophic blowout. It was just pure luck that it was contained so quickly and that the spill, for the most part, remained offshore. We at PVH do not wish to see a repeat of that. We believe the Washington coastline, as well as the shores of our neighbors to the north and south, are among the most natural and unspoiled in the entire world. Consequently, we have elected not to drill here. We will continue to concentrate our efforts in the traditional global areas: the Gulf of Mexico, the North Sea, and the Middle East.''

Another reporter spoke out: ''But what about the leases on the Hammer 4 site? You could sell them to someone else who might not be so generous.''

''Yes, you're right. That's why we've elected to place all of the Hammer 4 leases in trust with the Offshore Conservancy League. This will prevent any drilling at the site for at least the next twenty-five years.''

There was clapping in the background as the enormity of Cindy's statement hit home. By handing over the incredibly valuable prepaid offshore leases to the nonprofit national coastal environmental protection organization, PVH had insured that no one, not even the federal government, could get them back until the lease term expired.

Cindy was suddenly barraged with a broadside of questions. She responded for the next five minutes and then left the podium. The news conference was over.

Zackary Scott stood quietly during the whole episode. But Tim Marshall cursed repeatedly to himself as he listened to DeMorey. When Zack finally turned the TV off, Marshall couldn't stand it anymore.

''Zack, what in the hell is going on with those people? Are they out of their frigging minds?''

Scott just shook his head in disbelief. ''They're walking away from the Hammer 4 site like it's pocket change.''

"But there's millions of barrels of oil there—the flow test proved that! And what's this bullshit about the site only having marginal deposits?"

"I don't know." Zack paused for a moment—he was confused. "That's what I thought these bastards were after the whole time—the Hammer 4 oil. But now they've just given it away."

"Yeah, and to those Green Bigot bastards. I just can't believe that."

Zack walked back to the couch by his desk and plopped down. He felt sick, like all of the life had been sucked out of him.

"Tim, why would they go to so much trouble: sabotaging the well, kidnapping Wendy, and buying SCS, and then just give it all up?"

Marshall just shook his head back and forth. "I don't know. None of this damn business makes any sense."

Pearl Harbor

"Sir, as best as we can determine, this is where the projected course of that sub contact from Buoy Station A-119 would end up." The U.S. Navy lieutenant pointed his right index finger at a photograph on the conference desk.

Admiral Richardson leaned closer to the table, studying the black-and-white photo. The twenty-four-inch by twenty-four-inch contact sheet was an aerial image of a remote shoreline area. The jagged rocks of the coastline were ringed with a solid band of white. There had been a heavy sea running when the photograph was snapped.

The photo had been taken earlier in the day by a high-flying U.S. Air Force reconnaissance jet. The RF-16 had originated from an American-controlled air base in central Japan. Its flight plan, filed in advance with Japanese air controllers, called for it to fly northeasterly over Hokkaido Island, heading for the Russian coastline. The aircraft's officially reported mission was to photograph a Russian military installation in the northern Kuril Islands. The real mission, however, was to spy on the Nemuro Oil Complex.

"So this must be the main oil platform," Richardson commented as he pointed toward the center of the photo. The object looked like a huge industrial plant sitting in the middle of the ocean. Half a dozen other satellite plants were clustered around the main unit. They were all located farther offshore.

"Aye, sir," replied the thirty-year-old officer. Lieutenant Larry Williams looked like a recruiter's dream: muscular build standing a shade over six feet tall, short dark brown hair, tan face, and ice-cold blue eyes. "That's the main complex," he continued. "The other units are remote drilling platforms and production risers. They probably have a couple dozen wells on each satellite platform plus dozens more on the subsea wellheads."

"Subsea wells, what are you talking about?" Admiral Richardson knew a little bit about the offshore oil exploration business, but absolutely nothing about the mechanics of transporting oil once it was found.

Williams planted his elbows on the table top. "Sir, they're oil wells that are drilled some distance away from the main collection point, maybe a mile or more away. You won't see any of them in the photo, though. They're hidden entirely underwater."

The admiral turned away from the photo, running a hand through his graying hair. "There's no platform over them?" he asked.

"That's right. Everything associated with a subsea well is located right on the bottom: valves, control gear, monitoring equipment, everything. It's all automated, requiring no direct human contact. The oil flows up the production tubing to the subsea wellhead system, located on the ocean bottom. It then discharges into one or more underwater pipelines that lead back to one of the satellite platforms."

Richardson looked back at the aerial photograph. "Then all the flow lines end up at the main platform?"

"Correct, sir. The satellites pump the oil to the central platform complex. It's then collected and discharged into the shore pipeline."

"Where does the oil come ashore?" asked Richardson.

"Right about here." Williams pointed to the photograph. "You can see the disturbance in the shoreline where they cut a trench through the rock."

"That's all impressive to me. How typical is a setup like this?"

"Oh, it's perfectly normal. We've got a lot of similar setups in the Gulf of Mexico and the North Sea. And the Gulf of Arabia is loaded with similar platforms. The Nemuro Complex is one of the largest, though."

"Okay, if this is such a normal deal, why in the world would one of those behemoth phantom subs be heading right for it?"

"Sir, I have no idea. Maybe it's just a coincidence. Or maybe the boat was really heading for the west side of Hokkaido. It could have run through one of those passages."

"Pretty damn narrow and shallow in there for a monster like that boat."

The lieutenant didn't respond. Instead, he stood silently to the side as the admiral picked up another set of photos and began thumbing through them. The prints were the continuation of the recon flight as the jet passed over the Kuril Islands north of Nemuro. Richardson focused on the last contact sheet. A moment later he broke the silence. "What the hell's this? A ship?" SUBCOMPAC pointed to a tiny white spot near the middle of the photo. It looked like a blemish on the photo.

Williams bent closer to the table. "Oh, that. I took a look at that with a magnifying glass earlier. It's a drilling rig. And it's in deep water, so it means it's likely a floater, probably some type of semisubmersible."

"Is it Japanese?"

"No, I doubt it. I think it's in Russian waters." The officer picked up a plastic engineer's scale from the table top and measured the distance between the object and a nearby shoreline. "Yep, that's what I thought. That semi's on the Russian side of Friz Strait, not the Japanese."

"So someone else is trying to cash in on the Nemuro find?"

"It would seem so, sir. But I don't think they're going to find much out there. The Japanese claim that all of the oil in the Nemuro basin lies south of the Habomai Islands, not north where that rig's operating."

Richardson shifted position in his chair. "I didn't think the Russians had any gear like that."

"They don't, sir. They still lease most of the offshore drilling equipment, especially a deepwater rig like that one."

"So who owns it?"

"I don't know, sir. But it shouldn't be too hard to find out. I can have the negative of this photo blown up. Based on the semi's hull configuration and deck equipment layout we should be able to figure out the class. Once we've got that we can track down the owner."

"Good, I want you to get on this immediately. I need that rig ID'ed by tomorrow."

"Aye, aye, sir. I'll get right on it."

"Very well," replied Richardson as he stood up. He then walked out of the room, heading for the communications center. He needed to make an encrypted call to the Pentagon.

Seattle

It was now a few minutes past one in the afternoon and SCS's corporate headquarters was in chaos. The phone lines were jammed with callers—everyone from newspaper reporters to employees on vacation was calling the office to verify the statements from Cindy DeMorey's press conference. The announcement that PVH was acquiring most of Scott Coastal Systems was hardly news—just another business transaction. But her statement that PVH would permanently abandon the Hammer 4 oil field went off like a nuclear bomb. Already local and regional environmental groups were claiming victory in their long campaign to save the Washington coastline from offshore petroleum development.

Zackary Scott was still in shock over the whole affair. He refused to take any of the calls. He also instructed the company's executives, as well as the rest of the staff, not to talk with the press or environmental groups. SCS's receptionists were told to inform all of the callers that the company had no comment at this time but that it would be providing a press release at a later date.

Zack was blankly staring out of the window wall of his office when Tim Marshall walked through the doorway.

"Excuse me, Zack, but we need to talk."

"Come on in, Tim. What is it?"

"I just got a call from Warren Koons." Marshall paused for a moment. "Zack, he's not too happy with you right now."

Zack wasn't surprised. Koons was a Houston-based oil exploration syndicator. His firm specialized in finding investors for independent oil exploration companies like SCS. Koons had brokered the deal for the Hammer 4 tract, assembling nearly a dozen investors. It was his largest deal. In total, the group owned 25 percent of the development rights to the Hammer 4 oil fields. Koons himself had deferred his hefty commission, taking a piece of the pie instead.

"What did he have to say?"

"First of all he wanted confirmation on what that DeMorey woman—"

"How'd he find out about that so quickly?" interrupted Zack.

"Apparently, just before DeMorey went on the air here, PVH released a press briefing paper in Houston and a couple of other oil patch cities. A local CNN bureau rep in Dallas spotted the story and convinced Atlanta to pick it up nationally. It's been one of CNN's lead stories all morning."

"Damnit, that all had to be planned."

"Yep, it sure looks that way."

"What did you tell 'im?" asked Scott.

"That we were in the process of selling our interest in the leases but that we had no prior knowledge about PVH's intention to abandon Hammer 4."

"What else did you say?"

"Just that we were trying to confirm DeMorey's statements and that I'd get back to him when I had more information."

"I bet that went over like a lead balloon."

"Yeah, no kidding. Koons said that if we didn't kill this deal, he and the other investors would sue SCS and PVH into the middle of the next century. I don't think he was bluffing either."

"No, I'm sure he wasn't," Zack replied. "Those boys have invested millions in the deal, and if I were getting screwed like they were, I'd want blood, too."

"But legally, they don't have a leg to stand on under the terms of our partnership agreement. When we assign our interest to PVH, it will control the leases, and if it doesn't want to develop the Hammer 4 tract, there's nothing the minority partners can do about it."

"I know," Zack said, shaking his head. "Who would have

ever thought that the managing partner of the group would abandon the site. Koons and the others must be going crazy.''

Both men moved over a few steps to the left, sitting down on the soft leather chairs of an informal reception space next to Zack's desk.

Marshall was speaking. "You know, Zack, this all sounds fishy to me. Why would PVH give up developing the Hammer tract? The oil spill problem will get worked out and there's probably a couple of hundred million barrels of oil down there—at the minimum.''

"I don't know. I originally thought they really wanted the Hammer 4 field, too.''

Tim locked onto Scott's eyes. "Maybe we should take Shapiro's advice and call in the FBI.''

"No way! Not until I get Wendy back.''

Marshall sat silently. He didn't have the courage to tell his boss what he was really thinking: *You'll never see her again— she's already gone for good!*

Zack stood up and stretched. His lower back was throbbing again. Despite the pain his mind was clear. It ran in high gear. *Those bastards are up to something else—I know it. But what?*

Zack sat down again and then turned to face Marshall. "Tim, they've orchestrated this whole takeover thing perfectly—right from the beginning. SCS is just some kind of a pawn to them. Whoever is behind all of this has some kind of hidden agenda, and they're using me and SCS as a smoke screen.''

"To hide what?'' asked Marshall.

"I have no idea—yet.''

"So what are we going to do about it?''

"I've got to get some leverage on these bastards before it's too late. And the only way I can think to do that is to threaten to break the deal.''

"But what about Wendy?''

"They won't hurt her, not until they're finished with me. I still own SCS, so the deal won't close until I say so.''

"But, Zack, all the transfer papers are in escrow—you've already signed the sales agreement. The balance of the funds are supposed to be wire-transferred in a couple of days.''

"Doesn't matter. Shapiro can junk the whole thing today. All he has to do is instruct the escrow agent not to close the transaction because a last-minute internal dispute between the parties has come up. That'll stop the deal cold. No escrow firm is going to complete the transaction with one party contesting it.''

"But they've repeatedly threatened to harm Wendy if you don't close.''

"I know that! What do you think has been motivating me from the beginning of this whole damn mess? Pay the ransom and get your daughter back! What better leverage than that.''

Marshall remained silent, unsure where his boss was going.

"Tim, after what they did this morning, I'm now convinced they never planned to release her in the first place.''

"Why? That doesn't make any sense.''

"Oh, yes, it does. Think about this: You know that once I get Wendy back there would be nothing to prevent me and SCS from trying to rescind the whole deal—even if they try to kill us off. All I'd have to do is file criminal conspiracy and fraud charges against PVH, and with Wendy back home to corroborate the kidnapping part of it, we'd make life miserable for them.''

"I think I see what you're getting at. They must have thought we'd try that.''

"Exactly, Tim. And that's why they had the press release today—it was deliberately done to do a number on me.'' Zack paused as he changed positions in the seat. "By announcing the transaction before it was time to release Wendy, they've tied my hands behind my back. I can't do anything.''

"I see what you're getting at now. They can keep stringing you along, using Wendy as a carrot to get what they want.''

"That's right. They know I've got two choices right now: Go along blindly with whatever they're up to, or alternatively, kill the sale.''

"But if you kill the deal, they'll lose whatever it is they really want.''

"Yeah, maybe, but I'm not so sure about that right now. Think about this scenario: SCS files charges against PVH and asks a court to rescind the transaction.''

"That's just what we talked about—you'd get the company back.''

"Not necessarily. Without Wendy we'd have no proof

about the kidnapping. We don't have one shred of evidence to prove PVH was behind this whole thing. There's no ransom note, no police involvement, no physical evidence at all. It'll be just our word against theirs.''

"But Wendy's missing—"

"From a boating accident in Hawaii," Zack interrupted. "Remember, Tim, PVH will claim her body was never found. A smart lawyer will milk that fact for all it's worth.''

"Damn!" shouted Marshall. "I see what you're getting at now. We'd be in court for ten years over this deal and we might actually lose in the end.''

"Precisely," replied Zack. "They'd claim we invented this whole thing in order to queer the sale. And at the minimum they'd tie the development of the Hammer 4 site into knots. No one would be able to do a thing out there for years until the lawsuits were settled.''

Marshall nodded his head. "And you can bet that during all that time the environmentalists would be lobbying Congress behind the scenes, trying to get the site permanently closed.''

"Yep, and with the right connections, plus PVH's commitment to close the site if it wins, they just might succeed.''

"That's got to be what they're after—shutting down Hammer 4! But why? It's just plain crazy to walk away from that much oil.''

"I know that and that's why we've got to figure out what it is they're really after. Once we have that, then I'll have a fighting chance of getting Wendy back, and maybe the company, too.''

"But how do we do that?" asked Tim.

"I think it's time I called in a favor from our friend from back east.''

"MacDonald?''

Zack nodded his head.

Marshall remained silent for a few seconds. "Zack, do you really think he can help?''

"God, I don't know," Zack said as he stood up. "If anyone can do the job, it'll be Mac and his boys. Besides, what choices do I have left?''

"I see your point.''

Washington, D.C.

"Good afternoon, Mr. President," said the man as he walked into the Oval Office.

President Chandler looked up from his desk and smiled. "Hi, Jack. Come on in."

Secretary of Defense John (Jack) Stephenson sat in one of the three black leather chairs that faced the president's elegant oak desk. A set of bay windows behind the president displayed the immaculate grounds. The roses were in full bloom.

"So what's this important news you've got?" asked Chandler.

The forty-six-year-old former congressman from California momentarily glanced down at his notes and then looked back at the president. "Sir, it's about Japan."

Craig Chandler rolled his eyes. *Not again!* He was tired of having to continually deal with the economic trade war that had erupted between the two nations. "Let me guess—they want to shut down another one of our bases over there."

"Well, I'm sure that will be coming but that's not why I'm here." Stephenson paused to again consult his notes. "Sir, it looks like the Japanese may have built some type of new submarine that we know very little about."

Chandler sat up straight in his chair, his interest suddenly surging. An Annapolis graduate, the president had served aboard a nuclear submarine during his early career—long before he resigned his commission to become a politician. "Did they buy another Russian sub?"

"No, sir. Definitely not. This one they built from scratch." Secretary Stephenson reached into his file folder. He pulled out an eight-by-ten glossy print and handed it to the president. "This is an aerial photo of the vessel while it was under construction in Yokohama."

Chandler stared at the photograph. There was a white arrow painted onto the print, pointing to the center of a long, narrow object located in the lower right-hand corner. It looked like a pair of pipes side by side. "What's this?"

"Sir, those are twin cylinders. They're structurally tied together. They may not look like much in that photo, but that pontoon hull is bigger than any boat we've got. For that matter, it's bigger than anything anyone else has.''

"How big is it?"

"It's nearly a thousand feet in length and has a two-hundred-foot beam.''

"Christ Almighty! A thousand feet long?"

"That's correct, sir. It has more submerged displacement than any of our carriers.''

"That's just incredible." The president looked up. "Jack, what is this thing for?"

"We don't know, sir. We've been trying to find out and even managed to get a couple of our people aboard the thing to check it out but the results were inconclusive.''

"You've been spying on their military?"

"No, sir. We haven't violated any defense treaties. This vessel has been under construction in a civilian yard. It's not under military control—at least not yet."

"Okay, I'm glad to hear that. I've got enough problems with their government right now, and if they should find out we've got agents running around inside one of their military vessels, they'll go ballistic.''

"I know that, sir. Our people have been very careful. As near as we can tell, the Japanese Self-Defense Forces are not involved in this matter.''

"All right, continue on, please."

"Our agents were only able to get aboard for a short time. The sub was berthed inside of a cleverly disguised graving dock.'' Stephenson reached for another aerial photo. "This warehouse building is really a fake," he said as he pointed to the center of the photo. "The sub's hidden . . .''

President Chandler nodded his head as the secretary of defense continued with the briefing. Ten minutes later Stephenson finished.

President Chandler was now obviously upset. "All right, Jack, you've got my attention. Now what's this damn thing built for? Is it some kind of missile boat?"

"We don't think so. It's way too big and there are no provisions for any missile tubes.''

Chandler stared at his friend. "So what is it then?"

"We think it's some kind of cargo carrier, maybe a tanker.''

The expression on the president's face telegraphed his surprise. "You mean to tell me this thing's designed to carry products of some kind?"

"That's right. But we don't know what for sure, only that it's probably some kind of fluid."

"Like an oil tanker?" asked the president.

"Maybe, but we just don't know."

The president again started shaking his head in disbelief. "What are these characters up to with this thing? Is it some kind of prototype vessel that'll give them another edge in world commerce?"

"Sorry, sir, but we just don't know. Our experts are dumbfounded about this whole matter. They tell me that it's technically feasible to transport bulk products by submarine, especially with the volume this thing has, but no one can imagine why the Japanese would want to do that. Compared to surface transport, the cost of an underwater transport system would be at least two times as expensive. Besides, they still have the largest tanker fleet in the world."

"That's right," replied the president. "In fact, I remember Bradley from Commerce telling me the other day that the Japanese now have a surplus of tankers and are selling them cheap. Something to do with all of that oil they're getting from that new project."

"Yes, sir. I'm aware of that. Their domestic crude oil production from the Nemuro Complex has drastically reduced the need to import oil so they don't need as many tankers."

What a bunch of lucky bastards, thought the president. *How'd they ever find so much oil in their own backyard?* "If they don't need tankers, then what's this boat for—some kind of grand experiment?"

"We don't think so. In fact, a couple of these things may already be in service."

"What? How could that be?"

"Our subs and SOSUS gear have tracked some very big objects in the mid-Pacific. They're absolutely huge and have been operating at enormous depths."

"How deep?"

"We have one confirmed contact at over six thousand feet."

The president let out a low whistle. "Jack, what the hell is going on here? I thought you said this thing didn't have any military application."

"That's right, we still don't think it does. But nevertheless, we've tracked a couple of these behemoths at great depths."

"What were they doing out there?"

"Unknown, sir. Maybe some kind of testing. We only managed to follow them for a short distance and then they faded away. They operate at such great depths that we can't touch 'em. We don't even have a torpedo that can go that deep."

"Where do they operate from?"

"We only have a hint at that from some intell data that just came in from Pearl." Stephenson pulled out a nautical chart from his briefcase. It was an underwater map of northern Hokkaido Island. "One of our hydrophones off the Aleutians picked up an unknown contact operating at great depth. It was traveling at constant course and speed. When we projected the course ahead, it ended up here."

President Chandler stared at Stephenson's index finger. "That's the Nemuro Oil Complex."

"Correct, sir."

"But what would it be doing there?"

"We just don't know. However, we're certain they're up to something big. The money required to build these things is just phenomenal. And we both know they don't waste their yen." Stephenson looked directly into Chandler's eyes. "So whatever they're doing, these subs have strategic economic value—that much I'm sure of."

The president pushed his chair away from the desk, turning around to face the garden. He remained motionless for about half a minute before again facing the secretary of defense. "Okay, Jack, just what do you want to do about this?"

"Sir, we'd like to insert a special recon unit into the Nemuro Complex to have a look around. We think we might be able to figure out what those new boats are doing if we can check out the bottom areas around a couple of the platforms."

"What kind of unit?"

"A SEAL team, like we used in Yokohama. They'd go in underwater using . . ."

Stephenson spent another six minutes outlining the complex clandestine operation. When he finished, Chandler had only one question: "Jack, what's the probability they'll be discovered?"

"Not much, sir. They're really good."

"I need a number, Jack—a realistic one with no bullshit."

Stephenson thought for a few seconds. The SEALs selected for the mission were the best in the navy. Yet the mission was fraught with danger. A hundred things could go wrong. "Sir, I'd say the mission has a probability of success of around seventy-five to eighty percent."

President Chandler closed his eyes. *That means it has a probability of failure of between twenty to twenty-five percent. Damnit, another decision to make.*

The president was under enormous political pressure from members of the rival party. The American economy was once again in the middle of a full-blown recession and he was feeling the heat. The huge increase in energy costs, coupled with increased economic competition from the European Community and the Pacific Rim, especially Japan, had crippled America. The balance of trade deficit was again growing at an alarming rate. He had his hands full with trying to keep things from getting worse. He felt like a juggler struggling to keep half a dozen balls whirling in the air, knowing that if he dropped just one, the others would surely follow.

"Jack, I understand your concern over this matter, but this recon mission couldn't come at a worse time. If your people are compromised, we'd have a mess on our hands."

"But the—"

Chandler raised his hand, stopping the defense secretary in mid-sentence. "Jack, I don't want to upset the apple cart right now. If the Japanese government gets wind that we're spying on their most cherished natural asset, you can be sure they'll use it as an excuse to dump on us. Remember, they've still got billions in our Treasury bills and notes. If they suddenly decided to dump their investments, we'd really be up the creek for sure. I can't risk that right now."

"I understand, sir. But I'm really worried about those subs. God only knows what they're doing with them."

Stephenson was about to leave when he had a new idea. "Sir, I just had a thought. Would it be permissible to consult with the CIA about this matter? Maybe, just maybe, we could get one of their deep cover agents onto the Nemuro platform. He might find something interesting that would help us with the mission at a later date."

"If he gets caught, then we'll have the same problem as the SEAL team."

"Maybe not. If we set it up to look like an industrial espionage operation, it would go over a lot better than if any of our military people got caught."

"Yeah, you're right about that. The Japanese have been trying to infiltrate our high-tech businesses for years and we're forever weeding them out."

"That's right. sir. We do the same thing to them, and for whatever reasons, industrial spying seems to be tolerated a hell of a lot better than military operations. I don't think they'd make the connection if it was handled just right."

"How would you do this?"

"I'm not sure yet, but I think we'd get some civilian operatives working on it. That way we could isolate the government if things go wrong."

"You wouldn't use any of our professionals?"

"No, now that I think about it, we wouldn't have to. There are plenty of NOCS out there we could use."

"NOCS?"

"Yeah, civilian operatives working under nonofficial cover. No diplomatic immunity if they get caught."

President Chandler reflected for a few moments before responding. "I guess that would be acceptable—as long as you keep our military and mainline intelligence forces out of this situation. What I don't want is a bunch of navy SEALs or CIA agents being tried in the Japanese press as spies. Just think how we'd react if we discovered a bunch of SDF people spying on us."

"Got it, sir. I'll start setting up a civilian operation right away."

"Okay."

Hunts Point

Zack was home, alone. It had been a tough day. All of the premature press about PVH taking over SCS had been overwhelming. It seemed that the nightmare would never end.

It was almost eleven and Zack was drained. He was just about to turn in but he had one last task to complete. He had not yet been able to get hold of Dan Wallace. Zack reached for the phone and punched in the numbers. The phone rang four times and then Dan finally answered.

"Hello."

"Dan, this is Zack."

"Hi, Zack."

"Man, you're hard to get a hold of."

"I know. I've been doing some field work over on Molokai—I just had to get out of here for a while. All of this stuff's been getting to me."

"Hey, I understand." Zack paused a moment. "Dan, they let me talk with Wendy yesterday. She's okay and . . ."

Zack spent the next few minutes rehashing his conversation with Wendy. Dan's spirits skyrocketed at the news. He had feared that she was dead.

"And one more thing, Dan. Wendy said something about hoping that you got the Piper Alpha grant."

"The what?"

"She said she hoped that you got the Piper Alpha grant."

"Gees, Zack, I don't know what you're talking about. Piper Alpha grant, I have no idea what that is."

Zack remained silent for a moment, his mind racing. *She said Piper Alpha, I know that for sure.* "Well, maybe she was mistaken. Is there some other grant you're going after?"

"No, and she knew that. I already accepted the Bechtel fellowship last month. We celebrated that one together."

Zack was taken aback. Something didn't make sense. "You have no idea what she was referring to?"

"None, at least connected to research funding. The only Piper Alpha I'm aware of was an oil complex in the North Sea—the one that had that terrible fire." Dan paused. "In fact, I think I remember you telling me that you did some work up there before."

Jesus Christ! Zack thought. He hadn't made the connection until now. "Yes, now that you mention it, we did some sat diving for Occidental—on a pipeline in the Claymore field."

"I thought so. Anyway, her comment about the Piper Alpha funding is really weird. There isn't any such thing—as far as I know."

Zack was about to agree when it finally hit him. "Damn," he said, "I think I've got it."

"What?"

"She was trying to give me a clue."

"What do you mean?"

"The Piper Alpha complex. We spent a day there, taking a tour."

"What?"

"Wendy and I. She was with me for part of her summer vacation and I was in Scotland then, waiting for our divers to show up. A buddy of mine ran the Piper Alpha complex and arranged for us to visit. We stayed overnight. It was a real eye-opener for Wendy—she'd never been on an offshore platform. That was before SCS went into the oil exploration business." Zack paused. "About a week later the whole damn thing went up. Between the explosion and the fire, over half the platform was blown away."

"Wow, that all happened just after you were there?" Dan asked.

"Yeah. Wendy was back in L.A. by then so I called her from the job site and told her what had happened. She was crushed." Zack paused a moment. "I was, too. My friend didn't make it."

The Piper Alpha fire was one of the worst offshore accidents in history. The huge North Sea oil production platform, located 125 miles east of Aberdeen, exploded and caught fire on the sixth of July 1988. One hundred and sixty-seven crewmen were killed.

"So what do you think she was trying to . . ." Dan's voice trailed off as he figured it out. "Damn, she's being held on an oil platform, isn't she?"

"That's got to be it," Zack replied.

"But where?"

"If she's really in Japan, like those bastards claim, then it can be only one place."

"Nemuro?"

"Yep."

"Oh my God!"

25

THE RECRUITER

Pearl Harbor

Admiral Richardson was at his desk reviewing a top secret directive from the chief of naval operations. The special orders, transmitted through the navy's chain of command, had originated directly from the secretary of defense's office just an hour earlier. Richardson had just started to review the document for a third time when the phone rang. He punched the intercom button on the telephone and picked up the receiver. "What is it, Hansen?"

"Sorry to disturb you, sir," replied the male clerk-typist sitting in Richardson's outer office. "But Lieutenant Williams is here to see you again. He insists that you've been waiting for his report."

"Yes, that's right. Send him in."

A few seconds later, the young naval intelligence officer entered the office. Williams walked up to Richardson's desk. He stood ramrod straight as he snapped a salute. "Good afternoon, sir," he said.

Richardson raised his arm in a halfhearted response. "Sit down, Lieutenant."

"Thank you, sir."

"So what have you got for me?"

Williams glanced down at his notes for a couple of seconds and then faced Richardson. "Sir, we've identified the drilling vessel in the aerial photograph that I showed you yesterday. It's American owned and is operated by a Seattle firm—Scott Coastal Systems, SCS for short. A guy named Zackery Scott runs it.''

"Scott Coastal,'' Richardson said, nodding his head. "I've heard of it.'' Richardson had, in fact, just finished reading a joint FBI and CIA top secret briefing report on SCS. It was an attachment to the CNO's directive.

"What else have you got, Lieutenant?''

"Apparently SCS has joint-ventured with a Russian company, Okhotsk Sea Ventures. They're jointly exploring for offshore oil around several islands in the Russian Kurils.''

"Have they found anything yet?'' asked SUBCOMPAC.

"I don't think so. Our records indicate that they just started work on a new bore in Friz Strait. That's the passage that separates Etorofu and Urup islands. It's the new international boundary between Russia and Japan's Northern Territories.''

Richardson nodded his head in acknowledgment.

Williams continued: "The name of the drilling rig is *Deepquestor*.'' The junior officer paused as he removed several sheets of paper and an eight-by-ten photo print from his file folder. He handed the documents to Richardson. "Here's a blowup of one of our aerial photos plus a write-up on the rig from a trade journal.''

Richardson glanced at the aerial photograph. He was amazed at the resolution of the enlargement. What had been a tiny white speck on the original photo was now incredibly detailed. The topside decks of the semi were crammed full of equipment and assorted gear. The vessel looked more like a Detroit steel plant than a ship. He could even see people standing on the catwalks and open platforms.

After setting the photograph on his desk Admiral Richardson began thumbing through a photocopy of a five-page document. It was from a back issue of *Offshore* magazine. The article was a write-up on Scott Coastal Systems. It featured the *Deepquestor*. There was even a small picture of Zackary Scott at the beginning of the article.

"This Scott?'' Richardson asked, pointing to the picture.

"Yes, sir. The article talks a little about him. Started out with a harbor diving company and then branched into deep-sea diving, mainly for the oil companies. He really hit it big a few years ago when he moved into the oil exploration business. Apparently, he's had some big finds.''

Lucky guy, thought Richardson. ''What else have you got on him?''

''Apparently his company, Scott Coastal, has done some work for us on the mainland. Mostly classified, associated with our SOSUS gear guarding Bangor.''

''Have you talked with anyone from SCS yet?'' asked Richardson.

''No, sir. I thought I'd check with you first before pursuing it.''

''Good. Now here's what I want you to do . . .''

An hour and a half after meeting with SUBCOMPAC, Lieutenant Larry Williams boarded a navy Gulfstream at Hickam Air Force Base. The military executive jet took off ten minutes later. It was headed for Seattle's Boeing Field.

Seattle

Zackary Scott was in his office, leaning back in his chair. His feet were planted on the desk top. He had just finished a long telephone conversation with a former customer. *If anyone can do it, Mac can*, he thought.

Several years earlier, Zack met a very unusual man. Mac MacDonald was a former U.S. Navy special warfare officer who, upon retirement, started up an international security firm. The firm catered to the security needs of the megacorporations, providing a variety of services ranging from bodyguard training to developing computer systems that were immune to electronic eavesdropping.

Zack met MacDonald when MacDonald Security Consultants hired SCS to develop a new wireless long-range underwater diver-to-diver communication system. Zack never was told what the sophisticated hardware was for and could only guess what MSC was up to. Nevertheless, he grew to like and respect MacDonald. They eventually established a solid business relationship.

Zack was now forced to call on MSC for help.

Although it was not widely known, MacDonald and a handful of the several hundred MSC employees also excelled in a very specialized security matter: hostage rescue. Zack had just retained the firm to help him find Wendy. Later in the afternoon, a $250,000 retainer would be wired to MSC's headquarters in Arlington, Virginia.

After arriving in Seattle the previous evening, Lieutenant Larry Williams, USN, spent nearly the whole morning going over the FBI's files on Scott Coastal Systems. He was in a special FBI security area located in the massive Federal Building in downtown Seattle. The stack of file folders and bound reports on Williams's desk stood just over a foot tall. The bonanza of information had been recently compiled by the FBI as a consequence of the Hammer 4 oil spill. When the EPA filed criminal conspiracy charges against SCS, a special investigative unit from the Bureau's Seattle office launched the probe. Five agents were assigned to the mini-task force. In the space of just a few weeks they gathered a mountain of information on SCS and Zackary Scott.

The door lock to Williams's office snapped open with a click. The naval officer instinctively turned toward the sound. A second later the door swung open and a tall, lanky man walked in. Dressed in a conservative dark wool suit, Martin Doyle was the perfect embodiment of an FBI agent. Except he wasn't with the FBI. He was CIA.

"Oh, there you are," called out Doyle as he spotted the naval officer.

"What's up?" asked Williams.

"I just wondered if you had any more questions. I'm going to be leaving the office in about an hour for some meetings and thought you might like to talk."

"Great, your timing's perfect. I do have a couple of things I'd like clarification on."

"Fire away."

Williams moved back to his desk and sat down. He retrieved a pad of yellow legal-size paper and began scanning his notes. "Oh, yeah, here it is." He paused for just a second. "Martin, what can you tell me about this merger between SCS and PVH? I found several references to it in these files."

"We don't know much yet. It just happened—it's taken us by complete surprise."

"What is this PVH company?"

"Stands for Pacific Venture Holdings. We're tracking through the corporate ownership right now. So far we've only found a series of paper companies, with the trail leading first to the Bahamas and then to Korea and now to Japan. We've got some people in Tokyo right now making some inquires."

"Japan? Why would they be involved?"

Doyle shook his head. "Hell, I don't know. I was just assigned to this case like you. All I know is that our orders are coming right from the top and we have max priority."

"The top?"

"Yeah, the White House."

"Jesus, how do you know that?"

Doyle smiled. "Sorry, that's classified." What Doyle wouldn't admit to, however, was that it was his boss' secretary who had told him his orders had originated from the office of the president.

Lieutenant Williams looked back at the desk top, once again scanning his notes. He was puzzled by the whole operation. "Martin, do you think this PVH company is legit?" he finally asked as he refocused on Doyle.

"Hard to say. There are quite a few legitimate corporations operating in the U.S. but controlled through offshore holding companies. But then again, there are also some real badasses in the group."

"What do you mean by that?"

"Mostly druggies and other organized crime groups. They set up offshore corps and load them up with illicit cash. Then they start up some kind of legitimate business back in the States, or as may be the case with SCS, buy a perfectly legal U.S. company with the hot cash. Typically, what they'll do is have their offshore holding company loan its American counterpart the laundered money. The American corp will then buy real estate or a business or some other legitimate enterprise—paying cash from the loan proceeds."

"Why do they use loans instead of direct payment?"

"It's a tax deal," Doyle said. "If the money's brought into the U.S. as a loan, it isn't taxed as income. Only the interest is taxed and then that's deductible for the American corp."

"Hum, I see what you're getting at. The loans are never paid off."

"Right, they just carry them on the books. It's perfectly

legal because we can't regulate those offshore banks. Down there, they don't have to ask where the original money comes from—like our bankers do. All those offshore banks care about is the color of the money.''

Williams stiffened up in his seat. ''So you think this might be what's going on with SCS?''

''Possibly, but the dollars involved are enormous. So far we estimate that the sales price will be somewhere in the vicinity of one hundred and twenty million.''

''Cash?''

''Yep, that's what it's looking like.''

''Wow,'' Williams said. ''That fellow Scott is going to make a killing.''

''Yeah, he's going to do all right,'' replied Doyle. ''The bean counters tell me he'll probably net somewhere around sixty to seventy million.''

''No wonder he's selling out.''

''You'd think so, but there's a real twist to the whole thing that bothers me and a lot of others.''

''What's that?''

''That Hammer 4 tract. The Interior people tell me it's really loaded with oil—a couple hundred million barrels at the minimum and probably a lot more.''

Williams remained quiet for a moment as he worked the numbers in his head. ''Good Lord, at sixty bucks a barrel, that crude would be worth over ten billion.''

''That's right. You beginning to see the picture?''

''I think so. One hundred and twenty million is chicken feed. Why would Scott ever sell out at such a cheap price?''

''Yeah, that's what has been bugging me, too.'' Doyle then reached into his coat pocket and removed a pack of cigarettes. He offered one to Williams but the officer declined. Doyle ignored the No Smoking sign on the wall.

Williams waited for the CIA agent to light up before speaking. ''Maybe he thinks the government won't let him drill there anymore? These newspaper reports I read on the oil spill sure indicated that the environmentalists wanted the project shut down.''

''That's true,'' Doyle said. ''But if it were your company and you had the potential of owning one of the largest petroleum finds in North America, wouldn't you hang on for a while longer—fighting your way through the courts if you had to.''

''You bet. And if necessary I'd bring in more partners to share the costs.''

''Exactly, and with the potential pot of gold at the end of that rainbow you wouldn't have much trouble recruiting investors—I think they'd jump at the hint of an opportunity. And with the shortage of oil right now I think they'd eventually win the court battles to get the right to continue developing the oil.''

''So why's he selling out so cheap?'' asked Williams.

''We don't know.''

''Has anyone talked to him yet?''

''No, we're not ready yet.''

Williams again scanned his notes and then turned back to face Doyle. ''How about this woman from PVH—the one who made the announcement that they weren't going to develop the Hammer 4 field? That just doesn't sound right to me, if the oil's really there.''

''Quite frankly, we're all a little puzzled by that situation. We know damn well that no one's going to walk away from those leases or turn them over to the environmentalists. That would be economic suicide.''

''Yeah, I agree. There must be something going on behind the scenes. On the surface, none of this makes any sense to me.''

Doyle nodded his head. ''Yep, that's why we're continuing to probe Pacific Venture's ownership. Once we find out who the real owner is we'll have a better chance of unraveling this mystery.''

''But that's going to take time, isn't it?''

''Maybe. Our operatives in Japan may have some answers later today. I'll let you know as soon as we get something.''

''Great, the more I know, the better chance I'll have with Scott.''

''When are you planning to see him?''

''Admiral Richardson is pushing me like crazy. He wants an answer ASAP, so I guess I'll have to try tomorrow.''

''Good. We need to fast-track this thing if it's ever going to fly.''

''I know.''

* * *

Zackary Scott was in his office with Tim Marshall when the call came in. It was from Commander Halley Blake. "Hello, Commander," Zack said.

"Mr. Scott?"

"Yes. I'm on a speakerphone and Tim Marshall, my senior vice president, is with me."

"Oh, okay." Halley was taken aback by the third party to her call. "Well, I'm calling about the Hammer 4 situation."

"Did we get some more oil washing up on the beach?" asked Zack.

"No, no. The cleanup operation's doing fine but we've got a little mystery on our hands that I thought you might be able to help solve."

Zack turned toward Marshall and raised his hands as if to say "Now what?" He then said, "Fire away, Commander."

For the next several minutes Halley described what the *Pacific Voyager* had reported.

"Just what kind of explosion was it?" Scott finally asked.

"We don't know, but it was big. The ignition flash covered a couple of acres. We confirmed it from surveillance satellite imagery."

"Exactly where did this happen?"

"Less than a mile west of the Hammer 4 wellhead."

Oh, shit, it can't be, thought Zack. "I see what you're getting at, Commander, but I don't think our well had anything to do with that explosion. It's sealed up tighter than Fort Knox."

"I understand that—I'm not trying to implicate you or SCS. I'm just trying to come up with a logical explanation so I can close this file." She paused a moment. "Now, is it possible that your drilling operations or the capping of the blowout might have disturbed a shallow gas formation?"

"Let me answer that," whispered Marshall. Zack nodded his head.

"Commander, this is Tim Marshall. I'm familiar with the geology of the Hammer 4 bore. When we spudded in the casing we found no evidence of any gas-producing surface formations."

"Nothing?"

"That's right. Those bottom sediments are tight, clear into

bedrock. We only picked up our first gas signs at a depth of eleven thousand feet.''

Halley was caught off guard. She had thought she had the answer. ''Hum, well, I sure don't understand any of this.'' She paused a moment. ''What the heck could have blown up out there?''

''I'm sorry, Commander,'' Zack said, ''but I don't think we can help you with that.''

''Yeah, I guess so. Well, thanks for your time anyway.''

''Sure thing, call again if you have anymore questions.''

''I will. Good-bye.''

Marshall switched the phone off. ''What the hell was all that about?'' he asked

''I don't know, Tim. But whatever it was it doesn't concern us. We had nothing to do with that explosion.''

Zack was wrong.

The fax from Tokyo started printing out in the FBI's Seattle office at 9:03 P.M. Ten minutes later it was delivered to Lieutenant Williams. He was still in the cubbyhole office, reviewing the mountain of files on SCS.

The young naval officer scanned the two-page document. *Holy shit!* he thought as he sat down to reread it—this time slowly and carefully.

Two minutes later he tossed the paper onto the desk. *PVH is owned by Yoshida Heavy Industries? What the hell is going on?*

It was the next day and Zackary Scott was back in his office, sitting at his desk. It was late morning. He had just finished a telephone conversation with Captain Shay. The *Ranger* was still coming up dry. There was no sign of the *Odin* or her missing tow barge. *We're never going to find that damn BOP!*

Zack's thoughts were interrupted when his desk intercom came alive. It was his secretary's voice: ''Zack, there's a Lieutenant Williams in the lobby and he would like to see you for a couple of minutes.''

''Who?'' asked Scott as he stared at his speaker.

''Lieutenant Williams. He's with the navy. He doesn't have an appointment, but says it's urgent.''

"Hang on a minute." Zack dropped his feet to the floor and then punched the intercom line to Tim Marshall's office. "Tim, you there?" he asked.

"Yeah, Zack. What's up?"

"Are we doing any work for the navy right now?"

"Ah, no. I don't think so. Give me a sec and I'll check our job list."

Zack waited for Marshall to cue up his desktop computer. He answered about half a minute later. "Yep, just as I thought. We're not under contract with the navy or for that matter with any other service branches." Marshall momentarily paused. "Is there some kind of problem?"

"I don't know. Janet just told me there's some navy lieutenant in our lobby looking for me."

"You want me to screen this guy for you?"

Zack looked down at his watch. It was almost lunchtime. He knew Tim Marshall was planning to jog over his noon break. "No, I'll take care of it. Enjoy your run."

"Thanks, I will."

Two minutes later, Williams walked into Scott's office. Zack was instantly impressed with the officer. His uniform was immaculate and his handshake firm.

They were now both seated at Zack's conference table in the far corner of the office. After commenting on the spectacular view Williams turned his attention to Scott. "I'm sorry to barge in on you like this, Mr. Scott, but I was hoping you might be able to help me."

"With what?"

"It's a national security concern. And before we go any further I have to tell you that what I'm about to reveal to you is highly classified. Nothing I say can be written down or conveyed to others. You carry a top secret clearance so I know you're familiar with these procedures."

"Yes, go on."

Williams opened up his leather briefcase, removing a folded-up color map. He unfolded the document and laid it on the table. Zack's interest surged when he recognized the map of Japan.

"I assume you're familiar with Japan."

"A little. I've been to Tokyo a couple of times."

"Good, then you must have heard of the Nemuro Oil Complex." Williams pointed to the northeast tip of Hokkaido Island.

"Yes, of course. It's a colossal oil find." *Nemuro! What does this guy want?* thought Scott.

Williams removed another document from his briefcase. It was an incredibly detailed high-altitude aerial photograph of the Nemuro peninsula and the southern Kuril Islands.

"I assume this area is familiar to you also."

"Yes, I know that area well. In fact, one of my drilling rigs is moored nearby."

"Yes, sir. We're aware of that." Williams pulled out another aerial photo. The photograph was blown up to a larger scale. The unmistakable image of the *Deepquestor* dominated the print. The resolution was so detailed that Zack could actually see crew members on the open decks.

"My gosh, where'd you get that?"

Williams ignored the question. "That's the *Deepquestor* isn't it, sir?"

"Yes, but I don't ever remember seeing any photos like—" Zack stopped in mid-sentence when it finally dawned on him. *This thing was just made—over there.* "Was this taken from one of your satellites?" he asked.

"Sorry, I can't comment on that."

Zack placed the print back on the table. "Why are you here, Lieutenant?"

Williams evaded the question. "Sir, what can you tell me about the Nemuro Complex?"

"Like what?" asked Scott.

"How it's structured. Where would the oil wells be located. That kind of thing."

"Hell, I don't know. I've never been on it."

Once again Williams reached into his case and produced another photograph. It was a detailed blowup of a portion of one of the previous photos.

"Does this look familiar?"

"Sure," Zack said as he nodded his head. "I assume that's the main production platform."

"It is." Williams paused as he moved a little closer to the table. "Do you have knowledge of the underwater geology in the Nemuro area?"

"Personally no. But I've got people on my staff who do. You want me to bring them in here?"

"No. That won't be necessary."

Zack was getting tired of the cat-and-mouse game the navy officer was playing. "Lieutenant, what's going on here? Your own people probably know a lot more about that oil platform than I do. We're just trying to drill nearby, hoping to tap into a remnant of that field."

Williams looked Scott directly in the eyes. "You're right, sir. I'll cut the preliminaries and get down to the main event. Why are you selling your company?"

Zack stiffened up. "What the hell business is that of yours?"

Williams continued his evasion tactics. "Do you know who you're selling to?"

"Of course, PVH. It's a holding company for an oil and gas investment syndicate."

"But you don't know who really owns it, do you?"

Zack looked away from the naval officer, staring down at the rug. *What does this guy know? Why is he trying to grill me like this?* He turned back to face Williams. "Why don't you educate me, Lieutenant."

"Mr. Scott, it has taken our people a lot of time and effort but we've traced the ultimate ownership back to a single entity."

"A Japanese corporation, right?"

"Yes, it's a corporation all right. But that company is controlled by a single individual."

"One man?" Zack asked. He had been expecting the officer to say that the *yakuza* was the real owner.

"Yes, his name's Yoshida, Hiroshi Yoshida."

Zack sat up straight in his chair. "This guy's from Tokyo?"

"Yes. He's the CEO of Yoshida Heavy Industries—one of Japan's largest companies. I assume you've heard of it."

Zack nodded. "Only the name. I know nothing about it or this Yoshida character."

Lieutenant Williams pulled out another photograph and placed it on the desk in front of Scott. It was a color print of a man standing next to a limousine; he was about to step inside the passenger compartment. "This is a recent photo of Yoshida," Williams said.

Zack's emotions gave him away. His eyes seemed to widen to the size of saucer plates as he recognized the man. *That's the son of a bitch on the yacht in Vancouver!* The images of the underwater approach to the yacht, climbing aboard it, and then being chased by the submerged robot flooded back from his memory. *So that's who you are!*

"Have you ever met this man before?" asked Williams.

"No."

The naval officer guessed that Scott was lying but didn't press the issue. Instead, for the next ten minutes, he provided Zack with a detailed rundown on Yoshida and his empire. Scott listened quietly, occasionally asking for clarification on certain items. His face remained expressionless. The initial shock had worn off and Zack had regained control of his emotions.

When Williams finally finished, Zack stood up and walked back to the edge of the window wall. He said nothing. His mind, however, was like a whirlwind. Flashbacks continued to plague him: the *Kelda Scott* burning and then sinking; the wellhead spewing thousands of gallons of crude oil; his friends and loyal employees roasted to death. But the worst picture of all was what his mind fabricated: The image of Wendy, naked and drugged, being repeatedly violated by low-life scum, continued to haunt him.

Zack gritted his teeth as he flushed the terrible thoughts. He then began to focus on the positive: *Wendy's somewhere on the Nemuro Complex—this guy just confirmed it. But he doesn't even know it. I've got to let Mac know about this ASAP.*

For the first time in days, Zack didn't feel so helpless. Maybe he could really do something now. He turned around to face the naval officer. "Okay, Lieutenant, I think it's time that we get down to brass tacks. Now, just what is it you want from me?"

"I assume you're interested to know why Yoshida really wants to buy your company."

"Of course," Zack said. He was tempted to tell the officer about Wendy but stopped himself. It wasn't the right time.

"Well, we're interested, too." Williams paused. "Besides trying to secretly purchase SCS, this Yoshida character appears to be up to his eyeballs in a highly classified venture."

"What are you talking about?"

"I'll get to that in a moment, but first, I need to know something."

"What?"

"I assume you still control the *Deepquestor*?"

"Yes," Zack said as he sat back down in his chair. "SCS will retain ownership until the formal closing, and that will take place in five days."

"Good, now here's what we need . . ."

26

MOBILIZATION

Vladivostok, Russia

The gigantic U.S. Air Force C-5A Galaxy touched down on the long concrete runway just as the sun disappeared into China. The pilot engaged the thrust reversers and four jet engines roared in protest. Seven minutes later the cargo transport rolled up to a cargo terminal and stopped.

Less than an hour later, the cargo hold of the Galaxy was empty and the jet roared into the night, heading east. Sitting on the tarmac, next to a hangar building, was a sixty-foot-long truck trailer. It still had Washington State license plates on its rear end. On top of the trailer, shrouded in a thick green-gray canvas covering, was a cylindrical object. It was about twelve feet in diameter and occupied the entire length of the trailer. Unidentifiable, but quite noticeable, appurtenances jutted outward from the canvas in half a dozen places.

Lieutenant Williams was standing near the forward end of the trailer, watching as a Russian soldier jockeyed a tractor truck into position. After two tries the driver obtained the proper alignment and the universal coupling on the American trailer engaged its Russian counterpart.

Williams climbed into the cab. An army major, his Russian counterpart, was already inside, sitting next to the driver. "We're ready to roll," reported Williams.

The Russian officer nodded his head and then turned to the driver. "Move out," he said.

The giant truck-trailer combination began to roll along the taxiway. Six minutes later it drove through the main gate of the air base, pulling onto a narrow asphalt-paved roadway. The tractor-trailer combination seemed to fill the entire road with its bulk.

"How long will it take to get there?" asked Williams.

"About forty minutes."

Williams glanced at his watch. "Good. That should give us enough time to make the transfer before sunup—assuming, of course, your equipment is available."

"Yes, it is. I checked this afternoon. They are all ready for you."

Yakoda, Japan

While Lieutenant Williams and his special cargo rolled through the outskirts of Vladivostok, another American military cargo plane was completing its long flight across the Pacific. This time, however, the transport landed at an American air force base. The wheels of the C-141 Starlifter ground into the black asphalt runway at two-fifteen A.M., local time. Eight minutes later the jet pulled up to a holding area at the far end of the field, well away from the perimeter fence line of the base.

Fifteen minutes after the C-141 touched down, a huge U.S. Navy helicopter, a CH-53E Sea Stallion, landed near the tail of the cargo jet. The helo's three engines remained at high idle while it waited.

Inside the air force jet, the cargo master, a burly, middle-aged sergeant, was activating the hydraulic controls of the rear door system. Two clamshell doors rotated apart on each side of the tail assembly, exposing the cargo hold. An aluminum ramp was then extended downward to the asphalt surface.

Once the ramp was locked into position the sergeant turned to face his complement of passengers. He had to yell because of the noise from the Sea Stallion. "Okay, folks, that navy bird's all ready for you. Just head down this ramp and walk up its loading ramp."

Zackary Scott and Russ McMillin were the first ones out. Coast Guard Commander Halley Blake followed right behind. And finally, Finn Sorenson walked down the ramp. They all automatically ducked their heads as they walked under the helo's spinning rotors

When the special passengers climbed aboard the Sea Stallion, they were greeted by a man wearing green combat fatigues. He wore no insignia or rank. The only identification was the name tag over his right breast: HASHIMOTO.

While the CIA operative directed his passengers to the seating area, the Sea Stallion's loading ramp was retracted. The pilot then spooled up the engines to max power. Half a minute later, the huge helicopter broke its bond with the earth, roaring into the night sky. It flew toward the northwest; it was heading for the Sea of Japan.

Tokyo

Hiroshi Yoshida couldn't fall back to sleep. He lay wide awake on top of his tatami floor mat. The thick futon was pushed aside, exposing his night garment to the cool morning air. For several years now he had been experiencing a phenomenon common to many elderly people: He just didn't seem to need much sleep anymore. Consequently, he found himself waking up earlier and earlier.

He sat up in his darkened bedroom, leaning against a wall for support. He slipped on his reading glasses and then looked at the digital wall clock in the corner. Its luminous dial read 5:14 A.M.

Yoshida wanted a cigarette but ignored the urge for the time being. Once he had almost burned himself up when he fell asleep smoking. As a result, he never kept any cigarettes in his bedroom. He would have to get up and go into the living room if he wanted a smoke. He didn't want one that badly so he flipped on a light next to the bedding and reached for the telephone.

The telephone was an expensive model. It had a number of preset phone numbers programmed into its memory. He punched the numeral 9. It was his favorite number. Like most Japanese, Yoshida was superstitious when it came to numbers.

Nine was a good number; it was a sign of good fortune. The number 4, however, was the unluckiest number. It was to be avoided whenever possible.

Yoshida waited patiently for the international call to be completed. It was answered on the third ring.

"Hello," Cindy DeMorey said. She was inside the kitchen of her condominium, about to eat lunch.

"Hello, Cynthia," replied Yoshida, now speaking in Japanese.

"Uncle, it is so good to hear from you." Cindy paused momentarily as she looked at the wall clock. She made a quick calculation. "But it's so early in Tokyo. Is there a problem?"

"No. I just couldn't sleep anymore. I decided to call to check on the status of the purchase."

"Oh, everything's coming along fine. The attorneys tell me that the closing should take place on schedule. Scott appears to be cooperating."

"Good, I'm glad to hear that." Yoshida paused as he shifted the handset to the opposite ear. "Then we should go ahead and wire the balance of the funds?"

"Yes, I think that would be appropriate."

"I will see to it first thing this morning. Now, is there anything else we need to do over here to complete the transaction?"

Cindy took a few seconds before answering, going over a checklist of items in her head. The last mental entry jogged her memory. "Oh, what have you decided regarding the exchange?"

"Exchange?"

"Scott's security. What do we do about it?"

"Oh, that." Yoshida hesitated. He intended to keep Scott hanging to the very end by holding his daughter hostage. But now that the deal was as good as done, she was no longer needed. "I have not decided what to do about that yet. You do not need to worry about it."

"Fine, then there is nothing more for me to do here?"

"Yes, I think you should leave today. Have the attorney finish it up. I'll wire over the bonus payment for his firm and place it in escrow. That will keep him motivated." Yoshida didn't want his great-niece anywhere near Seattle when he sent the *yakuza* assassins to deal with Scott.

"Fine. I'll book a flight out tonight. I should arrive sometime tomorrow."

"Call the office with your arrival time. I will have a driver pick you up."

"Thank you, Uncle."

"Good-bye, my child."

Yoshida replaced the telephone handset in its cradle and then stood up. He walked over to a window wall and flipped a switch. The electric drive pulled the thick curtains away from the floor-to-ceiling wall. It was sunrise and the sky was cloudless. It would be a very nice day.

The brillant rising sun was a good omen and Yoshida felt like a great weight had been lifted from his shoulders. The nightmare was about to end. In just a few days he would control SCS, and Zackary Scott would be forever out of his life.

Sea of Japan

The skipper of the U.S.S. *Callaghan* was not used to waiting. Jogging at eight knots in the middle of the ocean was just not his style. He preferred to drive his 563-foot-long destroyer hard and fast. But his orders were explicit: Remain on station until contact is made.

He was just about to pour himself another cup of coffee from the bridge pot when the intercom came alive. "Bridge, CIC. We have a positive contact. Relative bearing zero-three-five degrees. Range eleven hundred yards."

It's about time, thought the captain as he set his cup onto the countertop.

The officer of the deck acknowledged the report while the skipper grabbed a pair of binoculars and headed onto the starboard bridge wing. The early morning air had a bite to it. The captain unconsciously shivered as the ship-generated wind blew over his body.

The sky was overcast but visibility was still good. It took him only a few seconds to spot the telltale blur of white water in the distance. *There you are,* he said to himself. He raised the binoculars to his eyes, focusing on the object.

By the time he had a clear image, the submarine's sail was

fully exposed. Thirty seconds later the remainder of the hull was in view. He recognized the hull. *That's the boat!* The captain just started to turn away when he noticed something different. *What the hell is that?* He could see something attached to the top of the deck, just behind the sail. It was big, about sixty feet long and almost as high as the fin itself. It was black, like the submarine, but it was not part of the hull. He shrugged off the anomaly: *Damn pig boats, they're always up to something weird.*

The captain returned to the warm bridge house and began issuing orders: "Make ready the launch. Get Air One up for SAR duty. Tell those people in the galley it's show time."

The forty-foot-long whaleboat rolled gently with the swells as its powerful diesel pushed it through the water. The five passengers were scattered between midships and the forward seating areas of the launch; the helmsman and tender manned the stern.

Zackary Scott and Finn Sorenson stood in the bow section. Halley Blake and Russ McMillin sat on a bench seat near the center of the craft. Commander Jeffrey Hashimoto stood next to the starboard railing, just behind McMillin. All five passengers carefully eyed the approaching submarine. The U.S.S. *Bremerton* looked like a black island.

Three minutes later the launch maneuvered next to the *Bremerton*'s lee side, about twenty feet forward of the sail. It looked like a toy alongside the long black hull. Despite the mass of the submarine, the long ocean swells rolled under its hull. As a consequence, the launch's two-man crew had all they could do to keep from smashing into the sub's steel hull.

At first Scott thought they might have to abandon the transfer because of the adverse sea conditions. But then the sub crew came to their rescue. A large rubber raft was inflated and tossed overboard. Then, by securing fore and aft lines from the raft to the sub's upper deck, the raft was moored alongside the hull. A rope ladder was deployed over the curved hull and two sailors from the *Bremerton* jumped into the raft. The motor launch was then able to tie onto the outer edge of the inflatable without worrying about hitting the hull.

The five passengers jumped from the whaleboat into the raft and then each climbed up the netting. Zack was the last to go.

As he pulled himself up the curved hull he noticed the green slime layer covering the special acoustic adsorping paint. *This baby's been at sea for a long time.*

When Scott climbed onto the top of the hull, a rating tried to usher him forward, toward the open hatch. But Zack protested. "Wait a second, I want to check something."

The sailor looked confused; he wasn't ready to deal with the civilian.

Zack recognized the man's dilemma. He turned aft, looking up at the sail. A man was perched atop the two-story-high fin, looking down at him. Zack waved as he yelled, "Skipper, permission to take a quick look-see at my property?"

The officer nodded his head affirmatively.

A minute later Zack was looking at *Little Mike.* The SCS submersible was mated to the afterdeck of the *Bremerton.* It looked like a baby whale riding on its mother's back. He spent the next five minutes examining the mini-sub's exterior surfaces. Everything looked in order.

As Zack headed back to the forward hatchway, he couldn't help but marvel at the efficiency of the U.S. Navy. Just a few days earlier, the fifty-ton submersible had been aboard one of SCS's work boats tied up to a dock on the Seattle waterfront. And then through a series of enormously expensive and secret operations, the mini-sub was moved almost halfway around the world. First it was lifted off the ship by special cranes and trucked in the middle of the night to McChord Air Force base in Tacoma. The mini-sub's entire exterior hull was then coated with a fast-drying gray-black paint. Later the same day it was loaded onto the largest cargo jet in the U.S. Air Force's fleet and flown to Vladivostok. Once in Russia, *Little Mike* was trucked to the port's industrial waterfront and loaded aboard the waiting *Bremerton.*

How in the hell did they ever get the Russians to do that? Zack wondered as he disappeared down the hatch.

Nemuro

It was a few minutes after ten P.M. when Wendy Scott heard the door lock open. It woke her instantly. Despite the ever-present noise from the platform's machinery, she heard the distinctive clicklike sound. Like her father, she was a light sleeper.

She pulled the blankets up to her neck. She wore only a pair of panties. "Who's there?" she called out. Her tiny cabin was dark.

The doorway to the cabin swung open and then she saw him. He was silhouetted against the doorway, backlit by an exterior light. Two seconds later the door was closed. He was inside. She could hear him breathing.

Wendy sat up straight, pressing her exposed back against the wood frame of the lower bunk bed. The two blankets slipped down, but the white sheet remained glued to her hand. She managed to bend her head just enough to keep from hitting the bottom of the mattress in the upper bunk. "What do you want?" she called out. Her voice gave away her fear.

"Do not be afraid. I've come to help you."

The shock of the male voice hit Wendy like a cold shower. For days now she had been locked up without any human contact—except for when she had talked to her father. Her meals were still delivered anonymously through the slot in the door. No one ever came to look in on her. The last voice she had heard was that of her father on the telephone.

"Who are you?" Wendy finally asked.

"A friend."

"Turn on the lights," she commanded.

"No, I can't. The guards might see the light through the door frame."

Wendy ignored the warning. She switched on a tiny reading lamp at the base of the bed.

The man was surprised by the light and flinched in response, trying to press his body into the corner by the doorway.

Wendy Scott leaned forward, examining the visitor. The Asian was young, about her own age. He was of average height and build. His short dark hair was neatly combed. His face was attractive.

"Why are you here?" asked Wendy. Her voice now calmer.

Yukio Nagai stared back at the *gaijin*. For nearly two weeks now he had passed by the cabin and wondered what was locked inside. At first, no one said anything—other than it was a special guest. But then he heard the rumors. Offshore oil platforms, like ships at sea, provide ripe breeding grounds for rumors. And the rumor he had heard was a masterpiece: Locked inside cabin 10A was an attractive foreigner. She was a *kinpatsu*, a blonde, his favorite.

But what really aroused Nagai's interest was why the woman was aboard. The American was a call girl—no, that was too polite—she was a whore. A real streetwise pro who had learned her trade in San Francisco's Tenderloin District. There wasn't anything she wouldn't do for money.

The rumor was that the *yakuza* had recruited her a few years back, encouraging her to set up shop in Japan. She accepted the lucrative offer and moved to Yokohama, where the business relationship blossomed. She serviced hundreds of shipyard and construction workers, crewmen from foreign vessels, and the occasional businessman who ventured out of his structured and controlled life to get a little taste of the underworld.

Going by the trade name of Wild Wendy, she became a star performer overnight. She was in incredible demand at all of the clubs and bars on the *gaijin* whore circuit. Her propensity to perform live sex acts with randomly picked patrons from the audience was legendary throughout the region. Everybody wanted Wild Wendy and would gladly pay for her services.

But somewhere along the line the *kinpatsu* ended up crosswise with her mob pimps. It was something about a dispute over money. As a consequence, she had been banished to the artificial island prison as punishment.

"I have lots of money," called out Nagai. His English was poor but understandable.

"Money, what are you talking about?"

Nagai was transfixed at the image in front of him. For days now he had fantasized over what Wild Wendy looked like. He had visualized her as older and tougher, almost callous. But the woman he was looking at now was young, soft, and glowing. And the way the light shown over her, it made her honey-blonde hair radiate. But what really made his loins stir was the sheet held across her chest. The nipples of her ample breasts protruded against the fabric. *She's naked under there.*

"How much for the night?" he asked.

"What?"

"How much do you want?"

"Who the hell do you think I am?" Wendy protested.

Nagai inched closer, shuffling his feet across the tile floor. He had a fistful of yen in his right hand; his left hand was busy unzipping his trousers. He hadn't been ashore in six weeks and he could hardly stand another day without relief.

Wendy Scott stared at the man as he slowly moved closer. His face seemed to be in some kind of trancelike state. His eyes were wide open. His mouth quavered. Then she noticed his fumbling at waist level. *What's he doing down there?* And before she could react, he was on top of her, his pants around his ankles.

Wendy let out a bloodcurdling scream and launched her right knee at his crotch. She then tore at the man's face with her fingernails.

Yukio Nagai didn't know what hit him. He had been expecting a cooperative whore, but instead found himself trying to screw a mountain lion. The blow to his testicles was the worst of it. Wendy's knee had connected perfectly with his exposed organs. The pain was as bad as it gets.

Nagai rolled off the bed, collapsing on the floor. He pulled his legs up into the fetal position and began moaning. Blood from the scratches on his cheek dripped onto the tile.

Wendy lay on the bed, exhausted from fear but still pumped up with what seemed like quarts of adrenaline. Her counter-attack had worked. She looked over the side. Her attacker was in no position to hurt her—for the time being. She then noticed the lower half of her bed. It was covered with yen notes. She picked up one, holding it to the light. *Money? He was offering me money? He must have thought I was a prostitute—but why?*

Before Wendy could complete her thoughts, the doorway to the cabin burst open. Two uniformed men rushed inside. Wendy instinctively pulled the blankets over her exposed chest.

The guards said nothing as they picked up Nagai by the armpits. After dragging him out of the cabin, they slammed the door shut and then relocked it.

Wendy sank back into her bed. She wanted to disappear. *Dear God, when am I going to get out of here?*

Tokyo

"Sir, I'm sorry to bother you, but we've just had a problem here."

Hiroshi Yoshida's back stiffened. He was sitting in a private booth at a Ginza bar, enjoying a late dinner with one of his female companions. The Nemuro Oil Complex's general manager was about to ruin his meal.

A few minutes earlier the manager had called YHI's central switchboard. The on-duty security officer then routed the call directly to Yoshida's personal cellular phone.

"What happened?" asked Yoshida.

"It was the Scott woman. One of our crewmen attacked her."

"Attacked?"

"Yes, sir. Apparently he thought she was a prostitute and he wanted to buy sex from her."

Yoshida rolled his eyes back. *What idiots,* he thought. "Is she all right?"

"Yes, sir. But I think it might be a good idea to remove her from here." He paused to consider his next words. "Sir, I have enough trouble with the unmarried men as it is now. Having a woman like that aboard will just create more problems."

"Put a full-time guard by the cabin for now. I'll be coming aboard tomorrow and will take care of it then."

"Excellent, sir. I am sorry to bother you, but you did leave instructions that you were to be notified if anything happened to the American."

"That's correct. You did as you were expected. Thank you."

Before the man could respond, Yoshida hung up.

Yoshida smiled at his companion. The young woman sitting across the table didn't ask any questions, but she could tell that her master was clearly troubled by the phone call.

What the hell am I going to do with Scott's daughter now? thought Yoshida.

27

THE MISSION

U.S.S. Bremerton

Zackary Scott and Finn Sorenson were sitting alone in the officer's wardroom. They were drinking coffee and eating sandwiches. They had been aboard the *Bremerton* for nearly twenty-four hours.

"Say, Zack, how fast do you suppose we're going?"

"I don't know, Finn. The boat's so smooth that I can't tell. For all I know we could be running along at anywhere between twenty to thirty knots."

Finn Sorenson shook his head and let out a low whistle. "No wonder they call these things hunter-killers. They're fast, silent, and deadly."

"Yep. Subs don't get much better than this baby."

Finn took a sip of coffee. He then turned to stare at a nautical chart mounted on a nearby bulkhead. The chart was of Japan's Hokkaido Island. At the northeast corner of the island the Nemuro peninsula was clearly identified. Someone had used a yellow felt pen to highlight the long, narrow peninsula of land that jutted outward into the north Pacific Ocean.

"What do you think we'll find when we get there?" asked Sorenson.

"I don't know. I'm still in shock over this whole thing."

"Yeah, I know what you mean. I can hardly believe I'm on a nuclear submarine, about to play spy." Finn took another sip from the mug. "Zack, when are you going to tell 'em about Wendy?"

"It's not time. If they knew about that, we'd never be on this boat."

"But you've got to say something."

"At the proper time—when I can control the situation—I'll let Maxwell know. But in the interim I don't want anyone else on this boat to know. Okay?"

Finn nodded his head. "Don't worry. I'll keep my mouth shut."

"Good, I'm counting on you."

Finn smiled at his friend. He did understand Scott's predicament and would have done the same thing if it had been him. As far as the U.S. Navy knew, Scott's only interest in agreeing to help out on the reconnaissance mission was the mystery surrounding the Nemuro Oil Complex and Hiroshi Yoshida's interest in SCS. The fact that Wendy Scott had been kidnapped by Yoshida's goons was unknown to anyone in the American government.

"Where's Russ?" asked Finn.

"He's still checking out *Little Mike*."

Finn smiled. "That's one helluva mini-sub you got there."

"Thanks, I'm real proud of her. I just hope she holds up through all this."

"Yeah, I know what you mean." Finn then decided it was time to change subjects. "By the way, Zack, I never did get a chance to ask you why Commander Blake is aboard."

"The navy wanted her along to evaluate firsthand what we find. She knows more about oil wells and offshore pipelines than anyone else in the Coast Guard or the navy."

"So she's going to be checking up on us?"

"That's right. She'll get the first look at whatever we find."

Finn placed his coffee mug on the table and reached for an egg salad sandwich. He took a bite and swallowed. "Do you know her very well?" Finn asked.

"Halley? Yeah, a little. I got to know her during the Hammer 4 blowout. She knows her stuff and so far has been fair in her dealings with SCS. That means a lot to me." Zack could sense Finn's obvious interest in the woman. "Besides, she's a great-looking woman, don't you think?"

"Boy, I'll say." *She's frigging gorgeous,* throught Sorenson. "Do you know if she's married?"

"Divorced, one kid. A girl in junior high, I think."

Finn's eyes lit up. *And she's available too.*

Zack picked up a ham and cheese sandwich and began to wolf it down. He was halfway through the second half when Finn began shuffling through a file folder on the table. It was filled with black-and-white photos.

"Zack, what do you think about these pictures of that phantom sub? It looks huge to me."

"Yeah, no question about that. But I just can't imagine what the Japanese would need with something like that."

"But it must be for carrying something—you know, like an underwater oil tanker."

"I know that. But why would they move it underwater?"

Finn was about to speculate on a wild idea he had just thought of when the doorway to the ward room opened. A second later Halley Blake walked in, followed by Commander Hashimoto. The two officers took up position on the opposite side of the table. Hashimoto spoke first. "Well, gentlemen, we'll be entering Japanese waters in a couple of hours. At that time—"

"Excuse me, Commander," interrupted Sorenson, "could you please show me where we are right now." Finn flashed a friendly grin. "I'm a surface sailor. This business of traveling underwater has got me buffaloed. I don't have the slightest inkling of where we are."

"Sure," replied Hashimoto. He pushed his chair back from the table and turned to face the wall-mounted chart. He placed his right index finger on the map. "We're right about here, in the southern end of the Sea of Okhotsk."

"Are we still in Russian waters?"

"No. We only hugged the Russian side of La Perouse Strait to avoid that Japanese destroyer that was patrolling off the northwest end of Hokkaido. We're in international waters right now."

Zack spoke up next. "I assume that warship didn't spot us."

"That's correct. According to our sonar people, we have absolutely no indication that any Japanese units are aware of our presence."

"But the Japanese have their own hydrophones. Won't they know we're coming also?"

"No. Most of their new ASW gear near Nemuro is located on the Pacific side of Hokkaido."

Zack caught on instantly. "And we're coming in from another direction?"

"Correct. We don't think they'll be expecting us to send a sub in this way." Hashimoto once again pointed to the chart. "By passing through the Friz Strait and then sneaking down the east coast of Etorofu, we'll be able to remain in the shadows the entire way. There aren't many Japanese sensors in those waters."

"But what about the Russians?" asked Finn.

"They guaranteed us free passage. They're just as interested in this Nemuro situation as we are. Besides, there isn't a lot they could do to stop us. Most of their SOSUS systems are—"

"SOSUS?" asked Finn.

"Stands for sound surveillance system—you know, underwater sensors that listen for submarines."

"Oh, yeah. Thanks, please go on."

Hashimoto continued. "As I was saying, most of the Russians' Kuril Island SOSUS systems are inoperative. They just don't have the funds to keep them going. As a result, we can operate right in their backyard and they wouldn't know it."

"Does that go for the Jap navy, too?" asked Finn. He then corrected himself. "Sorry. I should have said Japanese navy."

"No offense taken," replied Commander Hashimoto as he continued to face Sorenson. "I'm a full-blooded American." The officer was sincere. He had prepared himself a long time ago to face the brutal fact that the United States and Japan might once again be at each other's throats.

Hashimoto continued. "Now, regarding your question, yes, we can also operate in the Japanese Kurils fairly easily."

Zack spoke up next. "But Commander, what's to prevent them from installing their own sensors in Russian waters—or worse, to have one of their subs sitting on the bottom, waiting to ambush someone like us when we try to sneak in?"

Hashimoto smiled. "Mr. Scott, if they had tried that, we would have already known about it."

Zack shook his head questioningly. "What do you mean?"

"The Russian SOSUS sensors may be crapping out but ours aren't."

"You mean we have our own hydrophones in their waters?"

"That's right. We have a brand-new system on the bottom around Kunashiri and Etorofu islands. And believe me when I say we'd know if the Japanese—or, for that matter, anyone else—was operating in those waters."

"Commander," called out Halley Blake, "just how close to Nemuro will the *Bremerton* come?"

Hashimoto turned back to face the Coast Guard officer. "As I explained earlier, we're under specific orders to maintain a low profile. That basically means that the *Bremerton* cannot be detected under any circumstances."

"But the submersible has limited range," responded Halley.

"We know that. That's why, one way or the other, we'll get you close enough to get in. But then we'll have to back off. We can't wait around because of the risk of detection."

Finn commented next. "And when we finish, what then?"

"We'll come back in and pick you up."

"What if they spot us?" asked Zack.

"We won't be able to help you out. Our orders are to remain incognito at all times."

"So we'll be left out there hanging in the wind."

"That's correct, Mr. Scott. Just as we explained to you before. You clearly understood the risks then. That's why we went to all the trouble to set up the fallback story."

"I know, it's just that—"

Finn Sorenson interrupted again. "What fallback story are you talking about?"

Zack turned to face Sorenson. He had not yet been totally up front with his friend. "Finn, if they spot us and go after us, you know there isn't much of a chance that we'll make it out. We've talked about that before."

"I understand that, Zack. But what's this fallback story business?"

"I agreed that if we don't make it out and the Japanese discover what we're doing, the U.S. government will not be implicated."

"How can that be done?"

"Actually it's pretty easy. One of my drilling rigs, the *Deep-*

questor, is moored about two hundred miles north of the Nemuro oil fields. Right now it's spudding in a new hole on the Russian side of the Friz Strait as part of a joint venture with a Russian firm. We'll be passing right by it—submerged, of course."

Finn caught on instantly. "So if we're caught, everyone will think we came from the drilling rig and not a U.S. sub."

"Right," Zack said. "That's why we went through all the hassles of flying out to the destroyer and then transferring to this sub. That way no one can trace our movements back to the government. As far as anyone will know, the whole thing will be chalked up to industrial espionage—SCS spying on Yoshida Heavy Industries."

"That's right," Hashimoto said, "and that's why neither Commander Blake nor myself can accompany you. It has to be a civilian operation from head to toe."

Finn reacted. "Damn it to hell, Zack, this sounds just like another fucking cover-up."

Zack shrugged his shoulders. "I know, but what can I do?"

Hashimoto commented next. "It's absolutely necessary, Mr. Sorenson. If the mission falls apart and the Japanese prove that the American government was behind it, then it'll be an unmitigated disaster for us." He paused momentarily to collect his thoughts. "Right now, the Japanese central government is looking for the slightest excuse to close down all of our military bases in their country. And if we're caught spying red-handed, it'll create a tidal wave of opposition from the general populace that will give them the excuse. And please believe me when I say they'll kick us out so quickly that it will make your head spin."

"So what the hell are we staying there for now anyway?" asked Sorenson. "Why not let the greedy little bastards defend themselves."

Hashimoto wanted to stop the conversation but found himself unable to. He was asking this man to risk his life. The least he could do was to tell him why. "Finn, I'm sure you're aware of the balance of payment problem, and the trade war that's going on between us and the Japanese."

"Of course, but what—"

"Let me explain. What you haven't heard, because the press doesn't know about it, is that Japan is rapidly re-arming itself.

Its navy is growing like mad and in a few years it will be a match for our own.''

This was news to Zack. "How can that be?" he asked.

"Blame it on our Russian friends."

"What?"

"A couple of years ago, they secretly sold off a huge number of submarines to the Japanese government. It was part of the deal for Japan to get the Kurils back."

"Nuclear boats?"

"Yep, and that's not all. They also have over a hundred low-yield tactical nuclear weapons."

"You mean they've got their own nukes now?" asked Finn.

"Yes, plus a whole arsenal of medium-range missiles to deliver them."

"How did that happen—the Russian's sell 'em their old bombs?"

"No. Japan has plenty of plutonium from their nuclear power industry. They made 'em."

Halley Blake spoke next. She was just as shocked as Zack and Finn. "Commander, I can't believe the Japanese people would tolerate their government owning nuclear weapons—not after Hiroshima and Nagasaki."

"They don't know about it. Only a few top officials plus assorted general and flag officers know the real story. It's been well hidden."

"How'd we find out about it?" asked Scott.

"Sorry, I can't comment on that—I've already told you too much, but I had to let you know what's going on."

"Commander Hashimoto," Finn said, "what are they up to with all that hardware?"

"We're not certain of anything. We're still on speaking terms with their government. But there are others—industrial leaders, political right-wingers, plus a bunch of senior military officers—who want to see the Rising Sun replace the Stars and Stripes in East Asia."

"Well, they've already done that economically, haven't they?" Scott said.

"No question about that. Trade-wise, we're losing badly. Our energy costs are killing us while they're almost energy independent—thanks largely to the Nemuro Complex and their nuclear power industry." Hashimoto paused to sip a glass of water. "The only hammers we've got left are our bases. They won't dare pull anything while the Seventh Fleet is sitting right on their doorstep."

"And if we lose those bases?" asked Halley Blake.

"We might as well pull all of our ships back to Pearl Harbor. Our influence in the Far East will be over."

"And the Japanese navy will quickly fill the void," added Scott.

"Exactly. Who else is going to challenge them? China or Russia? Hell, they're both economic misfits right now. They won't be able to do anything other than cooperate."

"Commander," Zack said, "what you've described sounds just like what happened back in the thirties and early forties—Japan re-arming and then causing all that trouble in China and Indonesia."

"I know. It's scary, all right. They've done it once before so there's a real precedent. That's why this mission is so important. We need to know what they're doing with those phantom subs. We think they're somehow tied into their whole rearmament plans."

Finn Sorenson shook his head back and forth. He was having a hard time with what he had just been told. "You know, all that makes sense and I understand why you guys can't be implicated. But it still bugs me that we're going to be nothing more than glorified guinea pigs."

Commander Hashimoto raised his arms in a defensive posture. "You're right, Finn. And if you want to back out, we'd understand."

Zack turned to Sorenson. "He's right, Finn. There's no need for you to risk it. We can do it without you."

"No way. I'm going. I just wanted the straight poop before I decided to hang my fanny out in the wind. I now know what's going on and I'm ready."

Zack smiled at his friend. "Thanks, buddy. I'm real glad you're with me."

"Helm, all stop," ordered Commander Morgan Maxwell. The African-American officer towered above the other men inside the control. At six-foot-four, he had to continually duck his head when moving around in his submarine.

"Aye, aye, sir. All stop," replied the officer of the deck.

Maxwell turned to face his executive officer. Lieutenant Commander Matt Merlino was seated at an electronic console next to Maxwell. It looked like the instrument panel on the space shuttle.

For the past seventy minutes Merlino had been monitoring the ship's real-time position as it maneuvered through a series of turns and dives. A new and highly accurate inertial navigation system plotted the boat's every move, displaying its trail on a computer map of the ocean bottom.

"Well, X, what do you think?" asked Maxwell. "Are we in the right spot?"

"Looks good to me, skipper. Our coordinates match the target. So, if the engineers are right we should be within a couple of meters of it."

"Good, then let's see if we can hover here."

Maxwell turned back to the OOD. "Lieutenant, is our depth still holding?"

"Aye, sir. We're at seven-zero-zero feet and we have seventy-five feet under the keel."

"Good. Now what's the current like?"

"We've got one knot on a relative heading of zero-three-one degrees."

"All right, let's turn into it and jog in place. I want to hold these coordinates."

Maxwell turned to another man standing near the XO's station. "Chief, will you let our guests know that we're all set down here."

"Aye, aye, skipper," replied Chief Petty Officer Harry Appleton. He then exited the control room, heading aft. Appleton was the senior noncommissioned officer on the *Bremerton*. As chief of the boat, with twenty-five years in subs, he commanded as much respect as the captain.

It took Chief Appleton about a minute to reach his destination. He scaled a steel ladder, climbing up a dozen feet into one of the boat's emergency escape chambers. Designed to be flooded while isolated from the main pressure casing, the escape chamber could accommodate up to ten men at a time. Once the chamber was filled with seawater and the deck hatch was opened, the crew could swim to the surface.

Normally the deck hatch above the chamber would be sealed shut, unless the ship was on the surface. But today the hatch was open. Appleton climbed up another set of ladder rungs. His six-foot-two frame was nearly half the way through the sub's outer hatch when he stopped. He looked around, familiarizing himself with his new surroundings. *Ah, there they are!* he thought.

"Permission to come aboard, Mr. Scott?" called out Appleton.

Zack swung his head around, looking aft. He spotted the man; his head and shoulders were projecting out of the bottom access hatchway. "Come right ahead, Chief," he answered.

Appleton hauled himself through the lockout chamber and stood up. He was too tall for the confined space, requiring him to duck his head to prevent hitting the dozens of cable bundles, pipes, and other appurtenances that ran along the top circumference of the submersible.

Zack was now standing next to the navy NCO. "Welcome aboard *Little Mike*."

"Thanks." Appleton paused as he looked around the interior of the mini-sub. He spotted the other two men, both sitting down at control stations in the cockpit area. "Ah, the skipper asked me to tell you that we're on station now. He wants to know when you'll be ready to launch."

"Great. We're all set here. We've been running through our prelaunch checklists."

"That's good. If you're ready, then I suggest we make preparations for you to depart."

"That's fine with me, but wait a sec." Zack turned forward, facing his two crewmen. "Final call, fellows. You all set?"

Finn Sorenson, manning the engineer's station, raised his right thumb. Russ McMillin, sitting in the copilot's seat, nodded his head affirmatively.

"Okay, Chief. We're all set to go. Now, how do you want to initiate the launch?"

"Well, I think we'll have to improvise a little on the . . ."

Chief Appleton and Zack talked for a few minutes, going over last-minute details. Appleton was just about to head down the hatchway when he heard someone climbing the ladder from below. A few seconds later Commander Halley Blake was standing next to Scott and Appleton. "Zack, I just wanted to wish you and your crew good luck." She then turned forward, looking for the rest of the crew. She smiled broadly when she spotted Finn. He smiled back.

"Well, thanks, Commander," Zack said. "Maybe we'll get to the bottom of all this today."

"I wish I could go along, but I can't."

"I know that. But you can be sure we're going to look over that entire operation with a fine-tooth comb. We'll have lots of photos and videotape for you to examine."

"Good, I'm looking forward to it."

"Ma'am, I think it's time we go," interjected Appleton. "The skipper doesn't want to loiter around here too long."

"Yeah, okay, Chief."

As Halley dropped through the hatchway she waved to Finn. Sorenson waved back and then watched her golden hair drop from sight. *God, but she's beautiful.*

Zack heard Appleton close the *Bremerton*'s deck hatch. The vibration of the heavy hatch lid engaging the hull telegraphed through the mating collar into *Little Mike*'s deck plates. Back in Seattle, the special steel collar had been hastily welded onto the bottom surface of the submersible's hull. Designed to function like a giant suction cup, the device created an enormous bond when the water trapped in the annulus was pumped out.

"Okay, boys, looks like we're about set," Zack said as he sat down in the pilot's seat. Russ McMillin remained in the companion left-hand seat. Finn Sorenson was right behind Zack.

"Finn, you ready to disengage?"

"You bet, Zack. Just say when."

Zack turned toward McMillin. "Russ, let's hit the floods now."

"Roger." The copilot reached forward and tripped a series of switches. An instant later the water area surrounding the mini-sub's acrylic bow windows burst into light. High-powered floodlights mounted on the circumference of the hull illuminated the water as if it was the middle of the afternoon.

The *Bremerton*'s twenty-foot-tall sail and afterdeck were clearly visible.

Zack was the first to react. "Looks like good water clarity."

"Yeah, great," replied McMillin.

Finn Sorenson sat quietly in the back. He was awed. *Damn! We're really going to do this.*

"What's the current like now?" asked Scott.

McMillin checked one of the gauges on his panel. "My best guess is that as soon as we separate we'll be carried aft—the current should be around a knot."

"Okay, I'll compensate," Zack said as he reached forward, engaging *Little Mike*'s electric drive. The mini-sub's five-foot-diameter propeller began biting into the water.

A moment later Zack turned his head, looking aft at Sorenson. "Finn, go ahead and release the pressure. We're all set here."

"You got it." Finn reached to his right side, flipping the plastic guard that covered a recessed switch. A second later he activated the switch. "Venting now," he said.

Zack could hear the rush of seawater as it filled the mating collar's annulus. A couple of seconds later the mini-sub began yawing and pitching as its bond with the mother ship was broken.

"Russ, give me ten more pounds in the forward tank," ordered Zack.

"Roger." McMillin triggered a high-pressure valve, injecting more compressed air into *Little Mike*'s forward ballast chamber. Almost instantly a couple of hundred pounds of seawater were forced out by the expanding gas, causing the mini-sub to rise.

"Here we go," shouted Zack. He then turned the aircraft-like steering wheel to the right and advanced the throttle control to the stops. *Little Mike* sprinted ahead, shearing away from the gigantic black hulk of the *Bremerton*.

Within a minute the submersible was four hundred feet away from the mother ship. It was so dark, however, that the light from the floodlights could barely penetrate fifty feet ahead.

"What's our depth, Russ?" asked Zack.

"Six eighty to the surface. Ninety-five to the bottom."

"Okay, let's check our bearings."

Russ scanned the onboard sonar display. "Looks good, Zack. Our coordinates match up well within the tolerances."

"Good, then let's get going. Lay in a course of two-six-zero degrees, maintain one hundred feet to the bottom."

"Aye, aye."

"Captain, the propeller sounds are diminishing. The submersible is heading away."

"Very well, let's head back out to our standby position." Commander Maxwell stepped off the OOD watch station and walked over to the main chart table. His executive officer was already leaning over the edge, studying the underwater map.

"Well, Matt, what do you suppose they're going to find?"

"I don't know, skipper. But I'll say this much: It wouldn't surprise me if we never heard from them again."

"Yeah, I know what you mean. There's something all wrong with this mission."

"How close are we getting, Russ?" asked Zack as he continued to pilot *Little Mike*. The mini-sub had been running for fifty minutes. It was now on the outer fringe of the Nemuro Oil Complex.

"The main platform should be about two thousand yards dead ahead. The west satellite's closer." McMillin studied the computerized chart of the bottom for a few more seconds. "It's about twelve hundred yards off our port quarter."

"Okay, let's head over there first. I want to check out those subsea wells."

"Roger, come to a new heading of three-four-eight degrees."

"Right," replied Zack. He turned the yoke to the left while simultaneously watching the instrument panel. His eyes were glued to a television screen that produced an artificial, three-dimensional image of the water space directly in front of the submarine. Concentric fluorescent lines pulsed into the screen, creating a grid that formed a tunnellike picture. It looked like a video game display.

Little Mike was moving through the ink-black water at seven knots; its electric drive and ducted propeller assembly were for all practical purposes soundless. Even the *Bremerton*'s state-of-the-art passive sonar systems had lost contact with the tiny sub just a few minutes after it started on its mission. The background noise of the ocean masked the tiny vessel's soft hissing soundprint.

To conserve battery power, McMillin had switched off the floodlights as soon as they began heading for the Nemuro Complex. The resulting darkness of the abyss engulfed the mini-sub like a veil. It was so black that they might as well have been on the dark side of the moon.

"What's the bottom like now?" asked Zack as he continued to stare at the artificial horizon.

"Continuing to shoal. We've got about eighty feet under the keel."

"Okay, let me know when we hit thirty feet."

Before Russ could acknowledge, Zack spoke again. "Finn, how's our power supply?"

Sorenson quickly scanned the various gauges at his station. "Primary system is at eighty-three percent. Backup systems remain at ninety-nine percent."

"Good, that's well within the limits."

Zack continued to pilot *Little Mike,* occasionally adjusting the vessel's control surfaces to compensate for a crosscurrent that was flowing from the northeast.

"Coming up on thirty feet to the bottom," reported McMillin.

"Okay, hit the lights again."

A few seconds later, two floodlights mounted under the cockpit flashed on. Russ used a hand-held remote control to maneuver the lights until they were pointing downward at a forty-five-degree angle. Despite the power of the floods, the water still soaked up the light like a sponge.

"You see the bottom yet?" asked Zack.

"Negative, still too . . . no, wait a sec. Yep, there it is. I've got it now."

Zack glanced down, looking through the thick acrylic glass. The sandy bottom looked sterile. "Sand?" he asked as he once again eyed the artificial horizon. A new dark line was running along the bottom of the display. It was the bottom reflection.

"Yep, sure looks like it."

"Okay, how close are we now?"

"We've got about two hundred yards to go to the base of the west satellite. If we maintain this heading . . . Jesus Christ, pull it up, pull it up now!"

Zack was startled by McMillin's scream. Instinctively, he looked up from the display. *Oh my God!* A huge, black object was looming in the distance. They were almost on it.

Before Zack could react, however, Russ took over. He grabbed his set of the controls and yanked back on the yoke, sending the sub into a steep climb.

Little Mike cleared the object with just inches to spare.

"What the hell was that?" screamed Finn. He had witnessed the entire event but understood nothing that had happened.

Zack ignored Sorenson as he retook control of the mini-sub. Thirty seconds later the sub was powered down, drifting quietly with the current.

"Did you see the size of that thing?" asked McMillin.

"Yeah, it was huge."

"But what was it?"

"I don't know, but we're going to find out. Give me a reciprocal heading back to it."

Two minutes later *Little Mike* was hovering over an enormous subsea structure. The mini-sub was cruising above the object, running down its long axis. It was at least a hundred feet in width and seemed to stretch on for hundreds of feet.

"What the hell is this damn thing, another sub?" asked Finn. He was now kneeling down in the open deck space between the pilots' seats.

"No way," replied Zack. "It's not configured right."

"Uh oh," shouted Russ, "here comes the end of the thing."

They passed right over the object's semicylindrical end. It looked like a half-squashed giant sausage lying on the ocean bottom. And at its base, just above the bottom, was a two-foot-diameter pipe. It stretched off into the distance, quickly swallowed up by the darkness.

Zack turned *Little Mike* around and again lined up with the longitudinal axis of the object. "Okay, Russ, turn the cameras on. I want to get this thing on tape."

It took eight minutes to run down the entire length of the structure. Zack was dumbfounded by its size. "Good Lord, that sucker's over two thousand feet long."

"Yeah, and it's got a beam of about a hundred and fifty feet," reported Russ.

"What do you think it is?" asked Finn.

Zack shook his head. "I'll be damned if I know. All I can tell you is that it's the largest underwater structure I've ever seen."

"You know what it looks like to me?" asked McMillin.

"What?"

"It looks like a giant version of those rubber bladders that the military use. You know, for storing water and fuel at remote sites."

"Jesus, you're right. That's exactly what they look like." Zack paused for a second. "But what the hell would they want to store down here?"

"Oil?" piped up Finn.

"Oil! No way. Why would they do that? The Nemuro field is right offshore of their mainland. They can just pump it ashore—there's no need to store it underwater."

"But what else could it be for?" replied Sorenson.

Zack was just about to respond when Russ held up his right index finger to his lips, signaling silence. "You hear it?" his voice was a whisper.

"Hear what?" asked Zack.

"We've got company." Russ then switched on the long-range passive sonar. All three men heard the grumbling sound of machinery.

Zack instantly recognized the propeller noise. "There's another sub down here."

Zack and Russ immediately swung into action. Russ cut the floods back to the bare minimum while Zack guided *Little Mike* down. Within a minute the submersible was resting on the bottom, about ten feet away from the alien structure.

"Where's it going now?" asked Scott.

McMillin was monitoring the passive sonar display. "It's hard to tell. This thing next to us here is interfering with the signal—almost like it's absorbing the sound."

It must be made of rubber after all, thought Zack. "Well, is it coming or going away?"

"Away," Russ said. "It's definitely moving away. Wait a minute. Shit, now there's something else coming in."

"What?"

Russ turned up the volume control on the sonar's loud-speaker. Zack could still hear the grumbling sound of the sub, but mixed in with it was another sound. Something he had never heard before. It sounded like water flowing in a pipe.

What the hell?

Captain Sakyo Tokuda was standing next to the helmsman. Both men were monitoring the computer-controlled approach to the Nemuro Oil Complex. Tokuda's vessel, the *Sapporo*, was just a few minutes away from docking at its underwater berth. Another submarine, only a fraction of the *Sapporo*'s size, was standing by to assist. The powerful sub tug would be needed only if the tanker lost power at the last minute.

"We're coming up on the *Kobe*, sir," called out the helmsman.

Captain Tokuda stared at the computer screen. It projected a three-dimensional sonar view of the water space in front of *Sapporo*'s bow. Off to the right he could see the fuzzy electronic image of another underwater vessel. It was huge—almost as big as the *Sapporo*—but it wasn't a tanker.

"Are we well clear of the *Kobe*'s anchor points?" asked Tokuda.

"Aye, sir. We have a minimum separation of two hundred meters."

"Very well, continue with docking."

Captain Tokuda had visited the *Kobe* just once before. It was the most amazing vessel he had ever seen. He remembered the ship's interior with clarity, especially the derrick station. It was an impressive sight. The conical pressure housing surrounding the drilling hardware was over a hundred feet high. It towered over the main hull like an enormous shark fin.

Tokuda was a sub driver, not a driller, but he knew how the underwater drilling vessel functioned. Designed to explore for oil while submerged, the *Kobe* was truly a revolutionary vessel. It was like nothing else that had ever been built.

The *Kobe* had been moored at Nemuro for almost three months. After two years of continuous drilling in the South China Sea and offshore of Korea, the vessel was in desperate need of maintenance. Short of returning to a dry dock back in Yokohama, nearly every electromechanical system on the huge submarine was being overhauled at its underwater mooring.

While at berth or during drilling operations, the *Kobe* moored itself over the ocean bottom by deploying four self-embedding anchor systems, one from each corner point of the 850-foot-long hull. After achoring, immense ballast chambers built into fore and aft sections of the hull were charged with compressed air. The submarine then rose about fifty to seventy feet above the bottom until the anchor cables took hold. More compressed air was added, expelling additional seawater ballast, until the steel cables were stressed to several thousand tons of tension. The result was a rock-solid four-point mooring; the *Kobe* then became immune to all motion from currents and wave action.

As amazing as the mooring system was, it was nothing compared to the actual drilling operation. Although much of the heavy equipment was conventional—the drill pipe, the traveling block, the rotary table—operation of the drilling equipment was not. Everything within the drilling chamber was remotely controlled and completely stable, isolated from the surrounding ocean waters. Massive acoustic insulation, coupled with electronic sound masking devices, prevented mechanically generated noises in the chamber from broadcasting the *Kobe*'s underwater position. For all practical purposes, the drill ship was undetectable.

When the *Kobe* was moored and ready to spud in a new hole, the handful of operating personnel would vacate the drilling chamber and take up monitoring positions within a spacious one-atmosphere observation compartment located at the base of the derrick. From this location, the six drillers could control the entire drilling operation. Pressure-resistant robots, some in fixed positions, others mobile, took the place of the roustabouts, roughnecks, and derrickmen who are common to terrestrial and offshore rigs.

The mechanical surrogates were slightly more efficient than a human drilling crew. But efficiency wasn't the only reason the robots had been built. In order for the *Kobe* to drill underwater, the entire drilling chamber had to be pressurized to the same bottom depth at which the submarine was moored. And humans simply could not survive in those extreme pressures.

Tokuda was visualizing the automated drill string advancement process when the helmsman spoke: "Sir, we're approaching the outer marker. Do you want to make the final docking maneuver manually?"

"No, let the computer do it."

If Tokuda's vessel had been a real ship—one that floated on top of the water instead of hugging the bottom—he would have never turned control over to the computer. But underneath five hundred and fifty feet of coal-black water, with only acoustically generated images to judge distances, he stepped aside. He was redundant.

Seventeen minutes later the submarine was moored to its underwater slip. Its bow end was plugged into a towerlike structure that rose over a hundred and fifty feet above the bottom. Free to rotate with the current, the *Sapporo* looked like an ancient dirigible attached to its ground-based mooring mast.

"Captain, the docking maneuver is complete and we're ready to pump product."

"Very well, proceed."

The *Sapporo*'s chief engineer began activating a series of valves and hydraulic systems. Within just a few minutes crude oil began discharging from the submarine's cargo holds, flowing into a receptacle at the connection point on the mooring tower. A computer automatically adjusted the trim tanks to compensate for the heavier seawater that flowed into the partially evacuated holds.

After flowing downward through the tower's supporting column, the oil was discharged into a vast array of underwater pipelines that snaked along the ocean bottom. The flow was eventually routed to an underwater storage chamber located a few hundred feet away from the mooring. It would take almost twenty-four hours for the seventy million gallons of crude oil to be transferred.

"Now what's that noise?" asked Zack. He was sitting next to the sonar unit's loudspeaker. Finn and Russ were huddled around him. For the past half hour they had been listening intently to the myriad of strange noises that were overpowering the ocean's background sound.

"Sounds like some kind of pump," answered Finn.

"Yeah," McMillin agreed. "But there's something else there now. You hear it?"

Zack leaned a little closer to the speaker. There was a new sound. It was beginning to increase in amplitude. "You're right. Sounds like they're pumping something."

"Zack, do you think it's going into that bladder?" asked Russ.

"No, that sucker was full up with something. No way it could hold any more."

Finn broke in next. "You think it has anything to do with the underwater pipeline we saw? There could be more of these bladder things on the bottom."

Russ and Zack both looked at each other as Finn's words struck home. They had the same thought: *He's right!*

Ten minutes later *Little Mike* was following the two-foot-diameter black steel pipeline that led away from the storage bladder they had examined. The submersible had traveled only a few hundred feet when the pipeline flowed into another larger pipe, running perpendicular. Zack turned the submersible and followed the four-foot-diameter pipe for a few more minutes.

"There, just ahead," shouted Russ. "It's another one of those branching pipes."

Zack throttled back. *Little Mike* began hovering. He reached over and turned the sonar's loudspeaker to max. The electronic roar filled the cockpit. It sounded like the Colorado River. He turned to face McMillin. "Russ, let's check it out."

"Roger."

Within four minutes *Little Mike* was hovering over another one of the bladderlike storage devices. This tube, however, was nearly completely deflated. It looked like a giant flat bag lying on the sandy bottom. Hundreds of thick lead weights were also exposed. The ballast units were attached to the outer skin, running longitudinally along each side.

Zack was the first to spot the telltale bulge in the bladder. It was located at the connection point with the pipeline. The bladder was just beginning to swell up as oil was pumped inside. "Finn, you were right. These things are some kind of underwater storage containers."

"I thought so," replied Sorenson.

"But what could they be filling them up with?" asked McMillin.

"There's only one thing that makes any sense—it has to be oil," Zack said.

"But why would they do that? All they have to do is pump the oil from their subsea wells ashore. That's got to be much cheaper than this."

"Yeah, if this were a normal subsea oil field."

"What do you mean?"

Zack shifted in his seat. His back was beginning to ache. "Russ, there's something all wrong with this setup. I don't know what's going on but I'll bet you a steak dinner that the oil flowing into that bladder wasn't produced from any subsea well located around here."

"But where would—"

"Zack!" interrupted Finn. He couldn't contain himself anymore. "Remember those pictures the navy showed us. That's got to be it. It's an underwater tanker terminal, like I first thought."

Zack turned around to face his friend. "I think you're right, and if we're on the mark, that weird noise we heard a little while ago was one of those big fuckers."

"Like it was docking?" Finn said.

"Yep, I think so."

"That's just incredible," exclaimed McMillin. "What in the hell are these people up to here?"

"I don't know," Scott said, "but I can guarantee you this: Before we head back to the *Bremerton* we're sure as hell going to know."

It didn't take long for Zackary Scott and his crew to discover the riser. They simply followed the various branches of the underwater pipeline manifold until they encountered the vertical pipe section. The thirty-six-inch-diameter steel conduit towered above the bottom; it was held in place by a system of flotation collars and cable stays. It looked like a smokestack, reaching for the surface.

"Zack, what do you suppose this is?" asked Russ McMillin.

"I'm not sure." He hesitated a moment as he stared through *Little Mike*'s cockpit viewports. "It may be some kind of marine riser, but it's configured all wrong for a production unit."

"Yeah, that could be, but look at the joint with the manifold. Isn't that some kind of swivel?"

Zack studied the base of the vertical pipe section. There was a pronounced bulge around its connection to the larger horizontal pipeline. "You're right, Russ, that's one hell of a ball valve all right. It must have twenty-plus degrees of rotation."

"Why would they need something like that?"

Beats me, was what he was going to say, but he stopped himself as a new idea popped into his head. *Of course, that's got to be it.* "You know, Russ, this sure looks like a riser for a monobuoy mooring."

"Monobuoy mooring? Those navy photos didn't show anything like that around Nemuro."

"That's right. But then the photos can't penetrate into the water so they wouldn't see it."

McMillin looked at his boss with a puzzled look on his face.

"The buoy's submerged, Russ. It's for an underwater mooring."

Zack watched Russ's eyes widen. It was like watching a light switch on.

"Damn! If there's a phantom sub out there, then this is where it would be plugged in."

"Right on. Let's find out for sure."

Captain Tokuda was in his stateroom packing his duffel bag. His tour of duty, as well as that of his eight-man crew, was over. They all had three weeks off, and like most of the special YHI employees they were all looking forward to shore leave. Tokuda's wife and three children lived in Kobe. And in less than three hours he would be home.

Tokuda zipped up his duffel bag and took one last look around the Spartan quarters. It was clean and neat, just as he had found it four weeks earlier. The next captain of the *Sapporo,* due to arrive aboard the following day, would not complain.

Tokuda hoisted the heavy bag onto his shoulders and walked out. When he entered the control room the other members of his crew were already standing around. Their bags were also packed.

"Tetsuo," called Tokuda, "have we heard anything from the shuttle yet?"

"Yes, Captain. It's due to dock in about five minutes."

"Good, are the caretakers aboard the shuttle?" The *Sapporo*'s crew couldn't disembark unless the maintenance engineers had arrived to take over the detanking operation.

"Aye, Captain. They're aboard."

"Good." Tokuda dropped his bag onto the tile floor and then plopped down in his bridge chair. Just as he settled in one of the crewmen brought him a steaming cup of tea.

"Thank you," he said. The man bowed as he backed away.

"My God, look at the size of that son of a bitch," shouted Finn Sorenson as the bow section of the *Sapporo* materialized in *Little Mike*'s view ports. The hull looked bigger than a whale.

"Looks just like those navy photos," commented Russ McMillin. He turned to face his boss. "Zack, you really think this thing is a tanker?"

"It's got to be—nothing else makes any sense."

"Yeah, I guess you're right." Russ then turned his ear suddenly to the right, as if he had heard something. "Listen, you can hear the pumps or whatever they are. They must be off-loading."

The three men listened intently. The noise sounded like a washing machine on the spin cycle. Zack finally broke the silence. "Shit, that's not a pump. It's another sub—kill the floods!"

The exterior lights went off an instant later. And then Zack switched off the cabin lights. *Little Mike* was like a black hole in the water.

"Do you think they spotted us, Zack?" asked Russ.

"I don't know. But whoever's out there isn't using sonar to navigate by. We would have heard their pinging by now."

"What are we going to do?" asked Finn.

"We sit tight for a little while until that boat goes away."

But what if it doesn't go away? is what Sorenson wanted to ask but didn't.

* * *

"Captain, the shuttle is on final approach now. I have it visually." The *Sapporo*'s executive officer was sitting at a television console viewing the approach of an eighty-foot-long submarine. It was lining up with one of the two docking stations at the stern of the larger craft.

"Good, proceed with docking."

The robotically controlled submarine mated perfectly with the *Sapporo*. Dispatched from Nemuro's command center twenty minutes earlier, it followed a preprogrammed flight path, weaving its way through the oil field. By listening to preset acoustic beacons positioned throughout the vast oil field, it could navigate without direct human control just about anywhere within the huge complex.

"I don't hear that screw anymore. Do either of you?" asked Zack.

"Nope," replied Finn.

"No, it must have stopped," Russ said.

All three men waited patiently for another five minutes. Still no propeller sounds.

"What'll we do now, Zack?"

"Let's power up and get out of here while we can. I've seen enough for today."

"Welcome aboard," Captain Tokuda said as he bowed his head in greeting. He was standing inside Transfer Chamber 2. The shuttle craft's three-man detanking crew had just stepped aboard the *Sapporo*.

The newcomers returned the gesture and then their leader spoke. "Thank you, Captain. We trust your voyage went well."

"Yes, the ship functioned normally. There were no problems."

The voyage had been routine. Captain Tokuda and his assistants had made the two-thousand-mile trip to the South China Sea nineteen times.

"Excellent, Captain. Then I'm sure you'll want to go ashore right away."

"Yes, we're all scheduled to—"

Tokuda was interrupted by a loud warning Klaxon. The obnoxious noise roared inside the steel transfer chamber. Without commenting further Tokuda turned about and ran back to the bridge. The relief crew followed behind.

"All right, what's the problem?" called out Tokuda as he trotted into the control room. Four of his men were already huddled around one of the bridge consoles.

The nearest man turned toward Tokuda. "Captain, we've got some kind of pressure buildup in the port hold. When we started to detank we noticed a persistent increase in background pressure. At first we attributed it to the compression effect of the ram. But when it suddenly spiked to one point four times ambient, we knew something was wrong."

"Did you stop the transfer?"

"Yes, sir. We're in a standby mode right now. The pressure has stabilized."

"What do the gas sensors indicate?"

"We think that's the problem. Sensors fourteen to twenty indicate the presence of gas."

Son of a bitch! thought Tokuda. *That degasser must not be working correctly after all.* It was a common problem in the fleet.

Captain Tokuda was now embarrassed because he had forgotten to inform the relief crew about the one problem that had plagued the ship during the start of its return voyage. The sub's sophisticated degassing system didn't evacuate all of the natural gas from the crude oil. Somehow, a small amount of gas managed to get pumped inside the hull during product loading. And now, as the giant ram inside the port hull cylinder slowly moved forward, expelling the crude oil out of the bow portal, the residual gas trapped inside was beginning to compress. If the gas were to enter the subsea pipeline network, it would create havoc. The system was designed to convey only liquids.

"Close the mooring valve. I want that gas completely isolated."

"Yes, sir." The crewman turned away and directed the one man sitting at the console to carry out Tokuda's orders.

Fifteen seconds later the same man turned back to Tokuda. "The valve is closed, sir."

"Good, go ahead and activate the hull diffuser system. And make sure all of the gas is vented before continuing."

"Yes, sir."

Tokuda turned back to the detanking crew. The three men had stood by silently watching the captain and his crew handle the emergency. Although none of them said anything, they were all laughing inside. The great Captain Tokuda had finally made a blunder and lost face.

A minute later, nearly a thousand cubic feet of natural gas inside the hull was evacuated by a vacuum pump system. It was injected into the *Sapporo*'s gas diffusion system. The diffuser pipe, built into the top deck of the hull and stretching for nearly five hundred feet, exploded to life. In just eighteen seconds, millions of dime-size bubbles were expelled from the hundreds of tiny ports located along the pipe. The gas bubbles rose in a torrent.

Little Mike was right over the *Sapporo*'s hull, about twenty-five feet above the main deck when the venting started. The submersible was blacked out and Zackary Scott was piloting the craft by computer while Russ McMillin monitored the sub's sonar systems.

"We're right over the main deck now," reported McMillin.

"Okay, I think I'll turn—"

Zack stopped speaking when the leading edge of the rising gas torrent hit *Little Mike*'s underside. The turbulence was like that of a wild river.

"What the hell's going on?" yelled McMillin.

"Jesus H. Christ!" called out Finn Sorenson from behind the cockpit.

Zack fought the controls, trying to maintain his course. But *Little Mike* was out of her safe limits. "Russ, hit the floods— I gotta see what's out there."

An instant later, the submersible's cockpit section exploded in a cascade of light. The glare was almost blinding.

"What happened to the lights?" asked Finn, aware that the sudden brilliance was not normal.

Zack struggled to adjust his eyes to the glare. Looking through the cockpit view ports was like looking through a car windshield at night while driving sixty miles an hour in a blizzard—with the bright lights on! *God, I can't see a frigging thing. What is this shit?*

Russ was the first to figure it out. "They're bubbles. They're goddamn bubbles," he shouted.

"What?" screamed Zack. He was still having difficulty keeping the mini-sub on an even keel. It was starting to rock and roll like a bucking bronco.

"We're inside some kind of gas cloud. There are a zillion bubbles out there, and the light from the floods is reflecting back in on us." Russ reached forward, killing all but one of the bottom floodlights. The resulting change was dramatic. The reflected light subsided, revealing a spectacular backdrop just outside the cockpit. Legions of bubble streams billowed up around the view ports. It looked like some kind of psychedelic light show.

"Where's this crap coming from?" Zack asked. His eyes were once again glued to his computer monitor as he tried to maneuver *Little Mike* back onto the original course.

Russ leaned forward, looking down through the lower section of the acrylic nose section. He could see the dark hull of the submarine about forty feet below. Although most of the excess gas had been vented overboard, about a quarter of the ports were still flowing. "I'll be damned. Will you look at that?" he muttered.

"Look at what?" yelled Scott.

"Down there. The gas—it's coming from that sub."

Zack broke his eye lock on the computer screen and looked down. He could hardly believe what he was seeing. *What in the hell are these turkeys doing?*

28

THE DEBRIEFING

U.S.S. *Bremerton*

Little Mike's rendezvous with the *Bremerton* was right on schedule. The mini-sub attached itself to the hull of the larger submarine and then both vessels headed eastward into international waters.

As soon as his ship was secure, Commander Maxwell returned to the officers' wardroom. Commander Hashimoto, Zackary Scott, and Halley Blake were already waiting for him. Maxwell sat down at the head of the tiny dining table; his personal mug was already filled with fresh black coffee. As he took his first sip he turned toward Zack, nodding his head. "Please proceed."

For the next twenty minutes, the *Bremerton*'s CO listened to Zack as he described *Little Mike*'s recon mission.

After Zack summed up his report, Maxwell drained his mug. He then looked Zack square in the eye. He could hardly believe what he had been told. "All right, Mr. Scott, please tell me more about this sub. Are you really convinced it's some kind of underwater oil tanker?"

"Yes. What else could they be transporting in it?" Zack glanced at his notes. "And based on what I saw out there on the bottom, they may have ten to twenty million barrels of reservoir space."

Maxwell shook his head from side to side. "That's just an

incredible volume—it doesn't make any sense to me. Why would they import oil at this facility? It's supposed to be one of the highest producing oil fields in the Pacific."

"I know," Zack said. "It's ludicrous to store that oil on the bottom when it could be pumped directly ashore. There's an enormous complex of pumps and pipelines on the main Nemuro platform that should be able to pump oil ashore without the need for *any* seabed storage."

Halley Blake spoke next. "Maybe they want to store it on the bottom for some other reason."

"But why?" asked Zack. "There's just no reason for it."

"Maybe it's some kind of transient facility. You know, where it's off-loaded by a large vessel and then distributed to smaller ones."

"You mean like lightering?"

"Yes," replied the Coast Guard officer.

Zack shrugged his shoulders. "I don't know, Halley, maybe that's possible. But there's something else going on here that we're not focusing on."

Maxwell sat up in his seat. Scott had just hit a raw nerve. "Mr. Scott, you're right. There is something else going on here and it's a real mystery to me. Where's all this damn oil coming from anyway? That's what I want to know."

Zack raised his hands in desperation. "Hell, I don't know. All I can say is that they're obviously moving it over great distances." Zack turned to face Hashimoto. "Right, Commander?"

The CIA officer looked up. He had been busy taking copious notes of what Scott had reported. "Yes. We're convinced that these so-called phantom subs are running across the Pacific, but we don't know where they're originating from." He stopped speaking as he pulled up a leather briefcase. A few seconds later he removed a map, unfolding it on the table. It was a large-scale chart of the North Pacific Ocean. "So far, we've made several sightings of these monsters. One northeast of Hawaii and a couple south of the Aleutians."

Zack leaned over the table and examined the chart. Each one of the sightings was marked in red ink. "How deep were those subs operating at?" he asked.

Hashimoto retrieved another document. "Real deep, between three and six thousand feet."

Zack let out a low whistle. "And how fast?"

"They're not speed demons. We've only clocked them at around fifteen to twenty knots."

"At that depth, they must be incredibly difficult to track."

"That's right. When we've heard them, we're only able to follow them for a short while."

"Which way were they going?" asked Halley.

"Two eastbound and two westbound."

"Any projected courses?"

"Only one," Hashimoto said. "Our last contact, a remote bottom sensor off Adak Island, gave us enough info to develop a projected course. That's what brought us here."

"Nothing on the other direction?" asked Scott.

"Nope, nothing definitive as yet. Just that they're generally heading east."

Maxwell scratched his head. "So they could be loading these suckers up just about anyplace."

"Yes, skipper," replied Hashimoto. "Unfortunately, we just don't have a clue as to where they're buying the oil. We have absolutely no intell data on any oil producer that's loading product onto a submersible tanker."

"But someone is doing it," replied Maxwell. "They're getting the oil from somebody."

"I don't know about that, Captain," Zack said. He locked onto Maxwell's eyes. "Believe me when I say that if someone had developed a submersible tanker and was in the business of actively transporting product bought on the world market, I'd know about it. That type of development would be nothing short of spectacular. It would make headlines in my industry." Zack paused as he suddenly remembered something. "I have to admit, however, that the concept of a submarine tanker has been around for a while, so it's not just a pipe dream."

"What do you mean?" asked Maxwell.

"The Russians have been talking about it for years—as part of their plan to extract oil from their Arctic territories. There's a lot of crude under all that ice, but it's a bitch of a place to work in."

"I still don't follow you," Maxwell said.

"It's really a clever idea. Their plan works like this: Instead of working on top of the ice and then drilling through it to reach the ocean bottom—like what we do right now—the Russians plan to do everything in the open water under the ice. An underwater drilling rig would be used to find the oil and then it would be pumped into subtankers for transport to a conventional refinery.'' Zack paused. ''In fact, I have to admit that our company has been working on an underwater drilling device that could conceivably be used in such an operation, although we really weren't designing it for under-the-ice conditions.''

''Good Lord, Zack,'' Halley Blake said. ''Do you think that's what the Japanese are doing here—buying Arctic oil from the Russians?''

''No, that's not what's happening,'' interjected Commander Hashimoto. ''We know for a fact that the Russians haven't a clue as to where these subs have been operating.''

''I'm sure he's right,'' added Zack. ''The Russians haven't got the capital to undertake an operation like that. Besides, the economics of a subtanker system just aren't there—yet— whether the oil comes from under the ice or from conventional production methods. Surface tankers are faster, can carry more crude, and there are plenty of them around.''

''That may be all true, Mr. Scott,'' Maxwell replied, ''but nevertheless, the Japanese have built a couple of these things.'' He held up a glossy print of the sub photographed in Yokohama. ''And according to what you just reported, they're off-loading oil at Nemuro.''

Zack didn't reply. Instead he just shrugged his shoulders.

Maxwell turned to the CIA officer. ''Commander, if the Russians aren't involved in this and what Scott says about the oil industry is accurate, then where are they buying the oil?''

Before Hashimoto could respond Halley Blake spoke up. ''Maybe they're not, Captain.''

''What?'' asked Maxwell.

''Maybe they're not buying the oil.''

Zack's eyes lit up as the shock of the Coast Guard officer's words stuck home. *By God, you might have something there,* he thought.

''What are you getting at, Commander?'' asked Maxwell.

Halley turned to face the captain. ''Sir, maybe they're pirating the oil instead of buying it.''

''How could they do that?'' demanded Hashimoto, clearly surprised at her theory.

Halley focused on the CIA officer. "It's just an idea, Commander. Maybe they've tapped into an offshore pipeline someplace. They could run those subs in without anyone knowing about it, hook up to the pipe, and then siphon off the product. If they took their time doing it, the oil would probably never be missed."

Hashimoto was almost beside himself now. "You mean this whole thing could be a giant scam—YHI is ripping off oil from someone else?"

Halley shook her head affirmatively and then Zack jumped back into the conversation. "Commander, she's got something there. Think about this: The costs of developing these monster subs and then building the infrastructure to support them—like here at Nemuro and the shipyard in Yokohama—are just mind-boggling. It would never pencil out—but if they got the oil for nothing, then the whole picture changes."

"I'll be damned," Hashimoto said as the clarity of Scott's analysis sank in. He turned to face Maxwell. "Captain, that's got to be it—they're stealing the friggin' oil."

Maxwell stared back at the CIA officer. "But why would YHI do that? That Nemuro field's got plenty of oil. Japan doesn't need it. And besides, it's crazy for them to take a risk like that. If they ever got caught stealing another country's natural resources, there'd be a war."

"I don't know, sir. None of this sounds right to me."

Maxwell pushed his chair away from the table and stood up. "Well, maybe someone back in the Pentagon can figure it out."

"What are you going to do?" asked Scott.

"I've got to phone this in right now." He turned to face Hashimoto. "Commander, I want you to prepare a summary report for immediate transmission. How long will it take you to prepare it?"

"I'll need about an hour to type it up, code it, and then compress it."

"Okay, as soon as you've got it, let me know and we'll pop up to com depth and fire it off."

"Yes, sir."

The two officers started to leave the wardroom when Scott spoke up. "Hey, wait a second! What about me and my crew?

I'd like to run back in there and do a little more exploring. I think I know what to look for now."

"Sorry, Scott," Maxwell said. "But until I get new marching orders we're staying away from Nemuro. You did what was asked of you. We appreciate your help, but for the time being I'd like you to just sit tight. We'll hear back from Pearl later in the day."

"But I need to get back there to—"

"Sorry, it'll just have to wait," interrupted Maxwell. He and Hashimoto then disappeared into the companionway.

Zack rose from his chair. He had just started for the door when Halley called out. "Let 'em go, Zack. It won't do any good."

He stopped in his tracks and turned around. "I've got to get back out there. I'm convinced that with just one more recon dive we'll finally have the answers."

Halley could tell something was wrong. *He's holding something back,* she thought. "What answers?" she asked.

Zack wanted to tell Halley about Wendy, but instead kept his answer simple. "The answer to where that oil's coming from and why."

Halley nodded her head affirmatively. "Okay, that makes sense, but until Captain Maxwell gives his okay, you and your *Little Mike* are beached."

Zack nodded his head.

The Coast Guard officer looked back down at her notes. She remembered that there was something she had forgotten to question him about. It took her a few seconds to find it. "Oh, by the way, Zack, you mentioned something about encountering turbulence on your way out of the oil field. Could you elaborate a little more on that?"

Zack returned to the table, this time sitting in Maxwell's chair. "Yeah, that was really weird. We were heading right across the deck of that sub when it started. It was almost like they were venting a ballast tank."

"Why would they do that if it were moored? Wouldn't that upset the buoyancy of the hull?"

"Yeah, I guess it would. Maybe it has something to do with how they off-load the oil. There could have been some natural gas trapped in the hold and they blew it off."

"Natural gas? I thought this thing was designed to transport liquids only."

"Yeah, I'm sure." Zack stopped in mid-sentence. "Wait a minute. If that really was gas from inside that hull, then there's something fishy going on here."

"Like what?"

"If they were loading the oil from a conventional land-based facility, it would have already been degassed. But if they tapped into an underwater production pipeline or wellhead, like you suggested, then it would be quite possible to get gas mixed in with the crude. There's always some residual gas, even in the densest crude oil reservoirs."

Halley's eyes lit up. "Then that means that sub would have to have some way of getting rid of the gas in the crude during loading operations. Otherwise, it would screw up the buoyancy."

"Exactly. With the capacity of those tanks, that sucker would pop to the surface in a flash if it filled up with gas."

It was all beginning to make sense to Halley. The pieces of the giant jigsaw puzzle were finally coming together. "Zack, remember a couple of weeks ago when I told you about that apparent explosion that was sighted near the Hammer 4 site?"

Zack was taken aback by Halley's comment. *What's she getting at here?* "Yeah, I remember. You thought we might have had a formation breach that was—" Zack stopped in mid-sentence as he, too, made the connection.

Halley nodded but didn't say anything else. She could tell by the shocked expression on Zack's face that she had made her point.

Zack remained silent for a few moments before continuing: "One of those subs—it was there, venting gas!"

"Yes, and then the gas cloud somehow ignited. That's got to be what happened."

"But why?" asked Zack. "What would one of those subs be doing—" Zack again hesitated as a new thought flashed into his mind. It was like a stroke of lightning. *Yoshida! That bastard's been stealing my oil!*

Anchorage, Alaska

The Alaska Airlines MD-80 landed at Anchorage International at half past noon. The flight from Seattle was packed. All 112 passengers slowly filed off the aircraft, walking into the enclosed jetway that connected with the terminal building. One of the last persons to deplane was a tall, middle-aged man. He had dark hair and a thick, neatly trimmed beard. He wore an expensive dark blue business suit, custom-tailored to fit his trim build. He carried a leather attaché case in his right hand.

The man had managed to walk just a few steps down the long terminal corridor, following the crowd to the baggage claim, when he was intercepted. A short muscular man, no more than twenty-five years old, approached from the side. He was dressed in blue jeans and wore a thin nylon windbreaker. His right arm was raised to signal his contact. "Sir, over here, please!" he yelled.

Captain John MacDonald, U.S. Navy (Ret.), walked toward the man. "Hi, Jake," he said as he extended his hand.

"Afternoon, Captain," replied the contact.

The two men shook hands and then walked away from the main passageway, eventually moving next to a window wall that provided a view of the main runway lights.

"How was your flight, sir?" asked the younger man.

"Fine. I even managed to get a good hour of sleep." MacDonald paused as he removed a gold-plated cigarette case from his coat pocket. He lit up without offering the other man a cigarette. He knew the man didn't smoke. MacDonald inhaled and then began speaking. "So how's everything going?"

"Good, sir. The team's all set and the gear's been thoroughly checked out."

"The Herc show up okay?"

"Yes, sir. Right on schedule."

"Okay, that all sounds good."

The young man could hardly contain himself any longer. "Captain, are we really going?"

"I don't know yet, Jake. The Seattle people promise that we'll know within the next day or so."

"Well, I sure hope they make up their minds soon. This waiting around is for the birds."

"I know. It's always like this." - Mac understood the younger man's apprehension. Even after two decades of experience he still suffered from premission jitters.

"Sir, you want some lunch—there's a restaurant just around the corner."

"No. I had something to eat on the plane. Let's just head out to the team. I want to go through another full-dress rehearsal."

"Yes, sir."

Washington, D.C.

The president was standing next to his desk, looking through the windows at the garden court. He wasn't enjoying the view. He had a tough decision to make, one that would have enormous ramifications if he was wrong. He turned around and sat in his chair, once again facing the man who had brought the bad news. The secretary of defense, seated in front of the elegantly crafted desk, had just briefed the president on the encrypted radio report from the U.S.S. *Bremerton*.

"For the life of me, Jack, I can't see why they would risk so much by pulling a stunt like this."

"I agree, sir," replied Jack Stephenson. "On the face of it, it sounds incredible. But based on what the navy's been able to put together so far, I don't see any other logical scenario."

"But stealing oil! Christ Almighty, I just can't comprehend that." The president paused as a new thought developed. "Jack, is it possible that this YHI company is doing all of this on its own?"

"You mean without the government?"

"Yeah."

"I doubt it. The capital involved is enormous and the stakes are way too high for a single company to pull this off. The Japanese government's got to be in on it somehow."

"But they have plenty of reserves. Why would they stoop to such a despicable thing?"

"Maybe they're trying to conserve their own supply. Oil's getting short everywhere now and the price keeps going up.

By hanging on to their own reserves, they'd be just that much more valuable in the future.''

"I don't know about that. They would be taking a huge risk just to string out a few more years of production.'' The president shook his head back and forth. "Jack, there's something else going on here that we haven't keyed into yet. I'm sure of it.''

"Then we should continue with our investigation.''

"You mean send that mini-sub in again to collect more evidence?''

"Yes, sir. If they take samples of the oil from those bladders, the NSA people claim they can figure out where the crude is coming from. Then we'll know if they're stealing from us or our neighbors.''

"How the hell can they do that?'' asked Chandler. "Oil's oil, isn't it?''

"Apparently the chemistry of crude oil is quite variable and it's possible to identify a particular petroleum formation by breaking a sample into its individual components. The result is kind of like a fingerprint—no two formations are exactly alike so it's possible to pinpoint a sample's origin.''

"This can be done soon?''

"Yes, sir. The *Bremerton* can be in position to launch the mini-sub within ninety minutes of receiving your order.''

"And they'd send in those civilians again as a cover?''

"Correct. The *Bremerton* will remain in the shadows. If the probe is detected or somehow captured, we won't be directly implicated.''

"But they could get caught and talk.''

"I suppose so, sir,'' replied the secretary of defense. "If pressed hard enough I'm sure the civilian crew would spill the beans.'' He paused for a moment. "But that's the same risk we had when we sent them in the first time.''

"I know that, Jack. We've been lucky so far. But if we send them back in and they're caught this time, we'll be in deep shit for sure. It would just about kill any hopes of resolving this damn trade dispute.'' The president thought for a moment and then continued. "Damnit, Jack, we're scheduled to begin the final rounds next week—if they find out we've been spying—''

"Yes, sir,'' interrupted Stephenson. "I'm aware of the tenuous nature of the trade talks, but I think our timing is almost perfect. All we need is a little more evidence and then we can confront them—privately, of course.''

The president's eyebrows raised. ''You mean blackmail them into getting the concessions we want?''

Jack Stephenson didn't reply. Instead he looked down at his feet.

Chandler continued. ''If we're wrong about what they're doing or they catch us spying on them before we get the necessary evidence, how do you think that's going to look to them?''

''They won't like it.'' Stephenson said, now looking at the president.

''Damn right they won't, and I can just about predict how they'll react. If we wrongly accuse YHI, Tokyo will dump all over us.'' Chandler pushed his chair away from the table and stood up again. ''Hell, Jack, they know how weak our economy is and given the slightest excuse they'll yank out every dollar they've got left in the Treasury. That'll just about sink us.''

''I know that, Mr. President, but if they're as dirty as I think they are, they won't dare challenge us. We'll finally have 'em—right where we want 'em.''

''But we still don't know that for sure, right?''

''Yes, but if we go back in we—''

The President raised his right hand, stopping Stephenson in mid-sentence. ''Jack, isn't it true that you can't guarantee that those civilians won't get compromised?''

''Yes, sir. That's correct.''

''Well, then my decision is easy. Tell the *Bremerton* to withdraw. I don't want the Japanese government to have the slightest inkling that we've stumbled onto their secret. I want to get through the trade negotiations first. Once we've got things under control, we'll pick it up again, and at the right time we'll use this knowledge to our advantage. But for now, it's just too hot.''

''Yes, sir. I'll send out the orders immediately.''

U.S.S. *Bremerton*

Zackary Scott and Finn Sorenson were inside their double cabin lying on the bunks when Commander Maxwell walked through the open doorway. Zack had just waken from a nap; Finn was reading.

The sub skipper turned to face Zack; he was on the top bunk, Finn was below. "Mr. Scott, we've just been ordered to head back to Pearl."

"What? You mean we're done here?"

"For the time being, but I suspect that we'll be coming back."

Zack swung his legs over the side of the bunk and stepped down. He wasn't totally awake. "We're going back to Pearl Harbor?"

"Those are my orders."

"Jesus, how long will that take?"

"Four days," replied Maxwell.

"*Four days!*" yelled Scott. "I can't wait that long. I've got business to take care of. Can't you drop us off at Yokosuka?"

Maxwell shook his head. "No, I'm afraid I can't do that. There are too many eyes down there. The minute we showed up in that harbor, Japanese Self-Defense Forces plus a zillion others will know what we've been up to."

"What? How can that be?" demanded Scott.

"It's your submersible. It's still riding piggyback on our casing."

"Oh, yeah, I forgot about that."

Finn Sorenson joined in next. "Captain, how about taking us off with a helicopter."

"I'm sorry, Sorenson, but that's not an option right now. We're too far north to send out a helo. Besides, there are SDF ships and planes patrolling all over these waters."

"Look, Captain," Zack said, "I understand your situation, but give me a break. There's no way I can remain on board this sub for the next four days. I've got to stop the bastards that are trying to steal my company." *And save my daughter!* he wanted to add, but didn't. "Based on our little inspection tour, I've got more than enough grounds to have the sale rescinded."

"Mr. Scott, I don't know anything about that. Besides, there's no way you'll be able to use any of the photographs or videotapes you took from the submersible. My orders are to confiscate everything, and that means everything, including *Little Mike.*"

Zack was furious. He was standing toe-to-toe with Maxwell. Despite Zack's six-foot height, the black man towered over him. "Look, Maxwell, I want off this pig boat now. I don't care how you do it, but I can't stay here. Too many lives are at stake."

"My hands are tied, Mr. Scott. We'll be leaving within the hour." Maxwell had turned and started to leave when Finn spoke up again.

"Zack, I think you better tell 'im."

Maxwell spun around. "Tell me what?"

Zack gave Finn a dirty look. "All right, I guess it's time," he said. Zack paused, looking down at the deck for a moment. He then faced the submarine commander. "Captain, I haven't been completely up front with you and your people."

"What do you mean?" asked Maxwell. His voice was clearly agitated.

"I now have a pretty good idea of what's going on."

Maxwell stepped back inside the cabin and closed the door. "Okay, I'm all ears."

It took Zack nearly fifteen minutes to tell his story. Finn Sorenson helped out several times, adding his personal experiences and theories. After Zack finished, Commander Maxwell reacted. "Scott, that's just about the most incredible tale I've ever heard."

"I know, but it's all true. Now can you see why I need to get off this boat?"

Maxwell ignored Scott's question. "You mean to tell me that your daughter has been held hostage by this Yoshida character and that she might be somewhere on the Nemuro Complex?"

"Yes, I'm certain that's where they've been holding her. Everything fits."

"But how can you hope to rescue her?" asked Maxwell.

"Just turn me loose in *Little Mike.* I'll find a way."

"Yeah, and I'll go with him," added Finn.

Maxwell leaned back in one of the cabin's two chairs. His

mind was running at a furious pace. *I can't let him take that submersible back in there—my orders expressly prohibit that. But if I make him stay here, then he might lose his daughter. Shit! What should I do?*

The captain was about to once again tell Scott that his hands were tied when a new idea occurred. *Of course, that just might work. There's nothing in my orders prohibiting that.*

It was a bitch of a night. The wind was howling and the seas were mounting. The summer squall that raced across the ocean surface wouldn't last very long but it still packed quite a punch.

The U.S.S. *Bremerton* was broadside to the five-foot-high swells that swept in from the east. Its hull acted like a wall, creating a semishielded area on its lee side. Commander Maxwell was in the sail, looking aft over the hulk of *Little Mike*. He was using a night vision device to penetrate the coal-black darkness. The submersible endured the weather without incident; the mating collar firmly anchored it to the *Bremerton*'s deck plates. Maxwell ignored the mini-sub. Instead, his eyes were glued to the seven persons assembled on the open deck just aft of the piggyback cargo. Three seamen and a senior chief, all dressed in foul weather gear and PFDs, were coaxing an inflatable raft over the side. The other three, dressed in head-to-foot survival suits, were sitting on the deck.

While remaining focused on the deck party, Maxwell keyed his hand-held mike. "Chief, how you doing out there?"

"Okay, skipper," came the immediate reply. "We're just about ready."

"Good. Put Scott on."

"Aye, sir." The chief moved a few steps forward, squatting down next to his charges. He unclipped the mike. "Mr. Scott, the skipper would like to talk with you."

Zack reached for the microphone. "Scott here," he called out.

"I assume you and your people still want to go through with this—in spite of the weather."

"Yeah, I sure do, let me check with the others." Zack turned to face his companions. "Last call—anyone want out?"

Finn Sorenson shook his head negatively.

"No," Halley Blake said.

Zack keyed the mike again. "We're all going."

"Very well. I wish you the best of luck."

"Thanks, captain."

A few minutes later, Zack, Finn, Halley, and two of the seamen were in an inflatable raft. One of the enlisted men manned the forty-horse outboard, while the other sailor sat in the bow with Zack. Halley and Finn were seated in the middle.

Zack leaned over the side and pushed against the submarine's hull. The raft shot away. The helmsman gunned the motor. Thirty seconds later they rounded the *Bremerton*'s bow and headed into the oncoming seas.

There were white caps on top of the swells and it was pitch-dark. Despite the adverse conditions, Zack knew they didn't have far to go. Their destination was only half a mile away. He could see it in the distance. The *Deepquestor* had more lights on it than a Las Vegas casino.

29

A NEW HOME

Friz Strait

The *Deepquestor* was like a rock island. Submerged to its drilling configuration and moored to the bottom with eight anchor chain assemblies, two from each corner, it was designed to survive a typhoon. The squall's winds and waves buffeted the rig but had minimal impact.

Deep inside the floating factorylike vessel, on a mid-level deck, there was no sense of motion. What little noise penetrated the steel bulkheads and thickly insulated decks was masked by the resonance of machinery sounds and the hum of the fluorescent lighting. The small cluster of people gathered inside the room were immune to the events taking place outside. The twenty-foot by thirty-foot compartment was comfortably warm. The smell of fresh coffee permeated the air.

"Jesus, Zack," the long-bearded man said, "when the watch officer woke me up I thought I was dreaming."

"Yeah, I guess we surprised everyone."

"No shit! Here I am sleeping away and then I get this call from the bridge saying our boss is in some kind of small boat under the rig, waiting to be hauled aboard. I could hardly believe it."

"Well, none of us planned this," Zack replied. "It all kind of happened at the last minute."

Ian Flynn had been patiently waiting for Zack to provide

the details of the unscheduled visit. But so far his boss had talked only in riddles. The other visitors, a bearded, tough-looking character in his early forties, and a woman, several years younger but undeniably attractive, even with wet hair and no makeup, were equally cryptic. He couldn't contain his curiosity anymore.

"Zack, I gotta know! How'd you get here? This place is almost like the end of the world."

"On a sub," answered Scott.

"A submarine? What the hell were you doing on a sub?"

It took nearly half an hour to tell the entire story. When Zack finally finished, Flynn just shook his head in astonishment. He turned to face Zack. "What happened to Russ McMillin?"

"Oh, yeah. He wanted to come with us, but the sub skipper wouldn't let him leave."

"Why?"

"Because *Little Mike*'s still riding piggyback on his sub. The skipper wanted somebody to remain aboard who knows how to operate it if problems come up."

"I guess that makes sense," commented Flynn. He stood up and walked to an adjacent wall. A detailed hydrographic map of the Kuril Island chain was taped to it. He focused on the southern island group, just offshore of Hokkaido.

"You know, Zack," Flynn said as he turned around, "I've been wondering about that Nemuro area for a long time now. I've had dozens of conversations with our Russian partners about their earlier exploration attempts around Kunashiri and the Habomais." He paused for a moment to look back at the map. "Over the years, when Russia still controlled those islands, they punched in dozens of wildcat wells in this area." He pointed to a spot on the map with his right forefinger. "But you know, they only found a few marginal tracts of gas and just a trace or two of oil. And then, after the USSR breaks up and Russia gives the southern Kurils back to Japan, YHI suddenly announces a spectacular crude oil find offshore of Nemuro."

Flynn returned to his seat. "Geologically, the formations offshore of Nemuro are identical to those in the Habomais and around Kunashiri and Etorofu. And if there really was such a huge reservoir off Hokkaido, the Russians should have found evidence of its presence on their side of the Notsuke Strait a long time ago.''

"So what are you getting at?" asked Zack.

"Based on what you just told me about those phantom subs and underwater oil tanks, I don't think there's a huge reservoir at Nemuro. I think the whole thing is a fake."

Flynn's theory startled Zack and the others. They had all been thinking that Japan might be experimenting with a new system to bootleg oil. But Flynn's suggestion was so outrageous that it was frightening.

"Damn it," Zack said, "I never thought of anything like that."

Commander Blake spoke next. She looked straight at Scott. "You know, Zack, if Ian's right, a lot of this whole mess is beginning to make sense to me now." She paused for a few seconds to complete her thoughts. "If the Nemuro field is a phoney, and this Yoshida company is in fact stealing oil from other areas and bringing it in with those gargantuan sub tankers, then why have you been targeted? Why is SCS a threat to whatever they're up to?"

"That's what has been bothering the hell out of me ever since this whole damn mess started. I don't know why they want SCS. We're not working in Japan and we're certainly no economic giant, like Exxon or Chevron, so we could never challenge them in the offshore business."

"Yet they still persist, going to enormous means to get control of your company—why?"

"I don't know, Halley," replied Zack. "The only thing that used to make any sense to me was when I thought PVH wanted the Hammer 4 holdings. Those oil reserves are potentially huge and I could see why they would want to buy SCS. But when they announced that they were not going to develop the site my theory fell apart. From then on I was at a loss to explain anything—that is, until you came up with your idea about the gas release."

"Gas release? What are you talking about?" asked Captain Flynn.

For the next few minutes, Zack and Halley explained their theory on how a Japanese sub tanker was removing crude oil from the Hammer 4 site.

Flynn's reaction was immediate. "Well, that sure as hell

explains why they could afford to make themselves look like a bunch of goody two-shoes. By donating the Hammer 4 leases to that environmental group, everyone bought into their preservation line. But it was all a lie—they could still get to the oil any time they wanted.''

"Yep," agreed Zack.

Finn Sorenson spoke up next. "You know, Zack, that all sounds logical. But something still bugs me. How could they ever drill-in those wells off the Washington coast without somebody knowing about it?"

Finn's question was right to the point and Zack had already anticipated it. "It had to have been done from some kind of underwater drilling rig."

"You mean like on a submarine?" asked Finn.

"Yes."

"That's incredible." Finn then raised his arms and looked around the room as if he was seeing through the walls. "You mean something like this ship, the *Deepquestor*—with all of this gear on it—inside a submarine?"

Zack nodded his head. "Yes. In fact, SCS has been working on a prototype submersible drilling system."

He then spent the next couple of minutes describing the research project. When Zack finished, Finn shook his head from side to side. He was truly amazed at Scott's inventiveness. "Have you tried it out?" he finally asked.

"No. Not yet. We're still working on some of the computer software. It should be ready in six months or so."

Halley Blake rejoined the conversation. "Zack, I had no idea you had progressed that far with the technology. That's an incredible system."

"Yeah, well, I thought we were on the leading edge, but it looks like somebody else is way ahead of us—light-years ahead."

Halley frowned, reading Zack's disappointment. "I see your point. Apparently, the Japanese already have a similar system and it's fully operational."

"Yes, it sure looks that way."

Zack was thinking about all of the wasted time and money that SCS had spent on the development of his dream when Finn Sorenson interrupted his thoughts. "You know, Zack, if this Yoshida character doesn't want the Hammer 4 tract because he can steal the oil, then he must be up to something else, because they sure want SCS out of the picture."

"Yeah, I know that. But what does he want? Tell me, please, because I sure as hell can't figure it out."

Captain Flynn shifted his heavy body in his chair. "Maybe it's what we're doing with the Russians?" he said.

Zack turned toward the rig captain. "What do you mean by that, Ian?"

"Consider this: Both us and our Russian partners have let it be known for some time that our J-V group plans to drill a couple of wildcat holes in the southern Kurils. Even though Japan got their islands back, the Russians retained the right to develop offshore mineral resources around Shikotan and the north end of Etorofu. We will only have to pay the Japanese government an eight percent royalty on anything we find there. Now, just suppose—"

"But what about Kunashiri and the Habomais?" broke in Halley Blake. "The Japanese have complete sovereignty over them."

"That's right," Captain Flynn answered. "We can't drill in those waters. But around Shikotan and the north end of Etorofu we sure as hell can. In fact, we're supposed to head south to spud in another well off the north end of Shikotan later this year." Flynn paused to look at Zack. "Right, boss?" he asked.

"Yep, absolutely."

Flynn took another sip of coffee and looked back at Halley. "Now, I think that because we have the right to drill in the southern Kurils, it bugs the hell out of the Japs. They don't want us or the Russians poking our noses around in their territory, especially near their sacred Nemuro field."

Zack spoke next. "Then you must think they're afraid we're going to tap into their reservoir, especially if we drill near Shikotan?"

"On first glance you would think that. But, no, I don't believe that's what's going on." Flynn glanced back at the wall map. "I think both YHI and the Japanese government are scared shitless that we're going to continue to come up with dry holes in that area."

Zack didn't say anything at first. Flynn's statement didn't sound right to him. And then it hit him like a pail of cold water in the face. "I see what you're getting at, Ian. If we come up with a series of dry holes in that area, it's going to make the geology of the Nemuro field look even more suspicious. And if—''

"And if that field is a fake," interrupted Flynn, "like I'm beginning to really believe it is, then someone else is going to figure it out."

"That must be it," called out Halley. She was as excited as the others. "YHI's elaborate deception will be uncovered."

Zack spoke next. "That's got to be it, Ian. YHI doesn't care about SCS. All it wants is control of SCS so it can control the drilling around Shikotan."

"But, Zack," Finn said, deciding to rejoin the conversation, "what about the Russians? Won't they still own the drilling rights around those islands?"

"Yes, but remember they don't have the right drilling equipment for those areas. That's why they joint-ventured with us, and our JV agreement with them would still be valid even if SCS was sold. They'd have to work with whoever bought us out." Zack paused as he shifted position in his chair. His lower back was beginning to ache again. "Now, if someone from YHI were calling the shots on this rig right now, what are the Russians going to know?"

Finn hunched his shoulders as if to say: *I don't know.*

Zack continued. "Besides a dozen roughnecks, our Russian friends have only a couple of technical observers aboard, and their job is to coordinate resupply services." Zack locked on to Finn's eyes. "Now, I don't know if you're aware of this or not, but contrary to popular opinion, offshore drillers rarely know if they've encountered oil or gas when spudding in a deep hole."

"Why is that?" asked Finn

"Because of the enormous pressures involved. We do everything we can to prevent high-pressure subterranean formations from prematurely reaching the surface."

"You mean like in a blowout."

"Exactly. To control the pressure we fill the bore hole with a carefully concocted slurry of water, clay, and other chemicals."

"The mud?" asked Finn.

"That's right," replied Zack. "It continuously circulates through the drill stem and then flows back up the casing. Now, as the drill bit cuts into the rock, the tailings it creates are circulated back to the rig. We then analyze the fragments to see if we've pierced a petroleum-bearing zone.''

"So that's what the geologists look at?"

"Yes, mud samples are continually monitored as we drill deeper. When the right combination of things turn up in the logs, we stop and run a series of tests.''

"Okay, I think I see what you're getting at," Finn said. "Unless you're a geologist, you're not going to know what you've found.''

"Precisely. All the Japanese would have to do is salt the tailing samples with just the right amount of material and a dry hole suddenly becomes a marginal well site. However, additional bogus testing would indicate that there isn't enough oil to make the site marketable at this time.''

Finn Sorenson shook his head. "But, Zack, if there's really no oil there, what good do the fake well reports do?"

"That's the beauty of it, Finn. All they would have to do is create the perception that there really are petroleum-bearing formations in the vicinity of Nemuro, even though they're marginal deposits. That way, no one will be suspicious, like—''

"Like if they were completely dry holes!" interrupted Finn.

"Exactly. All they would have to say is that they might develop the satellite fields at a later date, if market conditions warrant the extra cost of extraction.''

"Clever, very clever," Finn said. "I think you've got something there.''

Tokyo

The 747 landed at Tokyo International at 7:05 A.M., local time. After sitting on a taxiway for nearly fifteen minutes, waiting for an opening at the main terminal, the jumbo jet taxied to its berth. Just as the pilot braked to a final stop, it seemed like all 327 passengers aboard the nonstop flight from Seattle jumped up from their seats. And in just seconds all of the aisles were plugged. After spending ten hours aboard the crowded aircraft, everyone was anxious to get off.

Despite the passengers' urge to deplane, they would be delayed an extra five minutes. Even the first-class ticket holders had to wait. A small army of flight attendants held off the hordes while the forward cabin door was opened. And then a man walked onto the aircraft. He was in a dark blue pinstripe suit with a white shirt and a red silk tie. He would have passed for any prosperous Japanese businessman except for one fact: He was built like a tank. Although he was only five foot eight, his bulk was massive. He looked out of place compared to the other slim passengers and crew.

The man squinted his eyes as he searched the forward end of the aircraft. He had glasses but was too vain to wear them in public. He spotted his target a few seconds later. He raised his massive right arm and began waving his hand. "Miss Cindy," he called out in Japanese. "Please come here."

Cindy DeMorey, standing in an aisle on the opposite side of the doorway, was tired of the delay just like the other passengers. But when she heard her name and then spotted one of Yoshida's bodyguards standing at the head of the jetway, she understood. As she made her way past the other passengers, politely asking them to move aside, Cindy felt the stares in her back. She could even hear the whispering, all in Japanese: *Why's she so special? Who's that goon over there? She must be a rich bitch!*

Just a few minutes after deplaning, Cindy's luggage magically appeared in the international VIP lounge. She was then whisked through a perfunctory passport check; the government agent didn't even bother to open one of the four suitcases she brought along. By the time the other passengers would finish the ninety-minute immigration and customs gauntlet, she would be in her hotel room in the Ginza.

The bodyguard loaded the luggage onto a dolly and, with Cindy following behind, headed for the special VIP exit. The limousine was parked outside in a no parking zone; a special sticker on its windshield made it immune to the airport police and their legions of tow trucks.

Ten minutes later, as the Lincoln raced down the highway, Cindy chuckled to herself while she stretched out in the spacious backseat. *Uncle, you sure know how to take care of a lady.*

The Kuril Islands

The helicopter raced northward, hugging the ocean surface in the still air of the late morning. It was a large aircraft, capable of transporting fifteen passengers plus a two-person flight crew. But today there were only three passengers aboard. They sat in the spacious main cabin, directly behind the flight deck. They should have been wearing survival suits, always mandatory for long flights over the water. However, they ignored the industry standard. Instead, the three men were dressed in expensive suits and ties.

The YHI representatives, dispatched from Tokyo headquarters the previous afternoon, were having a ball. The helicopter ride was smooth and exhilarating. The lousy weather of the previous night had been replaced by calm seas and windless conditions. Consequently, the company pilots were able to push the Bell 412 SP to its limits. Flying at 140 knots just a hundred feet above the wave crests was a definite "E" ticket ride. Earlier, while the 412 had hugged the shoreline, the men clustered around the port windows. One man fired off dozens of camera shots at the scenic coastline. But now that the aircraft was over the open sea there was nothing to photograph except water.

Despite the favorable weather conditions, the flight crew had its hands full. Compared to flying over open terrain, the ocean is like a desert. There are no landmarks. It is inherently easy to get lost. But the crew of the 412 were pros—they knew the exact position of the aircraft. While the pilot manned the flight controls, the copilot navigated. He monitored a GPS receiver that continually displayed the latitude and longitude of the aircraft. The system was accurate to within a few meters.

In addition to providing real-time earth coordinates, the device simultaneously issued recommended course corrections caused by wind drift. It also updated the distance and flight time to the selected destination. The digital readout currently indicated that the 412 was about a dozen miles and eight minutes away from its destination.

The copilot looked up from the digital receiver, scanning the water surface far ahead. He spotted a tiny speck on the horizon, right in line with the aircraft's heading. A moment later he keyed his intercom mike switch. "I think I have it, twelve o'clock, dead ahead."

The pilot looked toward the horizon. The speck had grown a little more noticeable. *Thank the gods*, he thought in Japanese. He was always nervous when flying over the ocean—it was almost as bad as having to fly in fog. "Roger, I have it. Looks like we're right on course."

"You want me to notify our guests?" asked the copilot.

"Yeah, might as well. I'm sure they're going to want to photograph their new toy before landing on it."

Captain Flynn was alone on the *Deepquestor's* bridge deck. He was sipping a steaming hot cup of tea, a weird Russian brand, when he heard the noise. It was a whomp-whomp sound. *Chopper,* he thought, as he turned to look toward the south. Even though the sun was behind his back, the glare off the water surface made it hard to see. He raised his right hand to his forehead, partially shielding the light. He spotted it a few seconds later. *There it is! Damn, but it's flying low.*

Flynn unconsciously sipped away at the bitter-tasting drink as he watched the helicopter close with the floating drilling rig. *I wonder where it came from.* About a quarter mile out it climbed a couple of hundred feet and began circling.

The chopper had just made its third orbit when Zackary Scott walked onto the bridge wing. "Hi, Zack," called out Flynn. "We got us a visitor."

"Yeah, I just heard about it from the bridge watch over the intercom. Is it military?"

"No, I don't think so. It looks like a civilian job to me."

Zack raised a pair of binoculars he'd borrowed from the bridge house. Although the aircraft was now moving at nearly a hundred miles per hour he was able to focus on its fuselage. He didn't like what he saw. "Son of a bitch," he whispered.

Ian Flynn heard him cussing. "What's wrong?" he asked.

"That bird's got a logo on it—a fat circle with a Y in the middle of it."

"Yoshida Heavy Industries?"

"Yep," replied Zack.

"What the hell would they be doing out here?"

"They must be getting ready to take over."

"What do you mean?" asked Flynn.

"Tonight, at midnight, they will officially own this rig, along with all of the others."

"Jesus, I forgot about that."

Zack hadn't. He had been thinking about it all night long, wondering how and when YHI would try to take control of SCS's assets. He now had his answer. As his mind kicked into overdrive, recalling one of the half dozen contingency plans he had developed, he lowered his head, staring at the blue-green water. Half a minute later he smiled to himself. *Yes, that'll work.* He looked up at the still-orbiting helo. *Come on, you bastards, land that thing!*

Tokyo

"Good morning, Uncle," Cindy DeMorey said as she walked into the expansive office. Technically it was still morning, but the noon hour was only ten minutes away.

Hiroshi Yoshida rose from his chair, a wide grin breaking out across his face. "Ah, Cindy, my dear, I trust you had a good flight?"

"Yes. The sleeping berth on the plane worked well and I was able to nap a little this morning." She paused as she sat down in a chair at the foot of his desk. Yoshida had already returned to his seat. "But no matter how many times I make the trip, I always feel worn out for a couple of days."

"I understand that. I, too, have a hard time with jet lag." Yoshida paused momentarily as he shuffled a few loose papers on his desk. "I assume everything is on schedule in Seattle."

"Yes, everything was fine when I left." Cindy reached into her handbag. She removed a pack of Salems and a solid gold lighter. After lighting up she continued. "According to the contract, we're supposed to take possession of SCS's foreign-based assets at midnight tonight, Tokyo time."

"That's correct. I've already made arrangements to take over the drilling rig in the Friz Strait." Yoshida glanced down at his wristwatch and then back at Cindy. "In fact, our transition team should be landing on it soon."

Cindy nodded her head positively. "That sounds good. But what about the woman? You know that Scott will never turn over the rest of his company until she's freed."

"Of course he won't," replied Yoshida. "I'm counting on that."

Cindy looked back at him with a questioning look on her face.

Yoshida continued. "She stays put as my insurance policy. I don't trust that man and I intend to make him dance for some time yet."

"But the exchange, it's still scheduled for tonight, isn't it?"

"Yes, but *you're* only going to give him a taste."

"What do you mean by that?"

Yoshida spent the next five minutes going over new instructions for Cindy. When he finished he sat back in his chair, waiting for her reaction.

"Uncle, this is very, very risky. You're going to make him crazy. A crazy man is unpredictable." She paused for a moment, thinking through his plan. "If you provoke him like that, I think he will come after you."

Yoshida smiled. "Cindy, my dear, that's precisely what I hope he does."

Nemuro

Wendy Scott stared out of the view port. The sea was calm today, not like the previous night with all of its windswept fury. She had the port cracked open just a little to let in the fresh fragrance of the sea. It helped keep her awake.

She was exhausted but didn't want sleep. The rape attempt was still fresh in her mind, and whenever she managed to drift off to sleep the nightmares returned. The dream was always the same: The brutish-looking man sneaks into her cabin. He silently looks at her for a few seconds before removing his trousers. And before she can react he hurls himself on her, smothering her body with his bulk. She tries to scream but his hand covers her mouth. She can't breathe . . .

During the dream, just when she was about to black out, Wendy always woke up with a jolt. It felt like her heart was going to burst from her chest. She would then lie still for up to ten minutes, waiting for the spasms to pass. She feared that something was wrong with her heart.

Wendy was not physically ill, nor had she been injured.

However, the agony she suffered was very real to her. The psychosomatic pain resulted from severe emotional trauma brought on by the combined effects of the rape attempt, her extended isolation, and the kidnapping.

As Wendy continued to gaze out the window, she rubbed her right hand over her sternum. The pain was gone but her unconscious wouldn't let her forget it. Wendy's awake mind, however, was focusing on more pleasant thoughts. She could see her mother's warm and smiling face. *Oh, Mom, I miss you.* And then she looked into Dan's eyes. She missed her lover more than anything. *I love you, honey, with all my heart.* Finally, Wendy thought about her father. She could picture Zack's handsome face with crystal clarity. He was aging, but he still looked young, and that gave her a great sense of comfort. While the parents of many of her contemporaries looked like they were one step away from the grave, her father was strong, both physically and mentally. And he would always be there for her. *Daddy, please come and get me. I want to go home!*

The *Deepquestor*

After repeatedly circling the *Deepquestor* for nearly ten minutes, the YHI helicopter finally touched down on the helipad. The pilot never bothered to radio for permission to land.

As soon as the twin turbine engines began to wind down, the port cabin door opened and the passengers filed out. The first man to exit was about thirty-five years old. He wore black-framed glasses with thick Coke bottlelike lenses. He was built like a beanpole. He carried a leather suitcase in his right hand and a black-body Nikon draped around his neck. The next man out was a twin to the first, except that he was partially bald and didn't wear glasses. Although the hair over his forehead was rapidly receding, the rest of his dark mane remained thick and full.

The last passenger was nothing like his predecessors. He was about twice the bulk of either one of the others and he towered over them by almost a foot. And he would have had a full head of hair if he cared to. Instead, he cut it razor-close along the sides. He kept just enough on the top of his head, however, to create a flat-top look.

"Good Lord, that son of a bitch is a monster," Ian Flynn said. He was standing on the bridge, looking aft toward the helicopter. "Who do you suppose he is?"

Zackary Scott was still standing next to Flynn, leaning against a steel guardrail. He pulled up his binoculars, focusing on the third passenger. As the image of the man's face burst into clarity, Zack reacted instantly. "So we meet again, you prick."

"What did you say?" asked Flynn.

Zack lowered the binoculars. "The big one down there . . . I had a run-in with him before. He's one of Yoshida's goons."

"You're sure?"

"Oh, yeah. He was my initial contact in Honolulu after they took Wendy."

"Damn it. Then we can't let him see you. No one's supposed to know you're here."

"That's right. And that goes for Finn, too." Zack paused for a second or two. "And Commander Blake. I don't want these guys to know she's aboard either."

"Okay, we can handle that. I think they're both in the galley, so why don't you go round 'em up and then head for some place inconspicuous—say, one of the engine rooms."

"All right," replied Zack, "that sounds like a good plan. We'll hole up in the starboard pontoon."

"Okay, but just what do you want me to do with these turkeys?"

"Find out what they're up to and then get the word to me. I'll decide what to do at that time."

"You got it, boss."

Captain Flynn met the three visitors on the main drilling deck. They had just worked their way down from the helipad. A deckhand following Flynn carried a cardboard box full of plastic hard hats and PFDs.

"Hello there," called out Flynn in as friendly a voice as he could muster. "I'm Ian Flynn; I'm the rig skipper." What he really wanted to do, however, was chew the intruders out from one end to the other. You never, ever land an aircraft on an SCS drilling rig without securing advanced permission.

The quasi twins bowed in unison; their huge companion didn't move. Instead he just stared back at Flynn.

The balding YHI executive was the first to respond. "Mr. Flynn, my name is Fukuda, and this is Mr. Suzuki." He gestured to his twin standing next to him. He then turned to his right. "And this is Mr. Kato." Fukuda paused for a moment as he turned back to face Flynn. "We represent the new owner of this vessel and we have come to take it over."

Flynn almost laughed out loud. *This little shit thinks he's going to take my rig. I ought to throw 'em overboard right now.* "What do you mean new owner?" asked Flynn, playing dumb.

Fukuda was startled. "This vessel, along with all of the other SCS drilling ships, has been sold."

"Sold!" yelled Flynn. "What the hell are you talking about? This rig belongs to Scott Coastal. There's no way it's been sold."

Captain Flynn watched as the twins turned to face each other; they were jabbering away in rapid-fire Japanese. *I think I shook the little pricks up,* he thought. *This package isn't wrapped up nice and neat like you thought, is it, boys?*

As the two YHI executives continued their cryptic discussion, Flynn studied the third visitor. He remained in the background, standing next to a steel bulkhead. He was now wearing a set of mirrored sunglasses, the kind U.S. Secret Service agents wear when guarding the president. When the man turned to his right, looking back over the length of the *Deepquestor*, his suit jacket parted. That's when Flynn spotted the bulge under his right armpit. *I'll be damned, he's packing.*

The twins stopped talking and turned back to face Flynn. Fukuda, the balding one, again did the talking. "There's obviously been some kind of mistake, Captain Flynn. Please take us to your radio room so we can straighten this all out."

"No, I'm afraid I can't do that—least not yet."

"Why not?"

"Because I gotta check you guys out first."

"Check us out?" questioned Fukuda.

"That's right. I'm going to make a few phone calls first. Then maybe I'll let you phone home."

"But this is preposterous. The agreement says—"

"Hey, buddy," interrupted Flynn, "if you don't like the arrangement, just climb back aboard that fancy whirlybird of yours and bug out of here."

"All right, all right," Fukuda said. "We'll wait for you to make your calls."

"Good, then put these on and I'll take you inside where you can get a cup of coffee and wait." Flynn's assistant began handing out the hard hats and life vests.

"Why do we have to put these on?" protested Suzuki, the twin with a full set of hair.

"Company rules. Nobody, and I mean nobody, walks around outside without a skullcap or a PFD."

Suzuki mumbled something in Japanese as he began to adjust the universal headband on the hard hat. He did it wrong and when he set it on his head, the plastic hat sank down to eye level. His partner laughed at his mistake.

"Here, let me fix that for you," Flynn said as he reached forward, grabbing the hat. In just a few seconds he corrected the problem and handed it back. This time the fit was perfect.

"Thank you," the man said sheepishly; he was clearly embarrassed.

A minute later, the three visitors began following Flynn. He purposely led them through a maze of walkways, ladderwells, companionways, and storage areas until they were deep inside the bowels of the ship. No matter how good their memory was, they would have a hell of a time getting back to their chopper.

Zack, Halley, and Finn were in the *Deepquestor*'s starboard pontoon, almost forty feet under water. The submerged hull, as big as a World War II submarine, housed two locomotive-size diesel engines in its aft section. The compartment was spotless and well illuminated. The air had a slight oily odor to it.

Zack was pacing across the tile floor of the engine control room when the intercom buzzer came to life. He immediately grabbed the handset. "Starboard engines," he answered.

"Hey, Zack, it's me."

Zack recognized Flynn's voice. "What've you got, Ian?"

"You were right, they're here to take over the rig."

"Did they say what their orders were?"

"No, not yet. Only that they represent the new owner. I've been playing dumb like you wanted. Right now they think I'm calling you in Seattle for instructions."

"Good, go back and tell 'em I won't release the vessel until the transaction is complete. You know what I want to find out."

"Got it. I'll get back to you shortly."

Zack set the intercom handset back in its cradle. He then turned to face Commander Blake and Finn Sorenson. "So far, so good. They've taken the bait. We're now getting close to setting the hook."

Tokyo

Hiroshi Yoshida and Cindy DeMorey were seated at opposite ends of the desk They were sipping tea and picking away at the *oyako donburi* when Yoshida's male aide walked into the private dining room.

The chairman of YHI lowered his chopsticks as the aide approached. The scowl on Yoshida's leathery face clearly telegraphed his displeasure with the intruder. Fifteen minutes earlier he had ordered the manservant not to disturb him during his noontime meal. "What is it, Hasumi?" he asked.

The sixty-year-old man bowed and then began speaking. "Excuse me for interrupting your meal, sir, but you have an urgent call from Mr. Fukuda. He insisted that I inform you immediately."

Yoshida's thin eyebrows raised in surprise. Fukuda would never interrupt him unless something was wrong. "All right, bring it here."

The aide walked to a nearby cabinet and opened the door. A portable telephone was housed inside. He removed the handset and carried it to the table.

Yoshida dismissed the servant with a flip of his hand. The man backed out, bowing as he passed through the doorway.

Before activating the handset, Yoshida looked toward Cindy. She sat quietly at the other end of the table, eating the delicious meal of chicken and eggs. "I'm sorry for this intrusion," he said.

"Please, don't mind me—go right ahead," she replied.

Yoshida switched the portable telephone transceiver on. "*Moshi-Moshi*," he said.

"Sir, this is Fukuda. We have landed on the drilling vessel." He hesitated a moment. "But there is a problem."

"What kind of problem?"

"The master will not release the ship to us. He just called the owner of SCS in Seattle and was told the transaction would only be completed when we produced evidence that the missing commodity was in working order. I do not know what he means by that, but apparently they are very serious about this requirement."

Damn it! Scott again! thought Yoshida. "What kind of evidence do they want?"

"They said you would know—something about a telephone conversation, like what was done earlier." Fukuda knew that the "evidence" Flynn had been referring to was Wendy Scott, but he continued his deception. His orders were to speak in code at all times when using an open radio circuit. "Sir, I do not understand what is going on here. These Americans are talking in riddles."

"All right, I know what has to be done." Yoshida looked at his watch; it was almost one P.M. "Tell them the call will be made at eight o'clock tonight, our time."

"Very good. Anything else?"

"Stay on that rig. As soon as we get this problem resolved, I want it out of there."

"Yes, sir. We will stand by."

Yoshida flipped the handset off and tossed it onto a tatami mat.

"Trouble?" asked Cindy DeMorey.

"Maybe. Scott's demanding proof that his daughter is all right before he'll release the *Deepquestor*."

"I can't say that that's a surprise."

"No, I suppose you're right."

Cindy watched as Yoshida began picking at his half-full bowl. She could tell he had lost interest in the meal. "Uncle, do you want me to handle this problem?"

He looked up. "No, I need to go to Nemuro tonight anyway so I'll take care of it from there." Yoshida paused for a moment—a new idea flashed into his head. "Cindy, why don't you come with me anyway? You've never seen the operation since it was completed."

DeMorey smiled. "Yes, I would like that very much."

"Good, then we shall go together." Yoshida returned the smile and then began eagerly attacking the *oyako donburi*. His spirits rose like the sun. He was more than pleased that Cindy would accompany him on the trip.

The *Deepquestor*

Captain Ian Flynn was standing next to his command station on the bridge. He was alone. The door to the adjacent compartment was closed. He picked up an intercom phone and punched in a two-digit number. The phone was answered on its third ring.

"Starboard engines."

"Zack, this is Ian again. I've got an update for you."

"Fire away."

"The boss Jap up here says that our Seattle office will receive confirmation tonight at twenty hundred hours, our time."

"Good, then get hold of Marshall and make sure he has everything set up ahead of time. I can't afford to have any last-minute glitches with the hardware."

"You got it, skipper. We'll run through a series of radio tests to make sure everything's working proper." The rig skipper paused for a moment. "Zack, what do you want us to do about these characters up here?"

"Aren't they going to leave now?"

"No, in fact, their helo took off a few minutes ago."

"What?"

"As soon as the guy finished his sat call to Tokyo, he opened his briefcase and removed a hand-held radio. Before I could react he sent out some kind of message. And about two minutes later the helo took off."

"Damn it, so we're stuck with these guys."

"I'm afraid so," replied Flynn.

"Where are they?"

"I've got 'em holed up in the library right now. I told them that once I got things under control I'd take 'em for a tour of the rig. That seemed to satisfy them."

"Good, just keep them there. We're all going to come up now. It's time I talk face-to-face with these guys."

"Okay, but remember that big fucker is packing some kind of pistol."

"I know."

* * *

While at sea for months at a time, life aboard an offshore oil exploration vessel can be hard, lonely, and tedious. The work shifts are often twelve hours long, and for many of the crew, especially the deckhands who handle the drill string, the work is physically brutal and highly dangerous. The grueling work conditions are partially mitigated by the high wages. The excellent food also helps. But after weeks and weeks of the same routine, crew members would literally go bonkers if they didn't have another outlet. For some men and women, working out in the ship's compact but well-equipped gymnasium helped relieve the boredom. For others, playing endless games of penny-ante poker in the lounge provided the necessary diversion. However, most crew members found solace in an area of the vessel that offered nothing more than simple peace and quiet. The ship's library was the only space aboard the vessel that reminded the crew of home.

Ian Flynn walked into the library at a few minutes after one P.M. The twenty-five-foot-wide by forty-foot-long compartment was located just off the main crew quarters. The deck-to-overhead shelves on all four walls were cram-packed with rows of hardbound books, paperbacks, and magazines. The *Deepquestor*, like all of SCS's semis, was stocked with the latest best-sellers and periodicals as well as an extensive selection of classics and hundreds of videos.

The three visitors were seated around a small table at the far end of the room. They were all smoking. While the twins jabbered away in Japanese, the large man was thumbing through a *Playboy* magazine.

Flynn slid into a chair next to the bald twin. "Can I bum one of those from you?" he asked, pointing to the man's cigarette pack, lying on the edge of the table.

Fukuda pushed the pack of Seven Stars across the table. "Thanks."

Flynn lit up, inhaled deeply, and then let out a thick cloud of smoke. "Not bad," he said. The Japanese brand was milder than he had been expecting. "Where are you guys from anyway?"

"Tokyo for us," replied Fukuda. He then looked across the table. "Kato's from Yokohama."

Flynn nodded as he inhaled again. "I was in Tokyo once—

a couple of years ago—I was heading to Indonesia to check out a drilling site and had a twenty-four-hour layover in Japan. An old navy buddy of mine who was stationed at Yokosuka met me at the Tokyo airport. Later that night we ended up in some bar in the Ginza.'' Flynn rolled his eyes back while breaking out in wide grin. "God, I had a great time. You have some of the friendliest women I've ever run into. There was this one gal, a real looker, and she . . .''

As Ian Flynn continued his story, the YHI men listened intently. All three found it fascinating to hear a *gaijin* tell a story about seducing Japanese women. The fact that the tale was getting raunchier by the minute only added to their interest. And none of them noticed when the library door opened and a man walked in.

Finn Sorenson ignored the giggling and laughing at the far end of the room. Instead, he pretended to be looking for a book. Half a minute later he retrieved a hardback from a wall shelf but didn't even bother to look at its title. He tucked the book under his right armpit and then slowly headed toward the opposite end of the room, casually examining the rows of books as he went.

"So Billy and I finally ended up back in this fancy hotel suite with these two babes. And there was this basket chair in the living room—you know, the kind that's suspended from the ceiling. Well, this one gal, the one with the big tits, cuts this hole in the bottom of it and then . . .''

Finn Sorenson was now opposite the table, directly behind two of the visitors: the gorilla and one of the twins. He glanced over his shoulder. Ian Flynn was really getting into the story.

"So here I am lying flat on the floor, buck naked, and she's in this basket right above me, you know, aligned just right.'' He briefly looked down at his groin area. Smirks broke out across the faces of the three listeners as they visualized the graphic image. "Then Billy and this other gal start winding her up in this thing, like a rubber-band-powered airplane. And then they . . .''

Finn reached into his coat pocket and felt the cold steel of the revolver. The short barreled .357 magnum belonged to Captain Flynn. It was the only firearm aboard the *Deepquestor*. He kept it locked up in the ship's safe.

"I tell ya I've never experienced anything like that before. It was fucking fantastic."

Fukuda was just about to ask Flynn a question about the technique when he noticed that the man standing behind his comrades had turned around. And then he saw the pistol.

Using both hands, Finn aimed the blue-steel revolver right at the back of Kato's head. A second later he pulled the hammer back. The characteristic double click of the cocking action broke the jovial mood around the table.

"Okay, you big bastard," Finn shouted, "keep your hands on the table or I'm going to blow your head off."

Kato slowly rotated his upper body toward the voice. The bearded gunman, a big man like himself, stood five feet away. His aim was steady. There was no question that Kato would die if he made the wrong move.

"What do you want?" called out Fukuda. He started to stand but Ian Flynn grabbed him by the collar, slamming him back into the chair.

"Order your gorilla to hand over his piece," Finn said.

"What?"

"His gun! The one under his left shoulder. Tell him to take it out, with his left hand."

"Just relax," Kato said, his voice calm.

"Well, so you can speak good English, too," said Captain Flynn.

Kato pulled his coat apart. He then removed the nine-millimeter Beretta from its leather holster.

"Put it on the table," ordered Finn.

The man complied and Ian Flynn scooped it up. He removed the magazine, pulled the slide back, and ejected a round from the chamber. "I see you keep this thing ready to go. What the hell were you planning?"

Kato said nothing.

Flynn stood up and slipped the automatic into his waistband. He then walked to a nearby wall-mounted intercom phone and picked up the handset. He punched in a two-digit code. "This is Ian," he said. "We're all set now."

A minute later, Zackary Scott walked into the library.

Kaishu Kato started to rise from his chair when he spotted Zack, but Finn forced him back down with a warning. "Get down, fucker, or you're fish bait."

Fukuda had no idea what was going on. The transition was supposed to have been trouble free, and Kato was only along as Yoshida's observer. Fukuda hadn't even known that the man was armed.

"How dare you hold us like this!" Fukuda shouted. "You're all going to be fired."

"Shut up!" Zack said. He was now standing at the head of the table, looking down on the three Japanese prisoners. "You aren't going to get this rig or anything else that I own."

"Who are you?" demanded Fukuda.

"Ask your friend over there. He knows."

Fukuda turned toward Kato.

"That's Scott," replied the *yakuza* thug.

"Scott!" yelled Fukuda. He then turned back. "But you're supposed to be in Seattle."

"Surprise."

Tokyo

"Foxtrot Two-One-Niner, you are cleared for takeoff."

"Roger Tower," replied the pilot. "Two-One-Niner rolling." He then advanced the dual throttles to the stops. The jet engines exploded to life and the Dassault-Brequet Falcon 20 raced down the two-mile-long runway.

About a third of the way down the concrete lane the pilot pulled back on the yoke and the executive jet climbed into the afternoon sky. There was a low ceiling over Tokyo and within just a minute the plane was swallowed up by the thick gray clouds. A minute later it pierced through the clouds into the sunshine. The blue sky was clear to the horizon in all directions.

"Oh, what a difference," Cindy DeMorey said as unfiltered light filled the cockpit. She was sitting in the copilot's seat, next to Hiroshi Yoshida. They were the only ones aboard the French-built executive jet.

"Yes, it is wonderful. I always love this."

"Do you fly often?"

"Not as much as I'd like. But I try to get up at least a couple of times a month, usually by myself."

"Where do you go?" asked Cindy.

"Nowhere in particular. I'll just head up or down the coast for an hour or two and then come back."

"You've been flying for a long time?"

"Yes. Ever since I learned in the military. I don't think I'll ever get it out of my blood. I can really relax when I get up here."

"Is it hard?"

"Flying?"

"Yes, to learn, I mean."

"No, actually it's fairly simple. With a good instructor and a couple of weeks of ground school you can learn."

"But that's with a little plane. What about big ones, like this?" Cindy spread her arms apart to emphasize size.

"Once you learn the basics, it's not hard to graduate into multiengine aircraft. In fact, I'm taking lessons right now so I can pilot a larger aircraft—one with four engines."

"You are?"

"Yes, and I'm just about done with it. I take my final flight test next week."

"What kind of plane?" asked Cindy

"Airbus Three Forty. YHI owns a dozen of them—all freighters. I've wanted to fly one of those things for years." What Yoshida did not volunteer, however, was his secret wish to pilot the "Cadillac of the sky"—the Boeing 747. In fact, his own advisers had recommended that YHI purchase the American jumbo instead of the European Airbus. But Yoshida refused; there was no way he would buy anything from Boeing. The giant American company had built the B-29 that wiped out his family.

Cindy was shocked at her great-uncle's revelation. "But aren't there some kind of limits?"

Yoshida looked across the center console and smiled. "You mean like my age?"

"Forgive me, I didn't mean it that way."

Yoshida laughed. "If I were flying paying passengers, like a regular airline pilot, then, yes, I'd never be able to do that. But as long as I stay healthy and pilot my own aircraft without carrying fare-paying passengers I can continue to fly just about anything."

"What's it like, you know, a big jet like that?"

"It's a dream to fly. Just about takes care of itself."

Cindy DeMorey looked away from her uncle, staring blankly ahead through the windscreen. *What an amazing man,* she thought. *He's like a little kid up here—he really loves flying.*

Cindy turned back to study Yoshida. He was now busy talking over his headset to a ground controller. Despite his advancing age he still looked like he was only fifty years old. And his mind remained quick.

Yoshida completed the routine call and then turned to face Cindy. "That was Tokyo. We've just been cleared all the way to Kushiro."

"How long will it take?"

Yoshida glanced down at the primary nav computer. "We should be there in about an hour and ten minutes."

"Then we'll be at Nemuro before sunset?" Cindy asked.

"Yes, easy. I've got a helicopter waiting for us at Kushiro. It'll only take us about half an hour from there."

"Sounds good. I can hardly wait to see it."

They talked for a few more minutes until Yoshida was again interrupted by a ground controller. While he completed the routine radio call, Cindy stretched out her arms and yawned. She then sank deeper into the seat, further relaxing her body. She still suffered from jet lag and inadvertently closed her eyes. Half a minute later she fell asleep.

Yoshida looked across the aisle at his great-niece. She was curled up in the seat, sound asleep. *Sleep well, my dear. I need you to be alert tonight.*

30

CAPTAIN HOOK

The *Deepquestor*

Zackary Scott and Ian Flynn were in a claustrophobic conference room next to the sediment laboratory. They had spent the last hour pouring over charts and subsurface surveys of the waters around the Nemuro peninsula. Flynn was just about to suggest a new tactic when the doorway to the compartment opened and Commander Halley Blake rushed in.

Zack could tell something was wrong. Her mouth was turned down and her cheeks were beet-red. "Zack, I think you'd better have a word with your Mr. Sorenson."

Uh oh! What the hell has Finn done now? thought Zack. He tried to smile as he responded. "What's the matter, Commander?"

"I think he means to kill those Japanese!"

"What are you talking about?"

"He's trying to drown them—I'm sure of it."

"You mean they're not locked up in the decompression chamber?"

"No. He's got them lashed to a crane basket and has been repeatedly dunking them in the ocean. He's calls it a modern-day version of keelhauling. I call it attempted murder!"

"Damn it to hell, what next?" Zack said as he headed for the door.

Ian Flynn followed Scott, almost knocking Commander Blake over as he ran by her.

A minute and a half later, Scott and Flynn reached the third deck level. They burst onto an open deck. Zack spun around, looking for Finn. "Where the hell is he?" he called out.

"There!" shouted Flynn. He pointed across the deck to the operator's cab of the port jib crane. Finn Sorenson was inside the glass enclosure, about twenty feet above the deck. He was facing seaward, away from Zack and Ian; the hundred-foot-long boom was cantilevered out over the water.

"What the hell is he doing?" yelled Zack as he started to sprint across the open deck.

Captain Flynn didn't respond. He was too winded from the steep climb. Instead, he gasped for breath and then took off in pursuit of Scott.

Zack ran to the guardrail next to the crane's base and stopped. He looked downward. "Holy shit!"

Flynn pulled up next to Scott a few seconds later. He took another deep breath and then looked toward the sea surface. He started laughing. "Jesus, Halley was right. He's really dunking those pricks."

Zack didn't respond. Instead, he watched the spectacle. The YHI visitors—the twins and Kato—were each lashed, spread-eagle style, to the *Deepquestor*'s main boarding basket. The basket, suspended from the end of Sorenson's crane boom, was eighty feet above the ocean surface and about fifty feet away from the nearest part of the semi's hull.

When Zack first spotted the basket, it was swinging wildly from side to side. Seawater was pouring off it like a waterfall. A few seconds later, the basket plummeted downward. It fell like the proverbial rock. *Good Lord, he's going to kill them.*

A boarding basket, a conical netlike maze of ropes that stretches eight to ten feet in height, is used to transfer personnel and limited cargo from a service boat to the deck of a semisubmersible and vice versa. To board the basket, you step onto the six-foot-diameter rubber base and grab hold of the ropes. The crane operator on the rig then engages the clutch and the basket blasts off. For the uninitiated, the ride is nothing short of bone-chilling. The speed of the descent—or the ascent, depending on your destination—is breathtaking. One second you're standing on the deck of a rolling service boat, the next you're accelerating through the air like a rocket. Disneyland's best ride is tame compared to a crane operator with a quick clutch hand.

As exciting as a normal trip on the boarding platform could be, the ride Finn Sorenson was now treating his Japanese guests to was nothing less than awesome. Finn had, in fact, invented a modern-day version of keelhauling.

Zack watched in utter amazement as the basket crashed into the green water. Spray billowed into the air like a geyser. And then the upturned basket, along with its unlucky passengers, bobbed in the five-foot-high seas. He could only see one head sticking above the water.

Finn re-engaged the clutch and the basket exploded from the sea. It accelerated upward at lightning speed until he slammed home the brake. The basket whipsawed around, expending its momentum like a bungee cord jumper. A few seconds later, as the basket continued to twirl around, Finn leaned out of the cab. The basket was now at eye level with the crane. Zack could just make out Finn's voice over the rush of the sea. "You bastards want some more or have you had enough?"

One of the men, it looked like Fukuda, waved his hand in submission.

After Finn Sorenson swung the crane boom around, he dropped the basket onto the deck. It hit hard, sending a shudder through the steel plates. Ian Flynn was the first to run up to the collapsed basket. Zack was right behind. The jumble of netting, cables, and bodies looked like something out of a demolition derby.

"Christ Almighty, what a bloody mess," yelled Captain Flynn as he began to peel away the coils of rope from one of Sorenson's victims. Each man's wrists and ankles were solidly lashed to the basket's webbing by layers and layers of gray duct tape. Zack knelt down and had just started to help when Finn roared in from behind.

"Don't help those fuckers yet," he ordered.

Zack stood up and turned to face his friend. "What the hell's the matter with you? You just about killed these fellows."

"And I might just finish them off yet." He then reached

into his pocket and pulled out an automatic pistol—the nine-millimeter he had liberated earlier from Kato.

"Now wait a minute," Zack said. "Put that thing away. There's no need for this."

"Yeah, well, think about this: I thought something looked familiar with this prick but I couldn't quite place it at first." Finn set his right foot on the back of the nearest waterlogged man—it was Kaishu Kato, looking like a beached whale. "However, when he stripped off his coat and started rolling up his shirtsleeves after climbing into the decompression chamber, I happened to spot this just before sealing the hatch up." Finn kneeled down and in one violent move ripped the soggy wet shirtsleeve from the man's right arm. Hidden underneath, and covering almost the entire length of the brown-skinned arm, was a magnificent tattoo of a dragon. The body was green and black and hideous. And fiery red and yellow flames blasted out from its mouth.

Zack still didn't understand, and had just started to protest when Finn continued. "I've seen this one before." He paused, looking straight into Scott's eye. "He was on the *Odin*."

It took Zack a few seconds to make the connection. And then he exploded. "You! You son of a bitch," he yelled. And then, without thinking, he cocked his right foot back and kicked the man in the side, right at belly level. The *yakuza* thug let out a weak groan.

Ian Flynn pulled Zack back just in time to keep him from really hurting the man. "For God's sake, what the hell's the matter with you?"

Zack shrugged off Flynn's grip and walked half a dozen steps away. It took him a minute to calm down. He then walked back to the others. "Not only did this bastard kill Finn's tug crew and a Coast Guard officer, but I'm certain he was part of the group that sabotaged the *Kelda Scott*."

"Oh, shit," mumbled Captain Flynn. He now understood. Captain Dan Barker had been one of Flynn's best friends. But he was gone—incinerated along with fifty-one other good people from the SCS drilling vessel.

At gunpoint, Zack and Finn marched the waterlogged trio across the open crane deck to an out-of-the-way spot near the base of the drilling derrick. Zack held the .357 magnum; Finn had the Beretta. Ian Flynn and Halley Blake followed in their footsteps.

Although the deck area was still out in the open, it was well sheltered from the stiff easterly breeze that had just started blowing, reducing both noise and windchill. But more important, the high-walled structures that surrounded the patio-size bay provided maximum privacy. None of the other crew members aboard the rig could see them.

"All right, you people," Zack said, waving the Smith & Wesson at the prisoners, all three now sitting on the deck, "I want the truth. Now, what the hell does Yoshida want with my company?"

Zack looked into each man's eyes. The first twin, the one called Fukuda, turned away without saying a word. The other man silently shook his head from side to side, as if saying "I don't know." Kato just stared back at Zack. His already narrow eye slits had decreased to a thin squint, a natural reaction to the sun's glare. Zack could feel the man's raw energy. It was like he was firing invisible arrows of hatred toward him. *This son of a bitch is crazy—watch out!* thought Zack.

Zack was just about to repeat his question when Finn intervened. In one fluid motion he stepped forward and let loose with his right leg. His heavy boot hit the unsuspecting Kato right in the side of his head. "Answer him, you murdering prick," Finn yelled.

Kato slumped to the deck.

"Stop it, you damn fool," yelled Halley Blake as she ran to intervene. Finn stepped away, slipping the pistol into his waistband.

A moment later Halley was standing between Sorenson and the fallen *yakuza* soldier. "I don't care what you think this man has done," she said, "you have no right to torture him. If he's guilty, then a judge and jury will set the punishment."

Finn was shocked at the Coast Guard officer's response. He had thought of her as a friend, maybe even a future lover. "Damn it, Halley, get out of the way. This bastard's a stone-cold killer! Hell, he even iced one of your own people. And now you want to protect his ass?"

"You don't have any proof, and until you do he is to be treated like any other suspect." She turned a half step to face Zack. "And if either of you harm this man before he can be turned over for prosecution, I'll personally arrest you. You know I can invoke my jurisdiction over this vessel at any time."

Zack started to respond, "Commander, what the hell are—" but stopped in mid-sentence. It happened in a flash. One moment the broken hulk lay still on the steel plating like a sack of grain. The next moment he was on his feet, lunging out with his right hand. He caught Finn with a vicious karate chop to the side of his jaw, knocking him silly. And then he grabbed Halley. In a heartbeat, he expertly wrapped his thick arms around her head and neck, totally immobilizing her.

Zack leveled his Smith & Wesson at Kato's head.

Kato pulled Halley closer, using her as a shield. "Back off!" he yelled. "Right now, or I'll snap her pretty little neck." His voice was clear and without a trace of accent.

Zack stood frozen. The magnum felt like a million pounds in his hands. *What do I do now?*

"I said get back, now!" Kato squeezed a little and Halley let out a weak cry—like a trapped animal.

"Okay, okay, just take it easy," Zack said as he stepped back, lowering the pistol.

Ian Flynn, standing next to Scott and silent until now, whispered softly, "Zack, I think this guy means it."

"Yeah, I know."

"Get up you two," ordered Kato. His two companions pulled themselves up. Their wet baggy clothes stuck like glue to their pencil-thin bodies.

"All right, Scott, here's the deal," Kato called out. "We're all going to walk over to one of your escape pods and then the three of us are going to get in it, with your lady friend here, too. You put us over the side and then we're going to motor ashore. Once we reach Etorofu, we'll let her go."

"No, Zack, don't do it," yelled Halley, "he's bluffing."

The man tightened his grip again. This time Halley started gagging.

"I'm not fucking around here, man. You cooperate or I'm—"

Before Kato could complete his threat, a loud blast shattered the quiet. The report of the nine-millimeter pistol echoed off the corrugated steel walls.

Zack watched transfixed as a tiny black hole suddenly materialized in the right side of Kato's closely shaved head, just forward of the ear. The man's eyes snapped open in utter shock. He seemed to hover for just a second before his massive body collapsed onto Halley.

They both hit the deck with a sickening thud. Halley, half buried by the man's bulk, was screaming in horror as a fountain of blood and brain matter poured out of the bullet hole onto her coveralls. The wound flowed like an artesian well.

Zack finally recovered from the shock of the killing and turned toward the shooter. Finn was still down. Blood was pouring from his mouth, but his hands remained tightly clasped around the automatic's handgrip.

"Jesus Christ," called out Captain Flynn as he finally reacted to the shooting.

Zack handed Flynn his pistol and pointed to the twins. "Watch 'em." He then ran to Halley, kneeling down by her side.

"Get him off, get him off me!" she screamed.

Zack pulled the heavy corpse off to the side, helping Halley to her feet. Her waist and thighs were drenched in blood.

"You all right?" he asked.

"He would have killed me, I know it. I could hardly breathe." She began rubbing her neck. It would be sore for a week.

Zack left the Coast Guard officer standing next to Captain Flynn, turning his attention to Sorenson. His friend was still down and in obvious pain. Zack knelt on the deck, removed the Beretta from Finn's grip, and then helped him to his feet.

Once Finn was up, Zack examined the injuries. The right side of Finn's cheek was caved in. Blood continued to seep out of his mouth.

"Finn, old boy, I think you've got a broken jaw there."

Sorenson nodded his head up and down and started to smile. A second later, however, he began gagging, spitting out more blood. When he finally stopped, about a minute later, the deck at his feet was covered with blood. And mixed in with the gore were a couple of broken teeth.

Despite the pain, Finn finally managed to mouth a few mumbled words. "I got the prick!"

Zack put his arm around Finn's shoulders. "Yep, you sure did, Finn. He won't bother us anymore."

Sorenson turned toward the remaining prisoners. They sat side by side, squatting like ducks. Neither man looked up. Instead, they just stared down at their wet stocking feet.

"Ask 'em now," Finn said.

"What?" Zack said.

"Tell 'em to start comin' clean now or I get to play Captain Hook."

Zack understood, and with Finn at his side he gave the two YHI executives an ultimatum: Tell everything they knew or Finn was going to make them walk the plank.

Twenty minutes later, Zack finally had some answers.

"Okay, Zack," Ian Flynn said as he keyed the intercom mike, "we're ready to jettison the cables."

"Good, we're just about all set down here," replied Zack. He was on the drilling deck, standing next to the moonpool. It was still early in the afternoon. The ocean surface was fifty feet below the ten-foot-diameter hole. "Just stand by until I give you the final word."

"Roger."

Zack turned to his side, focusing on a tall, lanky man standing next to an electronic console. "Johnny, you ready?"

"Yep. The preventer is completely engaged and the well's shut in. Just let me know."

"Okay, let's do it."

The man reached forward and tripped a switch, sending an electronic signal down a thin wire that was embedded within a heavily armored electrohydraulic cable. The four-inch-diameter cable, centered around a heavy-walled hydraulic hose, contained a hundred separate wires, each one connected to a different function. The entire cable assembly was attached to the thirty-inch-diameter marine riser; it extended downward through the moonpool, terminating four hundred feet below on the seafloor.

The energized wire was connected to a hydraulic pod located near the top of the blowout preventer. A logic circuit in the pod read the signal and activated a solenoid. The solenoid, in turn, opened a pilot valve that released hydraulic pressure from a locking device near the top of the BOP stack. A few seconds later the marine riser broke free of the wellhead.

"I've got positive separation," called out the BOP operator.

"Good, let's start hauling that sucker in."

Zack stepped away from the deck hole as a team of roustabouts began preparing to recover the riser. It was now just hanging from the heave compensator located over the moonpool. Broken into twenty-foot pipe sections, it would take a couple of hours to pull all four hundred feet to the surface.

Recovering a marine riser was normally done while the semi remained stationary. Zack, however, couldn't wait. He picked up the intercom mike and keyed the switch. "Ian, we're separated down here."

"Okay, skipper. We're ready to deballast."

"Proceed," ordered Scott.

Fifty-eight minutes later, the *Deepquestor* was riding forty feet higher. The upper surfaces of its twin flotation pontoons were now awash. The normally black hulls were covered with a greenish slime and thousands of tiny barnacles were plastered everywhere.

Zack walked onto the bridge just as Flynn killed the last ballast pump. Zack checked the ballast control panel and then turned to his friend. "Ian, it looks like we're ready to go."

"Yep. We're riding fine and all of our engines are purring like kitty cats." He paused momentarily. "Just say when."

"When!" replied Zack.

Flynn flashed a grin and then turned to his assistant. "Okay, Bill, the boss says it's time to break the mooring, so let 'em go."

"You got it, sir," replied the man. He began triggering a series of switches on his control panel. In five minutes all eight anchor chains that had moored the *Deepquestor* were allowed to spool off their individual reels. The chain links, each one weighing 108 pounds, thundered over the side like herds of stampeding cattle. The mile-long chain assemblies would be recovered later by dragging the bottom and reeling them back in.

"Zack," Flynn said, "we're now uncoupled and ready to make turns."

"Good, let's get the show on the road."

"What about the riser? We've still got a hundred feet or so to recover."

"I want to move out anyway. We'll keep hauling it—if we

lose it, we lose it. We don't have any more time to worry about it.''

"Right," replied Captain Flynn. He then turned toward the *Deepquestor*'s helm. The young Merchant Marine Academy graduate who had just triggered the anchor releases was now standing next to a console. It looked like something from a video arcade. "Okay, Bill. Turn right to a heading of two-zero-zero and go to flank speed.''

"Aye, aye, sir," replied the man as he started to turn the tiny steering wheel. "Coming right to a heading of two-zero-zero. Making turns for fifteen knots.''

The ungainly-looking structure was actually quite maneuverable, and in just a few minutes it was turned about and heading southward. Huge wakes of white water trailed behind the stern sections of both hulls.

Nemuro

To say Cindy DeMorey was impressed was an understatement. She had seen numerous photographs of the Nemuro Oil Complex but had never actually visited the offshore production facility. When the YHI helicopter set down on the flight deck of the main platform, she thought she had landed in the middle of a small city.

The main platform, referred to as Unit A, was gigantic. It covered nearly ten acres of water surface. Founded on multiple steel towers that rose six hundred feet above the seafloor, Unit A was the hub of the oil field. It supported dozens of vertical wells that led straight down to the seafloor. The steel conductor pipes were clustered near the center of the structure. Submersible pumps deep inside the well field pumped over half a million barrels of oil through the conductors each day. Once the crude was brought to the surface, the natural gas in the mixture was bled off and any formation water was removed. Another series of pumps on Unit A's lower decks then pumped the oil into a double-barrel submarine pipeline. Each of the three-foot-diameter conduits connected Unit A to the mainland, ten miles to the west.

Once ashore, the oil flowed into a gigantic tank farm located a few miles south of the Nemuro fishing village. Another network of terrestrial pipelines and pumping stations transported the oil seven hundred miles southward to the refineries clustered around Tokyo and Yokohama.

Nearly all of the subterranean energy produced at Nemuro was in the form of crude oil. However, a modest amount of natural gas was also recovered. Although the volume of gas was too marginal to support a commercial pipeline to shore, there was more than enough to satisfy the ravenous energy needs of the Nemuro Complex. A bank of gas-driven electrical generators, housed within an acre-sized compartment on Unit A, generated as much power as a small hydroelectric dam. And what little gas remained was burned off by means of a 120-foot-tall flare tower that angled away from one corner of the platform. The flame, usually only a flicker, occasionally burned like hellfire when power demands were relaxed.

Besides the vast array of oil production equipment on Unit A, the platform also served as the administration center and accommodation facilities for the complex. Dozens of offices and laboratories were grouped along the seaward side of the upper deck. And on the land side, facing the distant Hokkaido Island, were the principal living quarters. Over three hundred people called the Nemuro Oil Complex home.

A series of satellite platforms projected seaward from Unit A for distances up to several miles. Designated Units B through H, the seven remote production platforms were supported by skyscraper-size steel jackets that extended to the deep ocean bottom. The main deck for each satellite was about an acre in size. Several dozen wells penetrated the bottom near the center of each satellite. The upper decks of the platforms were crammed with equipment and machinery used to recover oil. The oil was then pumped through small pipelines to Unit A.

Clusters of subsea wells surrounding the various satellite platforms provided additional sources of oil. Located up to three miles from the remote platforms, the underwater wellheads were installed directly on the ocean bottom. The oil collected from these wells was then pumped to the various platforms by pipeline. The network of subsea wells and connecting pipelines surrounding each satellite platform looked like the tentacles of a giant octopus.

Although the remote platforms were continuously manned by a crew of up to a dozen persons, there were no quarters on the sat wells. Instead, workers were ferried to and from the structures by a fleet of helicopters operating from Unit A.

The infrastructure of the Nemuro Oil Complex had a first phase production capacity of 700,000 barrels of oil per day. This immense volume surpassed most of the fields in the North Sea and the Gulf of Mexico, making the Japanese facility one of the largest offshore oil finds in the world. However, less than one tenth of the oil produced at Nemuro actually originated from its vast network of seafloor wells. The rest was imported.

When Cindy DeMorey and Hiroshi Yoshida stepped out of the helicopter cabin, they were met by a coalition of Nemuro managers. The seven-man delegation, standing on the side of the helipad, bowed in unison as Yoshida approached. He returned their greeting and then began speaking, addressing Nemuro's general manager. He had to shout to overcome the noise of the still-freewheeling rotor blades. "Good to see you, Takashi."

"And you, too, sir," replied the forty-eight-year-old man.

Yoshida turned to his side. Cindy was standing a few feet behind him. The combined wind from the sea breeze and rotor wash was billowing her long black hair across her face. She used one hand to try to push the swirling locks aside, but her efforts were useless. It didn't matter, though. To the cluster of men facing her, she looked gorgeous, like a model from a high-fashion magazine. "Please, come here, my dear," Yoshida said.

Cindy stepped forward.

"Gentlemen, this is Cindy DeMorey. This is her first visit to Nemuro."

Once again the men bowed in unison. Cindy nodded her head in acknowledgment.

Yoshida turned his attention to the manager. "Takashi, I'd like a full briefing right away."

"Of course, sir. Please follow me to my office."

Five minutes later, Yoshida and Cindy were seated inside Takashi's spacious office. They were sitting around a small conference table, sipping tea and munching on a snack of rice cakes.

"Have you heard anything from Fukuda yet?" asked Yoshida.

"No, sir. He and the others are still aboard the *Deepquestor*, we're certain of that. Their helicopter returned here hours ago. The pilot informed me that Fukuda and his assistants would remain aboard to complete the transfer of ownership."

"Good, then it sounds like he has things under control there."

"Correct, sir. We haven't received any more calls from him, so I think you're right."

"What about the woman?" asked Yoshida. "How is she?"

Takashi looked past Yoshida, eyeing Cindy. He didn't respond.

Yoshida caught on instantly. "You can speak freely. Cindy knows everything." He smiled as he continued to speak. "In fact, she was the one who was responsible for securing the Scott woman for us."

Takashi nodded his understanding. "Sir, after the trouble we had the other night, she's gotten worse. She's not eating and appears to be regressing at an alarming rate."

"What happened to her?" asked Cindy.

Takashi turned toward the guest. "She was attacked by one of our crew."

"Raped?"

"Attempted, but he was stopped in time."

Cindy turned to face Yoshida. "I wasn't aware of this situation. This might compromise the final transfer, especially if we still have to arrange for the phone conversation tonight."

Yoshida's face broke into a frown. "I forgot to tell you. And yes, you may be right, this could be a problem. Do you have any suggestions?"

Cindy remained silent for nearly half a minute before finally responding. "Yes, Uncle, I think I know what to do." Cindy started to explain.

Takashi really wasn't listening to the woman's plan. Instead, he was thinking about what she had just said. *She called him Ojisan!*

Takashi's eyes widened when he heard Cindy refer to Yoshida as "uncle." He had heard the rumors that a *gaijin* had contaminated the Yoshida bloodline, but he never believed them. But now, as he stared at Cindy, he changed his mind. The beautiful woman sitting in front of him had Japanese blood in her all right. But it was her European features that dominated. He found the combination of East and West captivating, almost erotic. He wondered if she was married.

Wendy Scott was sitting in the lower bunk bed. Her back was pressed against the wall. Her knees were drawn up to her chest. She wore an oversize white T-shirt and cotton trousers. The fresh apparel had been anonymously stuffed through the slot in the door earlier in the day. She gladly welcomed the change of clothing. After more than two weeks of confinement, her original coveralls had been almost unbearable to wear.

Although Wendy stared ahead, looking through the cabin window, her mind wasn't focusing on the swells that continually swept by. Instead, she was praying: *Lord, please help me get out of here. All I want is to go home and be with Dan. I don't deserve this.*

Wendy started to repeat her plea when she heard the lock on the cabin door click open. The only other time she had heard the lock release was when she had been attacked. Before and after that traumatic event, her captors remained incommunicado, continuing her isolation except for a few brief interruptions.

Wendy instantly snapped out of her trancelike state and jumped onto the tile floor. She searched the claustrophobic room, looking for a weapon. She finally settled on the tiny wood stool by the desk. She raised it above her head, ready to slam it down on the intruder.

Cindy DeMorey pushed the door open and walked inside. She spotted Wendy just in time to step away from the blow. Wendy lost control of the stool. It slammed into the wall with a loud bang.

"Just calm down, Miss Scott," Cindy said. "No one's going to attack you."

Wendy stared at the woman. Her heart was pounding away like a racing freight train. She was almost out of breath.

Cindy stepped back toward the doorway and spoke to the guard who stood just out of sight. "I've got her under control,'' she said in Japanese. Cindy then turned around and offered her hand as Wendy started to stand. Wendy refused.

"What do you want?" asked Wendy Scott as she moved to the opposite end of the cabin.

"You will be going home soon. I need to explain a few things to you."

"Home!"

"Yes, we plan to release you soon." Cindy paused for effect. "But before that can happen you must cooperate with us."

"What do you mean?"

"You must make a telephone call tonight—to your father."

"Dad, is he nearby?"

"No. He's still in Seattle, but you will be able to talk with him by phone from your cabin."

"When?" Wendy could hardly wait.

Cindy glanced down at her watch. "In a few hours." She refocused on Wendy. "Now, when you talk with your father there are some basic rules that you must follow. If you disobey them, the call will be terminated and you may never be released."

Wendy understood. "What is it you want me to say?"

Cindy smiled. *Bright girl. She's coming around.* "First of all, you must . . ."

The *Deepquestor*

Zackary Scott was on the bridge deck when the Inmarsat began buzzing. He glanced at his watch. *Right on time.* It was 8:01 P.M. The *Deepquestor* had been under way for almost six hours, plowing southward through the ocean at fifteen knots. He walked over to the handset.

The Inmarsat unit was a telephone but it wasn't part of the ship's internal communication system. Instead, it was connected to its own computer, which, in turn, was hardwired to a parabolic antenna mounted on top of the wheelhouse deck. Housed in a solid white fiberglass dome, the antenna was pointed upward. It was aimed directly at a satellite that was parked in a geostationary orbit high over the central Pacific.

The satellite communication system allowed direct service

between ships at sea and the land. Immune to the effects of weather or atmospheric disturbances, the system provided exceptional quality voice links and high-volume data-transmission rates.

Zack picked up the phone. "*Deepquestor*, here."

"Zack, this is Tim." It was Tim Marshall. He was calling from SCS's headquarters. It was in the middle of the night back in Seattle.

"Has the call come through?" asked Scott.

"Yes, I'm going to patch it into your circuit right now."

"Okay."

Zack waited for Marshall to complete his work. About thirty seconds later, the line came alive. "Daddy, are you there?"

Thank God, she's still alive! "Yes, honey. It's me."

"Oh, Daddy, I'm so glad to hear your voice."

"Are you okay? Have they hurt you?" asked Zack

"I'm fine. But I want to go home. I hate it here."

"I know that and I'm working on it. It won't be long now."

"Please hurry, Dad. I don't—"

Wendy was cut off in mid-sentence as a new female voice broke in. Zack instantly recognized the caller.

"Mr. Scott, this is the last time we're going to do this. You know what needs to be done. Follow our directions and you'll get your security back. Otherwise, you know what will happen."

Up yours, bitch! is what Zack wanted to say to Cindy DeMorey, but he held his tongue instead. "Okay, okay. I'm convinced. I'll give the order releasing my rigs."

"Good. Then our transaction is about to conclude. You've chosen the right course."

DeMorey's line went dead before Zack could say anything. He waited for Marshall to reconnect the circuit. The phone buzzed. Zack again picked up the handset. "Tim?" he asked.

"Yeah, Zack."

"Did you pick it all up?"

"Yep, we've got a good recording. And like you predicted the incoming call was from a satellite. We traced the land signal back to a receiver in California at Santa Paula."

"That's where Inmarsat has one of their ground stations, isn't it?"

"Yes."

"Okay, that all figures. We know Nemuro uses the same sat system so it must be them."

"I agree. Everything points to that conclusion."

Zack didn't respond for several moments. He was reviewing his options. "All right," he finally said, "we're going to proceed with the plan." He paused for a moment. "Have you heard from MacDonald yet?"

"Yep, he called in about an hour ago. They're all set."

"Good. Then go ahead and give Mac the launch code."

"You got it, boss! Anything else?"

"No, it's up to me now."

"Good luck."

"Thanks, I'll need it."

Anchorage, Alaska

The cavernous hangar at the far end of Anchorage's international airport had only one airplane in it. The C-130 Hercules was parked in the center, opposite the main doors. Designed to accommodate several jetliners, the vacant building was a perfect staging area. With the huge sliding doors closed and the windows covered over with blackout paper, it provided maximum privacy.

The sixteen men that milled around the fully fueled Herc were growing impatient. They had been waiting nearly twelve hours.

When the phone started ringing in a nearby service office, everyone turned toward the single man who stood at the tail end of the aircraft. He was tall and trim, like most of the other men. And like the rest of the group he wore camouflage fatigues with shiny black leather boots. Although he was fifty-one years old, his thick beard and heavy mat of black hair made him look younger.

The man walked into the glass-enclosed office and picked up the handset. "Hello," he said.

"Mac, that you?" asked Tim Marshall. He was calling from SCS's Seattle office.

"Yeah. What's the word?"

"Zack just called in. He said it's a go!"

"Okay, then. We're outta here."

"Good luck," Marshall said.

"Thanks." Captain John (Mac) MacDonald hung up the phone and walked back onto the hangar floor. Most of his contingent were now standing just outside the doorway. "It's a go, gents," he said, raising his right thumb. "Let's get this bird warmed up. We've got a long way to go."

Ten minutes later, the four-engine propeller-driven Hercules roared down the runway. It was heading southwest into the black night sky, toward the distant North Pacific Ocean.

Nemuro

Wendy Scott was back in her cabin now. Three quarters of an hour earlier she had been moved to another compartment. It was the first time she had left her cabin since coming aboard. Unfortunately, she had no idea where she had been taken. She was blindfolded the entire time.

The woman she had talked with earlier was waiting for Wendy when she walked into the new room. The guards escorting her backed away and closed the door. The woman then guided Wendy into a chair and told her to wait. About five minutes later Wendy heard a ringing sound from a telephone. The woman picked up the handset and began speaking in Japanese. A few seconds later she switched to English. "Okay, Wendy, we have your father on the line now. He's calling from Seattle. Remember what I told you earlier."

Wendy could hardly believe it when her father answered. His voice was like a breath of fresh air. And as she lay in her bunk, she could recall his clear and steady voice with crystal clarity. *He'll get me out of here. I know he will!*

The *Deepquestor*

Finn Sorenson sat in a rickety old card table chair next to the deck decompression chamber. He was supposed to be guarding the two remaining Japanese prisoners—Fukuda and his look-alike companion, Suzuki. But there really wasn't much for him to watch. They were sealed up inside the steel cocoon. And except for two four-inch-diameter air vent valves, one at either end of the twenty-foot-long cylinder, the

DDC was impermeable. The occupants would never get out unless the steel bar jamming the opening mechanism of the hatchway door was removed.

Despite the built-in security of the unique prison, Zack had ordered the chamber monitored at all times. Finn volunteered for the first watch.

Finn was tired and his jaw hurt like hell. The bleeding from the broken teeth had finally stopped, but both sides of his mouth remained packed with thick pads of sterile gauze. His puffed-out cheeks made his face look like that of a giant chipmunk.

The *Deepquestor*'s paramedic had offered morphine to Finn, but he refused. Not only would the drug have dulled his senses, but it also would have weakened his resolve. He needed to feel the pain to remain focused, otherwise he would slip into the abyss of depression.

Only a few hours earlier Sorenson had killed a human being. Despite all of his brawling and tough talk, Finn had never taken a life. He was now struggling with his conscience. *I had to do it,* he repeatedly argued to himself. *There was no choice—he would have killed her. And besides, he was the SOB that killed my crew. He deserved everything he got.*

Finn relived the shooting over and over in his mind. And then he would visualize the trail of blood on the deck that marked the path where Zack and Flynn had dragged the corpse. He hadn't actually seen them toss the body over the side, but he created the image in his mind anyway.

Finn reached up with a hand and touched his right cheek. A spike of pain shot through his broken jawbone, once again breaking the spell of bad thoughts. *I hope that bastard's burning in hell right now!*

Finn was thinking about checking on his prisoners when an obnoxious buzzing sound broke his train of thought. *What the hell's that?* he wondered. He turned to his side and traced the noise to the DDC's exterior control console. He stood up and walked half a dozen steps to it. A red light next to a phone handset was flashing on and off. He reached for it and with considerable effort managed to produce a muffled but understandable response. "Sorenson here."

"Finn, this is Zack. Can you get Fukuda out of the DDC? I need him for a while."

"You bet."

"Good. I'll send down a couple of deckhands to bring him to the bridge." Zack paused. "Now, how are you doing?"

"Can't talk worth shit. But okay."

"Great, I won't bug you anymore. See you later." Zack switched off the intercom before Finn could reply.

Finn returned the IC handset to its receptacle. If it hadn't been so painful to speak he would have asked Zack why he wanted the little pencil-neck prick. But for now he didn't really care.

Hiroshi Yoshida and Cindy DeMorey were in the general manager's spacious stateroom eating dinner. Nemuro's principal chef, trained in Tokyo and Paris, had prepared a meal that combined basic Japanese cuisine with the fine art of French cooking. The result was a spectacular selection of dishes that ranged from smoked salmon to the finest veal. Manager Takashi, sitting cross-legged at the table, was pouring another round of California wine when a white-coated steward discreetly opened the dining room door and walked to his side. The man bowed politely before kneeling next to his superior. He delivered the message in a whisper and then handed Takashi a slip of paper.

Takashi nodded his head and dismissed the steward. A moment later he turned to face Yoshida, sitting to his right. "Good news, sir. Fukuda finally called in."

"Well, it's about time. I want to speak with him."

"Apparently he's not available right now. The *Deepquestor* is having some kind of radio problem. The voice transmission quality is very poor so he faxed in his report."

"Faxed?"

"Yes, sir. That seemed to work well and I have the hard copy right here." He started to hand the paper to Yoshida.

Yoshida raised his hand. "No, you read it—out loud."

"Yes, sir." Takashi cleared his throat and then began reading the message.

We now have taken control of the vessel. Z. Scott called in on-time, just before ship's radio system started to malfunction. He ordered his crew to turn the ship over to PVH. No problems during transition other than radio.

We will be finished terminating the mooring within the next hour or so.

Drilling at the site had only just started. As a result, it will be relatively easy to shut-in the well. We've already recovered the riser and should have the anchor lines reeled in within an hour or so. We'll be ready to depart shortly thereafter.

The Russian crew members will be put ashore at Podgornoye on Urup by the work vessel. They can make it back to the mainland from there. Please note that the Russian in charge plans to make a formal complaint through the Russian embassy in Tokyo. He repeatedly complained that they were never informed about the SCS sale and protests our ownership interest in their leases.

The American crew will remain onboard until we reach port. Captain estimates that our steaming time to Yokohama will be around three days.

When radio system is repaired, I will call in an updated report.

Signed, Fukuda

Takashi smiled as he looked up from the fax. "Well, sir, it appears that we now have control of the *Deepquestor*. This Mr. Scott should no longer be a problem."

Yoshida grinned back. He then raised his wineglass to toast the manager and Cindy.

Back aboard the *Deepquestor*, Zackary Scott was also handing out congratulations. "That was a great idea you had, Constantine. If we'd tried it like I suggested, I'm sure this little bugger would have given away the goods."

The tall, middle-aged man grinned as he replied, "You are welcome, Mr. Scott." He spoke with a slight accent. "I am glad I could help out."

It turned out that in order to create Fukuda's fake fax message, Zack had to have someone who knew Japanese. Constantine Benkevich was the ideal interpreter. He was Okhotsk Sea Ventures' chief engineer, responsible for supervising all of the Russian laborers aboard the *Deepquestor*. But he was also fluent in Japanese. His father had been a diplomat and for years the family was stationed in Japan. Young Constantine learned Japanese before English.

Zack was now staring directly at Fukuda. The YHI executive would not make eye contact with Scott. "Okay, Fukuda, you can go back and visit with your buddy." Zack then nodded to the two roustabouts standing by the slightly built Japanese. The huge Russians literally picked up the man by his armpits and carried him out of the radio room.

Zack turned to face Benkevich. "So, Constantine, do you think they'll believe the fax message?"

"Well, our chances are certainly much better than if we had let Fukuda talk directly. Like I said earlier, he would either refuse to speak at the last moment, or he'd send a subtle signal that something is wrong. The Japanese language is immensely complex and even though I've studied it for years, I still don't know many of its subtleties. There are dozens of ways to secretly signal that something isn't right: the wrong inflection on a word; the out-of-place phrase, the sudden inhalation before speaking."

The Russian paused for a moment. "And believe me, if Yoshida is really on Nemuro, I can guarantee to you that Fukuda would never lie to him personally—even with a gun to his head, as you had suggested. He would surely have cut his own belly before deceiving his master."

Zack shook his head. He had forgotten about how fanatic the Japanese could be. The worker's allegiance to his superior was still as strong as it had been during the days of the shogun and the samurai.

31

MAC'S MERCS

Over the North Pacific

The Lockheed C-130 Hercules was cruising at a smooth 320 knots, 22,000 feet above the Pacific Ocean, which was as black as coal, yet the pilot stared at the windscreen as if he was searching for something on the invisible horizon. His copilot, sitting in the right-hand seat, was fidgeting with a small boxlike object in his lap. It looked like a portable calculator but was far more sophisticated. Both men ignored the dozens of gauges and dials on the instrument panel. The eighteen-year-old propeller-driven cargo transport was on autopilot. All systems were running normally.

"Bob, you see anything yet?" asked the copilot. He was still working with the GPS receiver.

"No. It's so dark out there it's like we're flying in the inside of a cow."

"Well, I think we must be getting close. I've run three fixes so far and according to this little jewel we're about ninety miles out."

"Good, then we should see lights before long." The pilot paused as he scanned all four engine temperature/oil indicators. *Perfect!* The workhorse of an aircraft had performed flawlessly since taking off from Anchorage almost seven hours earlier. *Just hang together, baby, and we'll do fine.* The C-130 had another three hours of flight time before it would land at Seoul, Korea. "Bob, why don't you buzz Mac and let 'im know we're on final approach?"

"Yeah, okay."

The copilot keyed the intercom system. It was answered five seconds later with a blunt "Yeah, what ya want?"

"Say, Cap, we're about ninety miles out now. You want to get your people ready?"

"We've been ready for an hour. Just make damn sure you're on the money." The intercom line clicked off a second later.

"Gees, what a prick," the copilot said as he turned to face the pilot.

"Give 'im a break, Bob. Mac's a good guy. He's just a little worked up right now."

"Yeah, well, I guess I'll take your word for it, but I still don't like the guy." The copilot turned to look forward. The sky remained blacked out. "How'd you ever run into him anyway?"

"I met Mac about three years ago in a bar in D.C. Another buddy of mine introduced us. He said this ex-navy captain was looking for a Herc driver. Well, I'd been retired about a year and was getting tired of fishing and screwing the wife, so I decided to see what he was offering."

"Gees, three years ago. How many missions have you flown for him?"

"Ah, hell, I've been up about fifty times. But most were training exercises." The pilot paused as he leaned forward. He thought he saw a speck of light on the horizon. "But for real-live missions, this will be my sixth."

"Where else have you been?"

The pilot turned to his right, looking into the younger man's eyes. "Bob, one thing you gotta learn in this business is that we don't talk about what we've done in the past with new-comers—never. It's not like when you were flying for Uncle Sam where you can bend the rules now and then—to let folks know what you really did. You pull that around these guys and they'll cut your throat." The pilot let his words sink in for a few seconds. "Maintaining max security and keeping a low profile is the key to this whole operation. None of the bad guys know about us—they think we're some kind of super-spooks from NSA or the CIA. We want to keep it that way."

"Okay, I get the picture. I'll quit bugging you."

The pilot grinned. "Bob, you just get through this first mission and you'll get invited to the party. The group's real tight, but they gotta know they can trust ya before they'll open up."

The copilot couldn't really complain about being the odd man out. He had no empathy for the fourteen men back in the cargo hold—at least not yet. His sole motivation for risking his butt was money. A week earlier he had been dead broke, his meager air force pension bleeding profusely from the cash demands of an ex-wife and child support payments for four kids. However, the five grand he had received before starting the mission solved that problem. And the ten thousand he would be paid when the project was completed really whetted his appetite. *Jesus, fifteen grand for less than two weeks of work! Who do these guys really work for anyway?*

The pilot squinted as he stared through the windscreen. He should have been wearing his new glasses but left them in his shirt pocket. "I think I've got it, Bob," he said. "Eleven o'clock low."

The copilot looked ahead as the pilot adjusted the flaps, causing the plane to drop altitude. He could see a tiny flicker of light against the ink-black ocean surface. He then glanced down at the hand-held global positioning satellite receiver. "Right on the money," he said.

"Yeah, I thought so. Nice job. Now, get on the horn and tell Mac we've got it in sight. I'll take her down."

The copilot keyed the intercom switch again. "Captain, we've got the lights in sight and we're starting our descent. You've got about five minutes."

"Good. How we doing for time?"

"We're about three minutes ahead of schedule. The headwinds were a little weaker than we anticipated."

"Okay. We can live with that."

Five minutes later the Hercules leveled off at 18,000 feet. And within just forty seconds all fourteen men had jumped, one after another, from the aircraft's open tail ramp. The frigid and turbulent night sky swallowed them up like a black hole.

Zackary Scott was working his way up a series of open steel catwalks that linked the main drilling deck to the bridge when the alarm on his wristwatch started beeping. He stopped and looked up into the night sky. The night was filled with thousands of stars. While still scanning the heavens he reached down with his right hand and pushed a tiny button on his custom-made Omega Seamaster, shutting off the preset alarm. He cocked his head to the side, listening carefully. The drone of the *Deepquestor*'s engines was overwhelming. Even if he had been able to stop the engine noise, he wouldn't have heard the Herc. It was too high.

Zack momentarily looked down at his watch. It read 3:00 A.M. He then looked back up again. *I sure hope you guys are up there!*

I'm gettin' too old for this crap, thought Mac MacDonald as he pulled on a Dacron line, adjusting the trim of his parasail. The twenty-foot-long by twelve-foot-wide camouflaged nylon fabric was suspended over his head; it looked like a giant wing. Unlike a conventional rounded parachute that drifted uncontrollably, the parasail could be guided. By making subtle changes to the shape of the canopy, both the rate and direction of the descent could be controlled, allowing pinpoint touchdown accuracy.

MacDonald glanced down at his altimeter through the plastic cover of his full-face oxygen mask. He was just passing through the 11,000-foot level. His teeth were chattering. He had been airborne for ten minutes and the night air was freezing. Despite the rubber wet suit that covered his body, he was cold. *Jesus, I'm going to frigging freeze before I get down!*

After free-falling nearly a mile, MacDonald tripped the main chute. In spite of the thin air at 13,000 feet the parasail deployed normally. After adjusting the sail's initial trim he searched the black waters below, looking for the target. It wasn't hard to spot in the cloudless night. The glow from the floodlights on the main platform of the Nemuro Complex, a dozen miles away, stood out like a bonfire in the middle of the desert.

The former U.S. Navy special warfare officer was tired. At fifty-one years of age, he was nearly twice as old as the youngest member of his team, and his once-powerful and lean body was really beginning to deteriorate. He used to be able to ignore the periodic pain from his old wounds, but not anymore. The slightest exertion, like jogging (not to mention jumping out of airplanes!) aggravated his once-broken bones and prearthritic joints. Captain MacDonald wondered if this would be his last mission.

The other thirteen men who followed MacDonald out of the Hercules were also gliding through the night sky, each one homing in on the Nemuro Complex like an eagle searching for its prey. Outfitted in solid black garments, none of the men could see each other as they repeatedly crisscrossed through the blackness. For the lesser trained, the danger of a midair collision would have been paramount. For Mac's Mercs, however, the night flight was like a walk in the park.

The *Deepquestor* continued running southward as it approached the northeast tip of Hokkaido Island. It had slowed to a modest ten knots. The moonless night was so dark that the four-hundred-foot-long semisubmersible would have been invisible if the navigation lights hadn't been activated. An hour earlier all exterior lights on the vessel had been turned off. Everything was affected, from walkway safety lighting to equipment floodlights. The remaining low-intensity nav lights, one at each corner of the vessel and a fifth at the peak of the derrick tower, barely outlined the immense bulk of the rig's superstructure.

"Zack, we're just about in position now. Have you decided yet?"

Zackary Scott looked up from the chart table. He was now on the bridge. It was 3:00 A.M. Captain Flynn was standing a few steps away, next to the helmsman. The pilot house was quiet The only sound came from the low-frequency hum of the electronic equipment. "Yeah, Ian. Let's go for the zone just east of the main unit. We know what's there for sure. These other areas—I don't know yet!"

"Okay, just give the word and we're on our way."

Zack was about to comment when a new voice spoke up. It was Commander Halley Blake. "Zack, I think you're making a terrible mistake. I don't recommend that you continue with this plan of yours." Blake had been standing in the shadows of the darkened bridge deck listening to the crosstalk between Scott and Flynn.

"Too late, Commander. It's already started." He looked

upward for a moment. "Mac and his boys should be coming down right about now."

Halley shook her head. "This is all wrong."

Zack walked a few steps closer to the Coast Guard officer. "Commander, just who in the hell is going to help me get back my daughter—our wonderful government? Hell, those bastards are so scared of Japan's money that they're going to just stand by and watch her disappear and let SCS get swallowed up."

"But it doesn't have to be that way. We've got evidence, hard evidence of what YHI is up to. We can expose them in the—"

"With what?" interrupted Scott. "Do you have any of those photos or tapes we made in *Little Mike*?"

"Well, no. Commander Maxwell kept them all on the *Bremerton,* but I'm sure we can subpoena them from the navy if we need to."

"You're dreaming, honey. The Pentagon's going to slap top secret over everything associated with this mess. And even with your clout as an official investigator with the Coast Guard, you'll get nothing. Remember, you're still part of the military."

Halley stepped back, leaning against the railing of the chart table. She didn't respond at first. Instead her mind was racing with new thoughts: *He might be right. Without the photographic evidence all we'll have is our personal observations. And I'll never be able to say anything if gag orders come down from Washington. So it'll be up to Zack and his people. But no one's going to believe them without hard facts. They'll be laughed right out of court.*

"Okay, Zack, I see your point. But what can you gain by this tactic? It's only going to make things worse."

"Maybe, but at least I'm trying. Nobody else has done a damn thing yet."

Halley nodded her head in agreement. *God help you, Zackary Scott!*

Zack turned back to face Captain Flynn. "Ian, let's do it, now."

"You got it, Zack." Flynn walked a few steps to an adjacent panel and flipped a series of toggle switches, turning off every running light on the giant vessel. He next turned to face the *Deepquestor*'s helmsman. "Come right ninety degrees and go to flank."

"Aye, sir. Coming right ninety degrees. Increasing to flank."

While the young merchant marine officer began mechanically executing his orders, he couldn't help but think about what he had just heard. He had quietly stood behind the ship's wheel listening to the heated discussion between Scott and the lady Coast Guard officer. He didn't like what he had heard. And as the ship began swinging to the starboard, the consequences of the conversation finally hit him. *My God, we might all be killed.*

"How are we doing, Ian?" asked Zackary Scott. A few minutes had passed. He was now standing on the exterior bridge wing, next to Captain Flynn. The *Deepquestor* was charging westward at almost fifteen knots.

"So far, so good. I think their radar operator must be asleep. We haven't heard a peep over the radio yet."

"Good, how much farther do we have to go?"

"Another five minutes and we'll be in position."

"Okay, I'm going below. Give me a holler when we're there."

"You got it."

The lone operator in the Nemuro radar compartment wasn't asleep as Captain Flynn had speculated. Instead, he was busy thumbing through a new issue of *Penthouse Magazine*. He'd accidentally found the publication hidden under a stack of newspapers on a shelf near the radar display. One of his fellow operators from another shift had smuggled it aboard. Although he couldn't read a word of English, the graphic pictorials depicted in the uncensored magazine commanded his complete interest. For the past fifteen minutes he hadn't once looked at the radar screen.

Finally, after deciding that he would "borrow" the magazine for further perusal in the privacy of his tiny cabin, the man looked up. He spotted the radar blip instantly.

"What's that?" he yelled out loud to himself.

It took him another minute to figure it out. The unidentified slow-moving vessel that he had been tracking for the past hour had suddenly turned away from its southerly course and was now heading due west. Instead of safely passing along the outer limits of the Nemuro Complex, it was now lining up on Unit A—the main production platform.

He reached for the telephone handset.

Mac MacDonald hit the sea surface perfectly. He flared the parawing at the last instant, burning off excess speed in a controlled stall. He gracefully slid into the water, fins first. Just before his head submerged he jettisoned the canopy, freeing himself from the tangle of cords and nylon that would have engulfed him. He popped back up to the surface a couple of seconds later, minus his oxygen mask. And then, like a whale clearing its blowhole, he spit out a mouthful of water and took a deep breath. *What a frigging ride that was!*

As Mac regained his composure, he reached up with his gloved hands and began rubbing his forehead and cheeks. The ice-cold water coating his face stung the exposed flesh; it felt like someone had slapped him. A few seconds later he felt a new sensation as seawater began seeping through the seams and joints of his wet suit. New spikes of cold-induced pain began to erupt across his chest and down his spine. It would take several minutes before the thin layer of water sandwiched between the Neoprene suit and his skin would warm up. In the interim he would have to endure the cold.

MacDonald was already bone-chilled from the three-mile vertical descent. The near-freezing ocean just aggravated his already precarious situation. "Damn it to hell," yelled Mac as he vigorously treaded water, trying to generate more body heat, "this is worse than the damn North Sea."

While the ex-SEAL began to warm up, the rest of his team arrived. Within one and a half minutes all thirteen of Mac's Mercs slipped into the sea. Despite the fifteen-mile-an-hour crosswind, they all landed near each other. Five minutes later they were huddled around Mac, bobbing with the five-foot-high swells that repeatedly swept across the sea surface. It was like riding on a slow-motion roller coaster. Captain MacDonald was still cold, but he was improving.

"All right, everyone, listen up," Mac said, raising his voice just loud enough so he could be heard over the sea sounds. "Team One, take the east leg. Team Two, take the west." He paused momentarily, spitting out some water that splashed into his mouth. "You all know what to do when you get topside, so let's go kick ass!"

"Right on!" someone said. "Fuckin' A!" said another. And finally one of the ex-Marines bellowed out "Semper Fi!" Ten seconds later the group split into halves, each team heading for its respective target.

Captain MacDonald watched his charges swim toward the Nemuro Oil Complex. The giant Unit A platform, lit up like the proverbial Christmas tree, was about five hundred yards away. Even for MacDonald, it would be an easy swim.

32

FUSION

The *Deepquestor*

The *Deepquestor* was barely moving now. The semisubmersible's four engines supplied just enough power to nudge it into the oncoming wind. The rig was about halfway between Units B and D of the inner ring of satellite wells. The main platform, Unit A, loomed in the distance; it was about three quarters of a mile away.

Captain Flynn, Zackary Scott, and Halley Blake were huddled together on the *Deepquestor*'s bridge wing. The exposed steel catwalk hung over the ocean surface like a balcony; the ocean surface was a hundred feet below. The drilling vessel remained totally blacked out but its silhouette was visible in the reflected light from the Nemuro platform.

"Zack, do you think they know we're here?" asked Commander Blake.

"Yeah, they must by now. We're too damn close for them not to notice."

Captain Flynn spoke up next. "Zack, helm reports that we're just about over the coordinates." He was wearing a communication headset that was wired to the bridge's interior intercom system. His second in command was at the other end of the circuit, studying the digital output of the GPS receiver. "Do you want to hover here?"

"Yes, if you can maintain position with this wind."

423

"No sweat. I'll set up the computer right now." Flynn headed back into the enclosed bridge house to personally activate the ship's computerized dynamic positioning system.

Halley Blake inched closer to Zack. He was looking off into the distance. She turned to stare at the huge Nemuro Unit A platform. "Zack, do you think they made it?"

"I sure hope so, but I have no way of knowing—at least not yet."

"Who are those guys, anyway?"

Zack turned to face Halley. "Mac MacDonald used to be a SEAL—you know, the navy's elite commandos."

"Yes, I'm familiar with that organization."

"Well, Mac used to command a SEAL Team, based in Southern California. And from what I heard he was one of the best special warfare officers in the military. He's been involved in all kinds of secret operations: behind the lines work in the Iraqi war, counterterrorist operations in Europe, and drug interdiction in the States." Zack paused momentarily to scan the waters surrounding the *Deepquestor*. The rig was now stationary. "He made full captain in his early forties and was destined for flag rank when he somehow got crossways with the system."

"What happened?"

"I don't really know, other than he retired early, about five years ago."

"So you know him personally?"

"Yeah. We did some testing work for him a few years back on a new wireless underwater diver-to-diver communication system. That was several years after he started up his own firm—MacDonald Security Consultants."

"Consultants?" Halley said. "That's stretching it a little, isn't it?"

"Maybe now, but when he started out, that's what he did. He had clients all over the world, mainly big companies, Fortune 500 types, that were worried about terrorism and kidnapping. He critiqued their security programs and helped outline needed improvements."

"Then how'd he get into this business?"

Zack raised his outstretched hands. "I don't know. He never said. All I know is that he put together a team of around thirty

ex-military types. It now functions as a private counterterror-
ism unit. Most of the members are former SEALS along with
a handful from the army's Delta Force and a few Marines.''

"How can he do that?" asked the Coast Guard officer.

"Do what?"

"Have a private army like that? Isn't it against the law or
something?"

"Apparently not, because he's been quite successful."

"But it's still a mercenary organization. Mac's Mercs! Isn't
that what they call themselves?"

"Yeah, but that's just a nickname." Zack paused. "Believe
me, Halley, Mac's not a mercenary—he's a rescuer. And he's
very selective in what assignments he'll take on."

"Like this one?"

"Yes. Hostage rescue is his specialty. But even then, he's
selective as hell about who he works for. For example, when
I approached him a couple of weeks ago he refused to take
on my case until his people thoroughly checked out the situation. Only then would he agree to help."

"So you're paying him, right?"

"Well, of course. The man doesn't do this work for charity.
It's a business."

"It's still wrong. These things should be left to the proper
authorities. They're nothing more than a bunch of hired killers."

Jesus, she just doesn't get it. "Look, Halley, MacDonald
and his people are my only hope. With the exception of yourself and Captain Maxwell, no one else from the U.S. government will help. From the White House on down, they're all
too scared of Japan's money to intervene. So that leaves me
with just two choices: give up or fight." Zack paused for a
moment. "If Mac and his boys can rescue Wendy, the two
million I've already paid will be worth it. Hell, I would have
paid him ten million if he wanted that much. And maybe, just
maybe, if we're successful in what we're about to do here, I'll
save the company."

"Okay, Zack. You know I don't like it, but I understand
the situation. What do we do next?"

Zack smiled. *She's okay after all!*

* * *

The phone next to Hiroshi Yoshida's bed rang and rang. His subconscious mind, however, ignored the soft tone pulses. During the past twelve minutes he had been in maximum REM sleep, reliving another chapter of the war. For a reason that he could never quite fathom, he often dreamed about the surrender. Even though he had been confined to his barracks at the Chofu air base, it was like he had been a front-row spectator to the event. He pictured himself, then fifteen years old, standing on the deck of the U.S.S. *Missouri* in the middle of Tokyo Bay; he had been invited to witness the Japanese delegation as it penned the formal unconditional surrender document.

As the ceremony proceeded, young Yoshida watched in horror while his countrymen, each man decked out in full diplomatic attire, including black top hats, kowtowed to that mountain of a man named Douglas MacArthur. The five-star American general, with his corncob pipe parked in the corner of his mouth, reigned over the humiliating ceremony as though he were the Emperor.

Yoshida's hatred of the United States burned deep inside his gut as the reality of the dream once again set in—Japan had lost the war—*I lost the war! If only I had had a plane back then, I would have rammed the bastards—MacArthur, the traitors of our country, and all the others—right there in the middle of the harbor! It would have been wonderful!*

Yoshida finally awoke. Like all the other dreams in the past, this dream evaporated when his eyes snapped open. The phone was still ringing. He switched on the night-light at the head of the bed and reached for the handset. "Yes, what is it?"

"Sir, my apologies for waking you." It was the Nemuro general manager. "I would appreciate it very much if you could join me in the command center."

Yoshida glanced at the digital clock on the nightstand. "Good God, man, it's almost four in the morning."

"Sorry, sir. But I think you'll want to see this in person." He paused a moment. "We've had an unscheduled visitor tonight."

"What do you mean?"

"There's a drilling vessel one kilometer away. We think it's the *Deepquestor*."

"What? It shouldn't be near here until this afternoon!"

"I know."

Both of MacDonald's teams reached their respective targets at about the same time. The endless swells sweeping under the ten-acre platform made timing critical. The men waited until the crests lifted them to the proper point and then they latched onto one of the structure's four-foot-diameter diagonal braces, clamping their legs around the steel member like a vise. And then, with the use of special titanium grips attached to their gloves, they started shinnying up the forty-five-degree incline. It took only five minutes for all fourteen men to reach the first deck of Unit A.

Captain MacDonald squatted on the steel deck with the other six members of Team Two. They were all dripping wet; water pooled under their wet suit booties. Before climbing up the last few feet of the diagonal brace, each man had removed his fins, clipping them to chest harnesses. Once on the horizontal deck, they opened up their waterproof belly packs and began removing the contents. It took only a minute to gear up.

Each man slipped a balaclava over his head. With the exception of the eyes and a portion of the forehead, the black knitted woolen hood concealed all facial features. They next pulled on lightweight flak vests made of bullet-resistant Kevlar. Attached to the outside of the vest were assorted items: smoke canisters, grenades, ammunition pouches filled with thirty-round nine-millimeter magazines, pistol speed loaders, and first aid gear.

Mac's Mercs were armed to the teeth. They all carried the same armament: a Heckler & Koch MP5 submachine gun with suppressor; a stainless steel Smith & Wesson .357-caliber revolver with a four-inch barrel; and a K-bar combat knife.

MacDonald and the Team One leader also carried portable VHF radios. But they were to be used only for coordination during the final extraction process. The two commando groups operated independently of the other. There was no backup reserve force to call on if one of the teams encountered serious trouble. They'd have to solve the problem themselves.

In addition to the weapons and radios, one man from each

team carried a GMW missile. The guided multipurpose weapon was brand-new. Unlike its predecessor, the U.S. Army's unguided LAW rocket, the GMW was a guided missile. It was capable of destroying a variety of targets ranging from tanks and fixed gun positions to small boats. Operation of the weapon require a two-man crew. The spotter used a tiny tripod-mounted, battery-powered laser designator to illuminate a target. The missilere, separated from the spotter by at least a dozen yards, then locked the GMW's infrared sensors onto the reflected laser light. Once launched, the missile followed the light beam to the target. The weapon system is highly accurate to a range of three miles.

After inspecting his H&K, Captain MacDonald spun the open chamber on his revolver and then snapped it shut. He looked up. "Everyone set?" he whispered.

The men collectively nodded their heads.

"Okay, then, let's do it."

The team crept up a nearby stairway. They moved like tigers on the hunt.

Hiroshi Yoshida was standing on an observation deck fifty feet above the Nemuro command center. He was staring at a ghostlike image in the distance. "What the hell is Fukuda doing out there?" he asked.

"I don't know, sir. We've tried reaching them on the radio but there's no response."

"They weren't supposed to stop, and besides there's not a light on that thing."

"I know, sir."

"Well, get someone out there and find out what's going on."

"Yes, sir. I'll order a helicopter to investigate."

The Nemuro general manager turned around and headed down the stairway. Yoshida remained behind. He had a gnawing pain in the pit of his stomach. *Something's not right here,* he thought.

"Zack," called out Captain Flynn. "They're still trying to raise us on the radio. You want to talk with 'em yet?"

Zack glanced down at his watch. "No, not quite yet. Let 'em stew a little while longer."

"Okay."

MacDonald's team encountered their first obstacle on the third deck. A workman, one of the pump room operators, stumbled into the group of black-clad men as they started up another set of stairs. If the man had made any attempt to flee, he would have been cut down like firewood. Instead, he froze in his tracks, his eyes glued to the ugly submachine guns that were aimed right at his belly.

The point man, a former member of Seal Team Six who spoke fluent Japanese, began the interrogation. "Tell us where the American woman is being held." he ordered.

The workman said nothing. He was partially paralyzed from fear.

Another ex-SEAL moved forward and slammed the steel stock of his H&K into the man's midsection. He collapsed onto the metal grating.

As the worker gasped for breath, the interrogator leaned forward, his knife now in his right hand. He jabbed the needle-sharp point into the man's crotch. "Tell me where she is and I won't cut your cock off."

"I don't know for sure," the man said, his voice quavering. "I've only heard that she's somewhere on level six."

"Where on level six?"

The man pointed to the stairwell. "Up three more flights. That's all I know."

The interrogator looked back at MacDonald. Mac nodded his head.

Two minutes later the workman was bound and gagged. And after his body was hidden behind a storage container, he was injected with a tiny syringe. He would sleep for at least eight hours.

Zack checked his watch again. *It's time,* he thought. He turned back to face Captain Flynn. "Okay, Ian, let's talk to 'em."

Flynn handed a radio microphone to Constantine Benkevich. The Japanese-speaking Russian keyed the mike. "This is

Deepquestor calling Nemuro. Come in, please." His Japanese was perfect.

The reply was instantaneous. "*Deepquestor!* How did you get here so soon and why aren't you in the shipping lanes?"

"Ah, Nemuro, we made a lot better time than we originally planned but we've had some trouble here. About an hour ago our main generating plant went off-line. The voltage reduction gear burned up."

"You had a fire?" asked the operations watch officer.

"A small one, but it's out now. We lost all power to the bridge—nothing worked. We couldn't even radio that we had an emergency. We can only talk with you now because the chief electrician jury-rigged the radio so it would run off a portable generator."

"Are you in control now?"

"Yes, the ship's engines were not affected and we have plenty of mobility. But without electrical power to the bridge, we're having to operate them by hand."

A new voice came on the line—it was Takashi, the Nemuro general manager. "Fukuda, is that you?"

The Russian was ready. "No, this is Suzuki. Fukuda asked me to call. He's in the power plant right now."

"Why didn't you stay out at sea?" asked Takashi.

"The captain persuaded me to move here. He thinks you might have some of the parts in your storage compartments that we'll need. It's possible we can fix the generating plant and then be able to continue on to Yokohama. Otherwise, we'll have to anchor and wait for a tow."

"Okay, I understand your situation. Please stand by." Takashi turned to face Hiroshi Yoshida. The CEO of Yoshida Heavy Industries was now standing in the Nemuro command center. "Sir, do you wish to speak with Suzuki?"

Yoshida shook his head from side to side. He had only met Fukuda's assistant once. "No. Just tell him we'll send over a work crew to help repair the generator."

"Very good, sir." Takashi relayed Yoshida's message. Half a minute later the radio call ended.

Benkevich handed the microphone back to Captain Flynn.

"How'd it go?" asked Flynn.

"Perfect. They bought it like, how do you say, hook and sinker?"

Flynn laughed. "You mean hook, line, and sinker?"

"Yes, that is correct."

Flynn turned toward Zack. He had been standing in the background listening quietly. "Well, Zack, what do you want to do now?"

"We wait. It's all up to MacDonald and his men now."

Hiroshi Yoshida was exhausted when he finally returned to his cabin. He didn't even bother to take his robe off as he collapsed onto the bed. Just before switching off the nightstand light he glanced at the clock. It was almost four-thirty A.M. when he finally shut his eyes. He wondered if he would dream again.

MacDonald's team was now on the main deck level. They managed to stay partially hidden in the dimly lit companionways as they worked their way forward. Unfortunately, they had no idea where to look for Wendy Scott. There was no one around to interrogate. *Jesus H. Christ,* thought MacDonald as he looked down at his watch, *we're running out of time.*

While Team Two searched for the hostage, Team One set about its task with the precision of a well-oiled machine. The seven-man squad started with the central pump room. After surprising, and then drugging, the lone pump room technician, they attached two-pound bricks of plastique explosive to the bottom of the discharge ports. The twin steel pipes, each one thirty-six-inches in diameter, were connected to a bank of two-thousand-horsepower centrifugal pumps that were located farther aft in the compartment. Both lines were flowing at near the maximum design rate. Every minute, fifteen thousand gallons of oil flowed through the system. The crude oil eventually discharged into dozens of huge steel storage tanks located ten miles away on Hokkaido.

The bombs were armed with radio-controlled detonators. By remotely triggering a tiny transmitter, like an automatic garage door opener, the explosives would detonate. In order to deactivate the bombs, the detonators could be switched off by transmitting another radio code.

In addition to the main arming circuit, each bomb detonator was equipped with an antitamper sensor. If anyone tried to remove the C-4 bricks without first transmitting the deactivation code, they would explode. The charges were designed to punch baseball-size holes in the steel pipes.

After mining the pump room, the commandos moved to the central generating plant, located on deck level 3. This time, however, they had no choice but to use their weapons. One of the two workmen inside the control room spotted the intruders and ran for a telephone. He was cut down with a four-round burst from the team's point man. The technician was dead before he hit the steel floor. The other man gave up without a struggle.

After the survivor was sedated, two of the team members, both with electrical engineering backgrounds, went to work. In just five minutes they bypassed all of the control circuits for the power plant. The only way the four gas-burning turbines could now be shut down would be to manually shut off the natural gas flow. But that procedure would prove to be quite hazardous for anyone trying it. The chamber housing the valves was booby-trapped with half a dozen different types of antipersonnel devices. The least dangerous mine would simply blow a hand off; the worst would incinerate its victim.

The team leader was the last man to leave the control room. On his way out he flipped the door lock as he pulled the thick fire-resistant steel door shut. He then kneeled down and squirted three ounces of glue into the exterior keyhole. The epoxy would harden to a concretelike substance in five minutes.

The team leader checked his watch. *Right on schedule!* A moment later he took the lead and started down a catwalk that led to the flight deck. They had only one more task to accomplish.

Wendy Scott was still awake. She lay on the bottom bunk looking blankly up at the springs of the topside bed. She was both elated and terrified. Her brief telephone conversation with her father had been a godsend. *Thank God he knows I'm still alive,* she thought. But her other conversation, the one with the woman, still chilled her to the bone. *She'll never let me go!*

*   *   *

Team Two continued searching the corridors for victims until they literally ran into one. The off-duty electrician, a tiny middle-aged man, was jogging around the enclosed decks when he turned a corner and collided with the lead commando. Both men tumbled to the floor in a tangle of limbs.

After flipping the worker onto his back and placing a knife on his exposed throat, the Japanese-speaking American began his interrogation. He hit paydirt instantly. He turned to face MacDonald. "Captain, he says he knows where the woman is located."

"Well, it's about fucking time—convince him to lead us to her."

The commando smiled. He then leaned over and began whispering to the man. The worker's face mirrored the terror he felt inside. Half a minute later the team was once again on the move.

It took the electrician only a minute to lead Team Two through the deserted corridors to a part of the structure they had not yet explored. *This must be the quarters section of the rig,* thought MacDonald as he looked down the long hallway. There were dozens of cabin doors on each side.

The worker finally stopped by a cabin door on the right, about halfway down the compartment. He whispered to the translator. "She's inside there."

"Where's the key?" asked the American.

"I don't know," replied the man, surprised at the question.

The translator pushed the worker toward one of the other commandos for safekeeping. He then signaled for MacDonald.

Mac moved forward. "What ya got?" he asked, his voice barely audible.

"The gomer says she's inside here but I don't know. There's no guard around and this door doesn't look all that secure." He paused for a moment. "This sure ain't my idea of a jail cell."

"Well, there's only one way to find out, isn't there?"

"Yes, sir."

MacDonald stepped aside as another member of the team moved to the door. The man kneeled down and removed a thin steel lock pick from his vest. Fifteen seconds later the door's metal lock clicked open.

Bingo, thought MacDonald.

Two of Mac's men slithered into the room. One high, the other low. Not knowing what they'd find, they kept their weapons at the ready. The point man spotted her first. She was lying naked on the bed. She had only a sheet over her lower legs. *Christ, what a beauty,* he thought.

He moved forward, crouching down next to the bed. And then, as gently as he could, he cupped his hand over her mouth and whispered into her ear. "Miss Scott. Don't scream. We're Americans and we're here to rescue you."

Cindy DeMorey's eyes snapped open when she felt the hand cover her mouth. She never heard the man's words as she lashed out with everything she had: fingernails, feet, and teeth. The commando was expecting a grateful and docile hostage. Instead, he was attacked by a wild banshee. Somehow, he managed to stifle her screams, but he was getting the snot knocked out of him. She repeatedly bit through his rubber gloves and tore the hood off his head. Finally, in an act of desperation, the commando jumped on top of her flailing body and tried to pin her in place.

When Captain MacDonald entered the cabin he could hardly believe what he was seeing. One of his men was on top of a naked woman, struggling with her.

Mac rushed forward, ready to knock the man off the hostage. But then he discovered the mistake. He had committed Wendy Scott's face to memory. "That's not her," he said, his voice a little too loud.

"No shit," replied the struggling commando. His face was now bleeding.

Mac was temporarily stunned at the turn of events. But then he remembered. Scott had given him a whole series of photographs to study. A number of them contained shots of a beautiful Amerasian woman named Cindy DeMorey. *Well, this ain't so bad after all.*

A minute later, Cindy was under control. They had her spread-eagled on the bed, a commando securing each one of her limbs. Her mouth was stuffed with part of a pillow cover, and MacDonald was sitting on the side of the bed. He pressed his knife blade on her cheek, just below her right eye. "Now listen to me, Miss DeMorey, you don't have much time. Either you cooperate, like right now, or I'm going to slit your throat. You understand?''

Cindy looked into the eyes of the intruder. They were ice-cold. She nodded her head.

''Good, now, all we want is to rescue Wendy Scott. We know she's aboard and you're going to take us to her, right?''

Cindy again nodded her head.

''Good girl,'' Mac said. ''Now, you cooperate and we'll set you free when we're done. But if there are any screwups, and I mean *any*, I'll cut you. You understand that?''

Once again Cindy nodded her head.

A minute later, Team Two returned to the deserted hallway. The electrician who had led them to the wrong room remained behind. Drugged like the others, he was tucked away in Cindy's bed.

As the commandos headed down the hall, Cindy DeMorey was in the lead. MacDonald flanked her on the right side while another commando held on to her left arm. She wore a pair of foam sandals and a short, pink bathrobe, one that came halfway down to her knees. But there was nothing underneath the garment—time was critical and Mac wouldn't allow her to search for her misplaced underwear. And to insure her continued silence, Cindy's mouth was now sealed shut with a four-inch strip of duct tape.

The Team One leader couldn't believe his luck. One of the two choppers on the flight deck had already gone through a preflight checkout when they commandeered it. It was fueled, warmed up, and ready to lift off.

After capturing the two-man ground crew, the commandos grabbed the pilot and his three passengers. The six men were then herded into a nearby service hangar and administered knockout injections.

Team One was now aboard the Bell 412. Five of the men sat in the spacious passenger compartment; the starboard and port doors were open, allowing the commandos unobstructed fields of fire. If anyone approached the helicopter they would see them.

The leader sat in the copilot's seat next to the team's only flight-qualified member. While the rotors continued to turn at high idle, the commando-pilot began to familiarize himself with the aircraft's controls. With the doors open, it was like sitting inside a dishwasher.

"Can you really fly this thing?" shouted the team leader.

"Yeah, sure," replied the pilot. "They all basically work the same way—it'll just take me a couple more minutes to figure out where everything is."

The leader checked his watch again. *Damn it, where the hell are they?* He turned back to face the pilot. "Don't take too long. We're late. We may have to bug out of here any second."

The night supervisor for the Nemuro command center had just returned from the head and sat down at his console. He then scanned the half dozen remote TV cameras on an overhead display. He spotted the idling helicopter right away. *Hum, I wonder why they haven't taken off yet?* Before the supervisor went to relieve himself, the pilot had reported that he was about to lift off. He was supposed to ferry a crew of technicians over to the *Deepquestor*. But the helo was still sitting on the pad. The supervisor picked up a microphone and keyed the transmit switch. "Bluebird One, this is Command. Come in, please."

The commando-pilot heard the strange words over the aircraft's radio, but they didn't mean anything to them. The team leader, however, spoke Japanese. But he was not as fluent as he would have liked and he now had a new problem to solve.

"Bluebird One," repeated the supervisor, "this is Command. Are you having trouble?"

The team leader turned to the pilot. "Quickly, what can I say to make this guy believe we're okay?"

"Why not tell him we're waiting for someone else."

"Yeah, not bad." *Besides, that's exactly what we're doing,* he thought.

The leader reached for the headset. "Should I use this?" he asked.

"Yeah, slip it on and then I'll activate the circuit."

Thirty seconds later the Team One leader prepared to respond. He pushed the boom mike several inches away from his mouth, hoping the resulting distortion would mask his strange voice. The pilot then dialed the squelch control, trying to introduce static into the transmission.

"Command, Bluebird," said the team leader. He then continued, deliberately leaving out words. ". . . delayed . . . forgot . . . went to retrieve . . ."

"Bluebird, say again," ordered the supervisor. He could hardly hear the voice.

The team leader repeated his cryptic message.

"I barely copy you, Bluebird. Your transmission is very poor. Let me know when you're ready to lift off."

The team leader clicked the mike twice, signaling he had heard. He then turned to the pilot. "I don't know if they bought that or not. If Mac doesn't show up in five minutes, we're bugging out of here."

The pilot nodded his head while turning back to the console. He had everything just about figured out.

Cindy DeMorey led Team Two through a series of interior companionways that eventually opened onto an exterior walkway. The night air was chilly as she walked along the open steel grating. Wind-induced eddy currents were upwelling from below. She was literally freezing her butt off.

"How much farther?" asked MacDonald. He still had a viselike grip on her arm.

"Around the corner," she mumbled. The tape across her mouth had muffled her voice.

Captain MacDonald couldn't understand what she said so he ripped the tape off.

Cindy wanted to scream from the pain; pulling the tape away left a red welt on her cheeks.

"How much farther?" Mac asked again, his voice still a whisper.

"The room's just around the corner. There should be a guard by the door." Cindy felt MacDonald release his grip, but the commando on her other side remained glued to her arm.

Mac pressed his body against the steel bulkhead. He slid along the wall until he reached the edge of the corner. He dropped to his knees and reached into his vest, pulling out a tiny circular mirror; it looked like the type dentists use. He positioned the mirror so he could see around the corner. *There he is,* he said to himself. The guard was sitting in a lawn chair about ten yards away. He had a submachine gun on his lap.

Damn it, there's no easy way to take him from this approach. Mac knew there wasn't enough time to find an alternate route, so the decision was made. He flipped the safety of his H&K and stepped out.

The guard had just managed to pull up his weapon when Mac shot him: three silent rounds, right through the heart.

Wendy Scott heard the guard cry out in agony as he reacted to the impact of his fatal wounds. And then his weapon crashed onto the steel floor. *What the heck was that about?*

She had just managed to slip her long legs over the edge of the bunk bed when two black-clad men burst through the door.

Oh, God, no. Not again. She started screaming.

MacDonald managed to muffle Wendy before she made too much noise. "Keep quiet," he ordered as he tightened his grip around her mouth.

Wendy looked up at the masked man. All she could see were his brown eyes and thick bushy black eyebrows. She was so scared that she almost lost control of her bladder.

The man looked back down at her. "Miss Scott, we're Americans. We've come to get you out of here." He relaxed his grip just a little. "Now, if I take my hand away from your mouth, you promise not to scream anymore?"

Wendy nodded her head as best she could.

MacDonald pulled his hand away.

"You're really Americans?" she said, a smile breaking out on her pretty face.

"Yes, your father sent us and now we've got to get the hell out of here."

He half pulled Wendy off the bed. "Come on, we're leaving right now."

"But I'm not dressed. Let me pull—"

"No time," interrupted MacDonald. He then grabbed her arm and half carried her out of the cabin. Wendy was thankful that she had at least worn panties and an extra-long T-shirt that hung well below her waist.

The watch commander in the Nemuro security center leaned back in his chair, stretching out his arms. He then let out a long, groanlike yawn. He always ran out of steam near the end of his shift. This morning was no exception. Although he had been working the graveyard shift for nearly a month now, he was convinced that he would never get used to it.

Besides being dog-tired, the watch officer was bored stiff. With the exception of the offshore drilling rig that had showed up unexpectedly earlier in the morning, nothing out of the ordinary was going on. All of the remote-control TV cameras and sensing devices on the satellite rigs were normal. And the main platform's electronic security systems indicated that all remote systems were functioning normally.

The security officer couldn't even have a decent conversation with anyone. His assistant had called in sick at the beginning of the shift, leaving him alone in the security center. To break the monotony, he periodically checked in with the central command center, two decks above his tiny compartment. He was thinking about once again calling in when a new thought hit him. *I should check on Fuji.*

In addition to Nemuro's state-of-the-art electronic surveillance systems, there were also a dozen armed guards aboard. The guard section, quartered on Unit A, was split into three squads so that at least one of the four-man teams was on duty at all times. One man was always assigned to the central command center while the other guards continuously roamed the miles of walkways, catwalks, and companionways on the rig. And just recently, one of the three walking guards had been assigned to watch over a single cabin on level 6. The security officer hadn't checked on that guard's status for nearly an hour. He keyed his radio microphone. "Sentry Three, this is Security. Status report, please."

The security watch officer waited for a reply but heard only silence. He repeated his call two more times. Finally, frustrated, he made a new call. "Sentries One and Two report."

The responses were immediate. "Sentry One here," reported the first watchman. He was on level 3 near the east end of the platform. "Sentry Two here," called in the second roaming guard. He was on level 6, just a short distance from the guard station.

"Sentry Two, I can't raise Three. Check him out and then call me back."

"Yes, sir. I'm on my way."

The watch officer again leaned back in his chair. *Damn Fuji. I'll bet he fell asleep again.*

A minute later the security center's intercom speaker blasted to life as the roaming guard keyed his microphone. His voice was quavering as he shouted: "Command, this is Sentry Two. I just found Fuji. He's been shot . . . there's blood everywhere."

The security chief dropped his feet back to the floor. "What?"

"He's dead. Somebody shot him. And the woman in the cabin . . . she's missing, too."

Oh shit! thought the security watch officer. He was just about to hit the master security alarm when he hesitated. *No, not yet,* he decided. *If I do that, the intruders will know for sure that we're on to them. Maybe I can bottle them up before they try to escape.*

The security officer keyed his mike. "Sentry Two, check the immediate area and see if you can figure out where they went. Sentry One, get to the helo deck and secure it."

The security chief next triggered the intercom alarm in the quarters of the off-duty guards. The twenty-second burst of screeching noise was guaranteed to waken the soundest sleeper. When the alarm stopped, the officer shouted into the open mike: "Intruder Alert, Intruder Alert. This is no drill. Get to your security stations, now!"

Team Two's point man didn't have a chance. One of the Nemuro guards heading for the helo deck spotted the black-clad man as he rounded a corner and opened up with his Uzi machine pistol. The nine-millimeter rounds peppered his exposed legs. The commando plunged to the deck.

Captain MacDonald heard the rapid-fire shots just in time. He stopped the rest of the team from walking into the ambush. One of his men automatically moved to the edge of the corner and in a lightning move stuck his head out. He instantly drew fire. The bullets pinged off the metal wall. "I've got one shooter, ten meters away. Looks like an Uzi."

MacDonald didn't need to respond. His men took over. A short-fused fragmentation grenade was lobbed down the corridor. The surrounding steel bulkheads absorbed most of shock and noise, but the guard didn't know what hit him.

"Clear," shouted one of the attackers.

Team Two was once again on the move. MacDonald pulled Cindy DeMorey along like she was a rag doll. Wendy Scott was escorted by another commando. The point man, alive but unable to walk, was carried by two of his companions, one under each of his shoulders. A crimson trail marked their path on the steel deck.

The senior pump man from the day shift was an early riser. He wasn't supposed to take over until six in the morning but today he had decided to surprise the night shift crew. He was hoping they still had a kettle of water brewing. He liked to drink tea with his first cigarette of the morning.

The pump man walked into the main control room. Despite the insulation around the pumps, it was still noisy. He searched for his friends. *Where are they?* he thought as he looked around the huge compartment.

Hum, I guess they're off somewhere else, checking on something. He then unconsciously reached into his vest pocket and pulled out a pack of Seven Stars. He tapped the bottom of the pack, ejecting a cigarette. And then, while standing right next to a No Smoking sign, he lit up. The senior pump man was the boss of the control room. He could do anything he wanted.

He started walking down the manifold line, casually examining the discharge pipes. He was just about to turn around when he spotted it. It was just single loop of red wire, no more than an inch in length. But it hung just far enough below the invert of the pipe to make it visible. He walked up to the pipe and kneeled down. He bent his head under the pipe. *What the hell is that?* The man was looking at the back side of the detonator. However, from his angle of view it didn't look like a bomb. Instead, he thought it was some kind of new flow-monitoring gauge.

Now, who put that on there? he said to himself as he reached for the device.

The bomb exploded half a second later. The blast tore the pump man's right arm off just below the elbow. But that terrible wound didn't matter. A microsecond later a two-inch section of jagged steel pipe ripped into the man's head right above his left ear. It opened the skull cavity as if it were a can opener.

The momentum of the shrapnel snapped the man's head backward, flinging his half-consumed cigarette twenty feet away. It landed on a shelf six feet above the floor. It was still lit.

The detonation did not ignite the oil. Instead, it punched a fist-size hole in the pipe casing. The crude oil that was now blasting out of the opening covered the entire control room floor in just seconds. The flow was like a fire hydrant, except that the fluid was black and sticky.

The oil itself wasn't the greatest danger; it was the fumes. Natural hydrocarbon vapors are highly volatile, and when they are mixed with sufficient amounts of oxygen the resulting combination can cause a catastrophic explosion.

It took only a minute for the vapor level in the control room to reach an explosive concentration. And the smoldering tip of the pump man's cigarette supplied just enough heat to ignite the mixture.

Team Two was one flight below the helo deck when an enormous explosion shook the entire platform. The concussion from the blast knocked everyone to the deck.

Captain MacDonald was the first to recover. "Get up! Get up!" he shouted. He knew their time was running out.

As the others pulled themselves up, Mac reached for his portable radio. He was going to check with Team One's leader. However, when he keyed the mike a sickening feeling gripped his gut. The VHF transreceiver wasn't working. *Damn it!* he thought.

When Mac had been knocked to the deck by the blast, he had fallen onto the $3,000 radio.

When the blast vibrations reached the Bell 412, the leader of Team One made his decision. He had already waited six minutes longer than planned. He keyed his portable radio for one last time. "Mac, are you there? Come in, for Christ's sake!"

He waited fifteen seconds before turning to the pilot. "They didn't make it. Get us out of here!"

The pilot rotated the throttle to the maximum and pulled back on the collective.

* * *

Like everyone else aboard, Hiroshi Yoshida was brutally awakened. At first he thought there had been an earthquake, but the violent shaking lasted only a few seconds. A moment later one of his aides burst into his cabin.

"Sir, there's been an explosion in the pump room and there are intruders aboard."

"What?" asked Yoshida, still partially stunned from the rude awakening.

"The Scott woman—she's not in her cabin. And the guard's been killed. We think whoever took her set off the explosions."

Damn you, Zackary Scott! You'll pay for this with your life!

Finn Sorenson was the first to notice the trouble. Twenty minutes earlier he had joined his friends on the bridge of the *Deepquestor.* The incessant pain from his broken jaw and missing teeth had finally slacked off, mitigated by bed rest and a steady dose of codeine.

Finn heard the faint crackling noise as the nearly depleted shock wave from the distant explosion reflected off the wheelhouse walls. He then turned forward, looking through the windscreen. "Jesus, what the hell is that?" he shouted. His voice was still muffled by the padding stuffed into his cheek, but everyone standing around him understood.

Zack turned around and looked out the bridge windows. Flames were erupting from the side of the main Nemuro platform. "Oh, my God! Something's gone wrong."

Team Two made it to the helo deck a minute after the helicopter took off. They could see its flashing strobe as it flew away. Mac once again keyed his useless radio, hoping against hope that it would work now that they were out in the open. There was only static. Frustrated, he tossed the radio over the side. It crashed into the black water a hundred and ten feet below.

"What do we do now, skipper?" asked one of the commandos.

"I don't know."

The helicopter landed on the *Deepquestor*'s helipad four minutes after leaving the Nemuro platform. Zackary Scott and

Finn Sorenson stood on the elevated steel deck as it touched down. Zack's heart was almost in his mouth as he waited for the cabin doors to open up. *Please God, let Wendy be aboard.*

His hopes sank like a rock when the seven commandos walked away from the aircraft.

He ran up to the first man. It was the team leader. "Where's my daughter?" he shouted.

"I don't know. Something went wrong and the charges went off. Captain MacDonald and his rescue team never showed up. We waited as long as we could, but then had to get out of there."

Zack sank to his knees. There were tears in his eyes, but a bitterness welled up from deep inside. He exploded a moment later. "Yoshida, you motherfucker, I'll kill you."

Zack grabbed the commando's submachine gun before the man could react. He then jumped up and started running for the chopper. Finn Sorenson followed behind. "Zack," he yelled, ignoring the pain from his broken jaw, "what the hell are you doing?"

Scott didn't respond. Instead he started to climb into the pilot's seat. He hadn't flown a chopper in months, but he didn't care. With what seemed like a river of adrenaline flooding into his bloodstream, he reacted solely by instinct.

Finn reached the cabin door just as Zack pulled himself inside. Knowing he had only a second or two to react, he yanked the door open and lunged for Scott.

Zack wasn't ready for the assault from his friend. And as a consequence he never saw the punch. Finn hit him on the side of his head with his fist, knocking him out.

Zack slumped across the seat. Finn, his right hand smarting from the blow, grabbed Zack's right arm and pulled him out of the chopper. One of the commandos helped carry him back to the bridge. *Damn fool,* thought Finn. *He would have killed himself for sure.*

Captain MacDonald and Team Two were now taking gunfire. The guards dispatched to secure the helideck had finally shown up. They started firing the instant they spotted the intruders.

Bullets whizzed overhead and pinged off the metal equipment that sheltered Team Two. Three of Mac's men returned fire, but the guards were in an excellent defensive position.

"Mac, those guys have really got us pinned down. We can't get to them without getting cut to pieces."

"I know, I know. But there's got to be another way out of this."

Captain MacDonald crawled over to the edge of the platform, sandwiching his head between the steel grating and the lower guardrail. He looked downward. There was plenty of light refracting from several below-deck floodlights. He could see the edges of the lower decks. And then he spotted it.

He turned back to his companion. "Okay, here's what we're going to do . . ."

The chief supervisor in the Nemuro control center did everything he could to stop the flow of oil in the pump room. But nothing worked. None of the electrical controls to the pumps were functioning and he couldn't even get men into the main generating room to pull the turbines off-line. Somehow the door had been sealed shut. Meanwhile, the rupture in Port 1 continued to discharge 7,500 gallons of crude every minute. The oil invaded everything.

The crude oil fueled an enormous fire that had already consumed 8 percent of the platform. The automatic fire-suppression systems were useless and the firefighting teams that tried to smother the flames with foam were being literally baked to death by the oppressive heat.

In one last desperate maneuver, the supervisor ordered a diver overboard to manually close the main gas flow line. All electrical power to the platform would be lost, but at least the oil would stop flowing.

Hiroshi Yoshida pounded on Cindy's cabin door. "Cindy, wake up. We must leave now."

After repeating his plea two more times he turned to the steward who stood next to him. "Open it," he ordered. The man fumbled with a ring full of keys. A minute later the door popped open.

Yoshida was devastated to find the electrician sleeping in Cindy's bed.

* * *

Cindy DeMorey hung on to the commando's shoulder with a death grip. And her legs were wrapped around his waist like a clamp. She was absolutely terrified. They were hanging over the edge of the platform, suspended by a rope. The ocean was about sixty feet below.

"Hold still," ordered the commando as he struggled to rappel the last ten feet. He reached out with his free arm and grabbed the guardrail. A few seconds later he handed Cindy off to MacDonald.

"Got 'er," Mac said as he grabbed the half-naked woman. The commando pulled himself in.

"How are Pete and Jake doing?" asked Captain MacDonald. He was referring to the two commandos who remained on the helideck, covering Team Two's escape.

"They're running low on ammo. I gave 'em my vest."

"Okay, they'll break out after we leave. Now, let's get in this thing. It's time to go."

A minute later Mac sealed up the single-access hatch to Emergency Lifeboat 5. The self-contained fifty-person vessel looked like a giant orange flying saucer.

Mac turned around and looked at his fellow passengers. The two women sat on the starboard side with the wounded commando in between. The other three men from Team Two were on the opposite side.

"Okay people," Mac yelled as he sat down in a foam cushion seat, "buckle up. This is going to get rough." Thirty seconds later he triggered the emergency eject switch. The davits securing the ten-ton rescue vessel rotated outward, pivoting it away from the deck. Then the electrically operated cable locks snapped open, releasing the lifeboat. It slammed into the water forty feet below with a huge *whoooop!*

Mac felt as if the wind had been knocked out of him, but he quickly recovered. He pressed the Start button on the engine. It instantly burst to life. He then began piloting the craft away from the platform. The *Deepquestor* was still blacked out, but he could see its silhouette in the shadows. *Don't take off yet,* he thought. *We're coming!*

The remaining two members of Team Two heard the rescue boat launch.

"Time to get out of Dodge," replied one of the men.

"Right on," answered the second.

They laid down a heavy barrage of covering fire and lobbed their remaining grenades at the guards. Then, without ceremony, they leaped over the deck edge and fast-rappelled downward. They hardly used their friction brakes to slow themselves. Finally, when they were ten feet over the water, they released their lines and plunged into the ocean. The water was heavy with oil and the fumes stung their eyes. They didn't care, though. They could see the lifeboat's emergency strobe light as it slowly orbited two hundred yards away. The *Deepquestor* was about half a mile farther away. They began swimming like Olympic sprinters.

Hiroshi Yoshida rounded up one of the helicopter pilots and both men headed for the now-secure helipad. The raiders had escaped, but that wasn't Yoshida's main concern. Instead, there was a much more serious problem developing. The fire in the pump room continued to burn out of control. The diver had not been able to get to the underwater safety valve because the platform's dive center had been consumed by the fire. There wasn't any equipment left: no dry suits, hard hat gear, scuba tanks, masks, or anything else. And the fire had also disabled the underwater elevator system linking the Unit A platform to the submerged sub tug–shuttle terminal. The only way the flow of burning oil would stop was when the fire finally breached the insulated power plant bulkheads and burned up the generators—a process that might take hours. Then, without power, the gushing oil would finally stop.

In the interim, however, the burning oil would continue to spew all over the platform. The heat generated by the inferno was already so intense in several sections that half a dozen of the main structural supports had buckled, threatening to collapse the entire platform.

Yoshida and the pilot climbed into the Augusta A109C. Yoshida's personal helicopter had been parked near the aircraft commandeered by the Americans. There were several bullet holes in the windshield, ricochets from the intense gun battle, but nothing was seriously damaged. The pilot started up the engines. Five minutes later, they were airborne.

As the helo tracked westward toward Hokkaido, Yoshida caught a glimpse of the *Deepquestor* in the first rays of the rising sun. It was heading out to sea, toward international waters and freedom. The rage that had burned so feverishly in his heart now turned to the bitter cold of humiliation.

33

THE CHASE

The North Pacific

The *Deepquestor*'s port jib crane lifted the vessel from the ocean with ease. As the circular-shaped hull rose through the air, seawater cascaded from its internal ballast chambers. A minute later, it was resting on the deck next to the base of the derrick tower.

Zackary Scott and Captain Flynn were still scrambling down a steep ladderwell when the access hatch on the lifeboat popped open. A dark haired man with a full beard emerged from the opening. He climbed out and then jumped onto the semi's deck. The early morning air had a chill to it, causing his exhaled breath to form frosty plumes.

A few seconds later, a blond head appeared in the opening. Wendy Scott pulled herself out and stepped onto the outer deck of the emergency escape craft. Captain MacDonald then reached upward, helping her to the deck.

Zack arrived just as his daughter planted her feet on the *Deepquestor*'s steel plating. Wendy spotted him almost simultaneously. "Daddy!" she screamed, her voice filled with joy.

Father and daughter embraced. Tears filled their eyes.

"Are you all right? Did they hurt you?" asked Zack.

"I'm fine, Dad."

"Oh, honey, I can't believe it's finally over."

"Neither can I." Wendy laughed and cried for several more seconds before again speaking. "Dad, I never gave up hope. I knew you'd come get me."

"Well, sweetie, I had a lot of help."

"I know. Captain MacDonald and his men were wonderful."

Thank you, Lord! thought Zack. He then looked over Wendy's shoulder as he continued to hug her. MacDonald was standing a few feet away. "Thanks, Mac," he said. "Thanks for everything."

MacDonald nodded his head.

Captain Flynn walked forward, extending his right hand. "Captain MacDonald, I presume," he said, a broad smile breaking out across his tired face.

"Yes, sir," replied MacDonald, grinning back as he firmly gripped the man's hand.

"I'm Ian Flynn. I'm the skipper of this rig."

"Pleased to meet you, Captain."

Both men talked for a few moments until they were interrupted by a new voice: "Say, Mac, what do you want to do with her?"

MacDonald turned around and looked back at the lifeboat's hatch. One of his commandos was standing in the opening. Cindy DeMorey was next to him. Her hands were tied behind her back and she was still dressed in her skimpy pink bathrobe. Her bare legs shook as if she were standing on a dozen running washing machines. She was cold all right, but that wasn't what made her shiver. It was fear. She could feel the hate from Zackary Scott's eyes as he looked up at her, his daughter still wrapped in his arms.

Mac turned back to face Flynn. "Captain, do you think you could rig us up some kind of a brig? We got us a prisoner here."

"Yeah, no problem. I've already got two others locked up below."

Fifteen minutes later, Cindy DeMorey joined Fukuda and Suzuki inside the decompression chamber. Captain Flynn then ordered the *Deepquestor* to flank speed. The semisubmersible charged through the outer limits of the Nemuro oil field and turned north.

* * *

The *Deepquestor* continued to run at full bore. The bow sections of the parallel pontoon hulls knifed through the calm waters. Twin wakes of white foam merged into one long tail that extended nearly a mile to the southwest.

It was late afternoon now, and the semisubmersible continued to run parallel with the Japanese-controlled southern Kurils, staying well outside the twelve-mile limit. Etorofu Island, the most northerly of the reclaimed Kurils, was far off to port. The ship would continue on the same course for another six hours before turning northwest. It would then head for the Friz Strait. The deepwater passage separates the northerly tip of Etorofu from the Russian-controlled Urup Island. Once on the other side, the *Deepquestor* would be in far safer waters. The Sea of Okhotsk still belonged to the Russian navy.

Captain Flynn was on top of the bridge house, scanning the waters ahead. He preferred this location to the lower-level bridge wing; it allowed him to see the stern of the ship with his own eyes instead of having to rely on the vessel's closed-circuit television camera and radar. And today that was very, very important.

He turned around again and looked aft past the derrick tower. He raised his binoculars to his eyes and adjusted the focus. There was a pale plume rising into the atmosphere well beyond the horizon. The Nemuro Complex was still burning, but that wasn't what he was looking for.

"Do you see it anymore?" asked Zackary Scott. He was standing a few feet away from Flynn. The rest of the group—Halley Blake, Mac MacDonald, Wendy Scott, and Finn Sorenson—were standing about a dozen feet away; they were also looking toward the south.

"No, I think it's gone for good."

Everyone let out a collective sigh, followed up by a lot of laughing and back slapping. And then someone popped open one of the champagne bottles; Captain Flynn always carried a case of bubbly aboard the vessel. It was only to be used for special occasions, like completing a new well. But today there was even more cause to celebrate.

Even though Flynn was on duty he accepted a plastic glass of the bubbly fluid from Zack. He needed it—a couple of hours earlier he had been certain that he wouldn't live to see another sunset.

* * *

It all started when Flynn noticed the new target on the aft radar display. As soon as the Japanese Maritime Self-Defense Forces frigate passed through the Nemuro Strait, it started chasing the *Deepquestor*. The Chikugo-class vessel had a top speed of twenty-five knots, ten knots more than *Deepquestor*'s best speed. It could catch up with the floating drilling rig in just a few hours.

Captain Flynn, along with the rest of the *Deepquestor*'s crew, knew they were in serious trouble when the SDF vessel started broadcasting radio messages in English ordering the semi to heave to. Flynn refused to acknowledge the directive and pushed on. And in an act of desperation he ordered the radio room officer to start sending Mayday alerts, pleading for help. The universal signal went out on all available channels: UHF, VHF, CB, and even SAT COM.

When the Japanese frigate had closed to within five miles of the *Deepquestor*, it flared off to the starboard and began firing. There was no radio warning, no order to cut the engines, nothing. They just started firing. The projectile from the three-inch cannon arced high over the vessel, exploding half a mile away. The next two rounds bracketed the drilling rig. Now they couldn't miss. And they wouldn't have—if the Russians hadn't shown up.

The pair of MiGs raced eastward at nearly the speed of sound. They were so low that the frigate's surveillance radar didn't spot them until they were just five miles out.

The Russian pilots had achieved complete tactical surprise. All they had to do was release their antiship missiles and the Japanese warship would be history. The twenty-three officers and enlisted men crammed into the ship's tiny combat information center knew they were dead. They all heard the distinctive warning tones from the threat radar receiver. The wobbly sounds meant only one thing: The radar-guided missiles were locked on solidly to the ship. There was no time to implement countermeasures.

But the warbirds didn't attack. Instead, they broke off at the last moment, one heading over the bow, the other over the fantail. The roar of the double-barreled jet turbines on full afterburners shook the 305-foot-long ship from stem to stern.

The Russians had made their point, simply and dramatically: Back off or else!

The SDF skipper didn't wait for a second round. He ordered the ship to come about. Without any effective antiaircraft defenses other than a twin forty-millimeter AA gun, his charge was too vulnerable. The Russian jets could send his ship to the bottom in seconds.

The MiGs hung around for almost an hour, making certain the warship continued its southerly retreat. Then they headed northwestward, back to their landing field on Sakhalin Island. They dipped their wings as they passed over the *Deepquestor*.

Captain Flynn swigged down the champagne—it was warm but he didn't care.

"Well, Ian," Zackary Scott said, "would you like me to relieve you for a while?"

"Thanks, but not just yet. I'd like to see us through Friz Strait. Then you can have her."

"Fair enough."

Scott started to walk back toward the others when Flynn called out: "Say, Zack, what are you going to do about that bastard now that we've got Wendy back?"

Zack walked back to his friend's side. "First of all, I'm going to have the deal with PVH rescinded. With the confessions from Fukuda, Suzuki, and DeMorey, that should be a slam dunk."

"But do you think their statements will hold up—in court, I mean?"

"Sure. Remember, they made their confessions to Commander Blake, not us. And because they were made in international waters on a U.S. flag vessel under the direction of a federal law enforcement officer, it should be legal." Zack turned back to look at the Coast Guard officer. Halley Blake was engaged in a heavy conversation with Finn. They were both smiling. Zack, now grinning, turned back to face Flynn. "I think they're finally starting to hit it off."

"Yeah, it sure looks that way. I think it would be great if they got together."

"So do I!"

Flynn took another sip of the champagne before once again

addressing Scott. "So I take it that after all of this screwing around the *Deepquestor* won't be calling Yokohama its new home port?"

"Damn right! Thank the Lord we never formally relinquished title to any of our rigs—everything's still in escrow back in Seattle. As soon as we get a judge to rescind the deal, we'll get everything back officially."

"And Hammer 4? Didn't they say they were going to assign those leases to some foundation or something like that?"

"Don't worry! I'm going to get the Hammer 4 leases back, just like all my other property. And then we're going to sue Yoshida Heavy Industries for every fucking yen they've got. I'll go after YHI's corporate soul—Yoshida's going to pay dearly for sabotaging the Hammer 4 well, kidnapping my daughter, and killing all of those innocent people."

"But what about the oil in those subs?"

"Once we expose the scheme, we'll have everyone pissed at 'em. YHI will pay like hell then."

Flynn emptied his glass and then began shaking his head in utter disbelief. "Zack, I just can't believe those guys. How many places do you think they've been pirating oil from anyway?"

"Well, we know they've been working the Washington coast for at least two years, maybe longer. Fukuda confirmed that. But I've got a sneaky feeling they've been stealing oil from Alaska and off California as well. It'll take a while to search for their subsurface wellheads, but I'll bet you a steak dinner at the Canlis we'll find some in those areas."

"Anyplace else?"

"I wouldn't be a bit surprised if they've got a bunch of hot wells in Indonesia and off the Chinese coast. Those areas are right in their backyard. They'd be almost irresistible."

"But how could they keep this a secret for so long? This has got to be the biggest shell game ever conceived."

"It is. According to Fukuda, it all started years ago when YHI was halfway through development of the Nemuro field. That's when their crude oil wells started drying up. Turns out the reservoir wasn't nearly as big as first estimated—they still got some crude out of it, maybe a fifth of what they originally estimated, plus a little gas, but that was it." Zack took another swig of champagne from a bottle. "So, after having spent billions to build the project and touting to their own people that Japan finally had its own petroleum source, YHI was about to go bust.''

"But they didn't go bust," replied Flynn.

"That's right—old man Yoshida and a few of his lieutenants apparently dusted off an old contingency plan that had been lying around somewhere in their corporate archives. It was a wild-ass plan, but it was simple and effective: Develop an underwater drilling vessel to explore for oil and then develop the oil trapped in the world's deep ocean basins."

"Shit, that's what you've been working on, too, isn't it?"

"It sure is. And according to Fukuda, YHI stole some of the basic technology from SCS."

"But how? That whole system's still in development."

"Well, most of it is my own damn fault. Remember that grad student from Berkeley that worked for us six or seven years ago—his name was Willy Lai."

"Oh, yeah, the Chinese kid. He came out on my rig for a couple weeks."

"He was a grad student all right, but that was just a cover. Fukuda said he was a spy!"

"What?"

"Yoshida Heavy Industries was paying for his entire education, bachelor's through Ph.D., plus it promised to hire him to help work on YHI projects in China once he finished. In return, all he had to do was take summer jobs in a variety of high-tech corporations. He got lucky that year."

"Shit, you mean he worked on your drilling system?"

"Yep, I was too tied up at the time to do much checking on him, and the kid seemed to know his stuff, so I let him work on it. That was a big, big mistake."

Captain Flynn again shook his head in disbelief. "What a bunch of pricks! First YHI steals your ideas, then it steals your oil, and finally it tries to steal your company."

"Yeah, you're right. But it all boils down to just one person: Hiroshi Yoshida."

"That old fart must still have a pair of brass ones on him that are the size of grapefruits."

Zack laughed at Flynn's vivid description. "Yeah, maybe he does. But for some reason he's got it in for me." Scott paused for moment. "The only thing that I can figure out is that he was afraid I'd eventually discover that the Nemuro fields were a fake.''

''You mean by working with the Russians?''

''Yeah. If we came up with a bunch of dry holes near Nemuro, then maybe a lot more questions would be asked about what YHI was doing.'' Zack paused to take another sip of champagne. ''Anyway, we'll probably never know the full story. I've gotta believe the Japanese government is involved in this mess up to its eyeballs, and you can make book they'll do everything they can to cover it up. Hell, they'll probably protect Yoshida himself, making out that we're unfairly picking on his company.''

''You mean like Japan bashing?''

''Yep. The government will cry foul to cover its own ass. The Japanese people are decent and fair—just like us—and if they knew the real truth about what happened, they'd—''

''The truth—you mean stealing oil from its neighbors and allies?'' interrupted Flynn.

''Yes. The Japanese people are extremely honest, and they'd be terribly offended by what happened. The loss of face, I think that is the term they use, would be phenomenal.''

''I see what you mean. If the truth got out, then a lot of heads would roll.''

''Right. Their central government could even collapse.''

''So what do you think's going to happen then?''

Zack shook his head. ''Hell, I don't know. This whole thing's going political. No telling what our people in Washington will do.'' Zack paused. ''But I'll tell you this, I wouldn't be surprised if Yoshida comes after me again—he's never going to get over what I've done to him.''

''But he's finished,'' protested Flynn. ''His company's going tits up. What the hell can he do to you now?''

''I wish I knew.''

34

TAIRTARI

Over the Sea of Okhotsk

The ride was smooth as glass. The four giant turbofan jet engines purred effortlessly, pushing the 300-ton aircraft through the thin atmosphere at just over six nautical miles a minute. The western shore of Etorofu Island was twenty miles ahead. The long, thin, brown streak of rocks and earth looked like a mini-mountain range jutting up from the sea.

The descending sun was directly behind the Airbus 340's tail section. The shadow from the cargo-conversion aircraft danced across the ocean surface miles ahead of its advancing fuselage. The pilot looked down at his wristwatch. It would be dark in forty minutes. *Plenty of time,* he said to himself.

Hiroshi Yoshida glanced to his right. The copilot's seat was empty. And so was the rest of the cockpit. Yoshida was the only person aboard the widebody jet.

After escaping from Nemuro's main platform, Yoshida's helicopter landed at the Kushiro municipal airport. He then boarded his executive jet and flew it back to Tokyo. It wasn't until he had returned to his downtown office complex that the enormity of the developing Nemuro disaster really hit him. The lobby was crowded with reporters. They were all demanding to know if the rumors of the platform fire and spilled oil were true. He refused to speak to them, promptly finding sanctuary in his private office.

Alone and depressed, he considered all options. In the end, he always came back to the same conclusion: He was finished. His honor was lost and his personal disgrace would be monumental. *Zackary Scott, it's all your fault,* he thought over and over.

After brooding for several hours, Yoshida began to regain his composure. He then made an urgent call to the minister of defense. But the SDF frigate had not been able to stop the semisubmersible. The *Deepquestor* continued north, toward Russia.

The news filled Yoshida with hope as he realized that he still had a chance to redeem himself. He smiled as the irony of the new plan gelled. *Yes,* he thought, *by the grace of the gods, that will work!*

The YHI cargo jet had been preparing to depart for Singapore when Yoshida's limousine pulled onto the tarmac. The flight crew was astonished when the chairman of YHI walked into the A340's cockpit. None of the men had ever met him before, but they all knew him. He owned the plane and paid their salaries.

When Yoshida ordered the men to deplane, there was no hesitation, not even a single question. They simply filed off the portable stairway and climbed into the limo's backseat, as all loyal YHI employees would have. Yoshida was their master and his word was the law.

Yoshida turned back to the instrument panel, checking the autopilot settings. The plane was flying itself, following a preset flight plan. Two separate computer systems tracked the A340's eastward course, insuring that it flew within just a few meters of the prescribed course. It was heading for a specific set of earth coordinates in the Pacific Ocean off Etorofu Island's east coast.

At 28,000 feet, the jumbo jet was barely audible to the inhabitants of Etorofu when it passed overhead. It was just another silver speck in the heavens. No one paid the slightest attention to it.

Hiroshi Yoshida stared through the windscreen, carefully

examining the blue ocean waters ahead. There were a few clouds at 20,000 feet, but they hardly blocked anything. He was just about to scan an air chart on his lap when he spotted it. It was a minuscule white spot just a few degrees north of the aircraft's projected flight path. "So there you are!" he said to himself.

The coordinates provided by the Japanese frigate were surprisingly accurate. The *Deepquestor* was almost exactly where the warship had predicted it would be.

Yoshida reached into his coat pocket and pulled out a thin white scarf. It had a red ball in the center. Black and red *kanji* script covered the sides. He wound the soft cloth around his head, centering the red circle over his forehead. He knotted the ends in the back. The *hachimaki* was the same headband he had worn over a half century earlier during his only combat flight of World War II. He had missed his target then, but he wouldn't fail this time.

The party on top of the *Deepquestor*'s bridge house was still going full tilt. A dozen additional crew members, along with most of Mac's Mercs, had joined Zackary Scott and his friends on the roofside deck. It was a hell of a celebration. Someone had brought up a tape deck, filling the early evening air with soft rock and roll music. Finn Sorenson and Halley Blake were dancing together on one corner of the platform while three of the commandos surrounded Wendy Scott, trying to convince her to dance. A couple of the female crew members, along with a handful of the male hands, were laughing it up with Captain Mac MacDonald as he started telling off-color navy jokes.

Cold beer now supplemented the depleted champagne supply. A fifty-five-gallon barrel filled with crushed ice and Budweiser was the focal point of the party. The deck was already littered with dozens of crushed aluminum cans. And just about everyone, except for Captain Flynn and Mac MacDonald, was half bombed.

Flynn was still running the ship, calling in periodic commands to the bridge by means of his remote intercom. His one cup of the bubbly had been enough. MacDonald, however, avoided the booze; he drank Cokes instead. He had been dry for almost a year now, and as bad as he wanted one of those ice-cold Buds he managed to control himself. After abusing his body for most of his adult life, he had finally gotten help. He was bound and determined to keep it together.

Zackary Scott was standing off to the side, next to Captain Flynn. They were both listening to MacDonald. Despite his abstinence, the ex-navy captain was in fine form. "There was this dumbshit Marine major I met in a bar in Subic back in seventy-one. He was as drunk as a skunk, like the rest of us, but he didn't know I was a SEAL. So this numb-nuts challenges me to a . . . ."

Zack turned to face his friend. "Quite a guy, isn't he, Ian?"

"Yep, he's a real character." Flynn grinned. "You really gotta admire him, especially at his age. Anyone who jumps out of a damn airplane in the middle of the night, glides twenty miles to a little spot in the ocean, and then fights a major battle has got to be either a hero or a nut case."

"Maybe it takes a little of both to do what he does," replied Zack.

"Yeah, I guess you're right. Anyway, he came through, didn't he?"

"He sure did!"

Zack took another pull on his Bud when he noticed that Ian Flynn had turned his head. Flynn was looking over his right shoulder. His eyes were squinting as he stared into the setting sun, now just a few degrees above the horizon. A second later Captain Flynn reacted. "Jesus Christ, look at that!"

"What?" Zack asked as he turned around. And then he saw it.

The A340 was coming out of the red ball of the sun; it was headed right for the *Deepquestor*.

Hiroshi Yoshida held the wheel steady in his hands. Despite the 300-knot speed and the 500-foot altitude, the huge jet was smooth and vibration free. His timing was perfect as he passed over the forward half of the drilling rig. His starboard wingtip missed the top of the derrick tower by a mere hundred feet. *That ought to wake the bastards up,* he thought as he advanced the throttles and started climbing again.

Everyone on top of the bridge house hit the deck when the Airbus jet roared overhead. They all thought it was going to smash right into the ship, but it didn't. Instead, the noise from the four jet engines thundered down on them like a mountain avalanche.

As the plane pulled away, the partygoers began picking themselves up. Nearly everyone was in shock at the sudden appearance of the mystery jet.

"Christ, what kind of maniac would pull a stunt like that?" yelled one of the crew.

"The pricks must be nuts," commented another.

"That flight crew must be drunk'er than we are," shouted one of the commandos.

Zack was just as shocked as the others. Although his ears were ringing and his heart was racing, he kept his eyes glued on the giant plane. It had now climbed to a couple of thousand feet. It continued heading east.

Captain Flynn was still by Zack's side, watching the phantom jet maneuver in the distance. "Zack, what the hell was that all about?"

"I don't know."

Flynn pulled up his binoculars, focusing on the plane. A moment later he spotted the huge yellow-and-orange logo on the tail's vertical stabilizer. "Oh, shit, that sucker's got YHI markings on it."

"What?" shouted Zack.

Flynn handed Scott the binoculars. It took only a few seconds for Zack to confirm the sighting. "Oh, my God, you're right!"

"What's he up to, buzzing us like that?" asked Flynn

Zack just stood there, shaking his head. The reality of the situation had just hit him like a ton of rocks. *It can't be . . .*

Yoshida leveled out the plane at 4,000 feet. It was about twenty-two miles downrange. He had just completed a wide turn to the right and was now heading back toward the drilling rig. Half a minute later he adjusted the control surfaces, directing the aircraft into a shallow descent. After lining up the vessel with his new aiming point, he keyed his microphone. The aircraft's radio was now tuned to the *Deepquestor*'s VHF receiver. He ignored normal radio protocol. Instead, he made his demand: "*Deepquestor,* put Scott on right now." His English was perfect.

It took thirty seconds for the bridge crew to transfer the call to Flynn's headset. Ian handed it off to Zack.

Zack held one speaker to his right ear, speaking into the loose boom mike. "Who is this?" he demanded.

The A340 was coming head-on, this time racing into the sun. Thick plumes of black smoke billowed out from behind the aircraft. The plane was only fifteen miles out.

Yoshida keyed his mike. "You may think you have destroyed me, but it is I who will destroy you."

"Yoshida, is that you?" shouted Zack, now clearly astonished.

"Yes, Scott. Your death will be swift. Far more humane than what your countrymen did to my family in the war!"

"The war! What the hell are you talking about?"

Yoshida glanced through the windscreen. The distant drilling vessel was growing in size by the second. His salvation was just a few minutes away. He savored his final words: "Say your prayers, Zackary Jacob Scott, because you're about to meet your maker." Yoshida then flipped a switch on the wheel, turning off the radio.

Static filled Zack's headphones as he turned toward Captain Flynn. His face looked ashen. "It's Yoshida. He thinks he's a fucking kamikaze."

Yoshida made a few minor adjustments to the aircraft's controls. *Perfect,* he said to himself. The A340 was now only a hundred and fifty feet off the water, speeding forward at 315 knots. He ignored the low-altitude Klaxon that repeatedly blared out its warning: "Stall! Stall! Pull up! Pull up!"

The jumbo jet was aimed directly at the center of the floating drilling platform. The *Deepquestor* was just twelve miles out. Two minutes to impact.

When Yoshida announced his death wish, almost everyone on top of the bridge house began running for cover. Captain MacDonald and his commandos jumped off the twelve-foot-high structure, rolling on the steel deck as if executing a parachute landing. Several SCS crewmen followed, but they hit the deck wrong, breaking bones. Finn Sorenson and Halley Blake, along with other crew members, began climbing down the two access ladders.

Wendy Scott, however, remained on top. She was by her father's side, trying to get him to move. "Come on, Daddy, we've got to get out of here now!"

Zack wouldn't move . . . couldn't move. His legs were frozen to the deck by fear and rage.

Ian Flynn, however, had swung into action. He grabbed the headset from Scott and began issuing new orders. "Bridge, hard left rudder, go to flank."

The 15,000-ton vessel began turning to the port, but it moved like molasses. *Christ, we'll never make it,* thought Flynn as he stared at the oncoming Airbus jet. He wanted to run, too. Ninety seconds to impact.

Hiroshi Yoshida flipped the wheel switch with his right thumb. The autopilot was now engaged. Nothing would stop him. Seventy-five seconds to impact.

One of Mac's commandos found Cindy DeMorey in the deck decompression chamber, a couple of levels below the bridge. Without any warning, he yanked her through the hatch of the makeshift prison and headed topside. Fukuda and Suzuki remained locked inside the DDC. Seventy seconds to impact

Captain Flynn and Zackary Scott stood side by side, watching death approach. Wendy Scott, however, had collapsed to the steel deck at the base of her father's legs; she was too terrified to move any farther.

Like a heavyweight boxer about to go down, Zack could see the knockout punch coming. Nothing would stop it. He desperately wanted to scoop up his daughter and run for safety, but there was no place to escape to. When the monster-size jet hit, the *Deepquestor* would be destroyed. Sixty seconds to impact.

The commando dragged Cindy across the steel deck. She protested, fighting him all the way. She knew nothing of what was happening but sensed imminent danger.

"Stop fighting me!" he ordered. "We've got to get to the bridge radio so you call off that nut-case uncle of yours."

"My uncle?" she cried out. And then she saw it. The jet

was bearing down on the *Deepquestor* as if descending from hell. "Oh dear God," she screamed.

Forty seconds to impact.

Zack raised his right arm, shaking his clenched fist at the approaching jet. His words were bitter, filled with hate and fear: "Come on, you bastard. Get it over with!" Thirty seconds to impact.

Ian Flynn also wanted to run, but didn't. He was captain of the ship—it was his duty to stay with her to the end. Accepting his fate, he closed his eyes. Although he hadn't attended church in years, the words came automatically: "Our Father who art in heaven, Hallowed be thy name. Thy kingdom come, Thy will be done, On earth as—"

Bam! Bam! Bam! The racket from behind Flynn's position startled him, interrupting his prayer. He whipped his head around, searching for the source of the noise. "Damn!" he shouted.

Half a dozen of MacDonald's commandos were on the helideck, about a hundred feet from the bridge. The soldiers held their H&K submachine guns, minus silencers, at shoulder level and fired at the oncoming jet in controlled bursts. The A340 jet was still too far out, but they fired anyway. It wouldn't come into range until the last half mile of flight. Twelve seconds to impact.

While the submachine gunners filled the sky with lead, another commando prepared to fire. He was kneeling down at the far end of the helipad, one knee on the steel deck and the other up. A black plastic tube, six inches in diameter and about four feet long, was balanced across his right shoulder. His right eye was glued to the optical sight on the tube. *Come on, Mac, where the hell are you?* he thought as he waited for the GMW's red acquisition light to come on. The commando couldn't fire the missile until its infrared sensor spotted the reflected light from Mac's laser designator. Ten seconds to impact.

The starboard cockpit windscreen shattered when the first nine-millimeter rounds hit. But it had no effect on Yoshida. His mind was racing faster than the aircraft. Images of his mother and sister, his Uncle Tetsuo, flashed by. He would soon be at peace. Eight seconds to impact.

Mac MacDonald was about a hundred feet above the helideck, leaning over a catwalk railing on the derrick tower. He held the GMW's laser unit in both of his hands, aiming it like a pistol. There hadn't been time to reattach the device to its tripod mount. As a consequence, his aim was shaky. The pencil-thin laser bounced all over the sky. The weapon hadn't been designed to shoot down aircraft, but Mac had been forced to improvise. The machine gun fire alone wouldn't bring down the massive aircraft.

When Mac finally steadied his aim, homing in on the fuselage of the giant plane, invisible light from the laser reflected into the atmosphere. Seven seconds to impact.

The GMW's infrared sensor spotted the telltale splotch of light on the aluminum. A microsecond later the acquisition light inside the optical sight blinked on. The commando instinctively pulled the trigger on the pistol grip. The three-foot-long missile roared out of the fiberglass tube. Five seconds to impact.

The missile plowed into the A340's radar compartment, just under the cockpit. Shrapnel ripped upward, turning the thick bundles of instrument panel control wires into spaghetti. The autopilot disengaged and the plane abruptly yawed to the right. Three seconds later the monster jet slammed into the *Deepquestor*.

The outer forty feet of the port wing clipped the derrick tower about thirty feet below Mac's position. The severed wing tanks erupted into a fountain of flame. The rest of the cargo jet's fuselage raced across the top of the rig, spewing burning kerosene and broken aluminum. The aircraft finally smashed into the sea, the fuselage cartwheeling over the swells, about five hundred yards to the west.

MacDonald was shielded from the exploding fireball by the derrick's sheet metal enclosure. However, the shower of burning fuel spilled onto the decks below. Cindy DeMorey and her escort commando were directly under the tower when the Airbus hit. They were cremated in a heartbeat. Three other commandos on the helideck were splattered with burning fuel. Without hesitation, they all jumped overboard to escape the flames.

The *Deepquestor*'s upper decks were burning furiously from the spilled jet fuel, but the fires wouldn't last very long. Already, emergency response teams led by Captain Flynn and Zackary Scott were attacking the flames with rivers of foam and seawater.

EPILOGUE:

PAYBACK

The *Deepquestor* limped across the Sea of Okhotsk, finally mooring alongside an old concrete wharf on the Magadan waterfront. Before berthing at the Russian port, however, all of the drilling rig's injured crew were transferred by helicopter to shore-based hospitals.

Halley Blake and Finn Sorenson heloed out with the injured. Finn needed surgery on his broken jaw and Commander Blake had been ordered to report to the Pentagon. The Coast Guard commandant and the chief of naval operations wanted her personal report on the Nemuro incident.

Fukuda and Suzuki were also airlifted out. Instead of accompanying the other survivors, however, they flew out on a special U.S. Navy helicopter. The four Marines aboard the Sea Stallion had been dispatched to make sure that the YHI executives made it back to the United States. Both men would spend a very long time at a CIA interrogation facility.

Mac MacDonald and his surviving commandos remained aboard the *Deepquestor*. They would return home via a chartered jet that would meet them in Magadan.

Zackary Scott could have also arranged for a helicopter to transport Wendy and himself to the shore. But he elected to remain with his ship. Captain Flynn needed his help. The *Deepquestor* had been badly damaged by the fire. Zack supervised the temporary repairs while Ian Flynn piloted the vessel. The slow cruise across the sea also provided plenty of time for Zack to visit with his daughter and to plan for his future.

The fires at Nemuro burned for several more days, catapulting the disaster into the world's eyes. Hundreds of journalists descended on the northeast shore of Hokkaido, all looking for the story behind the headlines. But as the flames were extinguished and the spilled oil mopped up, the truth never surfaced. Instead, the journalists all bought into the official government line: A massive explosion had occurred in the main pumping plant, the result of an accidental pipeline failure combined with a careless worker who routinely smoked in hazardous areas.

Because of Hiroshi Yoshida's untimely death in an aircraft accident, the Nemuro general manager along with five senior YHI vice presidents were instantly targeted as the corporate culprits responsible for the embarrassing mess. At first there had been talk about a court trial to punish the men for pollution, but nothing ever happened. Instead, they all resigned, each one receiving a full pension.

Yoshida Heavy Industries was subsequently fined $20 million and ordered to restore all 110 miles of Hokkaido's oil-contaminated shoreline. The fate of the Nemuro operation itself, however, was another matter. The central production platform, along with the main subsea wells, had suffered irreparable damage. It would have to be abandoned. The government reported it would take several years to rebuild. In the interim, oil flow from the offshore field would plummet to only a fraction of its former volume. And once again, Japan would have to surrender itself to the world oil market in order to satisfy its insatiable hunger for black gold. The spot price of crude went up $5 a barrel on the announcement that the Nemuro field would be temporarily closed.

It was now four months later, long after the headlines over the Nemuro disaster had faded. There was snow on the grounds surrounding the White House. President Chandler was sitting at his desk in the Oval Office. The secretary of defense was seated in a chair directly in front of him. Both men were drinking coffee.

Chandler took another sip from his mug and then turned to face Secretary Stephenson. "Well, Jack, I think it's time."

"Yes, sir. We've kept him waiting for over half an hour."

"Yep, that's enough." Chandler then reached to his side and pressed the intercom switch. "Susan," he said, "we're ready now."

"Yes, sir. I'll escort him in right now."

A minute later the door to the president's office opened. A small man, only about five and a half feet tall, walked in. He was dressed in an immaculate black pinstripe suit. He was in his early fifties. His black hair was graying.

The prime minister of Japan stepped onto the thick rug of the Oval Office and then stopped. He looked toward the two Americans who moved forward to greet him. Both men towered over him. He bowed his head. "Good morning, Mr. President," he said. His English was good; there was only a slight accent.

"Good morning, Mr. Prime Minster," replied Chandler. He then reached forward to shake the visitor's hand. The smaller man's grip was like a vise.

President Chandler turned to his side. "Mr. Prime Minister, I'd like to introduce Secretary Stephenson."

Why is he here? wondered the Japanese politician as he shook the secretary's hand. The meeting was just supposed to be a courtesy call.

"Secretary Stephenson, it is indeed a pleasure to meet you." The prime minister paused for a moment. "If I had known that you were going to join us, I would have brought our minister of defense along."

"Oh, that's okay. I'll just be here for a few minutes."

"That's right, Mr. Prime Minister," Chandler said. "I asked Secretary Stephenson to sit in on our meeting. He has a videotape to show us."

The prime minister's right eyebrow arched for just a fraction of a second. "Videotape?"

"Yes," replied Chandler. "And I think you'll find it very interesting." Chandler turned toward Stephenson. "Jack, why don't we get started."

"Yes, sir. "

A minute later, President Chandler and the prime minister

were seated at a small conference table opposite the president's desk. The room lights had been dimmed and Stephenson was standing at the head of a table. A portable color television set with a built-in VCR was sitting on the table.

Stephenson switched on the machine. The screen snapped to life, displaying an aerial view of the Nemuro Oil Complex. Stephenson began his carefully orchestrated narrative. "Mr. Prime Minister, the tape you are about to see was taken a few days before the unfortunate accident at your Nemuro facility."

The TV screen blinked as a new image materialized. It was a surprisingly clear view of the bow section of the sub tanker *Sapporo*. The thousand-foot long vessel was moored at its underwater berth.

The prime minister's eyes widened in shock. He then sucked in a great breath. *They know everything!*

While Stephenson continued his detailed briefing, Chandler remained focused on his counterpart. The prime minister sat quietly but his body language gave him away. His face was turning beet red, and although Japanese aren't supposed to sweat, Chandler was sure he spotted a bead of perspiration on the man's forehead.

He's clearly embarrassed, thought the president. *This is perfect.* Chandler wanted to crack a smile but remained stone-faced.

The briefing lasted almost fifteen minutes. Stephenson finished with an underwater view of a secret oil well installation discovered off the southern coast of the People's Republic of China. The Chinese Communist government had no idea that the subsea wellhead existed.

Secretary Stephenson turned off the television and then left the room without further comment.

The prime minister stared at the table top for nearly a minute before finally turning to face President Chandler. The Japanese leader was a master at delay, indecision, and procrastination. But this time he had been outflanked. There was no way out. "All right, Mr. President, just what is it that you want from us?"

Chandler allowed himself to smile, just a little, as he opened up a leather notebook on the table top. The three sheets of legal-size paper inside were filled with over sixty separate items. "Well, let's see." The president paused for a moment as he scanned the first item on the list. He then looked directly into the prime minister's eyes. "First of all, about Yamato's campaign to flood the world market with its new hyper-drive supercomputer, I think it's time that . . ."